Ride Along

by

Mary Sikes

DORRANCE PUBLISHING CO., INC.
PITTSBURGH, PENNSYLVANIA 15222

The contents of this work including, but not limited to, the accuracy of events, people, and places depicted; opinions expressed; permission to use previously published materials included; and any advice given or actions advocated are solely the responsibility of the author, who assumes all liability for said work and indemnifies the publisher against any claims stemming from publication of the work.

All Rights Reserved
Copyright © 2013 by Mary Sikes

No part of this book may be reproduced or transmitted, downloaded, distributed, reverse engineered, or stored in or introduced into any information storage and retrieval system, in any form or by any means, including photocopying and recording, whether electronic or mechanical, now known or hereinafter invented without permission in writing from the publisher.

Dorrance Publishing Co., Inc.
701 Smithfield Street
Pittsburgh, PA 15222
Visit our website at *www.dorrancebookstore.com*

ISBN: 978-1-4349-3717-9
eISBN: 978-1-4349-3637-0

DEDICATION

This book is lovingly dedicated to the Houston police officers whom it was my privilege to ride along with when I served on the Harris County Grand Jury:

Sergeant H. K. Steinke	D. A. Van Ness	R. L. Hoyt
Sergeant Richard See	J. R. Cones	D. E. Calhoun
Sergeant R. A. Woodruff	R. J. McGovern	J. R. Bench
Sergeant A. R. Tharling	L. W. Hall	F. C. O'Neil
C. E. Adolph	W. G. Jackson	J. L Nicholson
J. D. Barnett	R. R. Hulett	W. J. Bench
L. G. Lee	D. R. Schmidt	F. K. Stephenson
W. E. Reese	G. D. Kuschel	E. W. Mitchell
H. E. Sharp	B. Gonzales	J. T. Keefe
J. L. Driver	D. F. Flores	D. W. Cook
F. A. Davis	J. W. Harris	M. J. Vassar
M. D. Wendt	R. O. Marcotte	T. A Britt
R. C. Hoefer	D. M. Barber	F. Savage
W. R. Elsbury	E. L. Doyle	C. P. Hall
R. R. Gilmore	R. B. Carbo	G. G. Gonzalez

And to all the officers I talked with while touring the different Divisions of the Houston Police Department:

Chief C. M. Lynn	Clyde Black
Captain Bond	Robert Warkentin
Captain Chuck Smith	Gene Babb
Captain Hickman	Richard Harston
Lieutenant Ken Garnett	Bill Elkins
Lieutenant Breck Porter	Officer Van Knox
Sergeant R. A. Branard	Janet Lee
Carolyn Stephenson	

Thank you for the most educational and unforgettable experience of my life!

Mary Sikes

ACKNOWLEDGMENTS

In the mid-1970s, during the three months of my grand jury service, I rode along every Friday and Saturday with both the evening and night shift patrol officers of the Houston Police Department. Those experiences provided the starting point of this book. The names have been changed to protect the innocent—and the guilty. The locations are left vague. The incidents shared with the reader are related as truthfully as my memory can make them, up to a point which changes the life of the grand juror in the story.

Although most of the story is fiction, the background is as authentic as my experiences and research could make it. Many people contributed their knowledge by answering a multitude of questions. All of the following individuals contributed something to the process of completing this book. My sincere thanks go to each and every one of them:

   Officer C. E. Adolph, Houston Police Department
   Sergeant T. A. Britt, Houston Police Department
   Michael Moore, Deputy Harris County Sheriff's Dept.
   Langley McKelvy, Deputy Constable, Harris County Precinct Four
   Chief Charles Bennett Thacker, Stagecoach, Texas Police Department
   Constable David Hill, Precinct 5, Montgomery County, Texas
   Chief Deputy Constable David Wood, Precinct 5, Montgomery County, Texas
   Chief Ron Cunningham, Magnolia, Texas Police Department
   Pat Coulson, Attorney
   Jeri Willen, friend, psychologist, proofreader, and editor
   Robert Lunaburg, friend and editor
   Janie J. Barnette, sister and proofreader
   Nance Hansen, friend, proofreader, and editor

If I have missed anyone, I apologize. I hope you enjoy reading the book as much as I enjoyed writing it.

Mary Sikes

Chapter 1
Houston, Texas

Friday, August 6, 1976 - 11:15 p.m.

The two men studied her with direct penetrating, judgmental eyes. Her eyes darted from their faces to their pistols, from their set jaws to their crisp two-toned blue uniforms, from their silver badges to the blue and white police car.

One of the Houston police officers opened the rear car door on the passenger side. Over six feet tall, with a husky build, his blue eyes were cold and his face showed no expression. He motioned for her to get in the backseat of the car. Her stomach knotted as she complied. The door closed behind her. The two officers got in the front seat and the car started to move. The tightness in her stomach was washed away by waves of uneasiness.

From under the dash the police radio crackled and growled in a language her ears failed to comprehend. She looked around. A heavy expanded metal screen separated the backseat from the front seat. The door and window handles had been removed. She could not open a window or a door. She was confined in a portable jail cell.

I shouldn't be here, she thought. It's a mistake! What was I thinking?

"So, Mrs. Cooper, you're on the grand jury, is that correct?" the officer in the passenger seat asked.

"Yes, I am."

"And you asked to ride in a patrol car?"

"Yes."

"Why?"

Why indeed, she wondered. When a friend had called and asked if she would be willing to serve as a prospective grand juror, she thought it her civic duty to say yes. Pleased when selected as one of the twelve on the jury, she thought the experience would be interesting and educational. At the welcome ceremony, the Harris County Sheriff had invited the jurors to ride with his deputies to learn about that side of the criminal justice system. When the Houston Police Chief Ledford extended the same invitation, her hand shot in the air. The chief looked at her as though she had some nerve interrupting his speech.

"Yes, ma'am?"

"Does that mean one ride, one night, or can we ride as many times with as many different divisions as we want?"

"You can ride as many times as you want, but I think one payday Friday night will be enough for you," he stated. "Call Community Relations. They'll make the arrangements."

So, here she sat in the back seat of a police car, still wondering why she did it. Her husband told her it was dangerous and pointed out that an officer had been shot and killed just a few months before. Her girlfriends admitted they would be scared to ride with the police. Her teenage sons thought the idea was cool but what did they know? *Am I as immature as they are?* Like them, she loved the roller-coaster rides at Astroworld and Six Flags. *Maybe I need to grow up and ask the officers to take me home. At the same time, as a free-lance writer, I can't afford to pass up this opportunity.*

"I want to see what police work is really like," she answered the officer's question.

"Well, Mrs. Cooper, we'll try to show you," he told her.

"Please call me Kathy."

"All right," he agreed. "I'm Calvin Henson. John Bailey is driving."

"You're not comfortable with me riding along, are you?" she asked.

"To be honest, not particularly." John answered. "Out here, partners take care of each other. Now we have to take care of you, too."

"I don't want to get in your way. I just want to observe," Kathy stated forcefully.

The men looked at each other. Calvin raised his eyebrows in question. John nodded.

"When we get a call," Calvin told her, "I'll tell you what to do when we get there. You will either stay at the car or follow us. I'll unlatch your door when we arrive but you will have to get out by yourself. Do you understand?"

"Yes, I do."

"If you follow us, stay behind us. Never get between us and whoever we are talking to. Understood?"

"Yes."

"Good."

"One thing," she said, "Don't tie this up in pretty red ribbons and don't worry about your language. I've heard all the words and used most of them."

"You may be in for a shock," John warned her.

"I don't shock easily. I'm not a lady, John." She knew she wasn't as tough as she was leading them to believe, but if she acted tough maybe she would be if circumstances required it.

"You rode along with Sergeant Schmidt on the evening shift, didn't you?" John asked.

"Yes."

"You make the shooting on Pinemont?"

"It wasn't our call but we went by."

"And?"

"And what?"

"Tell us about it."

"A family was having a birthday party for a five-year-old boy. The boy's father showed up, high on drugs, and shot the mother and her new husband. There were several small children that saw it all. It was sad."

"It always is when kids are involved."

"That must be the worst part of your job."

"Yeah, it is."

On that somber note, they all remained silent while John cruised east on Long Point where strip centers and businesses lined both sides of the street. When he turned north on Bingle, there was a crash behind them. John made a U-turn before the glass from a broken headlight finished hitting the pavement. He parked near the wreck and radioed for an Accident Unit.

"Stay by the car," Calvin told Kathy as he unlatched the door from the outside.

Kathy was relieved to see the drivers of both cars walking around, apparently unhurt. She stood by the car and watched John and Calvin direct traffic while the drivers got the cars out of the street. They started getting the information for the accident forms. When the accident unit arrived they turned it over to that officer and returned to the car.

"That stupid son-of-a-bitch!" John exclaimed. "Did you hear him try to blame it on us?" he asked Calvin. "Said we distracted him!"

Kathy smiled. The profanity was the first indication that the men might relax in her presence.

Calvin chuckled a deep Santa Claus-like 'Ha, ha, ha.' "Blue and white fever," he said.

"What?" Kathy asked as she got back in the car and they started cruising again.

"People seem to forget how to drive when they see a police unit. We call that 'blue and white fever,'" Calvin explained.

"I've gotten nervous myself," Kathy agreed.

In an effort to get to know them better she started asking questions and taking notes. John had five years as an officer, the first four years in Tulsa, Oklahoma. He applied to HPD to get away from the cold winters and for the bonus the department paid for experienced officers. He attended Houston's Police Academy and had just completed his six month probationary period.

Calvin had been an HPD officer for ten years, having grown up in the Houston area.

"Why did you become cops?"

"It beats working for a living," John answered with a chuckle.

"What do you mean?"

"If you ride along enough you'll understand," Calvin told her.

As she sat back to think about that, a car with a loud muffler passed them. John turned on the flashing lights and the car quickly pulled over. He stopped the unit behind and slightly to the left of the offender and left the lights flashing and the engine running. Calvin got out and unlatched Kathy's door without looking back. She stepped out to stand by the car and watch.

Sergeant Schmidt had told her about the dangers of making traffic stops. She watched apprehensively. Calvin and John approached the car, one on each side, using their flashlights to watch the driver. John hung back on the passenger side.

Calvin went to the driver's window and asked for his license and proof of insurance. Then he instructed the driver to get out of the car, get up on the curb, and stand there. He did. John watched him as Calvin looked around the inside of the car. Calvin then went to the unit and got on the radio. While sitting in the car, he wrote the ticket. He took the ticket to the man, who signed it. His license and a copy of the ticket were handed to him and he was allowed to leave.

John explained, as they drove off, that this was the standard method of making a traffic stop. "Calvin stood at the shoulder of the driver because it's hard for the driver to turn and see him, while I can see every move he makes. We tell him the reason we stopped him and ask for his license and insurance. Then we get the driver out of the car and out of the street. We check the inside of the car for drugs that are in plain sight. We're not supposed to move anything to find them without probable cause. The smell of marijuana smoke would give us cause to search the car."

"Not supposed to?" Kathy interrupted.

"Watch out, John. She's sharp!"

"Anything I see or you say is not going any further," Kathy assured them.

Calvin turned around, looked at her, considered a moment, and then turned to face the front. "Kathy, sometimes when we know we got a real bad one something might *accidentally* get moved. The arrest won't stand up in court, but we get the guy off the street for the night and we get some drugs off the street, too."

"That makes sense," she agreed. "And after you check the car?"

"We check wants and warrants on him and that the license plates belong on that car," Calvin explained. "If those come back clear, then we write him and turn him loose. He was cooperative, so I told him the ticket would be dismissed if he took proof to court that the muffler had been fixed."

"What exactly are 'wants and warrants?'" Kathy asked.

"Unpaid traffic citations," Calvin explained, "or warrants for felonies. If he has either, he's arrested and taken to jail."

"Does that happen often?" Kathy asked.

"Often enough to make it worthwhile checking," Calvin answered.

"John, I noticed you let Calvin do all the work while you just stood there."

"Do you know why?" John asked.

"You were standing by to back him up?"

"That's correct," John stated. "In a two-man unit, the man-on-the-ground, the one *not* driving, does the paperwork. The driver handles the radio, PA system, lights and siren. The man-on-the-ground writes down the time, type, and location of the calls and looks it up in the Key Map if necessary. We switch places each night."

John pulled the unit into a parking space in front of a doughnut shop on Long Point. He remained in the car to monitor the radio while Calvin and Kathy went inside. Kathy got some curious looks as she passed through on her way to the ladies' room. On her return, Calvin asked if she would like some coffee or something. She declined with thanks and they returned to the car with Calvin carrying coffee for himself and John. They were about to pull onto the street when a young man on a motorcycle sped by with a loud muffler.

"Shit!" Calvin exclaimed. "Every time I get a hot cup of coffee, this happens." He lowered the window and threw the coffee out.

John also discarded his, flipped on the flashing lights, and pulled out. The cycle rider turned north on Wirt. John pulled up behind the cycle at Hammerly. The cycle took off. John hit the siren and pursued at over seventy miles per hour. If the rider had made one mistake, they would have had him and the cycle all over the front of the car. The cycle stopped where Wirt dead-ended at Kempwood.

As the officers got out of the car the young man got off the motorcycle. Calvin unlatched Kathy's door. She sat there wide-eyed with surprise. Wow! That was exciting—and scary, she realized, as she got out of the car.

"I didn't hear you," the cycle rider said.

"That's what we want to talk to you about," Calvin stated, motioning the boy out of the street. He used the radio to check the boy's license and the cycle plates, then stood in front of him to write tickets for speeding and the faulty muffler. The young man became nervous and started to put his hands in the pockets of his windbreaker. Calvin's reaction was immediate.

"Son! Keep your hands out of your pockets!" The kid swallowed hard, realized it was a bad move, took them out very carefully and stood very still after that.

Kathy noticed that John, standing off to one side watching, had unsnapped the flap of his holster and his hand was on his gun. Covering his partner, Kathy realized. The degree of alertness they must maintain every moment for safety came as a surprise to Kathy, but made a lot of sense once she recognized it.

Later, cruising along Gessner, they heard an alarm ringing. John killed the headlights, drove past, and then came back, pulling up in front of the store.

"I'll take the back," he said, going toward the left side of the building.

Calvin approached the right front, a flashlight in his left hand and his pistol in the other. They had left the doors to the unit ajar, but in his rush Calvin did not unlatch Kathy's door. She could not get out of the car. Even worse, if something happened she could not get to the radio. Her tension increased until they returned several minutes later. They had not found any indication of entry.

Calvin was sorry he had forgotten to open her door. "We sure wouldn't want someone to jump in the unit and drive off with you."

"I wouldn't like that either!" she laughed, partly at that thought and partly with relief. "But if you needed help…"

"Get on the radio, give our unit number first," Calvin instructed. "Wait for the dispatcher to acknowledge by repeating our number. Give our unit number again, our location, and what the situation is."

"But don't ask for help or assistance," John added. "Ask for another unit to meet us. A two-man unit. That means we need some backup but we aren't in immediate danger."

"Why not ask for assistance?" she asked.

"Because every unit in the district will run it with lights and sirens," John stated. "It's difficult to hear the sirens of the other cars when your own is on. Accidents happen that way and men get hurt."

"So asking for assistance indicates a life-threatening emergency?"

"Yes," Calvin confirmed.

John reached for the radio mike. Calvin turned on the overhead light and got his clipboard and pen ready. Alerted by this, Kathy wondered, what next?

The dispatcher gave them a *prowler* call, a repeat of a few nights ago, Calvin explained on the way. This nut had repeatedly been bothering this one house. He and John had been out there a few nights before. At that time, the young woman's father had told them he had the prowler at the point of a shotgun. He told the prowler if he moved, he would blow his head off. The prowler shrugged, turned, and started to walk away. The father shot him in the buttocks. The prowler took off like a scalded cat. The gun had been loaded with rock salt.

John drove fast to get there, hoping to catch the guy this time. Another unit was already there. The prowler was not.

"He'll be here the next time," the young woman's father said. "I plan to shoot the bastard!"

"Don't kill him," Calvin advised. "He's committing a misdemeanor offense. The fine's only two hundred dollars."

"I'm not going to kill him, just stop him!"

"I hope you're a good shot, because if you kill him, you could be charged with murder," Calvin replied. He and John motioned Kathy back to the car while the other officers stayed at the scene.

"Why are they staying?" she asked.

"They'll file a report of the incident," John told her.

"But it was your call. Shouldn't you do it?"

"The other unit was first on the scene. They were already getting the information." A few minutes later, when a car going in the opposite direction dimmed their bright lights, one headlight went out. John made a U-turn and pulled the car over. Since it was about 3:30 in the morning, Calvin asked what he was doing out at this time of night.

"Just driving around," he answered, his breath heavy with the odor of alcohol. "Had a beef with my woman. I wanted to stay away from the house until she calmed down."

"Your wife?" Calvin asked.

"Naw. The bitch I'm living with. I'm just trying to avoid trouble at home. Look fellas, I'm on your side. I was on the force, even ran for sheriff and the whole bit."

Kathy was disgusted. The man reeked of alcohol, was unshaven for a couple of days at least, and his clothes looked like they had been slept in. She did not believe the Houston Police Department would have a man like him on the force.

They asked him to walk the white line on the side of the road. He did pretty well. They kept him talking for a long time. Kathy didn't hear all of it because at one point Calvin motioned for her to go to the car. She did, and stayed there. Finally they turned him loose but followed him for a couple miles, watching his driving.

"Borderline," John stated.

Calvin agreed. "If he had been weaving, we would have pulled him over again and taken him downtown for a breath test. Without being sure they'll blow a ten plus, it's a waste of time." He paused. "Thanks for going to the car back there, Kathy. I didn't want him to start swinging with you close enough to get hurt."

They cruised. No calls were going out, so at about five o'clock Saturday morning they took Kathy home. John threatened to come down her street with lights and siren going, but was only teasing. They complained about how quiet it had been that night.

"I got some of my questions answered, and I learned a lot. Thank you," Kathy said as she got out of the unit.

"Come ride along again," John invited. "We get tired of looking at each other all night every night."

"I will. Thanks," Kathy responded.

John nodded and said, "Goodnight."

Calvin walked with her to the front door, lighting the way with his flashlight and waiting until she opened it. "Goodnight, Kathy," he said with a friendly smile.

"Goodnight, Calvin," she said with an answering smile.

What an interesting night, she thought as she closed the door. Since they answered only one radio call, I didn't see much, but I learned a lot about radio procedure, which partner is responsible for doing what, and how to get help. The excitement of chasing the motorcycle and her concern for the officers checking the building with the audible alarm made the experience more intense than she had expected it to be. She realized that safety had been their primary concern; her safety and their own. Consequently, she never sensed personal danger. She felt kind of overloaded with information. It would take her a while to sort it all out. Riding along again would help. She smiled to herself. Police Chief Ledford was wrong. One night did not satisfy her. It was just a taste, and she wanted the whole meal.

* * * * *

Saturday, August 7, 1976 - 5:28 a.m.

In the master bedroom, Steve heard the front door open and close. He sighed with relief. She was home, home safe. He had slept little and lightly, waking up several times at the sound of sirens. Kathy was the adventurous type and he admired her for that. He had never forbidden her to do anything. But riding with the police?

Kathy quietly entered the bedroom.

"Hi, honey," he said.

Startled, Kathy jumped, then turned on the bedside lamp. "Good morning," she told him, leaning over to kiss him. "What are you doing awake so early?"

"What time is it?" he asked.

"A little after five."

"I heard you come in," he told her. "Well, how was it?" He watched her eyes light up before she answered. Damn, he thought, she enjoyed it.

"Interesting. Not much going on tonight, though."

"I heard sirens about midnight," Steve stated. Was she minimizing what happened? Or was it really a quiet night?

"Wasn't us," she told him, knowing he could not have heard the siren when they chased the motorcycle. "The officers turned on the lights a couple times to make traffic stops." She took off her clothes, dropped them on the cedar chest at the foot of the bed, and put on her pajamas. After she brushed her teeth, she yawned, stretched, and got into bed.

Steve was thankful Kathy was safe but uneasy knowing she would ride along again. Steve gathered her in his arms and held her tight until they both fell asleep.

Chapter 2

Saturday, August 7, 1976 - 3:30 p.m.

Getting ready for Sergeant Schmidt to pick her up to ride along for a second time, she thought about how shocked she had been when he arrived the afternoon before. He was the biggest man she had ever been in the same room with. The way the uniform fit, he was obviously in good shape; not fat, just big.

Her stomach churned with anticipation as she checked her reflection in the mirror one more time. She was satisfied with her appearance. The night before, she had worn royal blue to honor the Houston Police officers she met and rode with. Tonight, she was wearing navy blue.

The sergeant arrived. Kathy told Steve and their two sons she would see them in the morning. As the sergeant drove past a construction site on the way out of the neighborhood, the security guard waved at the car. The sergeant abruptly stopped, backed up, and drove in the entrance. Two cars were parked on the site, one with the trunk open. She tagged along behind the sergeant.

The security guard was in uniform, but unarmed. A young man and two little boys stood close together. She felt uneasy and could not determine why. There was nothing threatening about the situation.

"Is there a problem here?" the sergeant asked.

"They were taking stuff from the dumpster," the security man explained. "FHA requires that all construction trash be hauled away. It can not be sold, burned, or given away."

"We're putting the stuff back," the other man said, "but it doesn't make any sense."

"A lot of things the government does don't make sense," the sergeant stated, as he squatted down to speak to the children. "What are you and your Dad going to build?"

The two small boys looked at their father. He nodded and the older of the boys said, "A clubhouse, sir."

"Where're you going to build it?"

"In our backyard!" the younger boy exclaimed, not wanting to be left out.

"Are you going to get to sleep out in it?"

"Yes, sir," both boys answered with big grins.

"Sounds like fun," Sergeant Schmidt said and he stood up and turned to the father. "You can get scrap materials from some construction sites. Just ask permission first."

"Yes, sir," the father answered. "I'm sorry for the trouble."

"No trouble," the sergeant reassured him.

"Thanks for stopping," the security man told him.

"No problem." He shook hands with the two men, turned and shook hands with the boys. He and Kathy then returned to the unit and began cruising.

Kathy admired the sergeant for his gentleness and the warm, friendly way he treated the children like people instead of children. Because she still remembered the officer who helped her as a child, she knew those boys would remember him and how he spoke to them for a long time. This police incident would not make the newspapers. The public never got to read about an officer doing this type of thing. The papers only covered the sensational stuff, like shootings and chases, she thought—which reminded her of the shooting of the night before.

"Sergeant, have you heard anything about the victims of last night's shooting?"

He nodded. "The woman will recover, with some brain damage. Her husband died. The ex-husband is now wanted for murder."

Sick at the thought of how this would affect the children, Kathy groaned and shook her head. "The father hasn't been caught yet?"

"No. But he will be."

As they cruised, the sergeant checked the convenience stores they passed and watched for anything that did not fit, anything out of place, as he had the night before. Kathy asked questions about police work and the sergeant told of incidents to illustrate his answers.

When she asked if anyone had tried to fight him, he told of a young woman who he was trying to arrest for attempting to pass a forged prescription.

"She started kicking me in the shins," he said. "She was a tiny thing; maybe a hundred pounds. I didn't want to be rough with her. By the time I got her cuffed, my shins were black and blue from ankles to knees."

"Did you file assault charges on her?"

"No. I figured I'd get laughed out of court."

"You probably would have," Kathy agreed, amused.

He was driving north on Gessner a few moments later when he reached over, turned up the radio, and picked up the mike.

"Nine-thirty," he said.

"Nine-thirty, call 4411, urgent."

"Nine-thirty clear," the sergeant answered, then explained that 4411 was the telephone extension number for the North Shepherd substation.

He drove to the nearest service station with an outside payphone. Kathy said she would make a pit stop while he was calling. She was washing her hands when she heard a short squawk of the siren. She grabbed a handful of paper towels and ran to the unit.

"We've got a possible kidnapping," the sergeant informed her as he pulled onto the street before she got her seatbelt fastened. He got on the radio. "Nine-thirty."

"Nine-thirty," the dispatcher answered.

"Nine-thirty. Need two two-man units to meet me at Kempwood and Bingle."

"Nine-thirty clear. Eleven-fifty-two and eleven-fifty-three meet nine-thirty at Kempwood and Bingle."

"Eleven-fifty-two, Kempwood and Bingle. Clear," one unit acknowledged, then the other.

He drove as fast as traffic allowed with emergency lights only, ignoring the speed limit and carefully going through red lights and stop signs. At the convenience store at the intersection of Kempwood and Bingle, the sergeant and officers from the other two units talked to a young man named Matt, who had a three-quarter-inch cut on his left cheekbone.

"These two guys are holding my brother, Jerry. They got a shotgun. They hit me with it," he said as he wiped the blood from his face with the tail of his T-shirt.

"Why are they holding him?" the sergeant asked.

"They're mad at us."

"Why are they mad?"

"They just are."

"Look, son, we need to know what's really going on so we can help your brother. Now tell me the truth. Why are they holding him?"

The boy hung his head. "I got some pot from 'em and didn't pay for it. They sent me out to get the money." He wiped his face again. The cut did not appear deep enough to require stitches.

"Where are they holding him?"

"At our apartment. I can show you."

Matt was put in the back of one of the two-man units, and all three units headed for the apartment where Jerry was being held. Each building of the apartment complex contained four apartments—two on the ground floor and two on the second floor. Outside stairs went up to a balcony which gave access to both second floor apartments. Matt pointed out the building where his apartment was located. He remained in the back seat of the unit while the five officers and Kathy approached the building.

The apartment was on the second floor. The door stood open. The sergeant motioned for her to remain at the bottom of the stairs as the five officers drew their guns. She nodded, surprised at the adrenaline rush and how it heightened her senses. She stayed at the corner of the building, prepared to duck around it if necessary. The five officers approached the open door of the apartment with guns drawn. They entered and all remained quiet. After a few moments, Sergeant Schmidt called to her and motioned for her to join them.

In the apartment Kathy watched and listened as two young women pointed out empty spots where the TV, stereo, and other things had been. They said they had just arrived and there was nobody else there. The officers had checked through the apartment to make sure. One of the officers called Kathy over to show her evidence of a struggle. The door frame to one of the bedrooms had splintered when the door was kicked in. Some drops of blood were found inside that room.

The girls knew the men involved and described the car they were driving. One of the units remained to take the information for the burglary and theft report they would file. Matt was released from the other unit and joined the girls in the apartment.

"Put out a description of the car, then we'll check out the clay pit," the sergeant stated to the other officers.

On the way he explained to Kathy, "It's an abandoned clay pit off of Hollister and Hammerly that has filled with water. Kids go there to smoke pot, drink, have sex, and skinny-dip. This is just the kind of place the pusher and his friend would dump Jerry's body if they killed him."

"Is that likely?" Kathy asked.

"Pushers are mean about their money. They make an example of one that doesn't pay, so the others will. But they may have taken enough from the apartment to pay what Matt owed."

As they arrived at the clay pit, cars parked in the area left quickly. The officers watched the departing cars for one matching the description the girls had given. None were close. They got out of the units to check the area on foot.

Kathy remained at the sergeant's car, imagining all kinds of scenarios that might happen in the next few minutes. She was curious, tense, and excited. Nothing was found. Since the shift was ending, nothing more could be done.

"You going to stay for the night shift?" the sergeant asked as they got back in the unit.

"Yes, please!"

The sergeant smiled. He knew from her reaction that she was getting hooked. Well, there are worse things than police work to get addicted to.

Since Kathy started this ride along, her emotions had taken a trip from warm and fuzzy when the sergeant spoke with the little boys, through sadness and sympathy for the family involved in the shooting of the night before, to the tension of a hostage situation and possible murder. And she had enjoyed every moment of it.

Is this what John Bailey meant last night when he said that being a cop 'beats working for a living?' she wondered.

Chapter 3

Saturday, August 7, 1976 - 10:45 p.m.

The Northwest Substation, located on the edge of Houston in an undeveloped area, just off Hempstead Highway, was brightly illuminated. The station included a helicopter pad, a transmission tower, a fenced parking area for police vehicles, and a small public parking area at the front entrance.

Kathy and Sergeant Schmidt entered the building through an 'Officers Only' door, which opened on the rear of the lobby. At the center, night shift officers stood around a counter-high u-shaped desk waiting for roll call. Officers Calvin Henson and John Bailey smiled at her. Other officers had friendlier expressions than the night before.

"What did you say about bad language?" Calvin asked her.

"I've heard all the words and used most of them," she told the men.

"These guys might teach you a few new ones," Calvin told her.

"I'm here to learn," she told him, which brought smiles and chuckles.

Sergeant Watson, the night shift sergeant, glanced up. Through the window wall of his office he saw Sergeant Schmidt and Kathy as they came in the back door to the lobby. The night before he had immediately classified her: white, female, mid-thirties, five foot five, one hundred thirty pounds, brown hair and blue eyes, wearing a royal blue pantsuit. Tonight she was wearing navy-blue. He wondered if her choice of colors was deliberate.

Officers Henson and Barnett had given a good report on her behavior of the night before. He was comfortable with assigning her to ride with the officers again. He stepped out of his office, announced roll call, and motioned for Kathy to join them.

Kathy sat in the back of the roll call room, listening intently as the sergeant assigned beats, shop numbers, and partners for the shift.

"Hey, Sarge," one of the men called out.

"Who gets Kathy to ride along tonight?"

"Driskell and Richmond."

"Damn! Senior officers get all the breaks!" Chuckles followed this statement.

After John and Calvin's initial wariness about Kathy riding along the night before, the question and the officer's comment surprised her. She wondered if he was trying to say he would like her to ride along with him.

The sergeant had a few additional remarks about incidents of the past few days, including information on the kidnapping situation from the evening shift, and alerted them to some of the people they should watch for, and why. When he dismissed them, two of the officers approached Kathy and introduced themselves as Dean Driskell and Bob Richmond.

Dean Driskell was tall and slim, about six foot two, with a serious, intelligent face, and was about the same age as Kathy, mid-thirties. There was a sadness about him that piqued Kathy's interest. Bob Richmond, a few years younger, stood about five foot eleven, with a nice build and a perpetual look of amusement on his face.

Once on the streets, the three of them agreed on the rules. She would do what they told her to without question and they would show her police work without censorship or sanitation.

Dean drove inbound on Hempstead Highway as he headed for a coffee shop on Washington Avenue, but before they got to the coffee shop they got a call—an *aggravated assault* at Wirt and Westview.

When they arrived a few minutes later, they found a pretty Latin female crying near the payphone on the corner. A man and woman stood next to a pickup truck parked at the curb. All three approached the officers and all three started talking at once.

Bob motioned with his hands for silence. The three people quit talking.

"Who called the police?" Bob demanded.

"I did," the crying girl answered.

"And the two of you?" he asked the couple.

"We want to report a hit and run," the man answered.

"Is that your truck?" Dean asked, pointing to the pickup.

"Yes, sir."

"Let's go over there," Dean told them with a motion. Dean and the couple moved away.

Kathy didn't know which conversation to listen to. She tried to listen to both but gave up and listened to Bob talk to the girl.

When Bob asked what happened, the woman answered in rapid Spanish and many gestures. Bob stopped her and asked if she spoke English. She did, but slowly, and kept lapsing into Spanish. Gradually he got the story.

The woman had been with a man at the club down the street. He got drunk and wanted to go to a motel. The woman wanted to go home. He started slapping her around. When he stopped for a red light, she jumped out of the car and fell, skinning her knees. She raised her dress to show her torn stockings and bloody knees.

Bob used his flashlight to examine her knees. "Do you want the paramedics? Do you have any other injuries?"

She shook her head.

When Bob asked for information about the man, the girl told him the man's name, race, approximate age, and hair and eye color. She described the car he had been driving as light green with four doors.

Kathy knew that would not be much help without the make or license plate number. She looked around to see how Dean was doing with the couple he was talking to. It dawned on her that he was standing where he could talk to the couple and also keep Bob and the girl in sight. Kathy looked back at Bob and saw that he kept Dean and the couple in view. Kathy smiled, pleased with herself for noticing.

Bob was telling the girl that he would file a report on the incident. He gave her the necessary information about where, when, and how to file charges on the man who slapped her. She indicated that she was afraid to do that.

Finished with the couple, Dean joined Bob, Kathy, and the girl.

"How am I gonna get home?" the girl asked.

"Have you got money for a cab?" Dean asked her.

"Yeah, but don't you take people home when something like this happens?"

"No, ma'am. We're police officers, not cab drivers."

"You were giving her a ride!" she exclaimed, pointing to Kathy.

"If you want to go to jail, we'll give you a ride. That's where we're taking her," Bob explained. Kathy had trouble keeping a straight face, but did her best to play along.

"Oh! No, I'll…I'll call a cab. Thank you."

"You're welcome, ma'am," Bob responded.

The girl walked off toward the payphone. Kathy and the officers returned to the unit. As Dean drove them away, he called the dispatcher to get back in service. The dispatcher had a call waiting for them. They were to *call the station*.

"Eleven-thirty-seven, clear," Dean acknowledged. "Coffee!" he cried. "I need coffee!"

Dean drove to a convenience store on T. C. Jester and Dacoma, which the officers referred to as Station Six. He knew the coffee was good and there was a payphone for Bob to use. Evidently the men stopped here often, because the man at the counter called Dean by name, but he gave Kathy a curious look and raised an inquiring eyebrow. Dean introduced them. Smiling, the man asked how she liked riding along with the officers.

"I'm finding it very interesting."

"Look out for Dean, he likes good-looking women," he warned her.

Stepping to the counter with a cup of coffee, Dean stated, "I only look. My wife carries a gun."

"She does?" Kathy questioned in surprise.

"She's a cop," Dean explained. "She works in the jail."

Bob came in the store and headed for the coffee pot. "Want some coffee, Kathy?"

"No thanks. I don't drink coffee."

"A cold drink?" he counterman asked.

"Not now."

When they returned to the car, Bob explained about the call. Their snitch wanted to meet with them. "I told him you were riding with us, Kathy, and asked if it was all right to bring you along. He said okay. He's a young black. He's given us some good information in the past. When we get there, stay in the car while we ask if you can listen. If it's okay, you can join us." He turned to face her. "You can listen and that's all. Clear?"

"Yes."

When they arrived, she stayed in the car while the men asked permission for her to listen. Bob opened the door so she could join them. She listened while the snitch told of a dice game that was held every Saturday night. He told them the location, and said they would find drugs and probably guns, as two felons were usually at the game. Dean and Bob asked some questions about the building and the approaches to it.

When they finished and turned to go, Kathy asked Dean if she could ask the man a question. Dean looked at her in disbelief, wondering what the hell she wanted to ask. He looked at the snitch and the man nodded.

She thanked him. "I'm a writer. It's important for writers to understand why people do the things they do. These are other black men you are giving information about. They're your own people. Would you mind telling me why you are doing this?"

"Them are bad dudes," he answered. "They ain't no friends of mine. I got a wife and kids. If I walked out of that game and them dudes knew I had fifty dollars on me, I'd be knocked in the head and rolled 'fore I got off the block." He paused. "But I could walk through your neighborhood anytime, and your people wouldn't roll me. Call the police because I don't belong there, yes. But that's the worst that would happen to me in your neighborhood. I want my neighborhood to be like yours. Safe for my wife and kids and me."

Kathy thanked him and returned to the car with the officers.

"Goddamn," Dean exclaimed, as soon as he pulled out onto the street.

"Shit," Bob said. "You surprised the hell out of me, Kathy, asking a question like that."

"Did I do wrong?" Kathy asked.

"No," both men answered.

"Kathy," Dean said with wonder in his voice, "he told you the truth. He didn't read that somewhere, or make it up. He spoke from his heart."

Kathy realized the officers were as moved by what the snitch said as she had been. How many civilians had been lucky enough to experience what she had tonight, she wondered. How many women? Perhaps none!

Dean got back *in service*, and again cruised toward the coffee shop on Washington Avenue. Before they got there, a *silent alarm* at a doctor's office near Heights Hospital on West 20th went out.

"That should be a good one," Bob stated.

Dean was already reaching for the mike. Another unit took the call, but Dean called in as backup on it. He was driving north going sixty on Yale, where the speed limit was thirty-five, when a red VW bug passed them like they were parked.

"What the hell?" Dean exclaimed. "Goddamn, I wish we weren't on this call."

At that moment another unit called in saying that they would back up the unit that took the alarm call, which left Dean free to pursue the VW. He sped up to match the VW's speed, which was seventy-three miles per hour. Dean flipped on the emergency lights. The bug didn't slow down. Kathy thought the VW might flee, but a brief squawk of the siren got the other driver's attention and the car pulled over and stopped. The man cooperated. Bob wrote the ticket. The man signed it and left.

Dean cruised the Houston Heights area, an old neighborhood with many homes dating back to the late 1800s. An elegant neighborhood at the turn of the century, some of the magnificent homes had been restored. Some badly needed repair. Others had been torn down and replaced with contemporary homes for young couples wanting to live close to downtown Houston, the theater district, the museums, and/or the medical center.

"We still need to go by Juvenile for a copy of that report," Dean told Bob.

"Well, it's quiet. See if we can get out."

Dean picked up the mike, waited to be sure no one else was talking on the radio, then keyed the mike. "Eleven-thirty-seven."

"Eleven-thirty-seven," the dispatcher answered.

"Eleven-thirty-seven. Is it clear to get out on investigation at Central?"

There was a pause, then finally the dispatcher answered. "Eleven-thirty-seven, that's clear."

"Eleven-thirty-seven, clear and out to Central," Dean acknowledged and hung up the mike. "That ass. He always hesitates. If he can't make a decision quicker than that, he shouldn't be dispatching."

"It's safer with him there than riding with him," Bob commented.

"I take it that the officer you're talking about isn't a good one?" Kathy asked.

"Once in a while," Bob told her, "one will get through the Academy and probation that shouldn't. We're aware of it, the supervisors are aware of it, and all of us try to keep him from getting an officer killed. That's all we can do until he screws up bad enough to get suspended indefinitely."

"That means fired, doesn't it?" she asked.

"That's right."

"How'd he get a badge in the first place?"

"His father's a lieutenant," Bob explained.

"That's not right!"

"No, it isn't," Dean agreed. "But it happens."

Dean pulled the unit into a parking space behind the Central Police Station in downtown Houston. Kathy had not been here before. She noticed two entrances, one with double glass doors and the other a solid metal door with one small window.

"We're going to stop by the jail for a minute," Dean told Kathy.

"Oh! You *are* taking me to jail!" she exclaimed.

"Did you think I was kidding?" Bob asked.

"Yeah, I did."

"Cops don't kid around," Dean stated seriously.

Kathy knew they were teasing her. They wouldn't dare put her in jail, would they? She began to wonder when Bob took hold of her right arm and Dean took the other. Bob pushed a button beside the door, and shortly after an officer looked out the small window. The door was then opened and they were allowed to enter. The jailer gave Kathy a curious look, but when Bob explained that she was on the Grand Jury and riding along with them, she was welcomed and thanked her for her interest in police work.

Kathy looked around. There was a woman sitting on a bench to the left of the door, and three men in a cell on the right. Dean approached the high counter at the back of the small room, spoke to a cute female officer for a moment, then motioned for Kathy to join him.

"Kathy, this is my wife, Jean. Sweetheart, this is Kathy Cooper."

"Glad to meet you, Ms. Cooper," she said with a friendly smile. "Are you enjoying riding along?"

"Kathy please, and yes, I am enjoying it!" She stepped aside to allow Dean and Jean to talk for a moment. When they finished, Kathy turned to Jean. "Would it be possible for me to tour the jail while I'm here tonight?"

Jean's smile faded into a frown. "You sure you want to do that?"

"Well, I think so."

"She wants to learn all about police work," Bob said with a twinkle in his eyes.

Kathy picked up on his mischievous smile and wondered what unpleasant surprise awaited her.

Jean called the sergeant over, introduced Kathy, and informed him of her request. He agreed to the tour and sent for a female officer to take Kathy to the female floor of the jail. Dean and Bob decided to go to Juvenile Division while she toured. They said they would come back and get her when they were done. In the elevator on the way up to the women's floor of the jail, the female officer with Kathy explained that she was taking bail-bond papers to one of the prisoners for her to sign.

When the door of the elevator opened, the odors of unwashed bodies, stale beer and alcohol, vomit, urine, and worse things assaulted Kathy's nose. She made a face and a sound of disgust.

"Breathe through your mouth," the officer advised.

Kathy did, but it didn't help much. Cells lined both sides of an aisle. No walls, just bars, allowed her to see the entire cell block of prisoners. She watched as the officer opened one of the cells. One of the four women in it came to the door and signed the papers. The four cots that crowded the cell looked hard and lumpy and the toilet was in plain sight of anyone on the floor. A prisoner across the aisle came to the bars and started cussing and screaming at the officer, who ignored her. In the next cell, a woman was sitting on the toilet. In others, she observed one woman vomiting, one crying and moaning, and a third who looked like she was dancing to music only she could hear.

The officer followed Kathy's gaze. "She can't stand still. She's high on something. When she comes down she'll be as sick as that one," she said, pointing to the woman who was throwing up.

This was not a place Kathy ever wanted to spend any time. She and the officer returned to the jail entrance and Kathy thanked her and the sergeant. Dean and Bob returned and the three of them left.

As Dean started cruising the streets again, Kathy remained quiet, thinking about what she had seen in the jail and making some notes. The jail had been a shock. But, I'm glad I did it, she realized. It was just one more detail in the picture she was getting of police work.

Dean again headed for the coffee shop on Washington Avenue. This time they succeeded in getting there. The men got coffee and some doughnuts. Kathy got a cold soda. In the unit, they continued westward on Washington and pulled up at one of the used car lots. It was surrounded by a high chain-link fence. Inside the fence a dog starting barking furiously. The men got out of the car. The moment they spoke to the dog, the barking stopped and the tail wagging started.

Bob turned to Kathy. "Kathy, this is John Henry."

John Henry was a huge black and tan mongrel dog, who was so ugly he was almost cute. One ear stood up and the other flopped down. Kathy watched as he put his front feet up on the fence and stuck his nose through so the men could stroke his muzzle. Bob fed him the doughnut. Another dog, smaller, black and white, came forward cautiously, but would not come to the fence. Even another doughnut would not lure it close enough to determine if it were male or female.

"Looks like John Henry has a new pal," Dean commented. "We haven't seen that dog before."

"He's so skinny," Kathy said, "I can see all his ribs."

Bob threw a doughnut over the fence. When it landed in front of the strange dog, he was startled into stepping back, then stretched his muzzle forward cautiously to smell it and quickly devoured it.

"We need to bring some dog food next time," Dean said. Bob agreed.

After cruising for a while with nothing going on, Dean commented, "It's too quiet. I need some coffee to stay awake. Can you use a pit stop, Kathy?"

"If you stop, I'll use the opportunity."

Shortly, Dean pulled into Station Six at T. C. Jester and Dacoma. Obviously, this was a popular place with the officers, because a Radio Patrol Unit and an Accident Investigation Unit were already there. They asked how Kathy was enjoying riding along.

"I love it," she said with a twinkle in her eyes.

The officers all laughed. "Now you know why we're cops," one of them stated. The others nodded in agreement.

The accident investigator asked when she was going to ride with them. That took her by surprise. "You want me to ride with you?"

"Sure! Be nice to have a good looker along on a slow night," he stated, openly flirting.

She shook her head. "Too bad," she said with false sympathy. "I'm booked solid with Patrol until the end of October."

He walked off shaking his head and cursing under his breath as the other officers laughed.

"Nice going, Kathy. You don't want to ride with Accident. Not enough action. Stick with us and we'll show you what it's all about," one of the officers from the other unit told her.

When they got in the car she asked, "Do you think he was serious about wanting me to ride with him?"

"Accident Units are one-man. Driving around for eight hours alone can be boring. Having someone to talk to helps the officer stay alert," Bob informed her. "Besides, we love to talk about our job."

She sat back, stunned. In the beginning she wondered if she could get the officers to open up to her and wondered if they would resent her presence. Then she remembered roll call and the officer asking who got her to ride along tonight. It appeared that some of them, at least, welcomed her presence.

Back on the street, a *silent alarm* call came in. Dean drove at eighty plus getting there, and a second unit pulled in right behind them. The four officers checked while she stayed at the cars. No sign of entry. They couldn't figure out what would be worth stealing at this kiddy amusement park, anyway. Dean got on the radio and cleared the call by letting the dispatcher know they did not find any entry. Bob introduced Kathy to Officers Donny Wells and Art Donahue, who worked out of the North Shepherd station.

"Hey, Pretty Lady, when are you going to ride with us?" Officer Wells asked Kathy. "There's more action in our district."

"The men at Northwest have been treating me real good. Think you can match 'em?" she teased.

"Easy!"

She considered a moment, then nodded. "I'll try it next Friday night."

"Great!"

Back on the streets, they cruised, but no calls were going out on the radio. They talked about their wives and children, their hobbies, things that were right with the Department and things that were wrong with it.

"The thing we need mostly is equipment. LAPD has equipment that we should have, but the city is too cheap to pay for it."

"Such as?" Kathy asked.

"Handheld radios. The way things are now, if we get in trouble away from the car, we have no way to call for help. We have to handle it ourselves or get back to the car," Dean told her.

"We've had officers get killed that way," Bob added, "and officers have had to kill perps when they couldn't handle them alone and had no way to get backup."

"If you're involved in a shooting," Dean said, "it doesn't matter how right you were to fire your weapon, they still treat you like a perp until the investigation is over. Homicide and Internal Affairs *each* investigate it, and also the shooting team from the DA's office. Sworn statements are taken. Then it goes to the grand jury. And all that time, you can't work the streets. You're put on desk duty. All you can do is sit around and wonder if the Department is going to hang your ass out to dry to satisfy some political pressure. It's hell!"

"I take it you've been there," Kathy commented.

"Yeah. A couple times," he answered.

Two shootings, when most officers never fire their weapon in the line of duty? She realized he had been cleared in both cases; otherwise he would no longer be a cop. She wanted to know the details, but something about his manner warned her not to ask. At least not yet. Perhaps after he got to know her better he would be willing to share.

"Will that make you hesitant to shoot in the future?" she asked.

"No. I'll shoot. I'd rather be tried by twelve than carried by six."

Kathy had to think about that a moment. He would rather be tried by a jury of twelve than carried by six pallbearers. She would hear this phrase many times as she continued to ride along. She learned that the officers had thought about it. They were aware that they might have to shoot someone to stay alive or keep their partner alive, and they were mentally prepared to do it.

At about 6:00 a.m. Kathy was taken home. She thanked Bob and Dean, who invited her to ride along again. Maybe it would be busier next time. Bob lit her way to the door and waited until she was inside before he returned to the car.

* * * * *

Kathy succeeded in getting ready for bed without waking Steve—she thought—until he rolled over and took her in his arms. He just held her. She realized he worried about her when she was riding along. Concern she understood, but fear for her safety was keeping him from sleeping. That wasn't good.

She wanted to continue to ride along with the officers, but she also had to consider Steve and his feelings. They needed to talk about it. While trying to think of a good approach, she fell asleep and did not wake until about two in the afternoon.

Kathy showered and dressed, then joined Steve and the boys in the family room. They were watching a football game, of course.

"What happened last night, Mom?" Jacob asked.

She shrugged, as she considered what she could tell them. "The officers I was with met their snitch. He gave them information about illegal gambling. They went downtown to get some information. I toured the women's floor of the city jail. They checked a burglar alarm. Pretty typical night," she told them.

In the following weeks Kathy would learn there is no such thing as a typical night. Each is different and each can become chaos in an instant.

Chapter 4

Friday, August 13, 1976 - 3:00 p.m.

Evening shift officers Greg Sampson and James Dickens from the North Shepherd substation picked Kathy up at home for another ride along. Greg Sampson appeared older than the officers she had ridden along with so far. With light brown hair graying at the temples, he wore the uniform and accouterments easily, as though he had worn them all his life. As they got to know each other, Kathy found out that he had been wearing them for twenty-two years.

His partner, James Dickens, was ex-military police who had been on Houston's streets as a cop for seven months, having just completed his probationary period. In his late twenties, his whole demeanor illustrated his pride in his job, from the way he carried himself to his meticulous grooming.

"Ex-marine, James?" Kathy asked him.

"Yes, ma'am. How'd you know?"

"It shows. And my first name is Kathy!"

"Yes, ma'am. Kathy."

"Greg, have you spent all your years with HPD in patrol?"

"Mostly. Also Vice, Canine, and as a Criminal Investigator." After a moment he added, "I sure am glad I didn't know yesterday that you would be riding with us today. On a scale of one to ten on jealousy, my wife rates an eleven and a half. I got into a fight with a female prisoner one time and had to get her in a head lock. Got perfume and make-up all over my uniform. My wife didn't speak to me for days."

"How'd you find out I'd be riding along?"

"At roll call Sergeant Jenkins said, 'Unit eleven sixty-four, Sampson, Dickens, and Cooper.' 'Who?' I asked. 'You're to pick up Kathy Cooper. She's on the grand jury and will be riding with you as an observer.'" Before she could ask him how he felt about it, they received a *burglary in progress* call. The homes in the area were one-story brick bungalows with front porches predating World War II. Greg pulled up at the curb in front of the house. From the street they could clearly see that the front door stood open a few inches.

James reached back and unlatched Kathy's door from the outside. He and Greg drew their pistols and approached the front door and stood one on each side. Greg pushed the door open with his foot, then entered fast. James followed. Kathy got out of the back seat and moved to the front seat, keeping the car between herself and the house and staying within reach of the radio.

There it is again, she thought; the apprehension, the concern for the officers. Do they face this day after day after day? Do they get this knot in their stomachs each time? She waited, never taking her eyes off the entrance of the house.

In a few minutes Greg and James reappeared with three children who looked about six to eight years old—one boy and two girls. As they took the two little girls across the street to their house, Kathy tagged along. Greg explained to the girl's mother that they had been in the vacant house across the street and that it was not a safe place for them to play. The woman agreed and stated that the girls would be punished and that she would watch them closer in the future. The boy lived next door to the vacant house. They talked to his mother, who said he had been punished before for going in that house. She thanked the officers and began spanking the boy before the officers and Kathy were off the front porch.

"Taking the kids home," Greg explained after he got the unit back *in service*, "and talking to the parents is called *counseling in the field and releasing to parents*. If the attitude of the parents is good, most times that is what I do, rather than take the kids all the way down to Juvenile. All they do is talk to the parents and release the kids, anyway.

"I feel better now," he continued, "knowing you're not going to run inside on a burglary call. You did the right thing by staying by the car. I have to admit I was concerned for your safety in the beginning. It's hard enough to do this job right without having to worry about some ding-a-ling civilian female getting in the way and getting hurt."

Kathy couldn't help but laugh. "I can't remember ever being called a ding-a-ling. I'm as concerned for your safety as you are for mine. I'll stay by the car unless you tell me to come with you, and then I'll stay behind you."

"We'll make an officer out of you yet, Kathy," he said. "Have you thought about the Academy?"

"Not seriously."

"Why not?"

"I promised my husband I wouldn't work after we married and had children."

"We don't think of this as work!" James stated.

"I'm beginning to understand that," Kathy commented.

Greg reached for the mike. They received another *burglary in progress* call, located in an area developed about ten years earlier. The brick homes had well-kept yards with tall pine trees giving spotty shade. The house they went to had an attached garage, which was open. Greg pulled the unit across the driveway to block the car parked there. He and James bailed out with guns in their hands as a man walked toward them from inside the garage.

"Stop right there!" Greg shouted. "Raise your hands!"

"What the fuck? I called you!"

"Raise your goddamn hands!"

Reluctantly the man raised his hands and stood still. Greg and James quickly spread him out on the hood of the car in the driveway and patted him down. The whole time the man was cussing and complaining.

"What the hell are you doing? I'm the victim here!"

"Have you got some ID?" James asked.

"In my wallet in my left rear pocket."

Greg removed the wallet and flipped it open. The address on the driver's license was the same as the address of the scene. Greg nodded to James. They both holstered their pistols.

"Sorry, sir," Greg apologized as he allowed the man to stand up. "We received the call as a burglary in progress. We had no way of knowing you were the home owner."

"And I'm a black man and living in a white neighborhood!"

"Yes, sir. Sorry, sir."

The man opened his mouth to say something else, thought better of it, closed his mouth and just nodded. In the meantime, James had returned to the car and unlatched the door for Kathy. She joined the group to listen.

"I left for work about seven this morning and returned about twenty minutes ago," the man told them. "I found the garage door open. My golf clubs and cart are gone!"

"Was the garage locked?" James asked.

"Apparently not. I can't find any evidence that they broke in."

"I'll check it out," Greg stated and walked off to examine the garage doors.

Kathy followed along behind him. Neither of them saw anything to indicate forced entry.

"Did they get inside the house?" Greg called to the man.

"No!"

All the man wanted was an offense report number for insurance purposes. James used the man's phone to call Records to get a case number for the report he would file at the end of shift. Twenty minutes after receiving the call, they were back *in service* and James was angry.

"That stupid son-of-a-bitch!" James exclaimed. "He could have been shot. He told the dispatcher the burglary was in progress, when it wasn't. He just wanted a cop right away! The bastard!"

"Let's hope he learned his lesson!"

"Yeah," James paused. "Sorry, Kathy."

"For what?"

"My bad language."

"I've heard it before, James. No apology necessary."

Shortly after that, they got *out of service* to eat supper and miss the worst of the afternoon rush hour traffic. When they got back in service James took over the driving, as was usual on the evening shift. With the heavy traffic during the shift, one man got tired if he did all the driving.

After getting back *in service* they got a call, *a mental case walking in the street*. They found nothing at the location when they arrived, but James cruised around checking several streets in the area. Still, they found nothing. They informed the dispatcher that it was *GOA*, gone on arrival.

They cruised, made a couple of traffic stops, and talked. Kathy asked questions. They gave answers. She did not like all the answers, especially their attitude about female officers working patrol. It had not happened at HPD yet, but they knew it was being done in other large police departments.

Before Kathy had a chance to express her opinion, a *fight in a bar* call went out for another unit and the evening shift sergeant called for their unit to also respond. James drove to a beer joint on West Montgomery Road in a black area. The sergeant and two other units were already there. Those officers told them how, when they got there, about thirty guys came out of the place and melted into the night.

Kathy followed the men into the place. It was a dive, a dump, but it was quiet. Nobody saw anything. There was no trouble. Nothing happened. But there was a small amount of blood on the floor. A young black woman was using the pay phone. She was soaking wet and had a split lip.

When asked who hit her, she said, "Nobody. I got drunk. I tripped and fell in a ditch."

Even Kathy didn't believe her. But if she wasn't going to tell the truth and file charges, there was nothing the officers could do. They checked the bar's licenses and health cards. Finding everything in order, they left the building. Outside, Sergeant Jenkins, who was older than Greg and nearly completely bald, stopped Kathy.

"Greg Sampson is a liar," he told her. "He told me you were buck-toothed, knock-kneed, flat-chested, and fat."

Behind him, Greg was shaking his head in desperate denial. Kathy had decided the first night she rode along that if the men dished it out, she needed to be able to give it back.

"He explained that to me," she commented seriously. "He said I would be safer riding with him than with the sergeant, because the sergeant's a dirty old man."

When all the men, including the sergeant, laughed, she knew she was holding her own. They left the scene and headed for the North Shepherd station for shift change.

As they walked toward the 'officers only' back entrance at the station, James commented to Kathy, "You're a lot different than I expected."

"Oh?" she inquired.

"I expected you to be a frustrated female that wanted to be a policewoman and work patrol," James admitted.

Kathy smiled and shook her head. "Since childhood I planned on being a cop. I gave up the dream years ago. I understand why you love it and why one officer told me, 'It beats working for a living.' If it wasn't for my husband and kids, I'd like to try it, but only if I could do the job."

"That's the point," James stated. "You couldn't walk into a barroom brawl and command the respect and authority that the worst male cop would. Sooner or later, you'd find some smart ass you'd have to kill to control. Most situations men can handle without that."

"I know," she agreed. "But, it will happen in a few years. And the girls will have the training to do the job."

"I don't know. I hope you're wrong." Then he smiled, "Come ride with us again."

Greg followed Kathy into the lobby as James walked away. "James is right. You surprised me, too. Thanks for coming out. It was a pleasure having you ride with us. I hope you'll do it again," he stated sincerely.

"I'd like to. Thank you," Kathy answered.

"Come on. I'll introduce you to the night sergeant."

Chapter 5

Friday, August 13, 1976 - 9:50 p.m.

The layout of the Shepherd station was similar to the Northwest station. The building was older and smaller, and surrounded by businesses. Inside the lobby, the duty desk served as a gathering place for officers coming in to work the next shift. Greg Sampson escorted her to the sergeant's office and introduced her to Sergeant Ralph Strong, then excused himself.

The sergeant's welcome was reserved; not unfriendly, just cautious. About Kathy's age, he appeared hard as a rock, as though he worked out regularly. His features were regular and pleasant, but Kathy wondered if his face would break if he smiled, because she saw no laugh lines in his face.

"Mrs. Cooper," he said, "you asked to ride along with Officers Wells and Donahue, is that correct?"

"Yes, Sergeant."

"How do you know them?"

"I met them last Saturday night, and they invited me to ride along with them."

"Met them where?"

"At Peppermint Park. The officers I was riding with were handling an alarm call. Officers Wells and Donahue also answered the call. After they checked the building, I was introduced to them."

"You were riding out of Station Five?"

"Yes, sir."

He nodded. "If you'll wait out by the desk, I'll get back to you after roll call."

"All right," she agreed and left his office.

Kathy took advantage of the break to make a pit stop, wash her hands, wipe her face with a wet paper towel, and freshen her lipstick. As she stepped out of the ladies room, the men were coming out of the roll call room and leaving the building.

Sergeant Strong approached her with Officers Wells and Donahue. Officer Wells was the tallest of the three men, slim with dark, softly curled hair and dark eyes that twinkled when he smiled, which she would learn was often. Officer Donahue was average height and build, with light brown hair, blue eyes, and a relaxed stance and manner.

"Hey, you did come, Pretty Lady," Donny Wells said with a big smile.

"Donny! None of that," the sergeant ordered. "Mrs. Cooper, I hope you aren't offended by bad language, because with these two you're bound to hear some."

"Aw, Sarge, I'll be good," Donny promised like a little boy.

"Yeah, Sarge. We know how to treat a lady!" Art added.

"I'm not a lady," Kathy told them.

Sergeant Strong turned to Kathy with raised eyebrows. "I was trying to warn you, but maybe I should warn them!" he commented with humor in his eyes.

"We'll be fine, Sergeant. Thank you," she told him.

Kathy followed the two officers out to the parking lot and the unit that they would be using that night. They arranged their equipment in the car: Key Map, clipboard, flashlights, ticket book, rifle, and shotgun. As they pulled out of the station parking lot and headed north on North Shepherd drive, Donny got on the radio.

"Eleven-sex-sex SO," Donny told the dispatcher. The dispatcher acknowledged.

"This should be a busy night, Ms. Cooper," Art said.

"Call me Kathy," she told him.

"Yes, ma'am!"

"No, not ma'am. Kathy!"

Looking a little sheepish, he nodded. "Okay," and quickly added, "Kathy."

"Why should it be busy?"

"It's a payday Friday. It's warm and dry. And it happens to be Friday the 13th."

She laughed, partly from nervousness and partly because Chief Ledford had said one payday Friday night would be enough for her.

Donny picked up the mike and they had a call, a *disturbance at an apartment*. They were familiar with the apartment complex. Kathy tagged along behind them as they found the correct apartment, but no disturbance. After listening outside the door and hearing nothing, they knocked several times, but no one answered. As they returned to the unit, a gray-haired woman of about fifty pulled up in a car and got out. She had been drinking but did not appear to be drunk. She told them she had called.

"I want you boys to do something about what is going on up there in that apartment."

"It's all quiet up there, ma'am," Art told her.

"But he brought her here," the woman insisted.

"Who, ma'am?" Donny asked.

"That man I'm living with."

"Brought who here, ma'am?"

"My daughter. She's just a child."

"How old is she?"

"Twenty-one. She is good and innocent and I want her to stay that way. Oh, God, if only she'd find a nice young man, like you officers. You're both so young. Are you married?"

"Yes, ma'am."

"Both of you?"

"Yes, ma'am."

As the woman went on and on and on about her daughter, Kathy sensed the officers' impatience. She understood that the woman was lonely and wanted someone to talk to, but that's not the cop's job. Yet if they were abrupt and offended her, she would feel the cops didn't care and file a complaint.

Donny tried to tell the woman they would look for her daughter. The best thing for her to do was to go home and wait to hear from the girl. If the girl came home and found her mother gone, she would be worried. It was a touchy situation requiring tact and understanding on the officer's part.

Donny didn't sound understanding when they were back in the car. He was cussing vehemently as he drove the unit away. When he ran down, he apologized to Kathy.

"I've heard all those words, Donny. I even use them once in a while."

Donny sighed with relief. Kathy chuckled.

"I hate dealing with her nonsense calls," Art said, "when we might be really needed somewhere else."

"You've dealt with her before?"

"Several times," Art told her.

Donny got them *back in service*. The dispatcher had a call waiting for them, *a disturbance at a residence*.

"Mama's been drinking again," Donny stated.

"You're going to love this one," Art told Kathy.

"Why?"

"You'll see."

"You're not going to tell me, are you?"

"Nope!"

Kathy knew they were testing her, wanting to see how she would react to the situation. She tried to brace herself emotionally for whatever and realized that officers face 'whatever' every time they answer a call.

When they arrived, a man came out and talked to them. His wife was drunk and causing trouble. They asked him to sit in the back of the car while they checked it out. The man didn't seem to mind being locked in the back-seat. Kathy thought this probably had happened before, or he wouldn't be so calm about it. As Art and Donny approached the house, two little girls, about five and seven, came out of the door crying.

"Are you taking Daddy to jail?" the older of the girls asked. "Please don't. Mama's drunk and mad and she'll hit us. See where she hit me yesterday?" she said pointing to a small bruise on her arm. "Please don't take our daddy away."

The child was so pitiful, Kathy wanted to hug and comfort her. Donny took the girl's hand, told her everything would be all right, and led the girls back into the house. A boy of about ten stood just inside the door when they entered. He had Down's Syndrome. Donny and Art talked to the woman, then took her to the car. Art let the man out of the car and put the woman in. The man took the children back into the house. Art sat in the backseat with the woman and Kathy got in front with Donny.

Donny radioed in, "Female in transit. Time check." The dispatcher gave him the correct time. Art noted it down. As Donny started driving toward Central, the woman started whining about being a good mother and asked if Kathy had any idea why she drank once in a while.

"Cause I've got that retarded boy. Can you imagine what it's like to have a retarded son? Sure, I drink sometimes. It's just too much for a mother to bear. I'm a good mother. I've done everything for those kids. Everything. Given my whole life for 'em." She continued complaining and whining all the way to Central.

When they parked at Central near the jail entrance, Donny asked for another time check. After ringing the bell at the door and being identified, one of the jail officers opened it for them. The procedure for booking a drunk was simple. There was just one form to fill out.

While Art did that, Kathy stood to one side of the door and observed what was going on. The holding cells at the right had several men in them. To the left of the entrance along the front wall was a bench. Three women were sitting there, including the woman they had just brought in. Another unit brought in a husband and wife, both drunk. She was all wet and muddy. He was mad, still trying to get at her, and being held back by the arresting officers. He was quickly put in one of the holding cells.

"Don't you understand?" the crying woman blubbered. "I need to go home and take care of my children."

The woman was told to sit on the bench. Halfway to the bench, she fell. The drunk woman Donny and Art had just brought in jumped up to help the newcomer. Kathy watched as the first drunk woman pulled the shirttail of the second up, wiped the woman's runny nose with it, and helped her to the bench. Perhaps our drunk is a good mother when she's sober, Kathy thought.

A few minutes later, they left Central and got *in service*. Another call was waiting, a *burglary of an apartment in progress*. Donny headed north on Houston Avenue, driving more than the speed limit.

At the apartment complex they had trouble finding the apartment. In a project with multiple buildings, sometimes there is nothing to indicate the numbers of the apartments in each building. Art spotted the apartment across a courtyard and pointed. It was an upstairs apartment. Two panes were broken out of the lower window and it was raised. Without speaking, Art and Donny headed for the stairs that led to the second floor balcony.

Kathy watched until they drew their guns, then she ducked under the balcony and around a corner. She grew tense, concerned for them. All remained quiet. Then she heard a soft whistle. She stuck her head out.

"Come on up," Art said, motioning to her.

Upstairs in the apartment, Donny told her, "Look around and tell me what happened."

Kathy observed lamps tipped over, papers, beer cans, and ashtrays scattered on the floor, a box of laundry detergent poured over the mess, a partially burned Playboy magazine on one end table, and a camera, stereo, and television set sitting undisturbed in plain view. In the bedroom it became obvious that the apartment belonged to a man, because all of the clothes thrown on the floor were men's clothes. Drawers had been emptied. The bed had been stripped and the linens dropped on the floor. Toiletries from the bathroom had been poured over the clothes and linens. More torn up girlie magazines were scattered on the bed. The kitchen area was about the same, with the contents of cabinets, drawers and food from the open refrigerator thrown on the floor.

"Well?" Donny prompted.

"The television, stereo, and camera weren't stolen," Kathy stated. "Somebody's just mad as hell at this guy."

"Who did it?" Donny asked.

"I don't know," Kathy answered, puzzled by the question.

"Think about it."

Kathy didn't have a clue. She shook her head. "I don't know."

"A woman," Donny told her. "Probably a girlfriend that thinks he's screwing around on her."

"How do you know that?" Kathy asked, wondering how he could possibly know.

"The burned and torn up girlie magazines. A man would have done more physical damage and taken the magazines."

"That makes sense," Kathy agreed with a smile.

Afterward, Art wrote a note for the owner telling him to contact Burglary and Theft if he wished to file charges. They all returned to the squad car and got back *in service*. Donny drove to a doughnut shop. The men got coffee. Kathy made a pit stop.

"Do you guys eat?" Kathy asked when she returned. "Or is it just doughnuts and coffee?"

"This town shuts down about three o'clock. After that, we'll check out for breakfast or whatever you'd like, Kathy," Art reassured her.

They cruised. The guys talked about being a policeman and how it affects their lives, their wives and children, twenty-four hours a day.

Ride Along

"You're married," Art suggested. "You're living a normal life. Hearing people bad-mouthing the cops doesn't bother you or your wife. Then you become a cop. You're the same man, but the slams are slams against everything you stand for. Officers expect it and accept it. They hear it every day on the streets. If we don't get called names, we're not doing our job right.

"Your wife stands up for cops. It strains her friendships. Kids are so innocent. 'Daddy is a policeman,' they say proudly. The other children repeat slams they've heard at home. Children are cruel without meaning to be, but the cop's kid doesn't understand.

"Friends fall by the wayside. You can no longer relate to them or them to you. They say things like, 'Hey, Art. I was going down the street the other day and slid through a stop sign. This cop gave me a ticket for it. Now, I know you're not all bad, but… ,' and you have to sit there and listen to this shit. Or friends expect you to fix traffic tickets for 'em.

"You're torn between loyalty to friends and loyalty to the Department. So, you back off from these people, because they don't understand. You socialize with other police officers, talk a lot of shop, or limit your social life to family and relatives."

"Even some relatives become a pain in the ass," Donny added. "'Don't know why you want to be a cop,' they say. 'You could work for your Uncle so-and-so and make more money.' We're not in this for the money. We're in it for the involvement, to fulfill a commitment. To do something we feel very strongly about. Law and order. Civilians don't understand," Donny concluded.

"No, they don't," Kathy agreed. They were silent for a moment, thinking about it, when a question occurred to Kathy. "Does it also affect your sex life?"

Donny and Art glanced at each other.

"You want to answer that?" Art asked Donny.

"No!" Donny exclaimed.

"What I want to know is…the excitement, does it…Oh, hell!"

Both men burst into laughter. Then she knew that they were putting her on and they had not taken her question the wrong way.

"I suppose this will be all over the station at the next roll call," Kathy said with disgust.

"Probably," Art pointed out.

"I thought there was a code of silence," she stated.

"Between officers, yes," Art confirmed.

"You're not an officer," Donny pointed out.

Kathy's eyes narrowed. "You're doing it again!"

They laughed harder.

"Well, what's the answer?" she prodded when they regained control.

They admitted that their sexual appetites were healthy, but was it because they were policemen or because the personality of men was fitted for police work? Art admitted that some nights he needed sex to help him unwind and sleep. Donny agreed, but added that there were times when he needed it to confirm that he was alive, especially after a close call or a gory murder scene.

"Policemen have more opportunities," Donny told her. "There's something about the uniform that attracts the women."

Kathy was about to agree, when Donny turned up the radio and reached for the mike. It was 2:53 a.m. They were given a *discharge of firearms* call at a residence.

"Oh, shit! There goes breakfast," Donny moaned.

The neighborhood they drove to had narrow streets, no sidewalks, and small postwar frame houses. When they arrived, a man came out of the front door and pointed across the street. They looked around to see a car back out of a driveway and speed off.

"God! Damn! Get the hell in the car," Donny yelled. It was moving before she and Art slammed their doors. The unit was facing the wrong direction, requiring Donny to whip it around in a U-turn. He pursued at high speed with lights flashing.

"Watch your face, Kathy! Don't hit the cage," Donny warned.

Kathy had braced her feet and now raised her arms to protect her face if need be.

They lost sight of the car once, made one wrong turn, and Donny again made a U-turn. As they came around a corner they saw taillights in a driveway. The unit screeched to a halt as Donny stopped it across the driveway behind the suspect's car. The men bailed out, guns in their hands. They stayed behind and on opposite sides of the suspect's car, guns raised toward the driver.

"Get outta the car!" Donny yelled. "Get outta the car, before I kill ya!"

Slowly, the man got out. They kept him covered and went around to that side of the car. Donny grabbed the man's left wrist with his left hand. Art got the man's right one in his left hand. They laid him across the trunk, none too gently. Donny holstered his pistol and patted the man down before handcuffing him. Art put his gun away and they brought the angry, cussing man to the unit. Donny let Kathy out of the backseat and they put the man in. Art read the man his rights in between getting cussed.

"Let me see your flashlight, Donny," Kathy asked.

"Oh, God. Are you hurt? Where?" Donny asked as he started sweeping her with the light.

"No! He hit a fence coming out of the other driveway. There should be a mark on the car. I want to see it."

"Why?"

"We lost sight of the car for a second. I didn't get a good look at it to begin with. I want to be sure it's the same one."

"It's the same car," Donny stated.

"Show me!" she insisted.

They found the mark left by the collision with the fence. Kathy was convinced. They returned to the unit. Kathy rode in front with Donny. Art drove the suspect's car back to the scene of the complaint.

Donny parked the unit in front of the complainant's house and left the engine and air-conditioner running. Art got out of the suspect's car with a twenty-two caliber rifle which had been on the front seat. Kathy's heart skipped a beat as she realized that the outcome of the confrontation could have been much different. The rifle would be taken to Central, tagged, and kept as evidence.

The complainant and his wife came out on the porch to meet them. They were asked to look at the suspect. They identified him as the man who had shot at their house earlier. Because it was less than two hours since the shooting, this was a legal show-up.

"What happened here?" Art asked.

"We came home from playing dominoes," the complainant stated. "He was across the street, hollering and carrying on. 'I'll kill you and your GD dogs, too.' I walked over to see what the trouble was. He drew back a table leg. There's a busted table in the front yard. Anyway, he drew it back and I busted him in the mouth and came home. He must have gone and gotten a gun because he took four shots at our house."

"We recovered a rifle," Art announced.

The man showed them where one shot had gone through the hollow core front door and stuck in the wall across the living room. Two others were inside the outer wall of the house. The fourth went through the window and hit the complainant in the hip pocket. His billfold and credit cards had stopped it.

He and his wife both told the same story before Art started writing it all down. While he did that, Donny and Kathy recovered one bullet from the living room wall and one from the complainant's billfold.

When they returned to the unit, the suspect had been sitting in the car in handcuffs for nearly an hour. He started complaining that he had a broken arm and was in pain. Art took the man's car to his wife at the house across the street. She confirmed that the man had a broken wrist and was supposed to be wearing a brace on it which he wasn't wearing at the time of his arrest.

When Art returned, he and Donny moved the cuffs to the front and called for Sergeant Strong to meet them. Any time it appears that someone may lodge a complaint, they call the sergeant to look over the situation. Sergeant Strong wasn't worried, at least not about the perp. He turned to Kathy.

"You doing all right?" he asked her.

"Doing fine," she answered with a big grin.

He turned and frowned at Donny and Art suspiciously. They both put on innocent expressions. Sergeant Strong walked off shaking his head.

They all got in the unit—Art in back with the prisoner, Kathy in front with Donny—for the drive to Central. On arrival, they first went to Homicide to fill out forms and check charges to be filed. Aggravated Assault, they were advised. Second, to Burglary and Theft to check the charge, Burglary by Firearms. Third, to Patrol. Fleeing? No, it was Evading Arrest because they lost sight of the car once. Then to Identification for a copy of his rap sheet. He was taken to jail. Once he was booked, they went to Records Division to dictate the Offense Report on this incident and the Burglary of the apartment earlier in the shift.

"All this paperwork just to get this ass put in jail?" Kathy commented. "There ought to be an easier way."

"Everything we do during a shift must be documented. If it isn't documented, it didn't happen. Stopping to take a leak is the only thing not covered," Donny added.

John Bailey and Calvin Henson came into Records. Kathy had ridden with them on the previous Friday night shift.

"Hey, Kathy," Calvin greeted her. "You should have been with us tonight. We chased a kid on a motorcycle all over the county for speeding inside the city limits. When we tried to stop him, he took off. Went east on Long Point to Hempstead, north past Gessner to West Little York, west to Highway 6, south to Clay Road, and east past Bear Creek Park. We were right behind him and doing about a hundred when he went over the Addicks Dam on Clay Road."

Kathy grimaced. She knew these streets and roads and the Addicks Dam, which was an earthen dike around the east and south sides of the reservoir. The roads going over the dam went abruptly up a short hill, over, and down. This was something you did not want to do at a hundred miles per hour.

"I thought I'd lost it right there," he said shaking his head, his eyes still alight with excitement. "We were airborne for a ways, but landed okay. The kid made a left but I missed it. Went on past and took the next left, thinking he might head back our way. Sure enough he was coming at us. He tried a U-turn and crashed through a ditch and into a pasture. He got up and started to run. That was a mistake. John runs five miles every day. He was all over the kid. The bike was stolen."

"I always miss the fun," Kathy complained.

"Speaking of head-on," John said. "I was chasing two hijackers inbound on Washington Avenue one night. A central unit was chasing a drunk outbound on Washington Avenue. They hit head-on. Nobody killed. Talk about somebody getting what they deserve; it was beautiful!"

"Drunks and hijackers seem to be on everyone's blacklist," Kathy observed.

"We all have things we hate," John said. "The thing I hate most is hearing parents tell their kids they'd 'better be good or that policeman is going to get you.' Not good to frighten kids about cops. Cops should be considered friends; someone they can trust if they need help."

They left central at 6:25 a.m. The men had been on overtime since 6:00 a.m. They were just a few blocks away from Kathy's house when a guy ran the red light right in front of them.

"Oh, shit!" Donny exclaimed. "Can't let him get away with that."

He was pulled over and they got out of the unit. Art wrote the ticket.

"Did you see that, Kathy?" Art asked when he returned to the car. "It's daylight and we both took our flashlights. It's habit. We always take them on the night shift, so its automatic even after the sun comes up."

They dropped Kathy at her house at 7:00 a.m. She picked up the morning paper on her way in. It had been a long eventful night without breakfast. She headed to the kitchen to fix something to eat.

Steve and the boys woke up to the smell of coffee brewing and bacon frying. Kathy was starving and she was fixing enough breakfast for the whole family.

Steve walked up behind her at the stove, wrapped his arms around her, and kissed her cheek. "You're late this morning."

"Got tied up downtown doing reports," she told him.

The boys came into the breakfast room, said good morning, and asked what happened during the night. While they all ate, she described the condition of the apartment that had been broken into and asked them, "Who did it?" They didn't figure it out either. Then she told them a little about the man who shot at his neighbor, but she left out the brief chase. Steve offered to clean up the breakfast dishes. Kathy thanked him with a hug and a kiss and headed for bed.

Chapter 6

Saturday, August 14, 1976 - 2:20 p.m.

Jesse Banks picked Kathy up at her home to ride along with him on the evening shift out of Station One. He had heard talk about Kathy, that she was not judgmental, anti-police, stupid, or a blabbermouth. They talked of teasing her and getting back as good as they dished out. But Jesse wanted to find out for himself, so he asked the sergeant if she could ride along with him.

About six feet tall and average build, he was in his mid-forties. His features were pleasant, and became cute when he was amused, which appeared to be often because laugh lines were prominent. This man enjoyed life.

He was working a one-man unit, so Kathy sat in the front seat with him. As they left her neighborhood, the security guard at the construction site flagged down their unit. Jesse stopped the car and notified the dispatcher that he would be out on investigation at Mangum Road and Georgi Lane.

"Would that be the same as the 5000 block of Georgi Lane?" the dispatcher asked.

"Affirmative," Jesse answered.

The dispatcher then cancelled another unit that had been given the call.

Kathy got out of the car at the same time Jesse did. She again felt uneasy, as she had when she and Sergeant Schmidt stopped at the site. She looked around carefully, perceiving no threat. The feeling persisted the entire time Jesse talked with the guard and a man who had been attempting to take materials from the site. This was the second time Kathy had been present at the reporting of an attempted theft at this location.

Jesse informed the man that he would be filing a report of the incident, including the man's name, address, and information on his pick-up truck. The next time, he would be arrested for trespassing. The man left but he wasn't happy about it.

Kathy's uneasiness dissipated as soon as they left the site, so she dismissed it.

"How long have you been an officer?" she asked.

"Twenty-four years."

"Why did you decide to be a cop?"

He chuckled. "I did a lot of things as a teenager that I got picked up for. I never got away with anything. I figured if I couldn't beat 'em, I might as well join them. So, I tried it and found out I liked it. It was a lot of fun in the good old days.

"When we used to bust the whore houses, we'd wait outside the room until the dude got to stroking good. Then we'd kick the door. Well, you know he was all through when that door flew open. But, there he'd be, bare ass in the air. We'd prod the dude a little with the flashlight and tell him, 'If you can finish, you don't have to go to jail.' Then we'd tell the whore, 'If you can make him finish, you don't have to go to jail.' You wouldn't believe the antics that went on then."

"Oh, Jesse, you didn't!"

"Yes, we did."

"That's mean!" Kathy told him, but she was smiling, and when he nodded in agreement, she burst out laughing.

"We could get away with things like that in the fifties. Not now."

Kathy was still smiling when they got a call. Their unit was to meet Sergeant Thorp at a Chinese restaurant. The sergeant bought iced tea for Kathy and coffee for Jesse. Then he told Jesse to take her to some of the joints.

When they left, Jesse asked her, "What kind of joints would you like to see?"

"I don't know," she declared.

"Come on, Kathy. There must be some place in this town that you've wondered about and wouldn't dare go to without a police escort. Well, now you have one. So, where would you like to go?"

"A topless bar and a porno movie," she admitted with a blush.

"You got it." Jesse picked up the mike and told the dispatcher that he was *out of service* at a certain address. The radio went crazy with clicking noises. Jesse chuckled.

"What's that all about?" Kathy asked.

"They know you're riding with me."

"Oh." I should have known, she thought. Cops are observant. They had probably heard her address every Friday and Saturday evening for the past two weekends.

At the theater, they just walked in. No tickets. No questions. Kathy thought, a police escort is nice. Kathy and Jesse stood at the back of the audience rather than take seats. One man sitting near them turned, saw Jesse, and quickly moved to the other end of the row.

Five minutes of the movie was enough for Kathy. If she'd had popcorn, she would have barfed in it. How could people watch that crap, she wondered.

They have to be sick. Back in the car, Jesse radioed in that he'd be *out of service* at another address, which was a topless bar. Again, there was a lot of clicking on the radio.

"This place really doesn't get to rocking until later," Jesse told her as he held the door for her.

The dimly lit bar had tables spotlighted, on which the girls danced. Only one girl was dancing. Wearing only a G-string and four inch high heels, she had a pretty face but her make-up was overdone. Kathy couldn't decide if the girl was trying to look older or younger. Whichever, it wasn't working. Kathy envied her figure. The girl was trim with erect youthful breasts that obviously had never fed a baby. The girl moved well to the loud music.

The beat had Kathy unconsciously moving in rhythm to the beat as she watched, fascinated with the dancer's moves. Maybe I'll try some of those with Steve, she thought, not noticing the man sitting at the bar watching her. When the music stopped, he spoke to her.

"You going to dance next, honey?'

Surprised, Kathy shook her head.

"What's the matter? You bashful?"

"Yes."

"You move good. We'll let you get up there with your clothes on."

Again she shook her head.

"Come on. I'll buy you a drink if you dance for us."

"I don't think the guy I'm with would appreciate that."

"Oh? Who are you with?"

Kathy glanced over her shoulder at Jesse leaning on the end of the bar. She looked back at the man and motioned with her thumb. "The man in blue."

"Oh, shit!" the man exclaimed as he turned away.

Smiling with amusement, Kathy turned to leave. Jesse's stern expression made her wonder if she had done something wrong. They left the bar and got into the unit; Jesse laughed as he drove off. He had heard everything.

"He's right. You do move good! I'd like to see you dance myself. Wait till I tell the guys!"

"Jesse! You wouldn't!"

He just laughed louder and did not answer her. He must have said something though, because at the next roll call at Station One the men teased her about auditioning as a dancer at the titty bar. She took it good-naturedly and told them, "You should have been there."

Jesse got *in service*. A call was waiting: *suspicious car* behind an auto parts store. It was GOA (gone on arrival), meaning they didn't find anything when they arrived.

"Is it true that you are going to write something about police work?" Jesse asked.

"That's my plan."

"Make it more accurate than TV and the movies," he told her. "My wife won't watch a cop show or movie with me because I pick it apart. Did you see that new show the other night?"

"The one where stupidity and poor procedure got two cops killed right in the beginning?"

"That's the one."

"I changed channels. I couldn't watch it," Kathy told him.

"It just got worse."

"That's hard to believe."

"Also, talk to some of the wives. Get their slant on being married to cops. See how they feel when their husbands are assigned to Vice and are out every night in the joints hustling whores. It isn't easy for them to take."

"I'm sure it isn't," she told him. "I wonder sometimes how a cop stays married with all the crap they and their families have to take."

"A lot of them don't."

They got a call: *disturbance* at a restaurant. It was GOA.

"We aren't having any luck at all tonight," Jesse stated.

"That's all right," Kathy said. "I've been enjoying just talking, and I know you must have stories to tell."

"Oh, yeah. I could tell them all night."

"I'd listen all night," she said.

A few minutes later he pulled into the parking lot in front of a motorcycle dealership.

"Christmas Day, a couple years ago, the alarm on this place dropped."

"Dropped?"

"Went off, went down, dropped. I arrived to find the front plate glass window broken out. Inside, a man bombed out of his mind drunk was trying to hot-wire one of the cycles. When I walked up, he raised a two inch pipe about two and a half feet long. I figured if I stayed eight feet away from him I'd be okay. I told him to put the pipe down. The man did, reluctantly. I started toward him to shake him down and he picked up the pipe. I did a fast draw and shot.

"I couldn't believe it. The man didn't fall, didn't react at all. I had shot between his legs, just nicking the crotch of his pants, and killed the cycle behind him. 'Ain't gonna waste no more,' I told him. The man put the pipe down. I turned him around to pat him down and he turned on me and knocked me across the room. As he came toward me, I laid the flashlight up alongside his head and split it open. 'Goddamn, that hurt!' he said, and passed out cold.

"The dispatcher contacted the owner of the store. He came to secure the building, took one look at the cycle I shot, and demanded that I pay for the damage. You should have been there."

"I swear, I'm gonna shoot the next officer that tells me, 'you should have been there!'"

Jesse couldn't help laughing at her statement. "A threat like that could get you in a lot of trouble."

"Not if I don't have the means to carry it out!"

"You have learned a lot out here!" he said, surprised.

"*Any unit clear to check natural DOA in eleven-sixty-two's district?*" came over the radio.

"That's your beat," Kathy stated.

"You don't want to go on that, Kathy. The family will be in hysterics. It'll be a bad scene."

"I told you men, no red ribbons."

"Are you sure?"

"Yes."

Jesse sighed with exasperation. "Okay. Remember, you asked for it, so you'll have to see it through. No going to the car if you can't take it!"

"All right," she promised, not near as sure of herself as she pretended to be.

Jesse took the call. The ambulance was still there when they arrived. They had pronounced the man Dead On Arrival. The family told Jesse that the man, aged seventy-something, had come to his relatives' for dinner. He had some ice cream, sat down, seemed to have trouble breathing, took off his shoes, laid down on the couch, and seemed to go to sleep.

Kathy thought he looked peaceful, but the absence of life was obvious. The family was all calm and quiet, no tears, no trouble. The family asked Kathy if she was a policewoman. She told them she was on the grand jury and just riding along with the officer. They offered her a chair at the kitchen table and sat down with her. What did she do on the grand jury, they wanted to know. Kathy explained and answered their questions.

Jesse got the information he needed and used their phone to make the necessary notifications. He told the family that an autopsy would be done to determine the cause of death. The family wanted that. The man had been ill for some time, but they could not get him to see a doctor.

Jesse called for a body car to transport the deceased to the morgue. When it arrived, he and Kathy left. The family thanked them both for coming.

"They were so busy talking to you, that's the easiest natural DOA I ever made," Jesse stated at the unit. "Next time I get one, I'm going to swing by and pick you up to go with me."

It was near end of shift. Jesse headed for the station.

"Will you ride along with me again?" he asked.

"I'd be happy to," she told him. But, the next time she was in the unit with him, the situation was entirely different.

Chapter 7

Saturday, August 14, 1976 - 9:50 p.m.

As Kathy approached the sergeant's office, one of the older evening shift officers stopped her. In his late-fifties, Kathy estimated, his gray hair was thinning on top at about the same rate as his middle was thickening. His brown eyes were intelligent but tired, as though he had seen too much on the streets. In a slow Texas drawl and raspy baritone, he introduced himself as Joe Newman.

"You rode along with Jesse Banks on the evening shift, didn't you?" he asked her.

"Yes, I did," Kathy confirmed.

"Did he tell you about his first night on the street?"

"I don't think so."

"He was my rookie," Joe Newman told her. "We got a *shooting* call in Acres Homes. When we got there, I told him, 'I'm going in the back. You watch the front and waste the first dude out the front door.' I went in the back and through the house, checking the rooms as I went. I found nothing. When I came out the front door, I found Jesse's pistol under my nose. 'You told me to waste the first dude out the front,' he told me. 'Not me, damn it! I'm no dude! I'm a cop!' I said. He said, 'Can I see your ID, officer?'"

Kathy laughed. "That's sounds like Jesse," she said. "Thank you for sharing that story."

"You're welcome, ma'am. Good night," he said as he tipped his hat and turned to walk away.

"Good night," she answered, impressed with this old-school gentleman.

Through the window wall of the sergeant's office, she could see the sergeant and several of the officers gathered around the desk looking at a pornographic paper. They didn't realize she was there. Kathy just went in and sat down. She couldn't help smiling.

"Jesus, look at those tits!"

"They can't be real."

"I'd like to find out!"

"Look at the ass on this babe."

"I'd love to get both hands full of that!"

Oblivious to her presence, the comments continued adding to Kathy's amusement and education. When they finished the paper, Sergeant Ralph Strong looked up.

"Evening, Kathy," he greeted her.

The others looked around quickly.

"How long have you been sitting there?" Art Donohue demanded.

"Long enough."

Sergeant Ralph Strong and the men who had ridden with Kathy laughed. The other officers left with red faces.

"Who do you want to ride along with tonight?" Ralph asked.

"Has anyone asked for the dubious pleasure?"

"Just about everybody. Take your pick."

She turned to Art. "Do you mind having me aboard tonight?"

"Not at all."

At ten-thirty Kathy left Station One with Art Donohue and Dan Cannon. Dan was in his late twenties, blond with blue eyes deep enough to turn a woman's head. His smile was welcoming and his eyes twinkled with amusement when he learned Kathy was riding with him and Art that night.

On the street, they immediately received a *malicious mischief* call, and had trouble finding the house. The young couple complained about teenagers racing up and down the street in their cars and trucks from three in the afternoon until all hours. Also, they had seen boys in one car handing things out the windows to the smaller kids. The woman was concerned that it might be dope or something like that.

They were advised to call Narcotics and tell them what they had seen. Perhaps they would stake out the corner for a while and see if they could figure out what was going on. As for the racing, Art suggested that they call Station Five and have an alert slip put out. The men that patrol that district would check by, and just being around often would slow the kids down. The couple agreed to make both calls.

As they prepared to leave, Kathy asked if she could make a suggestion. Art nodded.

She turned to the couple. "We had a difficult time finding your house. You need to put up some house numbers that can be easily seen, just in case of an emergency."

"Oh, sorry about that," the man said. "We just moved in and we haven't gotten them up yet. But, I'll do it tomorrow."

Back in the car, Dan said, "Damn, I like this girl. I wouldn't have had the nerve to tell them to put up numbers, but she did. And she can get away with it."

"Did I do something wrong?"

"No, Kathy. You did it right. They took it okay."

A call came in: *see the complainant about recovery of stolen vehicle*. When they arrived at the parking lot of Northline Mall, they found the complainant—an older woman—and two teenage girls. The girls had spotted the car and brought their grandmother to be sure it was hers. The woman told them she had been there shopping that day. She had parked the car near the other end of the mall. When she came out, it was gone. She had looked all over for it, then reported it stolen.

Art checked the hot sheet. The car had been reported stolen. The complainant had the keys. Art took the keys, opened the door carefully, and checked the inside. Nothing seemed to have been disturbed. He went to the unit and called in to get permission from Auto Theft to return the car to the woman. He came back, handed her the keys, and told her it was hers and she could take it home.

"Art," Kathy said. "Aren't you going to look for prints or clues or something that might lead to catching the car thief?"

Dan stepped away from the group, with a coughing fit. Art gave her a lethal look. He explained to the woman that it would be a waste of time. The car was wet with dew, so no prints could be lifted. After sitting in the sun all day, any prints inside would just be grease spots. He had checked the inside and found nothing. The woman took the car and left.

Art turned to Kathy. "I almost hit you with my flashlight," he told her. "I thought you were serious until I saw that little smirk. That's when I wanted to hit you!" Then he laughed with her and Dan.

Moments later, they were going north on Shepherd when a car in front of them turned off and squealed the tires. Dan went after him, just to pull in behind and slow him down. The car wasn't speeding much, but it didn't slow down either.

"Let's see who they are," Art said, as the car approached a stop sign.

Dan turned on the flashing lights and the car ran the stop sign and turned left. The car ran over something in the street and blew the right front tire. It kept going, turning right at the next corner, and started to turn into the front yard of a house. As the car turned, the driver's door swung open. The driver missed the driveway, hit a car parked in the front yard, and came to a stop. Dan blocked the car and slammed the unit into park. He and Art bailed out with guns drawn.

The passenger in the car jumped out and tried to get to the door of the house. Art tripped the man, who fell face down on the ground. Art put a knee in the middle of his back and held him down while he holstered his pistol, handcuffed the man, pulled him to his feet, brought him to the unit, and frisked him.

Meanwhile, Dan approached the driver's side of the car. The driver started to get out, then got back in and shut the door.

"Get out of the goddamn car before I kill you!"

The driver reluctantly got out. Dan pushed him face first against the car. The man just slid down the side of it to his knees. Dan holstered his pistol, cuffed him, and brought him to the unit to search him.

When the passenger had been thoroughly searched, Art unlatched the back door of the patrol car, Kathy got out, and the passenger was placed in the unit. People came out of the house and asked what happened.

Dan found two .38 bullets in the driver's pocket and handed them to Art.

"Where's the pistol?" Dan asked the man.

Art looked up. "Everybody back up on the porch, right now!"

The people moved off. Art went to the driver's side and started searching the car. As he came around to the other side, one of the women started to get in the passenger side.

"Get the hell out of the car!"

"It's my car, sir."

"Right now it's my car!"

"Can I turn off the lights?"

"No, ma'am. That car belongs to me right now. Get out and stay out until we're finished."

The woman moved off. Art was talking to himself, "Where the hell's the pistol?"

Kathy looked around and saw one lying in the street. She walked over to it and stood with it between her feet. "Art, here's one," she called.

The woman came over to her. "Don't show him. Please don't show him."

Incredible! Kathy thought. Who does she think I am? Where does she think I came from? Didn't she see me get out of the police car? She called to Art again.

He came over and picked up the gun. It was a two-barreled thirty-eight caliber chrome plated Derringer. It had broken open at the breach when it hit the street. One bullet was missing. She and Art looked around for it and found it lying nearby. The pistol had been lying in the street about eight feet from the left rear corner of the car. Kathy realized the driver's door had swung open when the car turned because the driver was dropping the pistol in the street.

Dan and Art searched the passenger area and the trunk of the car thoroughly and found nothing else incriminating. They then took the prisoners out one at a time and searched them more carefully. The passenger had lost his shoes in trying to get away from Art. One of the women brought them over to the car. Art checked them and then gave them to the man.

They asked the driver if he wanted to turn the car over to his wife. He did, so Art gave her the keys and told her it was her car now. With the two arrested men in the backseat, Kathy, Art, and Dan got in the front seat and headed for Central.

First they checked wants. The driver had two unpaid traffic tickets. They checked for warrants for criminal offenses. Both men came back clear. Because Dan remembered something about hijackers using a chrome plated Derringer, they got a hold card from Robbery Division, which would give the detectives three days to investigate. Dan tagged the pistol, put it and the bullets in an evidence bag, and took it to the Identification Division where it would go to the crime lab.

Art and Kathy took the prisoners to the jail, then went to Records so he could dictate the report. Dan was taking care of papers for the District Attorney's office. Both officers wanted to know if they could put Kathy down as a witness, since she spotted the gun first. She agreed. It was just after 3:00 a.m. when they left Central. The radio was quiet for the first time all of that shift, until another unit radioed to them.

"Eleven sex-sex to eleven sexy-seven."

That had to be Donny Wells, Kathy realized.

"Eleven sixty-seven, go ahead."

"Are you clear and close to Acres Homes?"

"Location?"

"West Montgomery and Little York."

"Ten minutes."

"Eleven-sex-sex, clear."

Donny Wells and his partner Fred Oakes were waiting for them when Dan pulled up next to their unit.

"You want to do it now?" Donny asked.

"With Kathy riding along?" Dan asked.

"Why not?"

"Okay."

"Pick up some cans on the way."

"Clear."

"Do what?" Kathy asked.

"You'll see," Art answered with a smirk, enjoying paying Kathy back a little.

Both units drove off out West Montgomery Road. Dan stopped at one beer joint and the other unit stopped down the road at another. The two men-on-the-ground got out and started throwing beer cans in on the front floorboards of the units. They then drove out past the city limits and stopped in the middle of a straight stretch of road. The radios were switched to PA and the men started setting the cans up on the far side of the road.

Target practice?

Donny pulled a six foot length of toilet paper from his pocket and carefully tore off two squares. "Here, Kathy. Stuff your ears. When we start busting forty-fours, it's gonna get noisy."

Kathy stuffed her ears and saw that the officers were doing the same thing.

When everybody was ready, Art hit the spotlight and lit up the cans. Dan shot first with his thirty caliber carbine. Art tried the rifle next, then Fred fired off a load of three-fifty-sevens from his pistol. Donny set the cans back up.

"Would you like to try it, Kathy?" Dan asked, holding the rifle out to her.

"You'll have to show me how. I've never seen a rifle like this before."

He showed her how to jack a round into the firing chamber and how to sight it. "Put the bead in the center of the peephole, the peephole on the can, and squeeze the trigger."

They all stepped back to see what she could do.

Well, she thought. I could blow my whole relationship with the men right here. Take a breath, let a little out, hold it, sight, squeeze. Bang. She got it, and the second can too.

"Hey, hey!"

"That's all right, Kathy!"

"That's a nice rifle, Dan. Thanks," she said as she handed it to him.

"Sure."

Donny and Fred shot their pistols together. They each missed about one in six. They stepped aside to reload while Art and Dan shot their pistols. Donny offered to let Kathy try his little twenty-five caliber semi-auto pistol. It was just like the one she owned, except it had a hammer. He showed her how to pull the hammer back, slide the safety off, and reminded her to keep her hand below the slide.

"You've got seven shots," he told her.

Again they stepped back, and Kathy had second thoughts. It's no trick to hit beer cans across a two lane road with a rifle, but with a small pistol? That's a lot tougher. Afraid of disgracing herself, she prayed, please let me hit some of them. She took the proper stance, pulled the hammer back, and slid the safety off. She aimed and squeezed the trigger. Pow. A hit. Pow. Another hit. Pow.

"A little high," Art told her.

She took the other four shots and hit with all of them. One miss in seven shots.

"Goddamn," Donny said.

"She's tough!" Art exclaimed.

Dan said, "You're all right, Kathy!"

She handed the pistol to Donny and thanked him.

"Pretty Lady, you are something else!"

"Lucky," she said.

"That wasn't luck," Fred said. "She doesn't even blink," he told the others.

"Are you sure?" Donny asked. When Fred nodded, Donny said, "Let's see." He loaded the pistol up again.

Damn, thought Kathy. What do they expect of me? She started to refuse but Donny insisted. The men stood back. She shot seven times and got seven hits.

"Daaaamn!" Art exclaimed.

"What'd I tell you?" Fred asked.

"We gotta sign this girl up," Dan stated.

"You are hard to believe," Donny said, shaking his head.

"Would you like to try my three-fifty-seven, Kathy?" Art asked.

"No, thanks," she declined, knowing enough to quit while she was ahead.

The men each fired again, gathered up their stuff, checked to make sure everybody was loaded up, and headed back to town. They had just returned to their beat when they were advised to *call dispatch*.

Dan found a payphone and Art made the call. They were to find a man and tell him that his daughter had been cut and had been taken to Ben Taub Hospital. The family had been trying to reach him by phone and he didn't answer. They went to his apartment. After banging on the door and ringing the bell for some time, he finally opened the door. Art delivered the message. The man wanted to know how badly his daughter had been cut. Art told him that they didn't have that information. The man thanked them.

Dan headed the unit for Kathy's house. Art walked her to the door.

"Good night, Art. Thanks."

"We should thank you. You made a pistol case for us and showed us how to shoot," he told her.

"I think we all had a good time."

"I sure did. See you next weekend?"

Kathy nodded.

"Good night, Kathy."

"Good night."

I didn't blow it after all, she thought, surprised she shot so well. I'll have to thank Daddy for teaching me to shoot when I was a kid, she thought as she entered the bedroom. Steve was snoring softly. Glad that he was sleeping for a change, she undressed quietly, without turning on a light. As she crawled into bed, she almost wished he were awake so she could tell him about the target practice. It would keep until later.

Chapter 8

Tuesday, August 17, 1976 - 9:40 am

Kathy was folding a load of bath towels and thinking about the events of the past weekend, when the phone rang.

"Hello."

"Mrs. Cooper?"

"Yes."

"I'm Lieutenant Goodson at Community Relations at the Houston Police Department."

"Yes?"

"Would it be convenient for you to come to my office sometime tomorrow?"

"I have grand jury tomorrow. If we finish early, I could come by afterward."

"That's fine. Call me when you get done and I'll send a car for you," he instructed, and gave her his direct phone number.

"Can I ask why you want to see me?"

"We'll discuss it tomorrow." he told her and hung up.

Kathy stood listening to the dial tone for a moment. What the heck is that all about? Am I in trouble? Is he going to tell me I can't ride along any more? He didn't sound angry. He was polite, but he sure as hell didn't explain himself. She continued to wonder about the lieutenant's call. The boys came in from school as she folded the last towel and gave her other things to think about.

Wednesday, August 18, 1976 - 2:00 pm

The grand jury had completed its business for the day. Kathy called Kevin Goodson at Community Relations as he had instructed. He told her a car would pick her up in front of the courthouse in a few minutes.

Kathy spotted the unmarked car when it turned the corner. She stepped to the curb. The officer behind the wheel lowered the passenger-side window.

"Mrs. Cooper?"

"Yes," Kathy affirmed as she opened the door.

"I'm Charles Bishop. I'll take you to the lieutenant's office."

"Thank you. Do you have any idea what this is all about?"

Officer Bishop smiled and shook his head. He knows, Kathy thought, but he is not going to tell me.

"It's nothing bad," he told her.

He drove her to the Community Relations office, housed in a separate building on the grounds of Central, and escorted her through the outer office to the open door of an inner office. A tall, slim, nice-looking lieutenant in uniform walked around the desk and greeted her with his hand extended.

"Kevin Goodson," he told her. "I've been looking forward to meeting you, Mrs. Cooper."

"Call me Kathy, please." She remembered him from the news coverage a few years earlier when he was nearly killed in a traffic accident while trying to help a citizen with a disabled car on the Southwest Freeway. As he walked toward her, she noticed a slight limp. Otherwise he appeared completely recovered.

He motioned toward the couch in a sitting area. "Coffee?"

"I don't drink coffee, but thanks."

"Something else?"

"Not right now," Kathy declined, a little nervous about this meeting.

He dismissed Officer Bishop with a nod and sat in the easy chair to the right end of the couch, bending his right knee only slightly. A lasting effect of the accident, Kathy surmised. Classical music played softly in the background.

"Why did you want to see me, Lieutenant?"

"I'm curious," Kevin stated. "What made you decide to ride along with patrol? Not many of the grand jury women do that."

"I'm nosey. I want to find out what police work is really like for myself. Not what other people think it is or what they write about it."

"What does your family think about you riding along?"

"Our two teenage sons think it's cool. My husband doesn't sleep while I'm out there. I don't know what to do about that."

"I could arrange for him to ride along if you think it might help?"

"It might, if he'd do it."

"Let me know."

"I will. Thanks for the suggestion."

He nodded with a smile which faded into a lack of expression. Here it comes, Kathy thought. For some reason he is going to tell me I can't ride anymore.

"I've been told you've ridden along on two shifts each Friday and Saturday for the last two weekends." He met her eyes and waited for her to confirm what he had said.

"Yes," she confirmed with a nod. "The first weekend out of Northwest Station and from Station One this past weekend."

"You'll see some action there."

"I've seen action at both."

"Oh?"

She told him about the shooting on the first evening shift she rode along; of the adrenaline rush when they chased a speeding motorcycle on the first night shift; of the kidnapping and possible murder; and of being with the officers when they talked to their snitch about a dice game. Of the second weekend, she mentioned the three children in an empty house; the messed up apartment that had been broken into; the natural DOA; the porno paper incident; the stolen car that was not stolen; and finding the gun that was dropped in the street.

"And you plan to continue riding along."

"Yes. If I may." Kathy held her breathe.

"Of course you can. As much as you want."

Kathy sighed with relief. "Thank you. I was afraid you called me in to tell me I couldn't ride anymore."

He shook his head. "No. The reports I have on you are good ones."

"They've been reporting to you about me."

"Being on the grand jury is not a blank check. Riding along depends on the person's reason, attitude, and behavior on the street." He paused for a moment. "Kathy, you remind me of a little redheaded female officer who worked in the jail. A big drunk gave her some trouble one night. She was a little woman, five foot two, a hundred ten pounds or so. She hauled off and hit him right under the chin with her fist and cold-cocked him. Of course the fact that he hit the back of his head on a bench on the way down might have had something to do with him being out, but the girl did deck him because she caught him off guard.

"You catch people off guard, too. I think you'd make a good policewoman. Have you thought about the academy?" he asked.

"Yes. Years ago."

"And?"

"I got the required sixty hours of college, met my husband, fell in love, and got married. I've been a wife and mother ever since."

"You'd be an asset to this department."

Kathy didn't know what to say. She was stunned. Her heart skipped a beat or two. She gazed off across the room, considering the possibility. When she first found out she could ride along with the officers, becoming a cop was just a daydream left over from her teens. But here was a lieutenant implying that it was possible; not only saying that it was possible, but telling her that she would be an asset to HPD. She wondered if he was serious, and turned to study his face and manner for any sign of insincerity or deception. I don't see any, she thought, but maybe that's just wishful thinking.

"Kathy," Kevin interrupted her thoughts, "I'd like you to talk to Lieutenant Carl Stewart over at the Academy. It may take a week or so for me to arrange. Right now they're screening applicants for the next class. Would you do that?"

"Yes. I'd like to see the Academy."

"I'll arrange it and let you know." He got to his feet. "Come on, I'll take you back to…where's your car?"

"In the parking garage behind the courthouse."

"Okay, let's go." He turned off the music and lights as they left his office. They were in his car on the street before he spoke again. "Two other officers and I have an apartment here in town."

"I thought you were married," Kathy stated, confused.

"I am."

She turned to him. "Are you making a pass?"

"That surprises you?"

"Every time," she stated. "When I was younger, I didn't understand. I think I do now." When she paused, he motioned for her to continue. "I've always gotten along with men better than with women. I think men mistake my friendliness for availability."

"That's part of it," he stated. At her questioning look, he continued. "You're nice-looking, intelligent, articulate, and have a sense of humor, all of which attract men and make them…hopeful?" he said with questioning tone.

"Sorry," she shook her head.

"Damn! Integrity too!"

They both smiled.

At the parking garage he told her, "I'll call you about meeting with Lieutenant Stewart."

"I'll be looking forward to it. Thanks, Kevin."

Kathy drove home tired and excited; tired from hearing forty-three cases on the grand jury that morning, excited about visiting the Academy. On top of that, she had been told she would be a good policewoman and an asset to HPD.

Why did the lieutenant say that? Did he mean it? Or was he just trying to get in her pants? Was she getting this red carpet treatment because she was on the grand jury? Lieutenant Goodson indicated that was not the case. As a child I wanted to be a cop, she admitted to herself. When I married I gave up that dream. Still, it is kind of fun to think about, even though it's impossible. I'm questioning this too much, she told herself. I'm having a good time. I'm learning a lot. I'm meeting interesting people. Don't try to analyze it. Enjoy it, as long as it lasts.

* * * * *

Wednesday, August 18, 1976 - 6:45 pm

As Kathy cleaned up the kitchen after dinner, she thought about Steve. She knew that he was not sleeping when she was riding along with the officers. She loved him and did not want to worry him, but at the same time, this was an invaluable opportunity for her. For research, she needed to ride along as much as possible during her time on the grand jury. It would give her an insight into police work that few people ever experience.

Was there a way to relieve Steve's mind and still continue to ride along? What about Lieutenant Goodson's suggestion for Steve to ride along once or twice? Would Steve do that? If he did, would it help? Or make it worse?

She needed to talk to him, to let him choose to ride along or not. Steve was watching television in the family room. She sat in her favorite chair and waited until the program concluded, then got his attention.

"I have a question for you," she said.

Steve sat up, used the remote to turn the volume down on the television, and turned to Kathy.

"Lieutenant Goodson in Community Relations down at Central thought you might ride along with the officers, to get an idea of what it's all about. He said he'd arrange it, if you're interested."

"What brought that up?"

"Honey, I know you're…having trouble sleeping when I'm riding along."

"Missing a little sleep won't hurt me," he told her.

"I thought if you rode along a couple times, it might help you…worry less."

"If I rode along, and then ask you to stop, would you?" he asked her.

Kathy felt a sense of loss just from his question. "I wouldn't want to. But yes, if you asked me to stop, I would."

"You're willing to take that chance?"

Reluctantly, Kathy nodded. "Yes."

Steve stood up, stepped to her chair, and bent down to give her a kiss; a tender, loving kiss. "Honey, I don't like it, but I won't stop you."

"How can I reassure you that there's no danger? I've never been scared out there."

"You've only ridden a few times. You don't know what's going to happen the next time."

"No, I don't," she admitted, realizing that was part of the attraction. Not knowing what would happen next made it an adventure. She couldn't tell Steve that. He worried enough without her admitting that she found it exciting.

Steve did not have to be told. He could see it in her eyes whenever she talked about it. She seemed more alive somehow. He knew she was censoring what she witnessed on the streets for his benefit.

"Kathy, I know the officers will take care of you. Promise me you'll be careful and I promise I'll try not to worry so much," he offered.

Kathy nodded, knowing his promise was well intended but impossible for him to keep. She, on the other hand, had no choice but to be careful. If she got careless, if she got in the way, if she distracted the officers at a crucial time, riding along would end suddenly. The privilege would be withdrawn as quickly as it had been extended.

"I promise," she agreed. Kathy stood up and gave him a hug and a kiss. "I'll be in the study. I've got notes to type up."

"Okay," Steve said. He watched her leave the family room and enter the bedroom hall to go to the fourth bedroom which they had made a study/office combination. Kathy was intelligent, but was she street-wise enough to get out of the way if all hell broke loose? Have faith in her good judgment, he told himself. Trust her to do the sensible thing. With that thought, he tried to put the whole thing out of mind and tuned up an old movie to watch. When Kathy returned to the family room, Steve realized he had been staring at the television the entire time she was gone, without seeing or hearing any of it.

"Honey," she said, "I'm going to crawl in bed and read for a while."

"Read?" he said as he stood and gave her a mischievous look. "I had something else in mind."

"Really? Tell me!"

He stepped close to her. "I'd rather show you," he whispered in her ear, then kissed her neck several times.

"Ummmmm," she purred. "Yes, yes."

They turned off the lights and went down the hall holding hands, each looking forward with anticipation to making love to the other.

Chapter 9

The pattern for Kathy's time was set. She served on the grand jury on Mondays and Wednesdays and ran her errands and did housework on Tuesdays, Thursdays, and Friday mornings. She rode along with officers on the evening and night shift every Friday and Saturday, alternating between Station One and Station Five.

After the first two weekends, the men seemed comfortable with her presence and willing to answer the many questions she asked. She was learning. The men enjoyed teaching her. In fact, they began treating her like a rookie. "What would you do if...?" they would ask, and outline a situation. Sometimes her answers were good ones, sometimes they were not. They often told stories to illustrate points they were trying to make. Sometimes their stories were just funny. Kathy enjoyed the time with them as much as they seemed to enjoy having her along.

Some nights were hectic. Some were quiet. Every night there were traffic stops made, tickets written, and burglar alarms to check. Occasionally a truly memorable incident occurred.

Friday, August 21, 1976 - 11:15 p.m.

Kathy was riding along with John Bailey and Calvin Henson from Station Five for the second time. Their reluctance was apparent on her first ride along with them. This time, John's green eyes had sparkled with mischief as he greeted her.

"Think we can lose Calvin somewhere?" he asked flirtatiously.

"Not a good idea," she told him. "He's got the keys to the unit."

Calvin's deep ha-ha-ha chuckle made Kathy smile with delight that she had made him laugh. The war stories started as soon as they started cruising the streets.

"One night," Calvin said, "I was dealing with a fat, drunk woman. She must have weighed three hundred and fifty pounds. She was bad mouthing me and my partner, and we knew there was no way we could force her into the car. I commented on how fat she was. 'I'll bet you're too fat to get in the car. We'll have to call for the wagon,' I said. 'I can get in the car. You just watch,' she said. She did get in, and we closed the door and told her she was under arrest."

They had been cruising only a few minutes when a *shooting ambulance robbery* call at a shoe store went out for another unit. To back up the call, Calvin made a U-turn and hit the flashing lights to get through an intersection. In the next block they came up behind a car which pulled off on the right shoulder of the road, and a man came cartwheeling over the top of the car.

"Oh, my God!" Kathy cried.

Calvin hit the radio for an *ambulance* and an *accident unit* as he was pulling off the road into the gravel parking lot of a strip center. Calvin swung the car around so the headlights shone on the injured man. All three of them bailed out and ran to help the man.

Kathy knelt down beside him, blocking the lights from the unit shining in his face. He was an older black man who grabbed her hand and wouldn't let go. She told him to lie still, that an ambulance was on the way. Calvin got his briefcase and put it under the man's head. He had a small cut behind his left ear and his right leg was bent in the wrong place, undoubtedly broken.

She talked to the man, asking his name, address, phone number, date of birth, and other things she knew the officers needed. Squatting on the other side of the man, John wrote down the information as the man answered her questions. She continued to comfort him until the ambulance arrived. They were loading him into the ambulance when the accident unit pulled in. The ambulance left for a nearby hospital.

The driver who hit the man was nearly hysterical. The officers assured him that they had seen it happen and that it was an accident. It didn't help him much. John explained the circumstances as he turned over the information to the accident investigators. Kathy and the officers left the scene and got back *in service*.

It took several minutes for her to recover from the adrenalin rush that hit her when she saw the man cartwheel over the top of the car. She would remember the sight for a long time. She took several slow deep breaths and began to relax.

Calvin suggested that John tell Kathy what he had done the other night.

"No!" John stated.

"Then I will," Calvin threatened.

"You swore you wouldn't tell anybody."

"I swore I wouldn't tell any of our fellow officers."

"Well what do you think Kathy is?"

"She's special!"

"That she is," John agreed. "But I'll tell her. You'd screw it up."

"One night earlier this week," John told her, "we took a drunk to Station Five. When you book a drunk at the substation, you remove your pistol and lock it in a box outside the cell block before entering," John explained. "I put mine in the box and booked the drunk. When I came out, Calvin was standing there with my hat and clipboard. 'Let's roll,' he said. And we did.

"A little later we got a call: *burglars in the building*. I unconsciously patted my holster. It was empty. Calvin wanted to call and have another officer bring it to us. I said, 'No. We'll swing back by there later and pick it up.'

"When we got to the scene, I bailed out with the shotgun. Entry had been made, but the burglars were gone. The sergeant arrived and wanted to know what I was doing with the shotgun. I kept my holster out of his view and told him I wanted to be ready for anything."

"We swung by the station later and John picked it up," Calvin added, "after swearing me to keep the secret. He wasn't the first officer to do that."

"Did you ever do it?" Kathy asked.

"Just once," Calvin admitted.

"Well, that makes me feel better!" John exclaimed.

Calvin chuckled and Kathy laughed.

They made a traffic stop, checked an alarm with no sign of entry, and got out of service for breakfast at about 2:00 a.m. Afterward, they cruised and talked. They drove past a convenience store on Mangum road. John motioned toward the store.

"Do you think he's been back?" John asked Calvin.

"If it was me I wouldn't," Calvin answered.

"Kathy, we have a creep that frequents that store, or did," John told her. "He would come in and look at the girlie magazines until the store was empty except for the female clerk. He would walk up to the counter, unzip his pants, pull out his penis, and ask if she wanted it. One night he did this to an older woman working there. She looked over the counter and said, 'Not if that's all you've got!'"

They were still laughing when Sergeant Watson radioed for them to meet him. He had stopped a speeder. The man said his mother was sick and he was in a hurry to get home to her. The sergeant asked where she lived. He got the address and the phone number.

"Okay," the sergeant told him. "I want to be fair. I'm going to call your mother. If she is sick you can go to her. If she isn't, I'm going to write you for speeding."

"You might as well write the ticket," the man told him.

"No, no. I want to be completely fair." The sergeant called her. The man stood there with a look on his face that said he couldn't believe this was happening. The man's mother answered. The sergeant addressed her by name and told her, "We have a report that you're sick. I'm calling to see if you need medical attention or an ambulance."

"Aw, naw, sur. I's fine. I's in bed asleep."

"You're not sick?"

"Naw, sur!"

"Thank you, ma'am. I'm sorry I disturbed you." When the sergeant hung up, they all looked at the very disgusted and sheepish man standing there.

"Write him, John, for ninety-five in a fifty-five."

"With pleasure," John said, and he starting writing.

The remainder of the night was quiet. Calvin pulled up in front of Kathy's house and switched on the flashing lights. As he drove off he hit the PA system.

"Good night, Kathy."

She wondered how many of the neighbors heard, but nobody ever said anything about it.

* * * * *

Steve heard it and sighed with relief. Each time Kathy rode along with the officers, he felt like the father of a teenage girl waiting for his daughter to get home from a date. He kept trying to tell himself that she was with the cops. What could be safer? Was it the streets that worried him, or the fact that she spent hours in a car with men? He loved her for things he saw in her personality and character. Would other men see the same things and be attracted to her? How could they not be! While he trusted Kathy, he didn't trust the men. It wasn't only her physical safety he was concerned about. He was also concerned about losing her to another man. Kathy saw police officers as heroes. He knew she found riding along exciting. By comparison, marriage and motherhood had to be dull routine. What if they made a pass at her? Would she be flattered or offended? How would she handle it?

As Kathy came into the bedroom, he pretended to be asleep. She didn't need to know he had been awake all night. She wasn't fooled, but he didn't need to know that.

Chapter 10

Saturday, September 4, 1976 - 11:05 p.m.

Of the incidents Kathy witnessed, she usually heard about any follow-up at a later shift change. Seldom was she on hand to see it for herself. However, three weeks after Dean Driskell and Bob Richmond took her with them when they talked to their snitch about an illegal dice game, she was present at roll call when Sergeant Watson laid out plans to raid the game.

"Driskell and Richmond have this dice game they have been working on. Their snitch says we should be able to pick up some ex-cons with guns and maybe some wanted hijackers." He told which units he would call in, if possible. There would also be some units from Station One, if available.

"We're going in in force, or we're not going. We went in with too few once before and had to kill some niggers. We don't want that to happen again. If trouble starts, we want to stop it right away."

Kathy began to feel some tension and wondered how Dean and Bob were feeling. This was their show. She felt like she was part of it, and hoped to be present at the raid. When Sergeant Watson told Kathy to ride with Dean and Bob, she smiled. He chuckled.

"If we go in tonight, you'll be there," he told her.

"Thanks, Sarge."

"You'll be with me!"

"Yes, sir," she agreed as her smile faded.

Kathy left the station with Dean and Bob. They were cruising on their way to drive by the location of the game. They briefly stopped at Station Six for coffee, then continued cruising.

"I'm glad the Sarge is planning on a show of force," Dean commented. "Better to have too many men than not enough. People get hurt then."

"Yeah. That's good," Bob agreed.

Kathy knew then that they were concerned about the raid because they were unusually quiet. She was also concerned, and, she reluctantly admitted to herself, excited. They drove by the game. The place looked like it was packed, with lots of cars out front. The game was supposed to be in a building in the back. They notified the sergeant.

A few blocks from the game location, they met with two officers and a sergeant from Vice, Sergeant Watson, and two units from Station Five. Kathy was introduced and her presence explained. Dean unfolded a drawing of the target building and Bob started briefing them on the setup.

"This front building is about the size and shape of a three-car garage," Bob informed them, pointing to the different areas on the drawing. "That is a beer joint. There is space between the front building and the back one. Mostly it's full of trash. The game is supposed to take place in the back building in the room at the right-hand end, looking at it from the street. Behind the buildings and to the right are woods that go all the way to the street behind the location. There is a path from the back street, through the woods. It's wide enough for two people side by side.

"We will park on the back street, run through the woods, and hit the door to this room," he said, pointing to the location of the door. "It rained this morning. The path is probably muddy and slippery. Watch yourself."

"We are hoping to catch a couple of felons carrying," Dean added. "So stay alert."

"Any questions?" Sergeant Watson asked.

The Vice officers wanted a closer look at the drawing and had a few questions, but were quickly satisfied.

"Ms. Cooper and I will go in the front driveway to the back building," the sergeant stated. "She will remain in the car until the scene is secure." He waited a moment for comments. The men nodded in understanding. "Use Tac 2. Let me know when you are going in. Let's do it. Be safe."

They all headed for their cars. Kathy left with Sergeant Watson, who pulled up in a dark car a couple blocks away from the location of the game and waited. They would hear on the radio when the others were ready.

"When we go in," he told her, "you stay in the car with the doors locked. Honk the horn if anything breaks outside."

"Yes, sir," she told him. "I think that Dean and Bob are a little uptight about this. I know I am."

"Don't worry about them, Kathy," he reassured her. "They'll be fine. No one's going to get hurt, except maybe some niggers. Yeah, men get killed in this business, but not very often." He paused. "Dean's brother was an officer. He was killed out here on the streets."

Shock hit Kathy like a fist to her gut.

"I gave him the assignment that got him killed," Sergeant Watson continued. "I sent him across town to make an arrest. He and his partner heard a *hijacking in progress* call. They were on top of it. He dropped his partner off on one side and went around the other way and stepped around the end of the building as the hijacker made his break. The shooting started and he was hit in the head. Shot by his partner? Or one of the men from another unit? Or by the hijacker? Nobody knows for sure."

The matter-of-fact way he told this story was chilling. Yet Kathy heard regret and grief in the sergeant's voice, and perhaps guilt.

"I'm very close to Dean," he continued, "as I was to his brother. I know what he and his family have given to the department. I know the pressures Dean's under. His mother begged him to quit the day his brother died. He didn't. He stayed. He married a cop. They have a baby boy now."

She dug in her purse for a tissue to wipe her eyes. "I didn't know. I'm glad you told me." Then it came over the radio. "We're going in," Bob said.

The sergeant started the car and drove into the parking lot, around the side of the front building, and stopped with the headlights pointed at the door of the rear building. Kathy saw the other men running through the weeds and high grass toward the building where the game was located. Dean and Bob were the first through the door. The sergeant bailed out and wasn't far behind the others. They covered the place completely. There was a lot of shouting inside the building that Kathy couldn't hear from the car.

When the scene was secured, the sergeant returned to the car, radioed for the wagon, and got Kathy. He told her they had caught fifteen black males playing dice. One of them dropped a bag of marijuana when they broke in the door. He was seen and had been separated from the other men. The amount of marijuana was over four ounces; a felony amount.

She entered and looked around the game room. Black men were lined up around the walls, all with hands up high on the wall. Officers guarded them. In the room next door, the Vice officers were setting up to write out the complaints. Calvin Henson arrived in the wagon.

The prisoners were taken to the other room two at a time and the paperwork filled out. As the complaints were completed, each man was lined up against the wall outside and searched, then he was placed in the wagon. When the last two men were taken outside, both rooms were searched completely.

About 1:30 a.m. they all cleared the scene. Kathy rode with Dean and Bob as they headed for downtown. On the way to Central, the atmosphere was totally different than before the raid. Dean and Bob were like little boys who won a big football game. They had scored big and now they replayed the best moments.

"I could go through doors like that all night," Dean said with a big grin. "The look on their faces, grabbing the money and raising their hands. Beautiful!"

"And hiding stuff," Bob added, "and dropping things."

"Nobody dropped heat though," Dean commented.

"Well, personally, I'm glad they didn't," Kathy stated firmly.

"Gambling is a misdemeanor. Possession of a firearm by a convicted felon is a third-degree felony," he explained. "The snitch is going to hear about this! We're going to have to straighten him out. Put the fear of God into him!"

"It was a good bust," Bob said, "but we hoped to catch them packing heat."

They arrived at Central. Calvin pulled in with the wagon, right up to the door of the jail. They went inside. Kathy stood watching at one side of the door with the strap to her purse over her left shoulder. One of the jailers came up, took her purse, and told her to sit on the bench against the front wall. Before she could explain, Art Donahue stepped forward.

"Hey, what are you trying to do to my favorite lady?" he asked.

"What the hell is she doing with her purse?" the jailer asked.

"This is Kathy Cooper," Art explained. "She's on the grand jury and she's riding with Driskell and Richmond tonight. Don't go messing with her!"

"Oh, my God! I am sorry," he told Kathy, handing the purse back to her. "Please forgive me. Oh, God, I'm sorry," he kept telling her.

"It's all right," Kathy told him. "You didn't know." Kathy looked up to see Jean Driskell, Dean's wife, about to fall off her stool laughing. "You would have let him lock me up," Kathy accused her.

"Hell, yes!" Jean chuckled.

She was still smiling with amusement as Kathy, Dean, and Bob left the jail to go to Records. The two Vice officers were waiting to help with the offense report. They were not happy. Officers were lined up three deep at the booths where the clerks sat typing reports.

"This is going to take hours," one of the Vice officers said.

"What do you need in order to get the report done?" Kathy asked.

"A girl, a form, and a typewriter," he told her.

"Well, I'm a girl. Get me a form and a typewriter."

They did. Of course, they had to tell her what to put in the blanks on the form until they got to the body of it, where they told what happened. That was just straight typing. Most of the other officers were still waiting when she finished.

Dean looked over the report. "You didn't do any better than the clerks do," he complained.

"It's my first. Let me get some practice. After all, I wasn't good in bed the first time, either." Dean and Bob laughed, but the Vice officers stood with mouths open, not believing what they'd heard at first. Then they smiled.

"I find that hard to believe," one of them commented.

With the report done, Dean, Bob, and Kathy left Central at 3:30 a.m.

By comparison the rest of the night was uneventful. They got breakfast at the Washington Avenue diner, made a few traffic stops and wrote tickets, then cruised through Memorial Park and spoiled the fun of several couples who were parked.

At 6:20 a.m. they took Kathy home with lights flashing in front of her house. It had been a wonderful night! Exciting, productive, and fun! She was going to sleep good this morning. Later, she would tell Steve and the boys about the raid on the dice game and about nearly being jailed. They'll get a kick out of it, she thought.

Chapter 11

Saturday, September 11, 1976 - 3:50 p.m.

As Kathy was dressing to ride along on the evening shift, she found she did not have a clean blouse to go with either of her two blue pantsuits. She decided to wear her kelly green pantsuit. Knowing the shift started at three, she was ready shortly after. She waited and waited. She glanced at the clock. The shift started almost an hour ago. Maybe they got a call on the way, she thought, stepping to the front window in time to see a police car go by. They missed the house, she thought, turning to pick up her purse.

Jake ran in the front door. "Mom, your escort is out here writing tickets," he shouted.

"What?" she asked as she went out the front door.

Across the street and down two houses, Billy, one of the boys from next door, was standing by his motorcycle. Doug Shaw was writing a ticket. Billy's parents, other neighbors, and a dozen kids were scattered around watching.

"Where's the car?" Kathy asked.

"He's chasing after Tim," Jake answered, referring to a boy that lived around the corner.

Kathy stood and watched Doug write the ticket. When he finished, he walked to Kathy's house.

"This is all your fault, Kathy," Billy's mother yelled at her.

Kathy shook her head in denial and disbelief. Doug stepped up the Kathy.

"What happened?" she asked, amused.

"He had three violations," Doug stated defensively. "I only wrote him one, no helmet."

At that moment, Officer Gary Kaiser returned in the unit. Kathy said a hasty good-bye to her family and went to the car. One of the other neighbors said, "We'll see you in about ten days, after you get out, Kathy." She waved and got in the car and they left.

Gary chuckled and told them he had written two tickets for the other boy. "His father came out and started bad-mouthing me. I told him to butt out. He didn't, so I wrote another ticket. He kept at it, so I warned him once more to butt out or get in the back seat of the car. He shut up!"

"You missed Billy's father," Kathy stated. "He rode up a driveway, parked his motorcycle, and walked back to the house. He wasn't wearing a helmet either."

"Damn! Would have written him too, if I'd seen him!" Doug exclaimed. "I wrote the boy because his parents were right there, well aware that he was breaking the law and that they had done nothing to stop him. If the parents won't set a good example for these kids, then we have to."

Kathy had met and observed Doug and Gary during shift changes at Station Five. Referred to as 'the twins' because they shared the same birthday, Doug at thirty was a year older than Gary. Gary teased him about being over the hill. Friends through high school, they applied and went through the academy in the same class. They had been partners long enough for each to know what the other was thinking, which allowed them to anticipate what the other would do in any situation. That understanding of each other made them an effective team on the streets.

At six foot something, Gary's uniform did nothing to conceal his physique. Obviously he worked out regularly, without over-developing like a body-builder. Single, with a stable of girlfriends, to hear the others tell it, Gary loved practical jokes. He could see the funny side of any situation, somewhat twisted, as with most police humor. Yet, on the streets, he was all business.

Doug stood about five foot eleven, with wavy black hair women envied and green eyes that twinkled with amusement at his partner's antics. Quieter than Gary, he smiled often but rarely laughed. He seemed to enjoy a good joke, but took life more seriously than Gary.

"You should have been with us last night, Kathy," Gary said. "We nearly shot a man. He was holding someone at gunpoint. The victim finally got away. The man ran into an apartment. We had to go in after him. He was standing behind a wall. We told him to come out with his hands up. He didn't. We told him again. If he had stepped out with anything in the hands, it would have become a shooting. We cocked our pistols. He stepped out, hands up and empty. We laid him on the floor, searched him, and cuffed him.

"Good thing he gave up. I'd hate to wind up in front of the grand jury again."

"You've been there before?" Kathy asked.

"Once. That's enough. Bunch of bleeding heart liberals; they don't understand. I'd like to see them all locked up!"

Kathy knew she was being baited. "Well, here's your chance to put one of them in jail, if you've got the guts!" Kathy challenged.

"Score one for Kathy," Doug said with a smile.

Gary laughed. "You're different," he said, glancing back at her. "You try to understand. They don't."

They cruised, wrote a couple traffic tickets, and checked a silent alarm call. A little after 5:00 p.m., Gary pulled the unit into a driveway to a house in Spring Branch. A small single family frame house in an old neighborhood, it sported a fresh coat of white paint with dark green trim. Except for a scattering of bikes, balls, and other toys, the front yard was neatly kept. Four children stopped playing and ran to the car.

"This is my house," Doug explained. "Gary's going hunting next week. I'm loaning him my bow and arrows." Doug got out of the car and hugged a young woman who approached. He introduced his wife to Kathy.

The children climbed all over Gary in the front seat while Doug went into the house. When the kids saw Kathy, they backed off, thinking she was a prisoner.

"What'd she do?" the older of the two little girls asked, wide-eyed and a little fearful.

Gary explained, "This is Kathy. She's a friend of ours. She hasn't done anything. She's riding along with us tonight." That was better; a little. They still weren't sure about that woman in the back seat.

Doug's oldest boy was retarded. Four kids and one retarded. Hell of a burden for any couple, Kathy thought. Yet she sensed his wife to be cheerful and optimistic. Kathy couldn't help but admire her. Learning about his son helped Kathy understand Doug's more reserved manner.

After they left Doug's house, they got out of service for supper. Back *in service* afterward, they got a *discharge of firearms* call. The location was a little street that dead-ended at a gully. They found nothing.

They followed a smoking VW into a parking lot. The car had lost a belt. Doug and Gary talked to the three people from the car for a couple minutes. Went back to cruising the streets. At 8:15 p.m. a young man on a motorcycle popped a wheelie in front of the unit. They stopped him and wrote tickets for loud muffler and improper take-off from start position.

At 8:30 p.m. they got a *robbery ambulance* call. Another unit arrived at the fast-food restaurant first. A girl had been pistol whipped and was bleeding some. Gary got a description of the two men, and was told they were on foot. The other unit would do the report. Gary and Doug cruised the neighborhood looking for the men. They didn't spot them.

At 9:10 p.m. they got a call, *officer holding three prisoners*. It turned out to be a neighborhood security guard with seven prisoners, four young men and three young women, who were selling magazines door to door without a permit. Doug called for another unit to help transport the prisoners.

"Kathy, would you frisk the women?" Doug asked.

She put her purse on the front passenger seat and approached the women, not exactly sure of how to go about searching them.

"Be sure to check their pockets, between the shoulders, small of the back and around the waistband and ankles."

Kathy nodded and patted each one down carefully. She knew from what she had learned from the men that she was authorized to search the women the minute Doug asked her to. Still, she felt like she was invading the privacy of the women. They didn't seem to be bothered with being searched, making Kathy wonder if they had been through this before. She found nothing on them.

A second unit arrived to take the women to Central. The officers searched their purses and kept them. As Kathy finished with each woman, she was placed in the other unit. Doug and Gary loaded the men into their unit, and they left the scene for Station Five and shift change.

Chapter 12

Saturday, September 11, 1976 - 10:50 p.m.

Standing at the desk between shifts at Station Five, the men were telling Kathy about a big chase the afternoon before, and about other incidents in which three patrol cars were wrecked during the week. The one that they totaled was a wreck anyway.

"It was a real dog. You couldn't catch a five-year-old on a tricycle in it! We're glad to be rid of that one," Calvin Henson told her. She laughed and he joined in with his deep ha, ha, ha.

One of the other officers started to explain that each wreck required a letter to the chief, and of the possible consequences of being at fault for wrecking a Department car, when he was interrupted.

"Cooper!" someone hollered.

Kathy turned around and saw Sergeant Watson in his office through the window wall.

He motioned to her and pointed at his desk. "Get in here!"

She went to his office and stood in front of his desk. "Yes, Sergeant?"

He started by looking at her eyes, then down to her toes and back up again.

"You're out of uniform!" he stated harshly.

Kathy looked down at the green outfit she was wearing. "I thought you and the men would like to see me in something different."

"You see us in the same uniform every night," he pointed out.

"Yes, I do," she nodded, ashamed that she hadn't thought of that.

"If this happens again, it's days off," he threatened.

Kathy assumed that meant she would not be allowed to ride along.

"Do you understand?"

"Yes, sir."

"Dismissed."

"Yes, sir."

She turned and walked back to the men, eyes downcast and face red with embarrassment at being chewed out. She shook her head as she stepped up to the desk.

The men cracked up. She turned to see the sergeant come out of his office with a smile on his face as he announced, "Roll call." Suddenly she felt more a part of things than ever before.

Kathy left Station Five with Dean Driskell and Bob Richmond in unit eleven-thirty-seven. Dean was heading toward the diner on Washington Avenue when they got a call. "Unit eleven-thirty-seven call thirty-one thirty-one." Dean acknowledged and headed for Station Six.

The owner of the store was there. Dean introduced Kathy to him. "I've been hearing about you and wanting to meet you," he told her. "All the men say good things about you."

"That's nice of them," she said.

"Would you like something?" he asked.

"I was going to get a cold drink."

"Help yourself." But when she tried to pay for it, he refused to take her money.

Bob got done on the phone and said it was something about a report from the night before and clearing the slips. Kathy didn't understand, but Bob had taken care of it.

Back in the car on the street, Dean shook his head. "Kathy, shame on you!"

"What'd I do?"

Bob looked as puzzled as Kathy.

"She was sack-dragging, Bob," Dean told him.

"Oh, no. Not Kathy!" Bob stated.

"What are you talking about?"

"You didn't pay for your drink!" Dean pointed out.

"He wouldn't let me pay. So what?"

"When an officer gets a discount on a meal or something for free, that's sack-dragging," Bob explained. "It's against department policy!"

"Oh," she said, understanding that they were teasing her again. "Well, if you tell on me, I'll tell on you. You never pay for coffee."

"She's got a point," Bob said. And they all chuckled.

"If it's against policy, why do you two still do it?"

"Sack-dragging is an old police term," Dean explained. "Been around as long as there have been policemen. It's like a business man getting whiskey or something from salesmen at Christmastime. The salesman is trying to get their business. The store owners are trying to get the protection. A place that is frequented by police officers is a difficult hijack target and not likely to get hit. It's against policy, but there is no way to stop it. How can you argue with a guy that's glad to see you in his store and wants to give you something? It isn't easy."

"When you explain it that way, it sounds acceptable to me," Kathy said. "At the same time, there is the possibility of abuse, isn't there?"

"When a cop abuses it, the store owner quits giving him free coffee. The cop quickly gets the point."

"I'll bet he does," Kathy agreed.

They cruised for over an hour without hearing any interesting calls go out. Then the dispatcher gave them one they would have rather not gotten, a *suicide DOA at Spring Branch Memorial Hospital.*

When they arrived, Dean and Bob talked to a man who was the stepfather of the thirteen-year-old boy he had brought to the emergency room. He had found the boy with a hangman's noose made out of nylon rope around his neck. The man had taken him down, removed the rope, and rushed him to the hospital. He was *dead on arrival.*

"Do you have any idea why he did this?" Dean asked in a sympathetic tone.

"No," the man said. "The only problem with him is getting him up in the mornings to go to school. His grades are good; he just hates to get up."

Dean and Bob went in to look at the boy. Kathy didn't. When they came out they called Juvenile for them to take over the case. They were required to stay until the body was moved to the morgue. While they waited for the Juvenile officer to arrive, Dean and Kathy talked.

Kathy could tell it bothered him. He was tight around the eyes and mouth.

"Your wife worked in Juvenile for a while. She's seen these things before with children. How does she handle it?" Kathy asked.

"Sometimes she cries," Dean said. "A man doesn't, because he's a man. He feels he has to hold it all in. It affects us both. We show it differently. Any officer who is not touched by these things should not be a cop. A man with no heart is going to be a bad cop." He was quiet for a moment and then went on. "I had a brother who was a cop. He was killed on the job."

"Sergeant Watson told me about it," she answered.

"You don't know what it's like, Kathy. You'll never know unless you are there when a cop gets killed. Next time, and there will be a next time, go to the funeral. See what happens. The man who killed my brother was killed by other officers. The papers told of his widow and children that were left fatherless, but they didn't mention my brother's wife and kids."

Kathy now understood the sadness she had seen in Dean's face at their first meeting. No wonder he was slow to smile and rarely laughed out loud. She wanted to know more about a cop's funeral, but Dean was not the person to ask. She felt like crying but successfully fought it.

The Criminal Investigator, Calvin Henson, arrived and went into the cubicle to take pictures and fingerprints of the boy. When he came out, he asked Kathy, "Have you seen him?"

"No."

"If she wants to, I'll take her," Dean told him as though defending his territory.

Calvin left. The Juvenile officers arrived. Dean and Bob listened while they talked to the stepfather. They listened for changes in his story. There were none. The Juvenile officers went in to look at the boy, then took the man home. They would go over the scene there. Dean, Bob, and Kathy waited for more than an hour for the Medical Examiner. Finally the hearse arrived and they were told the Medical Examiner would not be coming. They waited until the body was loaded at 3:40 a.m.

When they left the hospital, they immediately got *out of service* for breakfast. There wasn't any joking, not much talk, and little appetite. Each of them was dealing with the memory of the call to the hospital. After breakfast they cruised and later made a pit stop at Station Six.

Bob and Kathy waited in the car while Dean was inside. A girl went in, stacked, midriff bare, with shirttail tied up under her breasts, no bra, and wearing hip-hugger short shorts.

"Watch Dean," Bob said.

They watched Dean as he watched the girl with eyes about to pop out.

"Sometimes it's hard to keep your mind on the job," Bob observed.

Kathy smiled with amusement.

Dean came back to the car. "Did you see that girl that came in?"

Kathy and Bob roared with laughter.

"Eleven-thirty-seven your location?"

"Eleven-thirty-seven T. C. Jester at Dacoma," Dean told him.

"Eleven-thirty-seven, *major ambulance call Katy and Bingle.*"

"Eleven-thirty-seven clear," Dean acknowledged.

Dean was headed in that direction when they heard another officer on the radio say something about explosions. Kathy looked off to the west and could see the red of a fire and smoke.

Officer Dickens came on the radio. "We're going to need all the units we can get out here. We've got a tank truck on fire."

Dean hit the lights and siren. As he took the Katy Freeway exit from Loop 610 and headed for Silber, the officer asked other units to block traffic at the loop outbound on Katy. They were past there already. Dean parked the car at an angle across a couple lanes at the Wirt exit. Bob warned Kathy to stay in the car. Dean opened the trunk to get out flares, but the box that was there the night before was gone. There was only one. They started waving cars off the freeway anyway. Several cars ignored them and drove right past.

Dean was cussing. Bob came back to the car and radioed for flares. Kathy watched from the back seat of the unit, so frightened that the officers would be run over that she thought she was going to lose what little breakfast she had eaten. A few minutes later another unit came through their roadblock and dropped off a box of flares which they put out and finally got the traffic blocked. Another unit behind them blocked traffic at the loop, and finally vehicles stopped coming.

Dean moved the car off the freeway to block the service road at Wirt. Kathy could hear a unit using the PA to find out if there were any witnesses and to locate the driver of the truck. They found him with minor burns and bruises. His truck blew a tire, rolled, exploded, and burned.

Day shift officers began arriving to take over, having come on duty as soon as they arrived at the substations. Dean and Bob were relieved of duty. As they were leaving, they crossed the railroad tracks that parallel the Katy Freeway and saw that a train was coming out from town headed for the fire site. Dean notified the officers at the fire.

The fire captain came on the radio. "Any officers to the east of the fire location, flag down that train. The fire hoses are strung across the tracks, power lines are down, and there's eight thousand gallons of gasoline on the ground."

Bob got out and put flares between the rails. The long freight train was already rolling at a good clip. The diesel engines on the train were cut as it passed the flares.

They could hear Dickens on the radio. "He won't stop in time!"

He didn't. The train cut the hoses. Kathy could follow what was happening at the scene by the radio calls. They heard the fire captain give clearance for the train to go ahead and get out of the way.

At 6:50 a.m. they left the scene and took Kathy home. She was worn out from worrying about Dean and Bob trying to get the cars stopped without flares with the traffic increasing as the city woke up. It had been very dangerous, even for her sitting inside the car, with fire engines, ambulances, TV news trucks, and idiots all speeding through their roadblock.

That situation was one she would not share with Steve and the boys. However, they would hear about the accident on the news and ask about it. I'll just tell them we set up a roadblock, she decided. The boys will get a kick out of hearing about the train cutting the fire hoses. Then she realized that she didn't even get to see the burning truck. She thought, I'll have to watch the news to see it!

Chapter 13

Sunday, September 12, 1976 - 7:10 a.m.

When Kathy arrived at home, Steve had already taken the morning paper into the house. She went to the kitchen, where Steve was pouring a cup of coffee.
"Good morning, honey," he greeted her with a smile, a hug, and a kiss.
"Good night is more like it," she told him.
"Busy night?"
"Mostly quiet, till end of shift. A tank truck crashed on the Katy Freeway. It was still burning when the day shift relieved us," she explained.
"How about some breakfast?" he asked.
She shook her head. "All I want is to do is go to bed and sleep until I wake up."
"You do that. The house will be quiet this morning. I'm taking the boys bowling," Steve told her.
With another hug and kiss, Kathy headed to bed, looking forward to several hours of renewing sleep, but the ringing phone woke Kathy at 10:30 a.m. It was Billy's mother, Peggy.
"Sorry to wake you, Kathy."
"It's all right. What can I do for you?"
"Well, I wanted to let you know that we really don't blame you for Billy getting that ticket last night."
That's mighty big of you, Kathy thought, without saying anything.
"I just had to call to find out what they did to Tim."
"They wrote him two tickets. One for no license and one for no helmet."
"What about the muffler?" Peggy demanded.
"The officer said he could see seven violations without looking hard, but they can only write four tickets at one time. He wouldn't have written more than one, but Tim's father came out and started bad-mouthing him."

"Really!" Peggy happily exclaimed.

"Yes, really."

"That's good. I'm glad they stopped the kid. Too bad they didn't arrest his father. But, Kathy, Billy didn't deserve a ticket. He's not like Tim. He was only out in front here. He hadn't had it out of the garage in over a week. It needed to be run and they come by and write him a ticket. Do you know how much that fine is, Kathy?" she asked.

"Yes," Kathy answered. "Twenty-seven fifty. Do you know what three times twenty-seven fifty is?"

"No. Why?"

"Billy could have gotten three tickets. No helmet, no license, and no glasses. He only got one."

"Well, that helmet law is so silly. After all, it's Billy's life. If he wants to ride without a helmet, that's his business!"

"No, it isn't. It's the law. If you disagree with it, work to change it. Ignoring it will only get him a ticket or worse."

"Well, maybe. But what ever happened to the practice of giving warnings instead of writing tickets for the first offense?"

"To begin with, this was not Billy's first offense. Every time he rides without a helmet, license, or his glasses, he's breaking the law. The officer wrote the ticket because you and Paul were standing right there. You were aware that he was breaking the law and you didn't do anything about it." Kathy sighed in exasperation, then continued. "If the parents won't set a good example for their children, then the police have to."

Her neighbor didn't have any more to say, except goodbye. Kathy knew she had probably damaged that friendship, but she didn't care. She was pissed, and realized for the first time the kind of flak the officers and their wives and families get from so-called friends and neighbors. No wonder officers are defensive and their relationships suffer. Friends and acquaintances expect to walk away, or drive away, without a ticket. It is not supposed to work that way!

In addition, Kathy was appalled at Peggy's disregard for her own son's safety and her attitude that Billy was better than Tim. She shook her head and crawled back under the covers, trying to calm down enough to get some more sleep. No wonder children were growing up with the attitude that anything they could get away with was all right! Some parents needed a reality check before that attitude ended in tragedy. Eventually Kathy got back to sleep, only to dream about motorcycle riders without helmets, headed for disaster, while she could do nothing to stop them.

Chapter 14

Tuesday, September 14, 1976 - 9:00 a.m.

Lieutenant Goodson from Community Relations had called the day before to set things up for Kathy's tour of the Academy. He was sending a car to pick her up at 9:45 a.m. As she opened her closet to get dressed, she had to smile. Never again would she be caught out of uniform. Today she chose to wear royal blue.

Riding along on patrol was exciting and educational. Kathy had started out observing, and the men had made her feel part of it by treating her like a rookie, teaching her like a rookie. She was learning a lot about people and herself. When the grand jury term ended, the riding along would also end. She wanted to stay involved. She wanted to continue to be a part of it. She wanted to be a cop!

Oh my God, Kathy thought, I do! I want to be a cop, she admitted to herself with surprise. She was stunned.

At the same time, it felt so right; the idea excited her and made her smile. It's a crazy idea, she thought, shaking her head. But could I do it? No, it's ridiculous. How can I even consider such a thing?

While I'm at the Academy, I'll find out what the requirements are, she told herself. Maybe I won't qualify. What a horrible thought! But I have to find out. I'll regret it if I don't. A sense of calm determination settled over her.

* * * * *

Officer Charles Bishop of Community Relations arrived exactly on time. On the way to Central, he asked what had been happening on her ride-alongs, and a few blocks from the house they were swapping war stories.

"I've been impressed with the officers," she told him at one point. "They seem as sincere in their desire to help people as they do about catching the bad guys."

"I'm glad to hear that, but there are a few officers I'd just as soon not get in the elevator with," Charles stated.

"May I ask why?"

"They're mean, cruel, even sadistic. They're good cops, but their attitude's bad. It's bust the bad guys, and they think everyone's a bad guy. No desire to help the public or to be of service to mankind. Just get out there and make those busts. Super tough cops! And there really is no place for them in the department. First bad mistake they make, they'll be suspended indefinitely without pay," he told her.

"You mean fired?"

"Yes."

"How do they get on the force in the first place?" she asked.

"Those tendencies don't always show up during training. Sometimes something happens on the streets that changes them. Some are just good at covering it up." He glanced at her. "I'm glad you haven't run into any of them, and I hope you don't."

At the Academy, Charles led the way. He first took her by the gym which was empty, and let her look around. The rope hanging from the ceiling caught her attention.

"Is that the rope?" she asked.

"That's the rope."

"All the cadets have to climb it and touch the ceiling, right?"

"Yes."

"Even the girls?" she asked, wondering if she could do it.

"Even the girls. If they try hard and can't make it, they can still pass the course. Some allowances are made to get the women through, because the department needs them for the inside jobs in order to get more men on the streets."

Kathy considered the implications of that. If this practice was common in professions dominated by men, then she could understand the resentment men had toward women's liberation. She knew some women wanted a free ride. Kathy didn't. She just wanted women to have an opportunity to try.

Charles escorted her to Lieutenant Stewart's office and introduced them to each other. The lieutenant, a tall good-looking man of six foot three, well proportioned, with very short light brown hair, blue-green eyes, and a modest tan, greeted her warmly in a rich, confident voice and offered coffee which she turned down.

"I'm beginning to think this department runs on coffee," she stated.

"It does, Ms. Cooper," the lieutenant agreed.

"Kathy."

"Carl," he nodded. "Lieutenant Goodson tells me you have been doing some riding along."

Kathy nodded and smiled. "Evening and night shifts every Friday and Saturday since the grand jury started."

"Really?" When she nodded, he asked, "Why?"

"Curiosity at first. Then I found out it's addictive."

Both Charles and the lieutenant chuckled.

"Also, I want to write something to explain to the public what being a cop is really like."

Lieutenant Stewart shook his head. "You have to be a cop to understand."

"And that's why I want to know about the Academy."

"What is it you want to know?" the lieutenant asked.

"Everything you're willing to tell me."

"What have the men told you about the Academy?"

"They've told me about the rope, and Charles showed it to me on our way to your office. They told me a little about the civil service test, background check, polygraph, and the interviews. They said that the final interview is a bitch."

"That's my job," Carl told her, amused at her language.

"Can you tell me about it?"

"Sure," he said with a shrug. "If I feel a young man is too immature, I suggest he withdraw for personal reasons. Then he can re-apply after one year with nothing held against him.

"In the case of the young girls, the screaming virgins just out of high school, I ask, very suggestively, 'When was the last time a man tried to get in your pants?' If the girl is embarrassed by the question, I suggest she withdraw like the immature men. Maybe after a year, if she goes out and gets laid, properly, and can learn to discuss sex openly and frankly without embarrassment, then maybe we can make an officer out of her. Women on the force deal with rape victims, child indecency cases, child molesting, exposure, and more. They can't do their job if they're embarrassed. These final interviews with the immature applicants are fairly low pressure and pleasant.

"When an applicant has already been eliminated for something in his background or something that showed up in the polygraph, the interview is easygoing and they are rejected. The applicant can find out why he or she has been rejected, but no one else can."

"So the interview is just a formality in their case?" Kathy asked.

"Yes."

"And if they're still in the running?"

"When the applicant looks good with a clean background, proper motivation, good attitude, maturity, et cetera, the interview is a high-pressure one. I do everything I can to make that person mad, to blow his cool, to want to come across that desk and kill me. He can get mad, but he must control it.

"Then I throw a hypothetical situation at him and ask what he would do. This is to find out of he can think quickly enough to make decisions in the field. They make mistakes. Any officer who works at his job will make mistakes. But on the streets they must act. They must do something. If they're able to think quickly, we can train them to make more right decisions than wrong ones." He stopped and got up to get himself a fresh cup of coffee. "Kathy, you want something? Charles?"

"Not right now," Kathy answered.

Charles joined the lieutenant at the coffee maker. When the lieutenant returned to his desk, he noticed a far-away look in Kathy's eyes. Suddenly, she looked him straight in the eye.

"Give me a sample of that interview," she requested.

He studied her for a moment as he sat down. She was serious. She almost seemed to be challenging him. "Okay. Can you pretend you're the applicant, a male applicant? I can get rougher with the situations."

Kathy nodded, "I can do that."

He hesitated a moment, in which his demeanor changed from warm and friendly to stern and authoritative. His total, abrupt transition to a marine drill instructor persona caused Kathy to feel like an applicant without pretending.

"This is your final interview," he stated in a firm voice. "Whether you get into the academy or not depends on this interview. You understand?"

"Yes, sir."

"All right. You're a rookie. It's your first night on the street. Your partner is a veteran officer. You have just left the station and he begins to tell you a few basics when you receive a call, a *disturbance at a bar*." He could see that her eyes were slightly unfocused.

In her mind, Kathy could visualize it, the inside of the car, the scratchy radio traffic, her partner driving. In her mind it was happening.

"As you pull up at the location, a chair comes crashing through the window. Your partner says, 'Go in and break it up. I'll back you!' What do you do?"

The look in her eyes focused for a moment. "I'd follow the procedure learned at the academy for making the arrest."

"Okay. You do that and he hauls off and pops you on the nose. You're sliding down the wall, dazed. Your partner steps in." He could see she was really into this. "Smash. He gets a beer bottle broken over his head. He's still standing, but out cold. The actor moves to cut your partner's belly with the broken bottle. What do you do?"

She didn't hesitate. "I shoot him."

"Where?"

"I aim for the center of his body."

"Good! But you shot him between the eyes. The man's dead."

She looked up at him and turned pale. "I'm a better shot than that," she said in disbelief.

Carl shrugged. "The man is dead!"

She looked away. "Oh, my God." She nodded, sick at the thought but accepting it as fact.

"He was forty-five years old. He'd worked for the same company for twenty-five years. The company went bankrupt. He lost his job. He went out and got blind drunk for the first time in his life and he got in a fight. Now he's dead!"

Kathy flinched and closed her eyes.

"His wife's a widow and his six kids are orphans. Can you live with that?"

Kathy squirmed as though trying to escape. She looked at the floor but found no answers there. The man was dead because she had shot him. Could I have stopped him some other way? No. There wasn't time. He would have cut my partner, probably killed him. She looked up.

"It won't be easy knowing I killed this man. But if I hadn't he probably would have killed my partner. That would be harder to live with."

"Will you think of this man the next time you're faced with a similar situation? Will you hesitate to shoot then?"

"I don't think so. I'll never forget, but I think I'd still shoot."

The lieutenant looked at her a moment. "Damn!" he exclaimed. He looked at Charles. "She'll do." He turned to her. She was pale, shaking and hugging herself as if she were cold. "Kathy?"

That broke the spell. Slowly the trauma of the scenario faded. She looked up and smiled weakly, embarrassed by her emotional reaction. "Yes?"

"How about a cold drink?"

"Yes, please."

Charles stood up and asked. "Coke okay?"

"Yeah, that's fine."

Charles left the lieutenant's office.

The lieutenant was thoughtful. He'd seen few applicants experience the scenario as deeply, as strongly as she had.

"What're the right answers?" she asked.

"There are none," he told her. "You gave the best set. But there are no right ones. Regardless of how the applicant answers, I make the situation worse. If he hesitates to shoot, and most of them try everything but shooting, their partner gets gutted with the broken bottle." He noticed she was still trembling, but her color had returned and her breathing had slowed.

She thanked Charles as he handed her the cold drink. The first sip betrayed her dry-mouth reaction to the hypothetical scenario. She gulped several swallows. If the men noticed, they did not react visibly.

"The situation seemed very real to you," Carl stated.

She nodded. "I could picture it all in my mind. Just as though it was happening." She took a deep breath and smiled. "I guess my imagination ran away with me." She sobered. "What would happen after an incident like that?" she asked.

"Your sergeant, lieutenant, captain, and probably the deputy chief would be called to the scene. Homicide and the Crime Lab would also respond. You'd be taken to Homicide to make a sworn statement. Witness statements would be taken. You'd be put on desk duty somewhere until the investigation was complete, and you would see a counselor."

"A shrink?"

He nodded. "The process of investigating an officer-involved shooting is a long one; a thorough one. It has to be. We have to justify our actions to the public. I've been involved in some of those investigations when I was working Homicide." After a moment, he continued. "Kathy, have you ever considered the Academy? You'd make a good officer."

Kathy's heart pounded with excitement. She nodded. "How do I apply?"

Lieutenant Stewart smiled. Charles chuckled knowingly.

"I'll give you a packet of information about applying. Just meet the requirements and go through the process."

"What are the requirements?" she asked.

The lieutenant told her about education, credit, work history, physical fitness, clean background, and, "age twenty-one to thirty-five."

"Thirty-five!" she exclaimed as her stomach knotted. "Are you serious? The maximum age is thirty-five?"

"Yeah," he nodded, mystified at her sudden paleness.

"Oh, shit!" Kathy's stomach turned over. Don't cry, she told herself, lowering her head and biting her lower lip.

Lieutenant Stewart and Charles exchanged puzzled glances and shrugged.

"Kathy?" the lieutenant said, concerned as he stood up and approached her. "What's wrong?"

"I'm thirty-six," she told him, fighting back tears.

Oh, shit was right, he thought. "Lie about your age," he advised as he sat on the corner of the desk.

"I'd get thrown out when they found out."

"Yeah, but look at all the fun you'd have in the meantime." That got a weak smile out of her.

"Any way around it?"

"No," he said, shaking his head with regret.

"Damn! I didn't think my age would be a factor."

"Take a look at the Sheriff's Department. They don't have the same age limit."

"But I've fallen in love with HPD."

"It's all police work. You'd make a good officer, Kathy. Think about it," he suggested kindly.

"I wonder how Steve would react."

"Ask him. He might surprise you," he suggested. "However, if he isn't one hundred percent behind you, don't do it."

"Why?"

"Being a cop is tough on a marriage. After six months, a year or two, the spouse says, 'It's the Department or me.' Most officers pick the Department. So, make sure it is going to be worth what it might cost you."

It was no mystery to Kathy why they picked the Department. They're hooked on the job, just as I am getting to be, she thought. Steve had never forbidden her to do anything—but becoming a cop? Would he accept that? She had wanted to be a cop since she was a little girl, since before she met Steve.

She loved him beyond reason, so she had to be sensitive to his feelings. She would have to think about how to approach the subject with him. She didn't want to do anything to damage their marriage.

As she stood, she promised to consider the Sheriff's Department; then she thanked Carl for his time and for all that she learned. He heard disappointment in her voice, but thought he saw a spark of hope in her eyes. She will try, he realized.

As they left the Academy building, Charles hoped he could lighten her mood. "Lieutenant Goodson instructed me to take you to lunch and then to tour any other division you wanted to see. There's a little greasy spoon place on Washington that looks terrible, but the food is good," Charles offered.

"Thanks, but I'm not hungry," she told him. "Would you just take me home, please?"

"Sure."

Neither of them spoke again until Charles left downtown, driving west on the Katy Freeway. He glanced at Kathy a few times, but her expression remained the same: defeated.

"Kathy?"

"What?"

"Don't let that stupid age limit stop you."

"You think it's stupid?"

"Yeah, I do. The department is missing some good people because of it." When Kathy looked at him with interest, he continued. "Military. They put in their twenty years and would be good candidates for the academy, and the age limit stops them. They go somewhere else. There is a group of them suing for age discrimination, so things may change."

"Soon?"

"Could be years."

"Damn. I'm not getting any younger. If I'm going to do it, I need to do it now!"

"So, do it now. Check out the Sheriff's Office. We may call 'em 'County Mounties,' but they're fellow officers, and we back each other up when needed." He considered for a moment. "You surprised me, Kathy," he admitted.

"I did? How?"

"Your answers to the barroom brawl. Like the lieutenant said, I tried everything but shooting."

Kathy smiled for the first time since they had left the lieutenant's office.

When Charles pulled into Kathy's driveway, she thanked him as she opened the car door.

"Anytime, Kathy," he said. "Give the Sheriff's Office a chance."

"I'll think about it."

"Ride with 'em. You'll see. It's the same."

Kathy nodded more to acknowledge his suggestion than in agreement. She shut the car door and stood in the driveway watching the car until it disappeared around the corner.

* * * * *

Kathy closed the door behind her as she entered the empty house. It was too early for the boys to be home from school. Good, she thought. It will give me some time to think. She changed into comfortable clothes, took a load of bath towels from the dryer, shifted a load of underwear from the washer to the dryer, and reloaded the washer with the boys' T-shirts. She carried the laundry basket of towels to the breakfast room and began folding them.

Too old! How dumb! What difference does age make if the person can do the job? Could she do the job? Could she make it as a police officer? Not with HPD! She was too old! When Lieutenant Stewart said, "Twenty-one to thirty-five," she didn't believe it. She didn't want to believe it. She felt crushed, disappointed that she wouldn't have a chance to work the streets with the men she had gotten to know.

Well, hell! I couldn't do that anyway. HPD doesn't assign women to patrol. That's another thing! If a woman made it through the Police Academy, made it through the same training as the men, and she had a desire to work patrol, she should be given a chance to prove herself. Maybe she couldn't help a partner load a two-hundred-fifty-pound unconscious drunk into the unit, but in other situations a women on the scene would be an asset. Sexual assault cases for instance, or calls involving children.

Observing the officers handle a variety of calls was one thing. Being the officer dealing with the calls would be something else. As an officer she would have to make judgments about people and how to handle them. Do I really want to be required to make decisions that affect other people's lives? Sure, some of them I would be helping. Most would resent me interfering in their lives, their fun. Do I really want to put myself in that position? Yes!

But that's not what I would be doing! Remember what Charles said this morning. Allowances are made for the females to get them through the academy because they are needed for the inside jobs to release more men for the streets.

How bad do I want to be a cop, she asked herself. Is it just a whim? Is it just that I'm hooked on riding along and want it to continue? Do I want to be a cop bad enough to take an inside assignment? Would I be willing to work in the jail? Or in Juvenile? And hope to get in patrol later?

I'd rather be on the streets, Kathy admitted to herself. That's where the excitement and the challenge are. It's not possible now, but someday it will be. Kathy believed that within a few years women would be assigned to the streets. If I'm already an officer when that happens, then a patrol assignment might be possible.

Since HPD is out, I need to look into the possibilities at the Harris County Sheriff's Office. With a phone call, I ought to be able to get some answers and arrange to ride along with deputies. Until she had answers, she would say nothing to Steve. First, she needed to know for sure that she would qualify for the Sheriff's Office. There might be something other than age that would disqualify her. If it was not possible, there was no reason to upset him by mentioning it.

The front door opened and the boys came in from school, hungry as always. She moved the towels she had finished folding from the breakfast room table and helped the boys assemble an after school snack. With a plan in mind, her appetite had returned, so she joined them, asking them about their day at school.

Chapter 15

Saturday, September 18, 1976 - 8:45 p.m.

Evening shift officers Greg Sampson and James Dickens were with Kathy in Records Division at Central. Greg was handwriting a report on a *burglary past* call from late in the afternoon. Except for that call, the evening shift had been fairly quiet, until 8:45 p.m.

A call went out for any unit, *officer having a problem with prisoners*. An officer was calling for back-up, and their unit was only three blocks away. Greg hit the lights and headed toward the location.

At the scene, they found a wrecker driver holding two auto thieves at pistol point. He had watched them hook a chain to a car in a used car lot and pull it off with an El Camino.

"I was going to radio for help, but hit the flashing lights by mistake. Those guys stopped and I jumped out with the pistol and held them for you."

Two other units arrived right after their unit. The two men were handcuffed and put in the backseat and read their rights. Greg arranged for the vehicles to be towed. Greg, James, and Kathy all rode in the front seat on the way to Central. The car thieves smelled so bad that neither officer wanted to sit in the back with them.

At 9:25 p.m. they arrived at Central. They went to Auto Theft for a hold card, which would prevent the prisoners' release for seventy-two hours, giving Auto Theft detectives time to investigate further. They checked for wants and warrants, found two traffic warrants on one of the men, and had taken both men to jail.

While Greg and James were getting the reports done, Kathy called Sergeant Ralph Strong at Station One to let him know she would be late getting to the station for shift change. He asked who she wanted to ride with.

"Art Donahue," she suggested.

"Have the duty officer call him in to pick you up when you get here," he told her.

* * * * *

They left Central at 10:35. When they arrived at Station One, Sergeant Ralph Strong was about to leave.

"Do you want me to call Art in, or would you like to work as my partner tonight?" he asked Kathy.

"You've got a partner," she told him with a big grin and sparkling eyes.

They left Station One at 11:15 p.m. in unit nine-twenty-two. Two minutes later, a *major DOA ambulance* call went out. He explained that there was a major accident with a death at the scene. That's one they run with lights and siren. As they approached intersections, she checked traffic on the right for him. Art Donahue and his partner, Dan Cannon, arrived just ahead of the sergeant and Kathy. As they bailed out, Art hollered at her.

"Sit on my car, Kathy!" He, Dan, and the sergeant ran off in the direction the driver had fled on foot.

"Right!" she hollered back. She noticed that a shotgun and rifle were in the car, which was sitting there with both front doors open. There was also a shotgun in the sergeant's car. Then she noticed the crowd.

Here I am, she thought, one white woman in a rubbernecking crowd of blacks, guarding two police cars containing three guns and a dead man in a wrecked car. She only had enough time to recognize her situation before another unit pulled in.

That unit got on the PA system and told everyone to move back. Witnesses were instructed to come forward. Everyone else was to get in their cars and leave. People started moving away from the wreck toward the street, but none seemed to be leaving. One of the men from the second unit asked Kathy if she was a witness.

"No." Before she could explain, he told her she would have to leave. "I'm riding along with Sergeant Strong tonight."

"Oh, okay."

Looking at the scene, Kathy could see that the accident had started when one car side-swiped another. It then went across the parking lot of a strip center and between the brick storefront and a utility pole. The space was too narrow and the passenger side of the car hit the utility pole. That side of the car was a mess. The passenger was dead. The driver had crawled out of his window and run off.

The officers returned to the scene. Ralph checked the utility pole. There were no wires down. Art radioed for an accident investigator, body wagon, crash bag, and a wrecker. Ralph pointed out the tamale wagon near the street and the fact it was doing a good business among the spectators. Kathy thought about the man lying dead in the car a few feet from where she stood. She was shaking. She wanted to look in the car, and she didn't want to look. Art came over to her.

"Have you been to the car," he asked. "Did you see the body?"

"No. I haven't," she answered.

"It's not a bad scene, Kathy. I think he died of internal injuries. I'll take you over there if you want to see," he offered.

"Not yet."

"Don't try it until you're ready," he advised and walked off.

She returned to the sergeant's car and waited while things got organized. The accident investigator showed up. The sergeant was ready to leave, when Art came up again.

"Kathy, I thought you were going to call me to pick you up," he said with a hurt tone.

"Well, the sergeant asked if I wanted to work as his partner tonight, so…"

"Pulled rank on me, did he? Okay. But you take good care of him. Keep him straight."

"I will," she promised, not knowing that later she would keep that promise.

She and Ralph began cruising again.

"Damn," she said. "A man died and I couldn't handle it. I'm out here to learn, to experience things, and I backed off."

"Don't be ashamed to have feelings," Ralph told her. "Don't be ashamed to let 'em show. If you ride enough, you'll get used to it. It will always bother you, Kathy, because you have a heart and because you care about people. Don't ever lose that quality."

Another unit bumped them on the radio, requesting the sergeant meet them. Officers Donny Wells and Fred Oakes needed to talk to the sergeant about getting an arrest warrant on a hijacker. A victim had identified the man from a series of photos.

"It's after midnight," he advised them. "You'll have to wake up a judge. Let me know if and when you get it."

As soon as they were back on the streets, a *beating victim ambulance* call went out. The sergeant flipped on the siren and got to the scene as quickly and safely as possible. In a room in a motel—a dingy, sparsely furnished place—they found Art Donahue and his partner Dan Cannon.

"Hey, Kathy," Art called to her. "Come look at this guy. He caught the leaded end of a pool cue in the mouth. Split his lip real bad."

"How bad?" she asked before going in to look.

"From inside one nostril all the way down and laying wide open," he said as he used a finger to illustrate the wound on his own upper lip.

Kathy looked. The man had bled some, but not as much as she expected. He needed medical attention at a hospital and agreed to go. He was the one hurt, still he stood aside and helped his wife get into the ambulance first. A real gentleman with a bloody towel held to his mouth.

Back on the street, a *disturbance call* went out. The sergeant must have been the closest unit because he got there first. Two other units rolled in shortly after, a two-man and a one-man. Inside the bowling alley, they found two men arguing by a coin-operated pool table. To get in line for a turn, people place quarters in a line near the coin slot. The men were arguing over whose quarter had disappeared from the line.

The sergeant shook his head. "It's a good thing it wasn't fifty cents! We'd be taking one of you in for murder," he said sarcastically, then got serious. "If I, or any of my men, see any of you on the streets again tonight, I'll have you busted. Now move out!"

The other units left the scene. Ralph took his time. He was just pulling out of the parking lot when a call went out. "I think I have a hijacker at the chicken place on Little York. Get me some backup." It was the officer from the one-man unit that had just been at the bowling alley.

Ralph hit the gas. They were only a block and a half away. The other unit was empty when they pulled in. The officer was in the parking lot next door. The hijacker was lying across the hood of a station wagon, arms spread out. The officer was right behind him with the barrel of his forty-five automatic against the back of the man's head, in the hollow at the base of the skull. Oh, God, Kathy thought. Am I going to see someone killed right here?

Ralph slammed the unit in park and ran to help the officer frisk and cuff the man. He was a big man, about six foot six of solid muscle; a big man for a single officer to go after. The man had run and thrown his sawed-off shotgun in a garbage can. It was recovered.

Right behind the sergeant's unit, two other two-man units pulled in, one of them a Sheriff's unit. Everything was under control.

The officer was proud of himself, and rightly so. "My first hijacker!" he exclaimed.

"Good job!" The sergeant told him. The other officers offered congratulations, too.

As soon as they were back on the streets, another *beating ambulance* call went out. Again they were first at the scene. An older black man had been sleeping when he heard the window in the front door break and someone enter the house. He got up to see about it and met the man in the dining room. The guy hit him in the head with a tire tool. The victim's forehead was cut and bleeding. There was also a welt along the ribs on his right side and an abrasion on his left forearm. Ralph cleaned some of the blood off the man's head so he could determine if he needed to go to the hospital. While he did that, he asked the man his name, age, address, and for a description of his attacker. Kathy wrote it all down in the notepad she carried with her.

"Take a look, Kathy. Do you think he needs stitches?"

"Yes, I think he does. He should also have x-rays of his head and his ribs where he got hit."

Suddenly, the man realized he was standing in front of a woman with only his undershorts on. "Excuse me, ma'am. I gotta get some pants on."

"Get some shoes, too," Kathy called after him. "There's lots of broken glass on the floor."

Art Donahue and Dan Cannon arrived just then. "What you got, Sarge?" Art asked.

Ralph held out his hand to Kathy. She tore off the page of information she had written down and handed it to him. He handed it to Art. "The man's going to the hospital. Kathy got the information. You write the report."

"Thanks a lot!" Art exclaimed, then turned to Kathy. "You left the major DOA too soon," Art told her. "The people at the scene chased after the driver when he ran. They brought him back. We had to call an ambulance for him."

"Why?"

"They beat hell out of him. He was spitting up blood."

"Why did they beat him up?"

"When a black man does something wrong, it reflects on all black men. Those that are straight resent the hell out of it, because it makes them all look bad. So, they chased him, caught him, stomped him good, and dragged him back to the scene."

Ralph pulled Kathy away before she got any more details. They had just gotten back on the streets when they were told to *meet the unit* at a certain location. The unit they met was Donny Wells and Fred Oakes, the two officers who earlier wanted to get an arrest warrant. They had to drive across town and get the judge out of bed, but he willingly signed the warrant. The judge was upset only because the system was keeping the officers off the street for so long.

Ralph called for another two-man unit to meet him. When they arrived, they all conferred. Donny told them they had a warrant for the hijacker, who would probably have a gun handy. Everybody was eager to go.

"Me and my partner," Ralph said, referring to Kathy, "will roll by and case the place, then come back and set it up for you."

In the car, Kathy turned to him, "Your partner?"

"Yeah."

He drove past the house slowly as Kathy used the flashlight to find and confirm the house number. They returned to the location where the other two units waited. The sergeant laid it out for them by drawing a diagram.

"The house is on the corner. The driveway goes into the backyard from the side street." He indicated that the second unit was to cover the back of the house. Donny and Fred would go in the front with him.

"What about Kathy?" Donny asked.

"She'll stay in the car until the scene's secured." He turned to her. "On the floorboards. This guy is a hijacker. He'll be armed. There may be shooting."

"I understand," she stated. But when he glared at her she added, "I'll do it," but she didn't like it.

The sergeant and Kathy led off. As they turned the corner a block away from the house, they cut the lights on the units. They rolled up quiet and dark.

As Ralph stopped the car, Kathy unbuckled her seatbelt and slid down on the floor so she could peek out the window.

She could see the two officers go to the back of the house, one at each rear corner, so that each could see the back of the house and one side. Ralph, Donny, and Fred went to the front door. Donny knocked, then knocked harder and harder. Finally, the door opened. It was the hijacker's father. He slammed the door in their faces.

"Open the door or we'll kick it in. We have a warrant for your son," Fred yelled.

Kathy saw and heard that much. Ralph told her the rest of it later.

The man opened the door. They went in to the boy's bedroom, flipped on the light, and he rolled over. They cuffed him right on the bed. A search of his room turned up a pistol. In searching his car, they found a shotgun. Donny and Fred got the privilege of taking him to jail. It was their arrest. They'd done all the work of getting the identification and the warrant.

"The parents are good people," Ralph told her when they were back on the streets. "I feel sorry for them. They had no idea what their son was up to. You spend twenty years of your life trying to raise a boy up right, and then he pulls something like this on you. Somebody always hurts. Somebody always cries over these people."

"Ralph," Kathy said. "We've got two sons, ages sixteen and fourteen. I worry about that. I think all parents do. When you've done all you can to teach them right from wrong, you have to give them a chance to do it. That's when you cross your fingers and start praying. But I don't believe it's all in the way they're raised. I think some are born with something missing that nothing can fix."

"The sociopath," Ralph commented. "Yeah, I've seen that. But some of these kids could go either way. Something happens and they go the wrong way."

She agreed, but neither of them had an answer.

Then, to change the subject and the mood, she confronted him. "One minute I'm your partner, and the next you have me hiding on the floorboards while you men have all the fun! It's not fair!"

He laughed. "No, it isn't."

"You wouldn't have done that if I'd been through the Academy, would you?"

"Probably not. But Kathy, men are going to be protective of the women. It's part of being a man."

"Even after they've had the same training?"

"I think the tendency would still be there. In a tight situation, it could get one of them hurt, maybe killed."

"I can see that. But it's going to happen. Women on the street, I mean," she clarified. "You know it is."

"And there'll be problems."

"And they'll be worked out," she said firmly.

They cruised. Ralph drove past the scene of the DOA accident from earlier. "See, Kathy? Everything is gone, even the tamale seller," he pointed out.

They stopped for a red light at Cavalcade and Elysian. They noticed that a car on Elysian was sitting through its green light, with someone sitting behind the wheel, the motor running, and the headlights on. Ralph pulled over to the passenger side of the car and used the hand held spotlight to see the man. He was sitting with his head back on the headrest, breathing heavily.

"He's probably passed out drunk," Ralph said. "But he might be sick. I'll check him."

He got out and walked around to the driver's door. He tapped on the glass and then opened the door. The man nearly fell out. Ralph pushed him back in and the man woke up. Ralph identified himself as a police officer.

"Leave me alone," the man said. "I haven't done anything." He tried to drive off.

Ralph slammed the car into park, turned the ignition off, pulled the keys, and told the man to get out. He wouldn't. Ralph told him again. He then pulled the man out of the car. The man came out fighting. Ralph managed to get the man handcuffed, but in front. The man started swinging with both hands together. Ralph was having a bad time with him.

Kathy looked around the car for some way to help. The only thing available was Ralph's shotgun. *I can't shoot him for being drunk and disorderly. What can I do?* Kathy considered using the radio, but she was a civilian and did not want to get Ralph in trouble. Ralph wrestled the drunk around to Kathy's side of the car and pushed him down on the ground. She already had the mike in her hand and handed it out the window to him.

"Nine-twenty-two," he said, holding the man down with one hand and a knee.

The dispatcher answered, "Nine twenty-two."

"Nine-twenty-two. Have a unit meet me at Cavalcade and Hardy."

"Clear."

He handed the mike back to Kathy. The man was trying to get up again and Ralph had his hands full. Kathy glanced at the street signs.

"Ralph, this is Cavalcade and Elysian! Not Hardy!"

"Tell him that, Kathy!"

She pushed the button and spoke across the mike. "Nine-twenty-two."

"Nine-twenty-two?" the dispatcher asked with surprise.

"Nine-twenty-two. Our correct location is Cavalcade and Elysian. We're having trouble with a prisoner," she told him.

"Nine-twenty-two. Cavalcade and Elysian?"

"Nine-twenty-two. Affirmative."

Kathy could hear sirens coming already.

"Nine-twenty-two. Will this be an assist?"

She looked at Ralph. He nodded.

"Nine-twenty-two. That's affirmative."

"All units," the dispatcher announced. "Assist the officer. Cavalcade and Elysian."

One unit arrived and two officers bailed out to help Ralph.

"Nine-twenty-two. We have one unit on the scene," Kathy said. A moment later she told them, "We have two units on the scene. The situation's under control. Everyone slow down, please!"

"All units not on the scene, disregard assist at Cavalcade and Elysian. The situation is under control," the dispatcher broadcast, but it didn't stop units from arriving.

The men from the first two units that came screaming in helped Ralph with the drunk. It took all five of them to get him cuffed behind his back and calmed down. With sheer manpower, they overwhelmed him. The third unit to arrive was Art Donahue and Dan Cannon. Art saw that things were under control and ran right up to Kathy, grabbed her upper arms, and shook her.

"Are you all right? Did that bastard get near you? Did he touch you? Are you hurt?"

"I'm fine, Art. I'm fine. Check on Ralph," she begged, her voice shaking as much as her hands. She had been so scared for Ralph and ashamed that she couldn't decide what to do. She looked around. Several two-man units and another sergeant had arrived, all of them running lights and sirens and floor-boarded, including a Sheriff's unit and the Harris County Emergency Corps.

Art came right back. Ralph was fine.

"Oh, my god," she cried. "What have I done, Art? Look at this. Five, six, seven units to handle one drunk." She sat down in the car, appalled at the danger in which she had put responding units by putting out *an assist*.

"It's all right, Kathy," Art told her. "Damn, it shook me up when I heard your voice!"

"Art was doing eighty," Dan said, "before he found out which way to go. He whipped the unit around in a U-turn. Just hearing your voice, we knew there was trouble. Sure got the adrenalin going."

"You sounded good, Kathy. Just like you. You did a good job," Art said.

"You told me to take care of him," she commented. "Did you rush to save me or the sergeant?" she asked. They took the fifth on that, but she knew it was for both of them.

Ralph came over to her. "You okay?" he asked her.

"Yes. Are you?"

"Just a couple of bruised knuckles. Thanks, partner. Thanks a lot."

"Oh, Ralph, I didn't mean to cause all this. I'm sorry."

"Hey. I needed help and you got it. You did the right thing. Forget it."

But she couldn't. She was afraid that this would end her riding along. Chief Ledford would surely hear about this and decide it was no place for her. She just knew that she would lose her permission to ride along.

Because officers Wade Ellis and Roger Dawson were the first unit on the scene, they would transport the prisoner to Central. Ralph and Kathy would meet them in Homicide. He wanted to fill out the report himself. At Central, they went up to Homicide. Ralph found an empty interrogation room and started filling out the hold card. Kathy asked if he would like something cold to drink.

"I sure would," he told her.

Kathy went down the hall to the Coke machine. Officers Ellis and Dawson were coming down the hall with the prisoner. She saw that he had gotten a bloody nose and a busted mouth in the struggle with the officers. Donny Wells was trailing along behind the officers.

"Hi, Pretty Lady. What's happening? Hear you had to put out an assist."

"Oh, Donny!" She told him about it while she got the drinks out of the machine.

"Way to go, Kathy. Ellis says you did a good job."

"You didn't hear it?"

"No. Been tied up down here. Take care," he said as he turned and walked away.

Kathy took the drinks back to the room. The drunk was complaining that those two officers abused him.

Ralph set him straight. "I'm the officer that abused you. If you have any complaints, file on me."

Kathy couldn't hold her tongue any longer. "Mister, any man who gets so drunk that he can't tell when a police officer is trying to help him, should get abused. We stopped because there was a chance you were sick. We stopped to help. And you started fighting because you drank too much. I am not a police officer, but I'd like to beat the crap out of you myself. You endangered this officer's life and all the officers who had to come to his assistance. You file any damn kind of complaint you want. Who are they going to believe? A drunk, or a member of the grand jury?"

"I'm a friend of the Sheriff," he said. "I gave to his campaign. He's going to hear about this. I'll have your jobs."

"How much did you give to his campaign?" Ralph asked.

"Seventy-five dollars."

"For seventy-five hundred I might be worried, not for seventy-five," Ralph stated.

When Ralph got all the information he needed, Ellis and Dawson took the drunk down to the jail. Kathy and Ralph went to Records to dictate the offense report. It didn't take long. They left Central and got *in service*.

"I'm worried," she told him.

"Because you sent out an assist? There won't be any trouble over it. A good sergeant fades the heat for his men, or woman, in this case," he reassured her.

"Fades the heat?" she questioned.

"Defends or takes the blame for them," he explained.

He pulled the unit into the parking lot of an all-night diner and got *out of service*. Usually Ralph only had coffee, but that night he joined her in eating.

They had both worked up an appetite. They began talking about porno films. He explained how difficult it was to get convictions.

"In one case I went to court on, the defense attorney for the ticket taker asked me if the movie had a plot. I told him, 'No.' He asked if I knew what a plot was. I went back to basic English and told him, 'A plot is a series of related events that has a beginning, a climax, and an ending. This movie did not have a plot, because it had no beginning or end. All it had was a series of climaxes.' The jury laughed and the judge nearly fell off his bench. We got a conviction."

After breakfast, Ralph took Kathy home. It had been one of the busiest nights she had experienced. She was tired and shivered when she thought of all that happened that night. She entered the house as quietly as she could, shut and locked the bedroom door behind her, stripped, crawled in bed naked, and woke Steve to make love to him. Or him to her. Or both.

Chapter 16

Saturday, September 25, 1976 - 3:45 p.m.

Evening shift officers Doug Shaw and Gary Kaiser from Station Five patrolled with Kathy in unit eleven-thirty-three. Gary told Kathy about working out of the Southeast Station. Many a night, he and his partner spent all night, plus overtime, at Ben Taub Hospital writing reports on people hurt in crimes of violence.

"One night they brought a burglar in that had taken a load of buckshot in the groin area. The doctor removed several pellets from vital organs and left the rest of them. I told him, 'You ruined his career, Doctor. Who ever heard of a successful burglar that rattles when he walks?'"

"That's pretty bad, Gary," she moaned.

A little after six, Gary got on the radio. "Eleven-thirty-three, is it clear to get out?" meaning *out of service for supper*.

"Eleven-thirty-three, not at this time."

They continued cruising, stopped a car for an expired inspection sticker, and found that the driver had no operator's license either. Doug started writing her NOL, when they got a *shooting ambulance* call. Gary hollered at Doug and he came running. Gary hit the lights and siren.

In the park, just off Watonga, they found a little girl of nine who had been shot in the left calf with a pellet gun. She had been playing with friends on the west side of White Oak Bayou. On the other side, some boys were playing with pellet guns, shooting at birds and other things. There were several witnesses. Doug and Gary talked to them and got all the information they could. Kathy and Gary went to the place it happened and found a few blood spots. Gary drew a diagram.

Doug had gotten the name of one of the boys involved and had his address narrowed down to a certain block of a street on the east of the bayou. There they asked the kids on the street where the boy lived. The kids pointed out a house and the officers went to the door.

When they asked the boy what happened at the bayou, he said, "I didn't shoot her and I don't know who did." He told them that it was probably a second boy who had run away and asked the first boy and another to bring his guns home and slip them in his bedroom window.

He told the officers the names of the other boys and where they lived. Kathy and the men walked across the street to talk to one of the other boys. His story was different. He said the first boy had shot near the girls, and that the third boy had left before this happened.

Two boys, two stories. It was time to round them all up. The parents of the second boy were allowed to take him to Juvenile. Gary and Doug picked up the first boy and then the third boy at the skating rink where he worked. Doug sat in the backseat with the two boys; Kathy sat in front seat as they headed for Central.

At 8:15 p.m. they arrived at Central and took the first and third boys to Juvenile so they could make their statements. Kathy and the men went to Records where Doug dictated a five and a half page report. Kathy and Gary stood around and visited.

At one point, one of the officers working in the District Attorney's Intake Center called Gary over and said he was going to tell Gary's wife that he had been flirting with a cute brunette. "You'd better leave her alone," he warned Gary.

"I can't. She's on the grand jury. She's riding along with us tonight," Gary told him.

"Damn! Thought I had you!" the officer exclaimed.

When Doug finished the report, they went back to Juvenile. The first boy would be kept in Juvenile until his parents came to get him. The officers took the third boy home and explained to his parents what had happened. Then they got out of service for supper. After they ate, at about eleven-forty-five, they headed for Station Five to go off duty.

Chapter 17

Saturday, September 25, 1976 - 11:55 p.m.

Kathy approached Sergeant Watson at Station Five and asked if she could ride with Dean Driskell and Bob Richmond.

"Dean is out sick and Bob is on special assignment," he told her. "He's sitting on that industrial plant that's been having trouble with strikers. How about Calvin Henson?"

"Sure. Calvin's fine. Is he riding alone tonight?"

"Yeah. Unit eleven-fifty-nine, criminal investigator unit."

"That'll be interesting," she said.

Shortly Calvin arrived to pick her up, "I hope you don't mind, Calvin."

"Of course not. It gets lonely in a one-man unit," he told her with a wink.

"Flirt!" she said.

They left the station and started cruising. Kathy noticed the rifle leaning against the front seat with barrel up, just to the right of the hump in the floorboards.

"Do you know Dan Cannon?" she asked.

"Yeah. He's over at Station One."

"I think your rifle's just like the one he has."

"It is. We bought them at the same time," he told her.

"Nice weapon."

He looked questioningly at her.

"Two of the Station One units took me out in the county one night for a little target practice. Dan let me try his rifle."

"How'd you do?"

"Two beer cans out of two." Kathy smiled, remembering how well she had shot.

Calvin glanced at her and saw her smile. "There's more to it, isn't there?"

"Yes," she admitted, then told him about hitting fifteen out of sixteen beer cans.

"Good girl!"

Calvin pulled over a man on a motorcycle at about 12:30 a.m. He had pulled into a trailer park to visit someone, he said. It checked out okay, so they left. A moment later, the man on the cycle passed them. Calvin and Kathy both wondered why. That was an awfully short visit with his friends. Calvin stopped him again. When he checked for traffic warrants, the man had two outstanding. Calvin arrested him and called for another unit.

Dennis Vaughn and his rookie met them. Calvin drove the cycle. The rookie drove Calvin's unit and Dennis drove his, all to Station Five. Dennis and the rookie got right back on the street. Calvin took the man inside and booked him, and then he and Kathy returned to the streets.

"Calvin, it seems a shame to take another unit off the street for that," she stated. "How much trouble would we have gotten into if I had driven the unit?"

"You trying to get me suspended?" he asked, horrified.

"That much?"

He shuddered. "I don't want to think about it."

"Sorry. Forget I asked."

"You're right about it taking a unit off the street when they might be needed elsewhere."

At 1:35 a.m. they got a *burglary of a residence* call. An older couple came home to find the back door open and all the lights on. The meat from the freezer and the TV were gone. The window in the kitchen had been broken out. Calvin dusted for prints and lifted three. The woman asked Kathy if she was a policewoman. Kathy explained about the grand jury.

The woman told her that several times kids in the neighborhood had put firecrackers in their mailbox at 3:00 a.m. What could be done about that? Since Calvin was busy looking for more evidence, Kathy told her to call Station Five and file an alert slip. This would be passed on to the unit patrolling that area. Patrol units would come by at the times the couple was having the trouble, and keep an eye on things.

When Calvin finished, they returned to the car and began cruising.

"Kathy, you really have learned a lot. The alert slip is what I would have told her to do. We're going to make a cop out of you yet."

"I wish."

Her tone held so much longing, he couldn't leave it alone. "What are you thinking?" he asked.

"That my husband would be against it."

"Is your family worried about you when you're riding along?"

"The boys think it's great. My husband worries." she told him. "Which to me is silly. I've never felt in danger riding along, not for me. A couple times I've been concerned for the officers I was with."

At 2:30 a.m. they saw a car parked in a strip shopping center lot with the lights on and the engine running. Someone was sitting in the car. They pulled up alongside and the car drove off. Calvin followed and pulled the car over. Suspecting that the woman was drunk, he asked her to turn off the engine and hand him the keys. In addition, she didn't have a driver's license. A check on traffic warrants showed that the woman was wanted. Calvin called for another unit to drive her car to impound, arrested the woman, and put her in the backseat of the unit.

Calvin searched her purse. He handed the purse to Kathy and put her to work. She didn't mind a bit. He dictated all the information on the woman's car to Kathy so he could fill out the paperwork to impound the car. The other unit arrived and they all headed for Central.

It never ceased to amaze her, the mounds of paperwork that were required. They arrived at Central at about 3:00 a.m. Kathy carried the purse, knife, and clipboard, and told the woman to follow her. Calvin brought up the rear. First stop, Traffic Warrants, where they picked up the warrant on the woman.

Then to Accident Division to run a breath test on the woman. She blew a point seventeen. Anything over point ten was over the legal limit. Then there were more forms, for driving while intoxicated. Next stop, the jail.

The officer working the door spoke to Kathy. "I've seen you around here a lot lately. Where do you work?"

"Patrol," Kathy answered.

He didn't buy it.

"Yeah, she's my partner," Calvin told him.

"Henson, I know you're a damned liar!"

So they told him the truth.

They left Central and were on their way back to Calvin's district when they got a call to *check for a runaway* on the Katy freeway near Wirt. As the call went out, Calvin drove past the kid. He disregarded the unit that had taken the call, stopped, and backed up, placing the unit so that the kid was in the headlights on Kathy's side of the car. She got out first.

The boy had one hand in his pocket. "Hold it right there, son," she told him. "And take your hand out of your pocket."

By then Calvin was around the car to talk to him. He was the runaway. Calvin checked his pockets and found a pocketknife. As he brought the boy to the car, Kathy opened the back door, then closed it after he was inside. Calvin and Kathy got into the unit and headed for Central.

Kathy picked up the clipboard to put down the answers to the questions Calvin was asking the boy: his name, age, address, phone number, and why he ran away from home. He said his Daddy told him to get the hell out. He was going to stay with a friend in Louisiana.

"It's dangerous to hitchhike," Kathy told him. "We had several boys picked up while hitchhiking and murdered here."

"Listen to her, son," Calvin told him. "She's telling it to you straight. This isn't a nice little town where you know everybody and everybody is nice.

Ride Along

Houston is a big city. We have a lot of bad people here, who will cheat you and hurt you, if you give them a chance."

They took the boy to Juvenile and left him with Jean Driskell, who had transferred from the jail.

When they left Central, they headed for Station Six. The owner had a message he wanted to get to Bob Richmond. Kathy bought some little cigars she knew Bob liked. Calvin drove out to the industrial plant where Bob was on assignment and parked driver's window to driver's window next to Bob's unit. Calvin gave Bob the message. Kathy passed the cigars to Calvin, who passed them to Bob. Bob unwrapped one and asked Calvin for a light. Calvin turned on his flashlight and shined it in Bob's face.

"Everybody likes a little ass, Henson. Nobody likes a smart ass," Bob pointed out.

Calvin and Kathy drove away laughing and headed for her house.

Three blocks from Kathy's home, they passed the construction site where she and other officers had stopped a couple times. She noticed a pickup and a man near a stack of building materials. Because she knew about thefts from this site, she told Calvin what she saw.

"Construction workers arriving early," he said.

"At five o'clock on Sunday morning?" she asked.

Calvin gave her a sharp glance and threw the car into a U-turn. He blocked the entrance with the unit. Leaving the headlights on high beam and pointed at the pickup, he got out of the car. When Kathy stepped out on the other side, she felt uneasy. Calvin motioned for her to stay at the car.

Kathy stood next to the passenger side of the unit and watched as Calvin approached the man at the pickup truck, which was parked perpendicular to the police unit and about eighty feet away from her position. The man at the bed of the truck turned to face Calvin as he walked up to the cab of the pickup.

She rested both forearms on the top of the door and leaned against it. She yawned, a big deep yawn. That bed sure is going to feel good tonight, she thought. This morning, she corrected herself.

Calvin and the man stood talking beside the truck. Two more men suddenly appeared behind Calvin's back, walking around the front of the truck. Calvin turned and stepped back from the truck, keeping all three men in his sight.

Oh, oh! If these three are up to no good, Calvin's in deep trouble, Kathy reasoned as she bent over to reach into the car for the radio mike. She looked away as she slid it from the holder mounted under the dash. Mike in hand and bringing it to her mouth, she looked up.

"Oh, shit!" she exclaimed as she saw the three men rush Calvin and take him to the ground. There wasn't time to call for another unit! Kathy dropped the mike on the passenger seat and reached for Calvin's rifle. She clasped the rifle in both hands and pulled it from the car, carefully keeping the muzzle pointed away from herself.

She looked up again. The fight was on, in fast-forward speed, while she felt she was moving in slow motion. They'll kill him if I don't stop this, she concluded. Bracing the rifle butt against her right hip with her left hand, she pulled the bolt back and released it to cock the firing mechanism and to load a cartridge into the firing chamber.

The three men were hitting Calvin, who was fighting to keep them from getting his pistol. The first man leapt to his feet and kicked Calvin in the ribs, then in the head. He had a piece of pipe in his hand. As she struggled against time to get the rifle to her shoulder, the man raised the hand holding the pipe over his head.

Hurry! she told herself as she snugged the rifle butt against her right shoulder. She took it step by step, as her father had taught her. Get your sight picture.

The man's hand reached the peak of his upward swing.

Put your index finger on the trigger.

The pipe started a downward arc.

Squeeze slowly.

The pipe was coming down, rapidly.

Squeeze.

The explosive sound of the shot and the recoil startled Kathy. She watched for a reaction. There was none, except that the man straightened up.

"Damn! I missed!" she swore, sighting for a second shot.

The man seemed to sway in place, then slowly, so very slowly, toppled forward, face down on the ground. Just like the slow motion death scenes in the Japanese movie, *Seven Samurai*, Kathy thought. How weird.

The other two men stopped hitting Calvin and looked toward the unit. Calvin wasn't moving. He was still in danger. I've got to get them away from him, she realized.

"Hands on your heads," she shouted, her voice deeper than normal to carry further; a trick she learned in drama class.

The men looked at each other, then back in her direction.

"Hands on your heads, now!" Watch their hands, she thought. Make sure their hands are empty. Will I shoot again if they aren't? she asked herself. Yes! I will! Don't make me do that!

"Get your hands on your heads!" she repeated.

Gradually they brought their arms up. Their hands were empty, Kathy noted as she wondered why they were moving so slowly. Finally, they accomplished what appeared to be a difficult task.

"Get on your feet!" she ordered, knowing she had to get them away from Calvin.

They looked at each other, then toward the unit again. For Kathy, whose brain was now operating at high speed, they were not moving fast enough.

"Get on your feet, now!" she yelled, impatiently.

The two men seemed to be fighting high gravity as they slowly stood up, still looking in her direction, as though trying to figure out who they were dealing with. Kathy had the advantage of being able to see them in the high beams of the headlights. She doubted they could see past the lights to her position.

"Walk toward me!" she told them. "Now! Move it!"

They started toward her, like they were walking in knee-deep water.

"Keep coming!" she told them. "Keep coming!"

When they finally reached a point about halfway between where Calvin lay motionless and where she stood, she ordered them to stop.

"Get down on the ground! On your faces!"

Gradually they got down on their knees.

"All the way down. Face down!"

They took their hands from their heads, placed them on the ground, and lowered their bodies to the ground, still operating in slow motion.

"Arms straight out!"

One of them did. The other hesitated, with his head raised, as if gauging the distance to where she stood.

"Get your arms out! Put your head down!"

Still he hesitated.

"Don't try it," she advised, aiming for another shot.

He must have thought better of it, because he spread his arms out and put his head down. Kathy watched for a moment to make sure he was not going to move. Resting the rifle barrel on the top of the car door, she reached into the unit and grabbed the mike off the passenger seat with her left hand. She took a deep breath, let it out and took another. Holding the mike at the side of her mouth, to speak across it, she depressed the button.

"Eleven fifty-nine," she said.

"Eleven fifty-nine?" the dispatcher came back.

"Eleven fifty-nine. Mangum Road and Georgi Lane. Shots fired. Officer down. I'm holding two at gunpoint."

"All units. Assist the officer. Mangum Road and Georgi Lane. Shots fired. Officer down. Female holding two at gunpoint. Repeat," and the dispatcher repeated the call.

I don't hear sirens, Kathy thought. Where is everybody? Am I going to have to shoot again? Hurry up, fellas! Why don't they come? She glanced at Calvin, who still was not moving. How badly is he hurt? Is an ambulance coming? I said *officer down* didn't I? They'll dispatch an ambulance. Why don't I hear them coming? What is taking them so long?

The man she shot was not moving either. She watched the two on the ground, but thought she would also see movement if there was any from Calvin or the wounded man lying beside him.

One of the men on the ground raised his head. Kathy tensed and took aim, ready to shoot again if she had to. Then she heard a siren, but a long way off. Be careful, she thought. Please be careful. But, hurry! I don't want to shoot again. The screaming siren came closer and closer and died as the unit skidded to a stop.

Two officers went past Kathy, seemingly taking their time. She raised the muzzle of the rifle and waited. One officer went to the men on the ground and started handcuffing one of them. The other officer went to Calvin.

Another unit arrived with siren screeching, then dying. Two more officers passed her position, apparently in more of a hurry than the first pair. The first officer of the second pair went to the second man on the ground and handcuffed him. The other went to the man Kathy had shot. She heard more sirens as more units arrived. They seemed to go on and on. One siren would die and another would grow louder as it came closer to the location. Flashing emergency lights gave the scene a strange, colorful strobe light effect.

Someone walked up behind her, reached around, and took hold of the rifle. Kathy resisted, turned, and saw an officer in uniform and released the rifle. Kathy realized that things around her were speeding up. Suddenly the officers were moving at normal speed, as Kathy's perception slowed down. Adrenalin, she thought. The relief left her weak and she began to shake.

She ran to Calvin on legs that didn't seem to work correctly. He was just regaining consciousness when she dropped to her knees beside him. Fighting, he grabbed for his pistol.

"Calvin, don't move," she told him. "An ambulance is on the way."

"What happened?"

"They jumped you," she told him.

"Who jumped me? Where are we?"

"Those three men at the construction site."

Calvin just looked at her as though he didn't know what she was talking about.

"We stopped to check a man and pickup truck on this construction site. But there were three men. They jumped you. I thought they were going to kill you."

"Three men?" he questioned in disbelief. "What stopped 'em?"

Kathy couldn't answer.

"Kathy, did you shoot him?" an officer asked, indicating the man lying next to Calvin.

She nodded. She didn't trust her voice. Calvin looked up at her with consternation. After a moment he smiled.

She fought to keep from crying. After that, she wasn't clear on events. Someone pulled her to her feet and moved her out of the way so the paramedics could get to Calvin, then stood beside her. When he let go of her arms, she just folded up and sat on the ground and let the tears flow.

Someone said, "He's DOA."

"No," she moaned, looking up.

"Kathy! The man you shot! The man you shot is dead. Calvin's okay. Calvin's going to be okay," someone told her.

Tears and sobs continued to rack her body. An officer handed her a handkerchief and she wiped her face, still trying to catch her breath and control the

Ride Along

shaking. She recognized it as adrenaline overload and knew it would pass. In the meantime, she felt out of control.

Someone was talking to her. It was Sergeant Watson squatting at her left side.

"Kathy!" he said sharply, not for the first time. "We need to know what happened."

She knew this was important. Fighting to stop the tears and control her voice, she told him, starting with spotting the truck and a man at the construction site as they passed, and Calvin coming back to check. She told her story carefully, not wanting to leave anything out.

"When he raised the pipe over his head to hit Calvin, I shot him. Then I got on the radio. Help came and somebody took Calvin's rifle away from me. Where is it?" she asked looking around. "I need to find it."

"I have it, Kathy."

She nodded. "Is he really dead? Did I kill him?" she asked hesitantly.

"Yeah," the sergeant confirmed with a nod.

"I wanna see," she stated as she tried to stand. Her legs did not want to work right. No one moved to help her up. Finally, she struggled to her feet.

The dead man had fallen on his face, but the paramedics had turned him over to check on him. He lay staring blankly at the dawning sky. There was a hole in his chest the size of a grapefruit. The smell of blood and other things hung in the air. The smell of hot copper, she thought, and feces. She turned away to see a gurney with Calvin aboard moving toward the ambulance.

"Calvin?" she questioned, going to him.

"They want to check me at the hospital."

She took his hand but couldn't speak for fear of the tears starting again. She walked to the ambulance with him. He was loaded inside and she watched the ambulance drive away.

The sergeant took her arm. "Kathy, come sit in my car."

"My purse is in Calvin's car." Kathy retrieved her purse. "Will you take me home, please?"

"That's not a good idea."

"Steve and the boys will be expecting me. It's just down the street." She was almost pleading.

"Kathy, it's important for us to keep you isolated until Homicide has talked to you. I'm sorry. I'll get a unit to go by and tell them what's going on. Will that do?" he asked.

She nodded.

He gently guided her to his car and she sat in the front seat. Still shaking and tears still threatening, she tried hard not to lose it again. She failed. There was no one to hold her, to offer a shoulder to cry on. Then she realized that it was how they would treat another officer. On the streets, they had been treating her like a rookie for weeks. At the moment, she wished they wouldn't. At the same time, she realized how easy it would be for one of the officers offering comfort to say something that would taint her memory. She understood, but she didn't like it.

The sergeant opened her door and bent over. "Kathy, your husband and family have been informed."

"Thank you. Is Steve coming?"

"We advised him not to. We'll see that you get home later."

"Am I going to need a lawyer?"

"Did you do anything wrong, Kathy?"

"No," she said weakly, as though unsure.

"Then tell the truth, as you remember it."

"Sarge, stop being a cop for a minute and be a friend. Should I have an attorney present?"

He hesitated to answer.

"It's like that, is it?" she asked.

He had trouble meeting her eyes. "Don't sign anything without one," he advised, then shut the door and moved away from the car.

Kathy was left to wonder how much trouble she was in. The car was parked with the headlights toward the place where the dead man still lay. She watched as cameras flashed, measurements were taken, and things were picked up and put in evidence bags. She looked behind her, toward the street. It was full daylight now. There were television station trucks and reporters and people from nearby houses and apartments. Officers were posted to keep all of them away from the scene.

Kathy turned away and began crying again, no sobs, just tears running down her face. She searched her purse for tissues, then realized she had a handkerchief in her hand. She tried to remember who had given it to her. She had no idea. The tears stopped. A good thing they did, she thought, because the hankie was soaked.

She was exhausted and numb. Clear thinking was impossible. She waited, not knowing what would happen next and not believing what had just happened. Unaware of time passing, Kathy waited, almost falling asleep a time or two.

Chapter 18

Sunday, September 26, 1976 - 7:10 a.m.

Finally the sergeant returned to the car with two people, a man and a woman. He introduced them as homicide detectives who were handling the investigation. They would take Kathy to Central and see that she was returned home later.

    The woman reached in, took Kathy's purse, and handed it to her partner. He searched it while Kathy was getting out of the car, then he handed it back to her. Kathy understood, but couldn't help resenting it a little. They escorted her to their unmarked unit, placed her in the backseat with the woman, and left the scene. Curious eyes stared at her as the car moved through the crowd. Kathy paid no attention to the people crowded around the scene.

    Nothing was said on the drive to downtown Houston. After parking the car behind the Central Station, the detectives and Kathy took the elevator to the third floor, turned right out of the elevator, and right again. Kathy looked toward the end of the hall. When she spotted a cold drink machine partway down the long hall, she realized her throat was dry from crying. She asked if she could get a drink. The man got her a cold soda and they proceeded through the double glass doors that led into the Homicide Division.

    Kathy noticed a walk-in closet on her right. As she passed the open door she glanced at the contents. She stopped, took a step back, and looked again. Clothes, a bed sheet, and other bloody items were hung from hangers or hooks. A sign on the door identified the closet as the 'Drying Room.' She didn't remember noticing the room when she and Sergeant Strong came to Homicide the night she put out the *assist*.

    In the main room, the usual drab green metal desks sat back-to-back in four pairs running the length of the room. Two men sat facing each other at one pair of desks. Otherwise, the room was empty. On the left, offices for ranking officers looked out over the front parking lot. Small interrogation rooms lined the wall on the far side of the room, and file cabinets stood against the third wall. The detectives took Kathy to an interrogation room.

With Kathy seated on one side of the table, the door was shut, and the detectives sat across from her, between her and the door.

"Except for not being handcuffed, I feel like a suspect," Kathy told them, beginning to feel more in control of herself as she recovered from the letdown after the adrenalin dissipated from her system.

"We need you to tell us what happened," the woman told her.

"Are you going to read me my rights?" Kathy asked.

The woman smiled. "No. We're just going to talk."

"I'm sorry," Kathy said. "I don't remember your names."

The woman re-introduced herself as Charlotte Saxon. "This is my partner, Paul Black."

"Mrs. Cooper," he said. "We know it's been a long night for you and we understand that you're tired. But we need to ask what happened while it is still fresh in your mind."

"Of course," Kathy agreed. She pushed her fatigue aside and concentrated on relating the events in clear, concise terms, starting with spotting the pickup and the man at the construction site. Step by step, she told them what happened, while Detective Black took notes. When she finished, the questions started.

"When you saw that there were three men, why didn't you radio for help?" Detective Black asked.

"There wasn't time."

"Why not?"

"I grabbed the mike to do that, but when I looked up they jumped Calvin and took him to the ground."

"Is that when you got the rifle out of the unit?"

"Yes."

"A thirty caliber carbine is not a weapon most women know how to use. Yet, you knew how to cock it and load a round in the chamber."

"Yes."

"Where did you learn how to do that?"

"I had fired that type of rifle before."

"You own one like it?" he asked.

"No, I don't."

"When and where did you fire a weapon like it?" Detective Saxon asked.

"I went shooting with a friend who owns one. He taught me how to use it," Kathy explained.

"What's your friend's name?"

She hesitated. "I'd rather not say. He doesn't have anything to do with this." Kathy knew she was being evasive, but she did not want to get the four officers who took her out for target practice in trouble.

Unfortunately, the detectives also knew that she was being evasive. The tension level in the room went up. They all felt it. The detectives wondered why she would not name the friend. What was she hiding? Detective Saxon changed the subject, with the intention of coming back to it later.

"You say Ray Jackson picked up a piece of pipe?"

"Who's Ray Jackson?" Kathy asked.

"The man you shot."

Without a name, Kathy realized, he was just a bad guy. With a name he became a person. The person she had killed. I didn't mean to kill him, she thought. I meant to stop him. I had to shoot. There was no other way. Was there?

"Are you sure about that?" Detective Black asked.

Momentarily confused and wondering if she had spoken out loud, Kathy asked, "Sure of what?"

"That he had a piece of pipe?"

"Yes."

"There was no pipe at the scene."

"What!"

"We did not find a piece of pipe at the construction site."

The bottom dropped out of Kathy's stomach. "But I saw it!"

"You were seventy-eight feet away. It was still dark. Are you sure?"

"Yes, damn it! The headlights were on high beam. It lit up things really well. He had a piece of pipe!" she insisted.

"Okay, Mrs. Cooper. Tell us one more time," Detective Black requested.

Before Kathy could begin again, the door to the interrogation room slammed open.

"This interrogation is over!"

Paul Black jumped to his feet. "Who the hell...?"

"I'm Ray Ulbrich," the man in the doorway stated. "I'm Mrs. Cooper's attorney." He handed each of the detectives a business card. "I'd like to speak to my client alone."

A friend of Steve's since grade school, Ray Ulbrich filled the doorway with his six-foot plus husky body. His carefully combed salt-and-pepper wavy hair, suit, tie, and briefcase gave him an air of authority, but with his large hands and square German jaw he still resembled the truck driver he worked as to get through law school. He practiced family law and had represented Steve and Kathy in that capacity ever since passing the Texas bar exam. The only more welcome sight to Kathy would have been Steve. However, Ray's presence was more appropriate at the moment.

"Of course, sir," Detective Saxon agreed, as she nudged her partner toward the door.

Ray looked around the top of the room. "No cameras or microphones in this room?"

"No, sir," Detective Saxon told him, as she left the room.

Ray Ulbrich closed the door behind her, turned, and went to Kathy as she stood up. They greeted each other with a hug.

"Thanks for coming, Ray."

"I got here as quick as I could, Kathy. How are you?" he asked, stepping back to look at her.

"Tired. I just want to go home," she told him, suddenly weak with relief and grateful that Ray was there to take over.

"I'll take you home soon. But I need to know what's going on first."

He picked up one of the chairs and brought it around the table to sit close to Kathy.

"Did they read you your rights?"

"No."

"Did you sign anything?"

"No. They just wanted me to tell them what happened."

"Did you tell them?"

"Yes."

"Tell me."

"It was about five o'clock this morning…" Kathy started. She related the events of the early morning shooting again. "They asked me how I knew how to use a thirty caliber carbine."

"What did you tell them?"

"That a friend had taught me. They wanted to know who. I can't tell them!"

"Why not?" he asked, mystified.

"Because he was one of the four officers who took me out in the county one Sunday morning at about three-thirty for target practice. They were on duty. If the police department finds out about it, they'll all be in trouble," she explained.

"Yes, they will," Ray agreed. "It's going to come out, Kathy. It has to."

"Oh, God," she moaned. "I promised that nothing I observed while riding along would go any further. I gave my word."

"I understand." Ray considered for a moment. "Call them. Tell them. Give them a chance to go to their supervisor and admit it before you have to tell the detectives."

"Okay," she promised, knowing that if the officers admitted doing something wrong, they would be in less trouble than if they tried to cover it up. "I'll call tonight before roll call."

Ray stood up and put the chair back in place.

"There's one more thing," Kathy stated.

"What?" he asked, looking down at her.

"They told me there was no piece of pipe at the scene."

Ray frowned. This was not good.

"What if they don't find it? How much trouble am I in?"

Ride Along

Ray could hear the anxiety in her voice. He wanted to reassure her by telling her that everything would be all right, but that was unrealistic if the pipe was not found. She needed to hear the truth, not false promises.

"If the pipe isn't found, you could be in a lot of trouble. This could get nasty," he warned. .

"How am I going to explain this to Steve and the boys?"

"Don't!" he stated emphatically. "Don't talk to anyone about this unless I am present. Except Steve. Anything you tell Steve is privileged. Anything you say to anyone else can be used in court against you."

"In court? You think this will go to court?"

"It could. It will go to the grand jury," he pointed out.

"If I can't say anything to anybody but Steve, how do I explain this to the boys and the rest of the family?"

"Why did you shoot Ray Jackson?"

"I thought he was going to kill Calvin. I had to stop him!"

"That's what you tell your family; that you shot because you thought Ray Jackson was going to kill the officer. And that is *all!*" He stood up, went to the door, and opened it. "Detectives," he called out to the room at large. "Is my client under arrest?"

"No, sir," both Detective Saxon and Black answered.

"Then I am taking her home. If you need to talk to her again, contact me first."

"Of course, sir," Detective Saxon agreed.

Ray held out his hand to Kathy as she stood up and walked to the door. They stepped out into the main room of homicide. Officers, some in plain clothes, some in uniform, occupied all of the desks. A dozen others stood around. Those who were seated stood, and all of them watched as Kathy and Ray walked across the room. Ray opened the door to the hall. Kathy turned back to face the room.

"Have you heard how Officer Henson is?"

"Yes, ma'am," Detective Black answered. "He's got a concussion and two broken ribs. He'll be fine."

"Thanks."

"Thank you, ma'am," Detective Black said.

Kathy stepped into the hall with Ray following her.

Chapter 19

Sunday, September 26, 1976 - 8:25 a.m.

As Ray drove toward Kathy's house, she put her head back and pretended to go to sleep. She didn't want to talk anymore. She just wanted to get home to see Steve and the boys. Kathy's thoughts were unpleasant and full of questions.

What happened to the piece of pipe? What if it wasn't found? She knew from her grand jury service that all shooting cases went to the grand jury, as this one would. She also knew that shooting investigations often took weeks, or even months. What would the grand jurors think? Would they understand that she had no choice? Would she be called to testify? Probably. Would they believe her? Would she be no-billed? Or indicted? On what charge? How long before this nightmare ended? Would it ever end, or was her life changed forever? How would she tell the boys that she killed a man? How could any child understand that? How would they be treated by their friends? By strangers? What would her parents and sisters think? Did Calvin go back and check the construction site only because I told him what I saw?

Yes, he did! It was all my fault. I nearly got Calvin killed. Knowing about the history of thefts and attempted thefts from the construction site, she had felt compelled to mention what she saw.

Was there some other way to stop the men? No. She knew there wasn't. All the retrospection in the world would not change the outcome. What happened happened, and she would have to live with the consequences. She could do that, but what about her family: Steve and the boys, her parents and sisters, her niece and nephew? How would they deal with it?

Would it bring the family closer together, or tear it apart? Contemplating the unknown future was unsettling, stressful, and a waste of time. She could not change the future any more than she could change the past. They would all have to deal with things as they happened. She knew it wouldn't be easy for any of them.

*****

As Ray turned the corner down the street from Kathy's house, he reached over and gently shook her. "Kathy."

"What?" she asked as she opened her eyes and looked down the street. Several television station trucks were parked on the street near her house.

"Say nothing. Go straight into the house," he instructed her. "I'll deal with the reporters."

"All right."

Ray pulled into the driveway. Before he had shut the car off, Kathy was out of it and on her way to the front door. Steve met her about half way, put his arm around her, and hustled her inside, shutting and locking the door behind them.

Their two sons greeted her with hugs and stricken looks on their faces. Arms around each other, Kathy and the boys went to the family room. The doorbell rang and Steve allowed Ray to enter. Steve and Ray talked quietly for a moment in the entry hall before Ray left the house and drove away.

Steve went to Kathy and gathered her into his arms. She clung to him as though drowning.

"Are you okay, honey?" He asked.

Concerned, the boys stood close.

She smiled weakly. "Yeah, I'm okay. Just tired."

"Come on," Steve said, taking her arm and leading her to their bedroom. He closed the bedroom door behind them.

"I killed a man," she stated.

"I know. We can talk about it later."

"No. Now."

"I can wait."

"I can't."

Steve sat her down on the edge of the bed and sat beside her.

"All right."

Again, she told of the events of the early morning shooting. "He was just lying there, eyes open, staring at the sky. With a big bloody hole in his chest."

Steve clenched his jaw, wishing she had not seen that, wishing he had stopped her from riding along. It took him a moment to push the picture of what Kathy had seen from his mind. "What would have happened if you had not shot him?" he inquired.

Tears filled her eyes and ran over. "They would have killed Calvin."

"Then you did the right thing."

"I know. But…"

"No buts! You did the right thing. Concentrate on that."

"I love you," she stated.

"I love you, too. Now, let's get you undressed and in bed."

Suddenly, exhaustion hit her. It was not just from being up all night. It was the letdown from the events of the early morning. She had been holding onto control for as long as she could. Here at home she didn't need to anymore. She could relax.

As she slipped out of her blazer, Steve took it and hung it in the closet. When he turned back to the bed, Kathy had lain down. By the time he had removed her shoes, slacks, and knee-high hose, she was sound asleep. Steve pulled the covers over her, gently kissed her, and left the room. He would be close if she needed him.

Chapter 20

Sunday, September 26, 1976 - 3:15 p.m.

Steve woke Kathy, knowing that if she slept any later, she wouldn't be able to sleep that night. Kathy staggered to the shower and woke up under a cool spray, then shampooed her hair and lathered her body under warm water. Awake and dressed, she walked into the family room. Steve stepped to her and gathered her into his arms. She held on to that warm safe place she did not want to leave.

"Did you get some rest?" Steve asked.

"Yes. But not enough." She reluctantly relaxed her grip on him. "We need to talk to the boys."

"I'll get them," he said, turning and walking away.

Kathy sat in her favorite chair and braced herself to tell their sons that she was a killer. Steve and the boys came into the room. Steve sat in his recliner. The boys sat on the couch. Neither Davy not Jake said anything.

"I have to tell you what happened this morning," she began. "But I can only tell you part of it. Ray Ulbrich said I cannot explain any further until the investigation is over. I hope you can understand and accept that for the time being."

Davy nodded.

"Sure," Jake stated.

She took a deep breath that she let out slowly. "Early this morning, I shot and…" her voice broke. She cleared her throat and continued. "I shot and killed a man because I believed he was going to kill the officer I was with."

"How'd it happen?" Jake asked.

She shook her head.

"That's all you can tell us?" Davy questioned.

"Right now, yes."

"What do we say when people ask us about it?" Davy asked.

She thought a moment. "Nothing. Especially if any reporters try to talk to you!"

"That's all we can tell our friends?" Jake inquired.

"It would be best to say nothing to anyone outside the family," she told them. "Just tell them you can't talk about it."

The boys glanced at each other.

"I know you have a lot of questions," she said. "I wish I could answer them. I will answer them as soon as I can."

"Okay, Mom," Davy agreed.

"This isn't fair. I want to know what the hell happened!" Jake exclaimed.

"Jake!"

"Yes, ma'am. Sorry."

"I want to explain. I'd like to answer…."

"This is for your mother's protection," Steve interrupted. "Try to understand that."

"Is she in trouble?" Jake asked.

"Probably not," Steve stated. "But the investigation isn't over. Until it is, this is the way things have to be!"

"Yes, sir," the boys said together.

"That's all," Steve dismissed them.

Jake went to Kathy and hugged her. "I love you, Mom." Then he fled to his room.

"I do, too," Davy said. "It'll be all right." Then he left the family room.

Kathy watched them leave the room. Steve watched her. She seemed to deflate as soon as the boys were out of sight.

"You handled it well," he told her. "They'll be all right."

The phone rang.

"I don't want to talk to anybody," Kathy stated.

"Okay," Steve agreed as he got up to answer it. "Yes. Hold on." He turned to Kathy. "It's your mother. I think you better talk to her."

"I can't tell her anything," Kathy stated.

"She's worried. Talk to her."

Kathy reluctantly got up and went to the phone. This was the first of many calls from family and friends that she would receive in the next few days.

Chapter 21

Sunday, September 26, 1976 - 9:45 p.m.

The phone on the duty desk at Station One rang.

"North Shepherd Police Substation, Officer Halbert," the duty officer told the caller.

"This is Kathy Cooper," she told him. "Is Dan Cannon there?"

"No, ma'am. He hasn't come in yet," he replied. "Can I help you?"

"How about Art Donohue?"

"He's not in yet either."

"Donny Wells?"

"Yes. He's here. Hold on a minute." He held the receiver out to Donny Wells. "It's Kathy Cooper. She wants to speak to you."

"Hi, Pretty Lady," he greeted her, with a much more serious tone than usual. "How you holding up?"

"As well as can be expected, Donny."

"I understand," he stated. He had a good idea of what she was going through, having been there once himself. "What can I do for you?"

"Donny, the homicide detectives asked me where I learned to use a thirty caliber carbine."

"Did you tell 'em?"

"No. Not yet. But I'll have to before this is over," she stated. "I wanted you and the others to know before that. I know I promised not to say anything about what happened on the streets, but…it'll get all of you in trouble, won't it?"

"Probably," he said, hoping she did not know how much trouble they could be in.

"Donny, I am so sorry."

"Don't be."

"But it's my fault!"

"No! It is *not* your fault. *We* violated policy, not you. You were just along for the ride."

"What will happen to you and the others?"

"I don't know, but don't you worry about it. You just take care of yourself, Pretty Lady."

"All of you take care, too. Good night, Donny."

"Good night, Kathy." Donny hung up the phone and looked over at Fred Oaks. He stepped away from the desk and signaled Fred to join him. At the same time, Art Donohue and Dan Cannon came in the back door. Donny and Fred met them about halfway to the desk.

"What's up?" Fred asked, when the four of them were standing together.

"Kathy called," Donny told them. "Homicide wants to know who taught her to use a thirty caliber carbine."

"Oh, shit!" Art exclaimed.

"Did she tell them?" Dan asked.

"Not yet, but she'll have to." Donny informed them.

"Yeah. She won't have any choice," Fred stated.

"No, she won't," Dan Cannon agreed.

"No way we can cover our ass on this," Art said.

"So…I guess we better talk to the Sarge," Donny suggested.

The others agreed. As a group, they approached Sergeant Strong's office.

"Can we talk to you, Sarge?" Dan asked.

Sergeant Strong motioned them to come in. They did. Fred closed the door behind them.

"What's up," Ralph Strong asked.

"It's about Kathy. She called," Donny stated.

"What about Kathy?" the sergeant asked with genuine concern. "Is she okay?"

"Yeah, but there's a problem." Donny hesitated. "Homicide wants to know who taught her how to use a thirty caliber carbine."

"I showed her," Dan Cannon told him.

"So, what's the problem?"

"We took her out West Montgomery Road one night," Dan explained.

"And had target practice?" Ralph guessed.

A chorus of four answered, "Yes, sir."

"While on duty?"

"Yes, sir."

"All four of you?"

"Yes, sir."

"Kathy will have to tell the homicide detectives about it," Donny stated.

"Yes, she will," Ralph agreed. "So you decided to get it out in the open now?"

Again the four all answered, "Yes, sir."

"Write it up, each one of you. I want your statements on my desk by end of shift."

"Yes, sir."

"I'll do what I can to fade the heat for you, but I don't know how much good it'll do."

"We understand that," Art said. "Thanks, Sarge."

The four of them turned to leave the office, when Ralph asked, "By the way, how did Kathy shoot?"

"Two beer cans out of two with the carbine," Dan told him.

"And thirteen out of fourteen with my twenty-five," Donny added.

"She outshot us all," Art admitted.

"It was beautiful to watch," Fred commented.

"Thirteen out of fourteen with a twenty-five?" the Sarge asked. "Damn!"

"You should have been there, Sarge," Donny added with a smile.

"Get out of here!" he told the four of them. As they left his office, he thought of his experiences when Kathy rode along with him and other incidents he had heard about from the men. As soon as her shooting was ruled justified, which he knew it would be, he planned on encouraging her to apply to HPD's Academy.

Chapter 22

Monday, September 27, 1976 - 7:10 a.m.

Reading the paper at the breakfast room table, Steve looked up as Kathy, in robe and slippers, came into the kitchen early Monday morning. He quickly gathered up the paper, folded it, and shoved it aside.

"Good morning," he said.

She nodded and yawned. "Morning." She put water in the teakettle and placed it on the stove to heat and took a mug from one cabinet and a tea bag from another. After setting them by the stove, she went to the table and reached for the paper.

Steve put a hand on it to stop her from picking it up. "It's bad," he told her.

"Let me see," she requested. When he released it, she opened it to the front page. There it was. The headline story.

UNARMED BLACK MAN DIES – SHOT IN THE BACK. A smaller headline declared, BY FEMALE GRAND JURY MEMBER – RIDING WITH HPD. It went on to tell of the man's widow and three children, with a picture of the widow crying. She was quoted as saying, "He was a good man. He never did anything wrong. Why did she do this?"

Kathy threw the paper down. This was just the beginning. It was going to get worse, if they did not find the pipe. What the hell happened to it? She shook her head and turned to the stove to make her tea. She needed to wake the boys, get their breakfast, and get them off to school before she dressed and left for the grand jury. School?

"Should the boys go to school today?" she asked Steve.

"Good question." He thought a moment. "Get them up and let's see what they think."

So Kathy woke the boys. She started breakfast while the boys were getting dressed. Davy came to the table first and started reading the paper.

Jake arrived, still half asleep until he saw the headline. "Unarmed?" he exclaimed.

"Read the article," Steve told him.

Jake quickly caught up with Davy's reading, and they were ready to turn to the completion of the article on an inside page at the same time. Jake finished first.

"Mom, this isn't right!" Jake stated.

"What happened to the pipe, Mom?" Davy asked.

"I can't answer that." she told him.

"Do you know what happened to it?" Jake asked.

"I can't answer that either."

"This is a bunch of…!"

"Jake!" Kathy cautioned.

"Well, it is!"

"I know," she assured him, carrying the boys' plates to the table. "While you're eating, think about this and decide if you want to go to school today or stay home."

"I need to go," Davy told her. "I've got a test in chemistry today."

"It's up to you. If you change your mind, call me. Oh, no, I won't be here."

"Mom, we know to call Dad," Davy pointed out.

"I've got a test today, too," Jake stated.

Kathy looked questioningly at Steve. He gave her a tiny nod of his head. Kathy wasn't so sure it was a good idea, but she voiced no objections.

Steve stood up, walked to Kathy, and gave her a hug. As he did, he whispered in her ear, "They'll be fine." A goodbye kiss, an "I love you" from each to the other, and Steve left for work.

Shortly after that the boys finished breakfast, rinsed their dishes, and put them in the dishwasher, gathered their school books, told Kathy goodbye, and left for the short walk to the high school. Kathy sat down at the table with another cup of tea.

Her thoughts were on the boys. She and Steve were adults. They would deal with whatever happened. Could the boys? How would their friends react? Teenagers can be cruel. She should be with the boys to protect them. At the same time she knew, however reluctantly, she had to let them grow up. Let them learn to deal with both types of people, the ones who try to understand and those who do not. It was going to be a difficult day for them.

She wished she could stay home in case they needed her, but she couldn't. The grand jury would convene at 9:00 a.m. and she needed to be there. Her mind was cluttered with family concerns, the events of Sunday morning, and her responsibilities as secretary of the grand jury. The ringing telephone startled her out of her thoughts. She quickly answered it, thinking it might be one of the boys. It wasn't.

"Kathy?" a deep voice asked.

"Yes?" she answered, not recognizing the voice immediately.

"I wanted to thank you for what you did."

"Calvin?"

"Yeah."

"Are you all right?"

"The headache's gone, finally. The ribs hurt like hell, but they'll get better, thanks to you."

"Thanks? I nearly got you killed! You only went back to the construction site because of what I told you I saw."

"Not true. I saw the same thing. I just didn't think about what day it was or the time of day until you brought it up."

"See? It was my fault."

"I screwed up, Kathy. Not you," he said, trying to reassure her. "I didn't *call out* with dispatch. If I had, another unit would have checked by. They knew I was one-man."

"You're just saying that to make me feel better," she accused him.

"You should feel good. You did what a partner is supposed to do. You pointed out something I missed and you covered my back."

"I killed a man, Calvin. I don't feel good about that."

"You never will." When Kathy did not respond, he continued. "Kathy, you did what you had to do, what you were supposed to do. What we taught you to do. I knew you were there and that you'd get help. I just had to keep fighting until help came."

"I wish it hadn't happened."

"So do I. I'm sorry I put you in that position."

"Don't be. It was my choice to ride along. I'm just glad that you're okay."

"Thanks again. Take care, Kathy."

"You too, Calvin."

Relieved to hear from Calvin and to know he was recovering, Kathy thought that his trying to take the blame for what happened was just chivalry that was inbred in Texas men. Their protective attitude toward women and children made them good cops and also made all the officers she had ridden with feel that women shouldn't be on the street. With women's lib pushing for equal opportunity in the work place, that attitude would change as women proved their abilities in many areas dominated by men. But it would take a generation, perhaps two.

She went to the bedroom to get dressed to go downtown. Thinking about her grand jury duties, she wondered if she could keep her mind on the cases. She doubted it. It would probably be better if she resigned. It would be best, she reluctantly decided. With that decision, she picked up her purse and the soft briefcase containing the records she kept of cases heard, indictments, no bills, and cases in progress. She left the house for the drive to downtown Houston.

Chapter 23

Monday, September 27, 1976 - 8:55 a.m.

Kathy entered the county courthouse and approached the grand jury room. She was intercepted by one of the grand jury clerks.

"Mrs. Cooper, Judge Parker would like to see you in his chambers," the clerk told her. "If you'll come with me, please."

"Of course," Kathy agreed. I think I know what this is about, she thought.

The judge rose from behind his desk and came around to greet her with a handshake.

"Please, sit down," he said, motioning to a sitting area at one side of the room. "Coffee?" he asked.

"No. I don't drink coffee."

"Would you like some tea, Mrs. Cooper?" the clerk asked.

"Yes, please, with a little sugar," Kathy said.

The clerk left, shutting the door behind her.

"This is about the shooting, isn't it?" Kathy asked the judge.

"I'm afraid it is," he told her. "One of the qualifications for serving on the grand jury is not being under investigation for a felony. In this case, I doubt felony charges will be brought, but to avoid the appearance of impropriety, I have to ask you to resign your position."

She nodded. "My mind wouldn't be on business anyway. I hadn't thought of the reason you stated." She paused. "Do you need it in writing?"

"That would be best," he stated. "I've taken the liberty of having a letter of resignation prepared for your signature." Having the letter ready for her was his way of trying to make things easier for her. However, now that the moment had come, he was mildly embarrassed at his presumption.

"Thank you," Kathy said, grateful for his consideration. Kathy opened the briefcase and pulled out the records she had kept of the grand jury proceedings. "Whoever replaces me will need these," she said, handing the papers to Judge Parker.

"Yes, thank you," he said as he took them.

A knock on the door announced the clerk bringing the tea and coffee things on a tray. She set it down on the table and left. The judge picked up the cup of tea and held it toward Kathy.

"Thanks, but I can't," she said. "Right now it wouldn't stay down."

He set the cup back on the tray. He wanted to say something encouraging to her but couldn't think of anything. "I'll get the letter." He went to his desk and returned with the letter and a pen. He handed it to her.

She took the pen, put the letter on the table, and was about to sign.

"Read it first," he advised.

She quickly scanned the short statement. "Personal reasons? That's generous, considering the circumstances." She signed the paper as firmly as she could with her hand shaking.

"One more thing," the judge said. "Have you consulted an attorney?"

"Yesterday."

"Good."

She nodded and got to her feet. "I enjoyed serving. I'm sorry I can't complete my term."

"So am I," the judge told her, shaking her hand.

Kathy turned to the door, then back. "Is this going to affect the indictments the panel has already returned?"

"No reason it should."

She nodded. "Good." She turned and left the room.

Judge Parker stood in the open doorway and watched her walk away. He felt pity for her and what she would be subjected to in the next few weeks or months. The press was having a field day with this. The repercussions were going to touch a lot of people.

Chapter 24

Monday, September 27, 1976 - 2:25 p.m.

Ray Ulbrich was working on a brief when his secretary announced that John Everett was holding on line two. John Everett and Ray Ulbrich had been classmates in law school. While Ray went into family practice, John became a criminal defense attorney and excelled at it. The two had remained friends over the years, but with their busy schedules they seldom talked unless one of them needed something.

Ray picked up the phone and punched the proper button. "Morning, John."

"Good morning. How's your family?" John asked.

"Doing good. And yours?"

"Great. Carolyn just passed the bar," John replied. "I'd planned on having her join my practice, but she turned me down."

"Smart girl! You work too hard," Ray teased. "What is she going to do?"

"She's going with the DA's office."

"That's a switch. What can I do for you John?"

"I heard that you are representing Kathy Cooper. Is it true?"

"Yes, it is."

"I'd like to offer my services to her. Can you arrange a meeting for me?"

"I can, but aren't you a little premature? She hasn't been charged."

"Ray, if they don't find that piece of pipe, she will be."

"Probably," Ray admitted. "But John, she can't afford you."

"In this case she can."

"Pro bono?"

"Yes. You understand why."

"Yeah, I do." Ray thought a moment. If she gets indicted she'll need a good defense attorney, and John was one of the best. However, he felt John was rushing things. Approaching Kathy with John's offer at this time would only add to her anxiety. "Let's wait and see what happens."

"Why delay?"

"I think it's best for my client at this time."

John accepted the pointed reminder that by making his offer he was indeed poaching.

"Understood. I'm available if she needs me."

"I'll keep it in mind and pray it doesn't come to that."

"We both will. Let's get together for lunch soon."

"Absolutely," Ray agreed, knowing it wasn't likely to happen. "Give my best to your family."

"You, too."

Ray hung up the phone, forced thoughts of Kathy from his mind, and turned to the unfinished brief.

Chapter 25

Tuesday, September 28, 1976 - 1:50 p.m.

Ray Ulbrich had called Kathy that morning. Detectives Saxon and Black wanted to speak to Kathy again. Ray set up a meeting at his office for two o'clock that afternoon. Kathy really didn't want to think or talk about the shooting anymore. However, she thought, maybe it will be easier with Ray present. Kathy dressed carefully for the meeting, but she could do little to hide the fatigue around her eyes.

She, Ray, and the detectives met in a small conference room at Ray's office. Coffee, tea, and cookies were provided. Kathy turned everything down, rather than take part and then hope her stomach wouldn't reject it. Detective Saxon prepared to take notes by opening a small spiral notebook and getting out a pen. Ray asked the detectives if they were going to read Kathy her rights.

"That's not necessary at this point," Detective Black stated. "There is just one thing we want to clear up."

"And that is?" Ray asked.

"Her ability to operate the thirty caliber carbine."

Kathy looked at Ray. He nodded.

"I told you a friend taught me," Kathy stated.

"And the friend's name?" Black asked.

Reluctantly Kathy answered, "Dan Cannon."

"How can we get in touch with Mr. Cannon?"

"Officer Cannon works night shift patrol out of North Shepherd."

"He's a police officer?" Black asked with surprise.

Kathy nodded.

"How did he happen to teach you?"

"He and some others took me out for target practice."

"Other officers?"

"Yes."

"To a range?"

"No."

Black and Saxon exchanged glances. They both had a good idea of what happened, but they needed to hear it from Kathy.

"We need to know the details. When, where, who, et cetera."

Kathy again turned to Ray, who again nodded for her to go ahead and explain. Feeling miserable for having to tell, and hoping that the officers didn't lose their jobs, she worried more about them than herself at that moment. Reluctantly she told them who the officers were, where they took her, and when it happened.

"They were on duty?"

Kathy nodded.

"They left their beats?"

She nodded again.

Detective Black looked down at the table and covered his mouth with a hand to hide his smile. He had done the same thing a few times when he was working night shift patrol. It wasn't that unusual. It wasn't condoned, just ignored. The supervisors knew it was done. They had done it themselves as patrolmen. If they didn't know about it they didn't have to do anything. The fact that the officers took Kathy along proved she had a good relationship with them and that they trusted her. Obviously she knew it was against department policy, or she wouldn't have been reluctant to answer questions.

"Thank you, Mrs. Cooper," Black told her as he got to his feet. "That's all we needed."

Saxon gathered her things and rose to join her partner as they expressed their thanks for Kathy's time. They left the conference room. Kathy and Ray remained for a few minutes.

"I feel like I betrayed them," she said, holding her head in her hands.

"You warned them, didn't you?"

She nodded.

"You didn't have any choice," Ray told her.

"You don't understand. They could lose their jobs. They're good cops. They love being cops. They never wanted to do anything else. If they lose their jobs they'll never be cops again, anyplace." Kathy understood what they would lose because she felt the loss of not being able to ride along anymore.

"Do I need to remind you that if they had not taught you how to use the carbine, Calvin Henson would probably be dead?"

She looked up at Ray and wondered if they would feel it was a fair exchange. The price could be extremely high—their jobs—but a man's life is priceless!

Chapter 26

The next several days were a blur of phone calls from family and friends and the press requesting interviews. Kathy finally left the phone off the hook unless she wanted to make a call.

The press and television coverage got worse in some ways. They began attacking the mayor, who was not very popular at the moment for other reasons. The mayor was blaming the police chief, who was suddenly considering retiring after twenty-five years with the department. Judge Parker was also mentioned, but only in the context that she had served on his grand jury panel from which she had resigned right after the shooting. The media was asking tough questions, all slanted to favor Ray Jackson. Some of the editorials attempted to make Kathy look like a gun-happy vigilante. The civil rights and black activist organizations were fanning the flames and demanding her arrest.

Steve and the boys were handling it better than Kathy expected. She was worn out from worrying about them. Her parents and sisters were supportive. Her mother was furious at the way Kathy was being treated by the media. Her father had his hands full trying to keep his wife calm.

Some of the neighbors kept their distance and had trouble looking Kathy in the eye. She tried to understand. She was the same person she had always been. She hadn't changed, but their perception of her had. She had trouble concentrating, and knew most of the time that she wasn't thinking straight.

Worst of all she had nightmares; recurring graphic images of Calvin's head being smashed like a cantaloupe. Her terror-induced outcries woke Steve more than once. Steve did his best to comfort and reassure her. Both of them were losing sleep. Kathy found herself being short with the boys. She came to understand why stress led some people to alcohol and/or pills. She was determined not to resort to using that kind of crutch.

After three nights of little to no sleep, she called a long-time friend who was a psychologist. He told her that because of their friendship he could not help her. Whoever she saw must be licensed to practice in the state of Texas to insure that anything Kathy said would be privileged information and could not be used in court. He recommended a woman he knew who had a good reputation.

Kathy made an appointment for Thursday morning of the next week. In the meantime she tried to cope with stress, nightmares, and impatience. She just wanted this to be over. She wanted to get on with her life; what was left of it. She was looking forward to seeing the psychologist on Thursday. But she wouldn't keep that appointment.

Chapter 27

Tuesday, October 5, 1976 - 3:05 p.m.

On Tuesday afternoon when Jesse Banks finished a report call and got back *in service,* he received another call: *meet the DA investigator* at a convenience store on Mangum Road. As soon as Investigator James Tucker explained his mission, Jesse went to the payphone and called Station One and asked for Sergeant Schmidt.

"Sarge, this is Jesse Banks. I got a call to meet a DA investigator to assist in serving a felony warrant."

"You need back-up?"

"No. I'd like to be excused from this call."

"Why?" Sergeant Schmidt asked, puzzled. It was not like Jesse to refuse an assignment.

"The warrant is for Kathy Cooper. She's been indicted for murder."

"What?"

"The first grand jury no-billed her. The DA took it to a second one and they indicted her," Jesse explained.

Jesse held the receiver away from his ear as the sergeant let loose an explosion of German curse words. This was an election year. Obviously the DA had given in to media pressure and pushed for an indictment in Kathy's case.

"Damn politicians!"

"Sarge," Jesse continued when the sergeant ran out of expletives. "I know Kathy. She rode with me."

"Every cop in northwest Houston knows her," the sergeant pointed out. "Take care of business, Jesse. Make it as easy for her as you can."

Jesse acknowledged the order and hung up the phone.

* * * * *

Word of Kathy's indictment and arrest spread through the Houston Police Department as fast as a wind-driven grass fire during a drought. Officers who knew her were furious. Most of the others were appalled that the woman who saved the life of a fellow officer received such treatment at the hands of the District Attorney and the grand jury. Assistant District Attorneys (ADAs) who present cases to the grand juries can slant their presentation to favor the state or the defendant. They also make recommendations for indictments or no bills.

Mostly the officers blamed the DA, knowing he had taken the case to a second grand jury after the first no-billed her. The officer's comments about it were not recommended for those with tender ears. Donny Wells alone cussed for several minutes without repeating himself, to the approval of everyone at the station. Roll calls and coffee rooms throughout the department reverberated with two questions. What happened to the piece of pipe? Secondly, how could they help her? The answer to that question was obvious.

Chapter 28

Tuesday, October 5, 1976 - 3:55 p.m.

Kathy drove into her driveway and parked on the right-hand side in front of the garage. As she got out of the car, two cars pulled up across the driveway. The front car was a blue and white HPD unit, the other dark gray. Jesse Banks got out of the police car and joined the man in a suit who stepped from the gray car.

Kathy walked toward the men, meeting them half-way to the street.

"Hi, Jesse," she said with a smile.

"Kathy," Jesse said in a flat tone of voice. "This is James Tucker. He's an investigator for the DA's office."

Kathy faced Tucker. "Mr. Tucker, if you have any questions you'll have to contact my attorney."

"No questions, Mrs. Cooper. I have a warrant for your arrest for the murder of Ray Jackson."

Kathy felt the bottom drop out of her world. It took her several moments to catch her breath before she could speak. "I understand," she said, although she really did not.

"I'll be transporting you downtown," Jesse told her.

"May I tell the boys what's going on first?"

"Where are they?" Jesse asked.

"They should be inside."

"Sure," Jesse nodded.

Kathy turned toward the front door and reached into her shoulder bag for her house keys. Jesse took hold of her wrist with one hand and slipped her purse from her shoulder with the other. It was instinct on his part, and Kathy realized she had made a mistake.

"Sorry. I need my keys."

Jesse looked through her purse and handed it back to her. The three of them went to the front door. Kathy unlocked it and entered first, with Jesse and Tucker right behind her.

"Davy. Jake," she called out. "Come out here, please," she said, putting her purse down on a table in the family room.

"Hi, Mom," Jake said as he came into the room, then looked questioningly at Jesse, an officer he had met, and the stranger. "What's going on?"

At that moment, Davy entered the room. "Mom?"

"You know officer Banks. This is James Tucker," she said, indicating the investigator. She didn't know what to say next.

Jesse stepped forward and held out his hand to the boys. "Davy. Jake," he said as he shook hands with them. "Mr. Tucker has a warrant for your mother's arrest. I'll be transporting her downtown."

Davy asked, "What's the charge?"

"Murder," Tucker answered. "She's been indicted for the murder of Ray Jackson."

"What! That's ridiculous." Davy stated.

"That's bullshit!" Jake exclaimed.

"She was protecting the officer!" Davy protested.

"They can't do this!" Jake exclaimed.

"Yes. They can," Kathy told him. "They're just doing their job. I need you two to call Daddy and tell him what's happened. Have him call Ray Ulbrich. Tell him they're taking me…" She turned to Jesse. "Where are you taking me?"

"To the County Jail, 301 San Jacinto," he informed her and the boys.

"Tell him," Kathy instructed.

"Yes, ma'am," Davy said.

"Can Mr. Ulbrich stop this?" Jake asked.

"I don't know. He'll do what he can, I'm sure. Don't worry. It'll be all right. I'll be home later." She tried to reassure the boys with a group hug. From the looks on their faces, it didn't work. She stepped back and turned to Jesse and Tucker.

"Kathleen Mavis Cooper, you are under arrest for the murder of Ray Jackson," Tucker stated. He proceeded to read the Miranda warning to her. "Do you understand your rights as I've read them to you?"

"Yes, I understand."

"I have to cuff you and pat you down," Jesse reluctantly told her. "It's policy."

"I know." She smiled at his discomfort. She turned around and brought her hands behind her back.

Jesse took a pair of handcuffs from a pouch on his gun belt and stepped up behind her. She flinched as the cold steel of handcuffs closed around her wrists with the rapid clicking of the ratchet mechanism. The weight of the handcuffs surprised her. These were not a toy, but serious restrains. For the safety of the officers and their prisoners, they had to be.

With a deep breath let out in a long sigh, Jesse started at her neck and moved down. His hands checked between her shoulders and her armpits. From behind her, with the backs of his hands he checked under her breasts. Davy and Jake had never seen anyone, including their Dad, touch their mother that way. With difficulty Davy maintained control, but Jake lost it.

"Stop it! Get your hands off her!" Jake exclaimed, his face red and his fists clenched.

Davy stepped in front of his brother and put his hands on his chest. Jake slapped Davy's hands away.

"JACOB!" Kathy warned.

Jesse stepped around Kathy to confront Jake.

"Son, I mean no disrespect to your mother. She's a special lady. One I admire and respect. I didn't want to make this arrest. But I felt she'd be more comfortable with someone she knew than with a stranger. I wanted to make this as easy for her as I could."

Silence prevailed for a moment while Jake's color faded and his fists relaxed. "And I'm making it hard for her."

Jesse nodded.

"I'm sorry, Mom."

"It's okay," she told him.

Jesse stepped back behind Kathy to resume the search, feeling around her waist, then below her waist where men would have pockets. Kathy's slacks had no pockets. The boys stood watching quietly until Jesse used the back of his hand to check her crotch. Jake turned and fled the room. A moment later the door to his bedroom slammed shut. Jesse continued, running both hands down each leg and around each ankle. Jesse took Kathy by the arm.

Tucker led the way to the front door and opened it. He turned to Jesse. "The media's out here."

"Keep them away from Kathy when we go out," Jesse instructed and turned to Davy. "Don't answer the door. If they bother you call 911 and have officers give them trespass warnings."

"Yes, sir," Davy answered.

"Get me out of here, Jesse," Kathy pleaded, head lowered.

"Hold your head up, Kathy! Walk tall and proud. You haven't done anything to be ashamed of."

She looked sideways at him, raised her head and gave him a weak smile. He was right. Don't ever show any weakness to the enemy. And right now the media was her enemy. She braced herself to maintain no facial expression while running the gauntlet of reporters and cameramen.

Tucker led the way out the door. Kathy and Jesse followed. Jesse held her upper right arm with his left hand. Davy shut the door behind them and Kathy heard the deadbolt slide home. With Tucker running interference, Jesse walked Kathy directly to the HPD unit. She looked straight ahead at the car and ignored the questions shouted at her by the reporters. Jesse opened the back door and helped Kathy inside. He wasted no time going around to the driver's seat, starting the car, and driving away.

"Kathy?" Jesse questioned. "Are you okay?"

Kathy looked at him through the expanded metal cage. "You gotta be kidding. I haven't been okay since the shooting."

"You did the right thing," he told her. "It's the fucking media. They'd try to hang Jesus Christ if he'd shot Ray Jackson. Who, by the way, was an ex-con and the worst kind of turd around. Assaults, drugs, burglaries, auto theft. You name it, he's done it. And he wouldn't hesitate to kill a cop if he got a chance."

Kathy thought about that. It helped to find out that Ray Jackson had a prison record. Still she had feelings and thoughts about the shooting that she couldn't bring herself to share with her husband or her attorney—the satisfaction she felt when she looked at his dead body, and the feeling of being cheated out of hurting him the way he had hurt Calvin.

They passed the construction site as they left the neighborhood. A crew was erecting an eight-foot chain-link fence. Too late, she thought. If they had done that at the beginning of the construction, I wouldn't be sitting in the backseat of a police car in handcuffs.

Leaning back against the seat pressed the handcuffs into her wrists and against her back. If she sat forward, her face came close to the cage. Because there were no seatbelts in the back of the unit, a sudden stop would throw her into the heavy expanded metal. The men had warned her of that danger when she rode along. She turned sideways in the seat.

Even with Jesse in the front seat, she felt alone. He was doing his job as an officer. She was a prisoner, who had no control. The loss of control left her feeling vulnerable. Her uncertain future made her anxious. The unfairness of it all made her mad, fighting mad, but there was no way to fight it. This would play out according to the rules of the Criminal Justice System. Kathy tried to resign herself to the situation. Like a case of the flu, this too would pass, one way or another.

As Jesse approached the county jail, Kathy's thoughts shifted from turmoil to writer mode. She began observing and mentally noting details of a new experience. Having never been arrested before, although she was not looking forward to jail, she realized that this was another aspect of police work and the Criminal Justice System. It could be a valuable experience for a writer if she looked at it that way.

Chapter 29

Tuesday, October 5, 1976 - 5:20 p.m.

At the county courthouse, which also included the county jail, Kathy started noticing everything. Jesse drove down the vehicle ramp that led to the basement entrance to the county offices and courtrooms. Also located on that basement level was a small area for parking 'authorized only' vehicles, as well as the entrance to the county jail. A television crew had beaten them to the jail.

"Damn vultures!" Jesse exclaimed as he parked the unit. He came around and opened Kathy's door, he took her arm as she got out, locked up the unit, and guided her to the jail entrance.

Tucker had pulled in right behind them and caught up with them at the door. Jesse and Tucker were identified through the small window in the door and allowed to enter. Jesse escorted Kathy to a bench along one wall and asked her to sit down.

Tucker proceeded to the booking desk and handed the warrant to the booking officer. He filled out the necessary paperwork and motioned for Kathy to step over. Jesse removed her handcuffs. She was told to empty her pockets and remove her jewelry.

"I have no pockets," she stated, removing her watch and reluctantly tugging at her wedding ring. She had to wet her finger to get it off. She had not taken it off since Steve slipped it on at their wedding, eighteen years earlier. She bit her lower lip as she dropped it into the small valuables bag with her watch. Both thumbprints were then put on the booking papers.

"Put her in that empty cell," the deputy ordered.

Jesse nodded and walked her to the indicated cell. Tucker swung the cell door open. As Kathy started to step into it, Jesse pulled her back, wrapped her up in a bear hug, and whispered in her ear. "Hang in there, Kathy. I'll help you any way I can. Just call the station."

"You know a good defense attorney?"

Jesse shook his head as he released her. "Cops and defense attorneys work opposite sides of the street," he pointed out with a little smile.

Kathy stepped back and looked into Jesse's troubled eyes. She wasn't sure whether he wanted to cuss or start hitting people. He turned abruptly and quickly left the jail. Kathy stepped into the cell.

"Good luck, Mrs. Cooper," Tucker said as he shut and locked the door, then exited the jail.

Kathy sat on the bench for only a few minutes. A female deputy sheriff opened the cell door and motioned for Kathy to step out.

"Grab the bars. Feet back and spread 'em," the deputy instructed.

Kathy complied and found herself being searched again, with quick, firm hands. Kathy was then directed through a medal door of bars, which clanged closed behind her. The deputy followed Kathy, two steps behind and slightly to one side, as she was escorted through the processing.

Two sets of finger prints were taken. She was photographed from the front, left profile and right profile. Directed out of the room, down another hall and into an area marked as Medical Evaluation, which consisted of her complete medical history, what medication she required, etc. Had she ever had any thoughts of suicide, a history of mental problems, depression, illnesses, injuries, surgeries, physical conditions, food and drug allergies, or special dietary requirements, and did she have any health issues at this time?

The deputy next took Kathy to Pre-Trial Services. The deputy behind the desk looked at the papers brought to him by her escorting deputy.

"You're Kathy Cooper?" he asked. "You killed Ray Jackson to protect an HPD officer, didn't you?"

"I've been read my rights, Officer. I'm not saying anything."

He smiled. "Smart lady. That was a good thing you did. Sorry you're having to go through this." He looked down at the papers again and frowned. "I don't understand this," he looked up at Kathy and her escorting deputy. "Bail's denied."

"I thought everyone was entitled to bail out of jail," Kathy stated.

"They are, except in Capital cases." When he saw Kathy turn pale, he quickly continued. "This isn't a Capital case! Someone made a mistake, but you'll be held here until your arraignment."

"When will that be?"

"At least two days."

Kathy had expected to be able to bond out when the paper work was done. Now it appeared that that was not going to happen. Her shoulders slumped with disappointment and she started to lower her head in defeat. Then Jesse's words came back to her: "Hold your head up, Kathy." She turned the motion into a nod indicating acceptance and pulled her shoulders back, almost in an act of defiance.

"Your attorney may be able to straighten this out sooner. You do have an attorney, don't you?"

"My husband is taking care of that."

He handed the paperwork to Kathy's escort. "I hope this all works out for you."

"Thank you."

The deputy and Kathy proceeded to the elevators and rode up to the fourth floor, the women's floor. When the elevator stopped and the door opened, the odor of unwashed bodies and other unpleasant things was familiar, but not as strong as at what she had experienced at the jail at HPD. Another barred metal door opened. The paperwork was passed to a deputy. Another door clanged shut behind her.

The deputy motioned Kathy through a side door. A female deputy waited on the far side of a table. Kathy realized that all the deputies on the women's floor were female.

"Strip," the one at the table told her. "Put everything on the table."

She began undressing. As she put each article of clothing on the table, it was checked and placed in a large bag. When she was down to her skin, she began shivering. It wasn't cold in the room. One of the officers searched through Kathy's hair, her mouth, ears, and nose, and slipped on a rubber glove for the cavity search. It was humiliating, even though Kathy understood it was for security reasons.

She was instructed to shower in another room. Issued a brown, shapeless dress with large orange-and-white plaid patch pockets, two pairs of plain white cotton panties, and a pair of plastic sandals, Kathy was instructed to get dressed. She was also given one sheet, one blanket, one towel, and a small hygiene kit that contained a bar of soap, toothpaste, toothbrush, comb, and disposable razor.

The entrance of the women's cell block was entered through another metal door with bars. The paperwork was passed to a deputy inside the cell block and the door closed.

"Last cell on the left," the inside deputy instructed Kathy.

Just past a small control booth on the right, in a barred, open area, surrounded on three sides by cells, a dozen or more black females sat at tables watching television, playing cards, or talking. A few approached the bars as Kathy came into view.

"We got us some fresh honky meat," one commented. "Hey, sweet thing come in here. I'll treat you right." The woman proceeded to make come hither motions and kissing noises.

"Knock it off!" the deputy ordered. The women paid no attention and continued to taunt Kathy as she passed by.

"You know who that is?" a second woman asked. "She's that honky bitch that killed Ray Jackson. I seen her on the TV."

"Damn you!" a third woman shouted. "He was a hell of a man!"

When Kathy glanced their way, the hate in their faces surprised her. She looked away and ignored them, but their jeers reminded her that she had killed a man. A man some people cared for. A man some grieved for. She remembered Sergeant Ralph Strong's comment: "Somebody always cries over these people." Kathy stepped into the last cell on the left.

"You missed dinner," the deputy stated. "I'll get you something to eat. You want coffee, tea, a soda, or water to drink."

"A diet soda, please," Kathy answered.

The solid metal cell door closed and Kathy looked around. The six-foot by ten-foot cell contained a platform with a thin mattress, a small desk, a toilet, a sink, and a mirror, all made of stainless steel and all attached to the walls. The door had a two-foot by six-inch vertical window off to one side and a hinged horizontal opening for a food tray.

Kathy set the sheet, towel, and hygiene kit on the end of the bunk. She opened the blanket and wrapped it around her shoulders. She sat down on the cot, back against the wall, and pulled her knees up against her chest. With her arms and the blanket wrapped around her body and legs, she hugged herself. Alone in a private cell and out of the sight of others, she fought unsuccessfully to block the tears.

She thought of Steve and the boys and what this situation was doing to them. Steve and she would survive it, but how would it affect the boys? She was more concerned about Jake than Davy. How would they deal with it if she was convicted of murder? If she had to serve time in prison, so be it. Even if she was acquitted, nobody walks away clean from a murder charge. Doubt would always remain in people's minds. It would follow her through the rest of her life. Murder! How unfair! When she squeezed that trigger, it was the only thing she could do; the only thing there was time to do. She had made the right choice. What was it the officers had told her? They'd rather be tried by twelve than carried by six. Yes! And I would rather be tried by twelve than the alternative–Calvin Henson being carried by six. Slowly she regained control, wiped the tears from her face, took a deep breath, and tried to relax.

Chapter 30

Tuesday, October 7, 1976 - 7:55 p.m.

One of the deputies brought Kathy a bologna sandwich with mustard and cheese, a peanut butter and jelly wafer, and a diet soda, which was not the flavor Kathy preferred, but it was cold and wet. She ate about half of the sandwich and saved the peanut butter and jelly wafer for later.

Without her watch, she had no idea what time it was when a deputy opened her cell door and announced that her attorney had arrived to see her. She was taken down the hall, out of the cell block, and escorted to a booth which was open at the back. Through the window she could see Ray Ulbrich and another man waiting for her. Ray motioned for her to pick up the telephone receiver on her side of the window as she sat down.

"I'm glad to see you, Ray!" she told him. "Thanks for coming."

"Are you all right, Kathy?" he asked.

She shook her head in the negative. "How are Steve and the boys?"

"Upset, of course, but mostly concerned about you."

"I'll be okay," she stated, glancing at the man with Ray.

"Kathy, pick up the phone in the booth next to you," Ray instructed.

She looked around the left-hand wall of the booth and took that receiver in her left hand. The cords on the receivers were just long enough for her to hold one to each ear.

"Kathy," Ray said, "this is John Everett. He's a criminal defense attorney."

She nodded to Mr. Everett. Kathy knew his reputation. He was well known for his defense of some notorious people. He was the attorney Kathy would want if she was guilty. Once, when asked if it was true that he charged everything his clients had, he answered, "Yes. And everything they ever will have."

"I've heard of you Mr. Everett, but I don't think I can afford you," Kathy told him.

"Mrs. Cooper, you don't have to worry about that."

"Yes, I do."

"No, ma'am, you don't." He looked at Ray, then continued. "A defense fund has been set up for you."

"Defense fund?"

"It was started by officers of the Houston Police Department."

Kathy closed her eyes, hoping to hide the tears that suddenly filled them. "God bless 'em," she murmured, then quickly opened her eyes. "Will the department approve of that?"

"It already has," Mr. Everett stated.

"Chief Ledford announced it on the news tonight," Ray told her. "Along with comments about the DA's misplaced priorities and his personal belief that you will be cleared of the murder charge."

"The national news has picked up the story," Mr. Everett added. "By tomorrow, contributions will be coming in from all over."

Kathy put the receivers in her lap and wiped the tears from her face with the sleeve of her dress. It took her a moment to regain control.

"Mrs. Cooper," John Everett continued, "would you like me to represent you in this case?"

"What do you think you can do for me?"

"I think I have a good chance of getting you acquitted. I'll be able to assess that after you and I have gone over the facts of the case. Not here. In my office, after your release."

"When will that be?" she asked.

"Your arraignment is scheduled for Friday morning."

"Friday? This is Tuesday! I have to stay here until then?"

John Everett nodded. "Unless I can get it moved up, and I will try in the morning."

"What exactly is an arraignment?" she asked.

"It's a court appearance to establish your identity and for you to enter a plea," Everett explained. "The judge will set the amount of your bail and I'll get you out of here as soon as the paperwork can be done."

"What if he sets a high bail?"

"It doesn't matter. I'll take care of it," Everett stated. "Do you wish me to represent you?"

Kathy glanced at Ray, then addressed Mr. Everett. "May I speak to Ray privately for a moment?"

"Certainly." Mr. Everett agreed and hung up the receiver he was using.

"What's bothering you, Kathy?" Ray asked.

"Most of the people he has represented have been guilty as sin. I'm concerned that if he represents me, people will assume I'm guilty."

"Let them. It's what the twelve on the jury think. And believe me, if he can't convince them of your innocence, no one can," he told her.

Kathy nodded and motioned for Mr. Everett to pick up the receiver.

"Yes, Mrs. Cooper?"

"Yes, Mr. Everett, I do want you to represent me."

"In that case, call me John," he said with a smile.

"Okay. I'm Kathy."

"Do you have any questions?"

"Yes. They have me in a cell all by myself. There's no TV and nothing to do."

"That's to keep you out of the general population of the jail, where you would be in danger of getting beaten up, or worse. It's for your safety."

"Oh!" She thought of the black women taunting her as she was escorted to her cell, and the hatred she saw in their faces.

"When a person is arrested, the arresting officers and later the jail personnel are responsible for the health and welfare of that person," John Everett explained.

"I see. But I'm going to go nuts with nothing to do." She turned to Ray. "Can you get me some books to read? And a deck of cards?"

Ray shook his head. "Nothing can be brought into the jail."

"The money you had when you were booked was deposited in your account," John told her. "You can use that to buy books and cards at the commissary."

"I didn't bring any money with me. Just the clothes I had on, my watch, and wedding ring."

"I'll deposit some money into your account before I leave," Ray said. "You'll be able to use that in the morning."

"Thank you, Ray."

"Anything else?" John asked.

"No."

"Good. One thing I must impress on you: don't discuss the shooting with anyone except your husband. Do not discuss it with your sons, your parents, your siblings, or friends. They could be subpoenaed to testify to anything you say to them. So say nothing!"

"Ray warned me about that, but I did talk to two detectives in Homicide."

"Did they read you your rights?"

"No."

"Did you sign anything?"

"No. I just told them what happened."

John Everett nodded. "Good. I'll take it from here and we'll talk again soon. Try not to worry, and get some rest."

"I'll try," she said, knowing that was unlikely. "Thank you both for coming. Ray, tell Steve and the boys I'm okay and I love them."

"Will do. Take care."

Kathy nodded. The men hung up the receivers and Kathy reluctantly followed suit. As soon as she did, the feeling of being isolated returned. In spite of the encouragement from Ray and John, her spirits fell.

Knowing that the officers believed in her helped, but none of them would be on the jury that decided her future. That would be left up to twelve civilians who would have little or no understanding of police work. *I hope John Everett is as good as his reputation,* she thought.

Back in her cell, she made up the bunk with the sheet she had been issued, washed her face, and brushed her teeth. She had just lain down when she heard orders shouted outside her cell. She got up and opened the food tray slot and listened. Other prisoners were ordered to return to their cells. Moments later she heard the clanging of cell doors being closed and "lights out in ten minutes."

She returned to the bunk, pulled the blanket over her tired body, and tried to get comfortable on the thin mattress. Her last thoughts before falling asleep were of Steve and the boys and how much she loved and missed them.

Chapter 31

Wednesday, October 6, 1976 - 6:00 a.m.

That first night in jail, Kathy slept fitfully. Strange noises woke her several times. After a while, she recognized them as doors to the cell block and cells opening and closing. A few times she heard voices, but made no effort to hear what was said. Each time, she changed position, and sometimes managed to fall asleep before the noises began again. It was not a restful night.

It was further disturbed when the nightmare came again. Just before the moment when the piece of pipe came down on Calvin's head, the lights in the cell came on, startling her awake. Her heart pounded. Her mouth was dry. Her hands shook from the dream. In fact, her whole body trembled.

Longing for Steve's arms around her, she sat up, wrapped the blanket around her, and tried to breathe slowly and deeply. Her heart slowed gradually and the shaking ceased. It's just a dream, she told herself. But she knew that if she had not acted that night, it might have come true. She could live with the nightmare. It would go away, eventually. Had it become reality, it would have followed her through life, making life itself a nightmare. She thanked God again for the fact that she had the means and the knowledge to act that night.

The noise of the breakfast trays being delivered to the cell block prompted her to get up, use the toilet, wash her hands and face, and brush her teeth. She finished just as her tray was pushed through the slot.

The meals were no better or worse than any institutional food she had experienced in college and in hospitals. The portions were more than adequate for her appetite, and she seldom ate more than half of the food at any meal.

Kathy was allowed to go to the commissary late in the morning. She bought a deck of cards and a couple of police procedural murder mysteries. The police procedures related in the stories had fascinated her since the first one she had read in her early teens. In an effort to savor the books and make them last, she limited herself to one chapter, then played solitaire until she won a game.

In the two days before her arraignment, she played every solitaire game she could remember her grandmother teaching her. She tried not to cheat, but at times she was so anxious to get back to one of the books, she fudged a little.

She looked forward to showering every day. It gave her a short break from the confining six-foot by ten-foot cell. The cheap soap was drying her skin and her hair, but there wasn't much she could do about that.

Mealtimes were welcomed because it gave her the only sense of time passing that she had. Without a watch or visible clock, most of the time she had no idea what time it was. Even a TV would have helped, but she didn't have one in her cell.

Nights were the worst. There was nothing she could do when the lights went out except try to sleep. Each night the noises on the floor bothered her less, but the nightmare came at least once each night, leaving her shaken and tired every morning.

Chapter 32

Friday, October 8, 1976 - 8:45 a.m.

Kathy had just laid out another of the endless games of solitaire when her cell door opened. "Mrs. Cooper," the deputy said. "It's time to go to court for your arraignment."
"Finally," Kathy said, relieved.
The female deputy escorted her to the cell block door, where another deputy waited to escort her to the entrance to the back halls of the courthouse. There, a male deputy waited with a pair of handcuffs in his left hand. Kathy frowned at the sight of the cuffs.
"It's policy," the tall, well-built, light-skinned black deputy explained.
The black deputy took over escort duty, guided Kathy to the holding area behind the courtroom, and stood guard on her for what seemed a long time. She wished she could have dressed in her own clothes. The brown shapeless shift was not a good color on her, and the handcuffs definitely were not her idea of jewelry.
When her case was called, she was escorted to the door leading to the courtroom. The deputy acting as court bailiff waited while the handcuffs were removed. Glad she would not appear in handcuffs, Kathy stepped through the door to the courtroom. Television and flash cameras pointed her way. Blacks, who filled the near side of the courtroom gallery, began chanting, "Murderer, murderer, murderer."
Shocked, Kathy took a step back and stumbled into the deputy behind her. He caught her, pulled her back into the hall, and shut the door. Still, she could hear the commotion in the courtroom as the judge banged his gavel and called for order. With Kathy out of sight, the noise from the courtroom gradually ceased.

When all got quiet, another deputy opened the door to the courtroom and motioned Kathy forward. She took a deep breath. The first time she entered the courtroom, all she saw were the angry blacks and the cameras.

This time she noticed Steve and the boys sitting in the front row of the far side. Steve appeared to not have slept since her arrest. She had never seen him look so tired and concerned. The boys appeared to have held up better, but they also looked worried. She wanted to touch them, to hug them, to comfort them, but no physical contact was allowed.

John Everett stood in front of the judge's bench. He held out his hand to her. They shook hands and faced the judge.

A third deputy asked, "Are you Kathleen Mavis Cooper?"

"Yes, I am," Kathy answered with a nod.

The bailiff read the indictment aloud and handed the papers to the judge.

"You've been charged with the murder of Ray Jackson," the judge stated. "How do you plead?"

"Not guilty, Your Honor," she stated.

The judge turned to the prosecuting Assistant District Attorney, Lloyd Maddox. "I see you've requested the defendant be held without bail, Mr. Maddox. Why?"

"This is a murder case. There's a flight risk, Your Honor."

The judge looked at John Everett.

"Mrs. Cooper's family and relatives all live in the Houston area, Your Honor. She is not a flight risk," John told the judge.

"Your Honor, her in-laws live in Brazil," Maddox stated.

"Is that true, Mrs. Cooper?"

"Yes, Your Honor."

"Do you have a passport?"

"No, Your Honor."

The judge nodded and turned to Maddox. "The court will notify the authorities that Mrs. Cooper is not to be issued a passport. Bail is set at fifty thousand dollars cash or bond." He banged his gavel once. "Next case."

The blacks once again broke into shouts, protesting her release, or perhaps the low amount of bail the judge set.

"I'll have you out of here in an hour or less," John Everett told her.

The bailiff tugged on her arm to escort her from the courtroom. As she turned she noticed officers in uniform sitting behind Steve and the boys. She thought it strange that so many were appearing in court on the same day, and then realized that most were familiar faces. The door closed behind her before she could acknowledge their presence. She was again handcuffed for the walk through the back halls to the women's area of the jail. On the way, the escorting deputy spoke to her.

"Prisoners are released through the bonding office. The lobby is public. We'll arrange for you to exit through the jail entrance. We'll notify your husband and attorney and keep the basement clear of media and others."

Moved by his consideration, Kathy looked up at the black man. She could only think to say, "Thank you."

"Our pleasure, ma'am," he said with a smile as he looked down at her.

A female deputy opened the door to the women's jail, the handcuffs were removed, and Kathy was escorted back to her cell. She gathered up the cards and the books, sat with them in her lap, and waited impatiently to be released. She could hardly wait to see Steve and boys. It seemed to take forever, when in fact she was released in less than an hour.

Escorted from the cell block, down the elevator to the basement and through the areas where she had been processed, she retrieved and changed into her own clothes. After signing for her personal property, she slipped on her wedding ring and watch. As she approached the door leading to the parking area in the basement of the courthouse, she grew nervous about what waited outside.

However, when the door opened, Steve and the boys were standing at Steve's car. After hugs and kisses all around, Kathy and her family got in the car, Steve driving with Kathy beside him, and the boys in the back seat. As Steve drove up the exit ramp, officers moved spectators and press aside and stopped traffic so Steve could pull out without stopping.

Chapter 33

Monday, October 12, 1976 - 9:55 a.m.

On Monday following Kathy's release from jail, she and Steve arrived at John Everett's office for a conference. The receptionist showed them right in, took their requests for tea and coffee, and closed the door behind her. With handshakes all around, they sat down.

"How are you two holding up?" John asked.

Kathy shrugged. "I just want this to be over."

"Steve?"

"I'm all right," he answered.

After knocking on the door, the receptionist entered with hot tea for Kathy and coffee for the men, then left the room and closed the door.

"Kathy," John said. "Everything said in this room is privileged. I can not and will not repeat any of it outside this room. Steve can listen. He's your husband. He can not be compelled to tell what he hears either. Do you understand?"

"Yes, I do."

"Steve?"

"Yes."

"Tell me what happened that night, Kathy," John asked.

"Where do you want me to start?"

"Just before the incident."

"You know about me riding along with the officers?" she asked.

"Yes."

"That Saturday, night shift, I was riding with Calvin Henson. It was about 5:00 a.m. Sunday and he was taking me home." Kathy again told her story, step by step. "I put the rifle to my shoulder as he raised the pipe over his head to hit Calvin. I shot him. I got the other two to move away from Calvin and

I got on the radio to get help." She was shaking by the time she finished. Reliving it was difficult, even though she had gone over it many times in her mind.

"I've heard the tape of you on the radio. You sounded tense."

"Tense? I was scared for Calvin."

"You did a good job."

"I made a mistake somewhere, or I wouldn't be here."

"Tell me again about the pipe. Where did he get it?"

"I didn't see that. When I put the rifle to my shoulder he already had it in his hand," she stated. "I don't know where it came from," she said shaking her head.

"What kind of pipe was it?"

"I don't know," she shrugged.

"Describe it."

"It looked to be about this long," she said, holding her hands about fourteen inches apart. "It was about this big around," she made a circle of her middle finger and thumb. "It was dark," she added with a shrug.

"Okay." John thought for a moment. "You want to add anything to what you've told me?"

"I don't know what it would be. I didn't have any choice, John. There wasn't time to do anything else. Calvin wasn't moving. I was afraid they were going to kill him. I knew I had to stop them." She was shaking again.

Steve reached out, took her hand, and squeezed. "What's next?" he asked.

"I'm going to have an investigator talk to Officer Henson and the officers who came to the scene that night. Something may develop from those interviews. We'll wait and see." He paused. "In the meantime, stay home as much as possible, Kathy. If the press becomes a nuisance, call the police and have them arrested for trespassing, if necessary. Any questions?"

"I have one now. Was I indicted just because no pipe was found?"

"Basically. HPD referred it to the DA without charges. The first Grand Jury no-billed you. The DA took it to a second one, which indicted you. The press has been crucifying you. The civil rights people have been demanding your arrest, and it's an election year. Probably all of that contributed to your indictment." He sighed. "Try not to worry, and call me with any questions or if you think of something to add to what you've told me."

She and Steve thanked him and left his office. They didn't talk much on the way home. When they did, it was to discuss how to keep the effect of all this on the boys to a minimum.

Chapter 34

Days passed slowly for Kathy. Time seemed to stand still. She and her family got back into their routine, but nothing was the same. She doubted if it ever would be. Not even close, she decided.

Friends called less frequently. The press finally had other stories to sensationalize, but she knew it would all begin again when her trial started.

She tried to fill her days with chores around the house. She tried to read, but found her eyes following the lines of print without anything getting through to her conscious mind. After three attempts at the same book, she gave up.

At least once a week she called John Everett for an update. There was nothing to update. His investigator had to wait until Calvin returned from sick leave to talk to him about the night of the shooting.

She hadn't typed up her notes from the last two nights. After retrieving the notepad from her purse, she went to the study. She tried, but it was too painful, her thoughts too chaotic for her to concentrate. Perhaps someday she would be able to use the notes for an article or a book, but not now, not with this murder charge hanging over her.

In the meantime, she couldn't seem to accomplish anything. She had craft projects planned, even started a couple, but quickly lost interest. Like a robot, she went through the days doing what had to be done – meals, laundry, shopping, cleaning, bill paying. When those things were caught up, she sat and stared at the walls. She had lost all the joy in life. Would she ever get it back, she wondered. Her smiles all felt forced and she hadn't laughed in weeks. Her lack of appetite made meal planning difficult and enjoying a meal nearly impossible. Fatigue caused her to fall asleep any time she sat still for a few minutes, and nightmares frequently invaded her sleep at night.

Her mother and sisters called every day. Because she wasn't allowed to talk to them about the shooting, they tried hard to make small talk. Kathy had to admit that she was too wrapped up in her own problems to enjoy the conversations. In fact, she came to hate to hear the phone ring.

She could talk to Steve. However, there were some feelings and thoughts that she had about the shooting that she wouldn't share with him. In keeping those thoughts and feelings from him, she felt dishonest. They were ugly, disturbing, and would only add to his worry.

The psychologist she saw once a week didn't help. The woman couldn't understand what it was like on the streets with the police. Kathy stopped going after four visits.

Mostly she felt lost. Hope faded away as time passed. She needed to maintain a positive attitude for her family and avoid sinking into depression. She didn't feel positive. She didn't feel negative either. She felt in limbo. It was frustrating, like treading water, and she was getting damn tired. She felt better when she got angry about the situation, but she couldn't sustain that for long before worry returned.

Then one day, almost two months after the shooting, John Everett called. He wanted to see her and Steve in his office the next morning at 9:00 a.m.

Chapter 35

Wednesday, November 24, 1976 - 9:05 a.m.

Once they settled down in John Everett's office with coffee and tea, he brought them up-to-date on the investigation.

"Officer Calvin Henson has been interviewed. Basically, he confirmed your story up to the point when he was kicked in the head. He was unconscious when you fired the rifle. The officers who responded to the *assist the officer* call told what they each did on arrival. None of them saw a piece of pipe.

"Kathy, I'm sorry. We didn't get any information to help us."

Kathy looked completely defeated. He didn't blame her.

"There is nothing to support getting the case dismissed. So, we will be going to trial," he stated. "There are several ways we can go. We can request a change of venue, a bench trial, or a jury trial."

"What's a bench trial?" Steve asked.

"The judge hears the case without a jury. There are some things in favor of that. Because of the press coverage, it may be difficult to get an impartial jury in Harris County. A judge is supposed to be objective. Not all of them are. If I have doubts about the judge, we can request a jury trial or change of venue. There are advantages to each one.

"The disadvantage with a change of venue is staying in an out-of-town hotel for the duration of the trial, which could be several weeks. The advantage would be a more impartial jury pool, especially if the trial was moved to a county with a strong law-and-order population.

"A jury trial here would allow you to stay at home, keeping your expenses and mine down. The decision is yours, Kathy."

"The verdict has to be unanimous, one way or the other, doesn't it?" she asked.

"Yes," he confirmed, "it does."

"And if they can't all agree, it's a hung jury?"

"Yes."

"And I could be tried again?"

"Unfortunately, yes. However, the courts are so crowded with cases pending that a re-trial isn't likely, except in the most extreme cases."

She thought a moment. "Getting an acquittal would prove my innocence."

"Yes, Kathy," he said kindly, "in the eyes of the law. However, once indicted there is no way to *prove* your innocence to the public, unless we can prove someone else is guilty. That's not possible in this case. We have to prove that the shooting was justified because you believed that the officer was in danger of being killed."

"He was!"

"I know," he agreed.

"Then there's no way to clear my name?"

He shook his head. "It doesn't work that way."

"Then I'll always have a felony record," Kathy said, dejected.

"No, no! When you're acquitted, I'll petition the court to expunge the records. It will be as if it never happened. It's a felony *conviction* that you want to avoid."

Still, people will always remember that I killed a man, Kathy thought. For the rest of my life it will follow me, affecting the way people see me and treat me.

"Kathy, what do you want me to do?" John asked.

"Which way will be the quickest?" she asked.

"It may not be the quickest, but I think a jury trial here would be best."

"Why?" Steve wanted to know.

"The press coverage will be better; the public here will learn the details and see that she was justified in her actions. It's the way the system is supposed to work and the way the public expects it to be handled. A change of venue or bench trial might make them wonder if we have some ulterior motive, as in avoiding the judgment of your fellow Houstonians."

Steve and Kathy exchanged a look, and each nodded at the same time.

Kathy turned to John. "A jury trial here," Kathy decided.

John smiled his approval of that choice and of the accord he sensed between Kathy and Steve. "Good," John confirmed. "I'll start working to get a court date set. Do either of you have any questions?"

Kathy and Steve exchanged a look, and both shook their heads in the negative.

"Call me if you think of any," John stated, getting to his feet.

Kathy and Steve rose as they both shook John's hand and thanked him before they left the office and headed home.

* * * * *

Wednesday, November 24, 1976 - 7:45 p.m.

Kathy and Steve were in the family room watching a movie on television. Steve tried to concentrate on the movie, but his concern for Kathy kept getting in the way. He often glanced at her, noticing that she stared at the screen but her thoughts were elsewhere. She didn't smile, chuckle, or laugh at the humor in the comedy they were watching. She hadn't even picked up her crocheting, which in the past she usually worked on while watching TV. Mostly he was concerned about depression.

She showed signs of it: lack of appetite, disinterest in the usual things, and communicating only when necessary. Kathy was an extrovert. She liked people. She liked being involved in things. Her present behavior was atypical, as though hiding from reality by retreating to a dark corner somewhere. She needed to talk about the shooting, the coming trial, and the future. He didn't seem to be the person for her to talk to. He had tried several times. She talked of the shooting only in terms of the facts, the events of that night, never about her feelings during the incident or afterwards. She expressed concern for the boys and Steve, but didn't share her concerns for herself or her doubts about her future. If the future was scary for him, and it was, it must be terrifying for her, he thought.

Steve felt ineffectual. Kathy needed help and he did not know how to help her. He reassured her often, hugged her, kissed her, and expressed his love and pride in her at every opportunity. Still, he knew it wasn't enough.

The psychologist she had seen a few times hadn't helped, either. When he suggested she find another, she shrugged it off as though it was too much for her to deal with. Kathy needed someone to talk to, someone she could confide in. He had no idea where to find such a person.

The movie ended. Steve turned off the television.

"Time for bed," he told Kathy.

She looked up at him and reluctantly nodded. Sleeping meant nightmares, unless she was exhausted, which she wasn't, or a sleeping pill, which she hated to take for fear of becoming dependent on them. She rose. Steve followed her down the hall to their bedroom, wishing he had a solution.

Chapter 36

Wednesday, December 8, 1976 - 1:30 p.m.

John Everett met Kathy and Steve in the hall outside Judge R. J. Harrison's courtroom for a hearing on pretrial motions. They entered together and sat in the gallery until the case was called. Kathy and John stepped through the gate in the railing to the defendant's table. Steve took a seat behind the railing near Kathy.

The motions were argued and the judge ruled on each one. John Everett moved for a change of venue, stating it would be difficult to get an unbiased jury in Harris County because of all the adverse publicity in this case.

"A change of venue is not necessary to get an impartial jury," Mr. Lloyd Maddox, the prosecutor, stated. "That's the purpose of voir dire."

"I agree," Judge Harrison stated. "Motion for change of venue denied."

"Your Honor," John addressed the judge. "The defense requests a questionnaire be prepared for the prospective jurors prior to voir dire."

"This is a first degree murder case. Not capital murder," Judge Harrison stated.

"Yes, Your Honor," John Everett agreed. "But the defendant has a right to an unbiased jury, and a questionnaire will ensure that right in spite of all the adverse publicity in this case."

The judge turned to Maddox. "Does the State have any objections?"

Maddox suspected that the questionnaire was what John Everett wanted all along. "No, Your Honor," he stated, realizing he had been outmaneuvered.

"Motion granted. Questions are to be submitted by the end of business Friday. We're going to trial, gentlemen," Judge Harrison said, reaching for his court calendar.

Kathy blanched. She knew this day was coming, had in fact prayed for it. Now that it was here, she was past worried. Steve reached over the railing to touch her shoulder. She turned to him, her face tense and pale. He reached out and took her hand. It was shaking. He didn't know how much more of this she could take. He wished that he was going through this instead of her.

"I'm not going to start a murder trial in the middle of the holidays," the judge announced. "January third, nine a.m., to get the jury panel and distribute the questionnaire. The following Monday, January tenth we'll start voir dire." He looked up. "Any conflicts?"

Both attorneys said they didn't have a conflict.

"Happy holidays, gentlemen," he said, standing to leave the bench.

"Thank you, Your Honor," John said, turning to see Kathy and Steve holding hands. He felt sorry for Kathy. He knew this waiting was hell. It always was for the innocent. He wished there was some way to help her deal with it.

As the three of them left the courtroom, Kathy asked, "What questionnaire? And what is to start on the tenth? I didn't understand that."

The three of them stopped in the hall. "Voir dire?" John asked. She nodded. "That is the process of qualifying jurors. The questionnaire will give some background on the prospective jurors. Each side questions each prospective juror to eliminate any that we feel will not be objective and impartial in deciding the case. The background on each will give us ideas of things we need to investigate in the questioning."

"And…what kinds of things…what are you looking for?"

"In this case, racism will be an issue. Also, civil rights activists, male chauvinists, and anyone who is anti-police or anti-law-and-order, and any older person from the 'a woman's place is in the home' generation. We want younger people with open minds and middle-of-the-road views," he explained.

From the look of consternation on her face, it was clear that she hadn't considered these attitudes and the possible influence they might have on the verdict.

"Steve, take her home," John instructed. "I'll be in touch!" He turned and walked away.

Steve took Kathy's hand and they headed for home to wait some more.

Chapter 37

Monday, January 3, 1977 - 8:05 a.m.

The month of December dragged by, in spite of all the holiday activities. Finally, the first Monday in the New Year arrived. The clothes Kathy would wear to court were laid out on the bed. She sighed. For a woman who owned only two dresses, one for weddings and the other for funerals, she had resisted John Everett's instructions about what to wear. In the end, she had reluctantly gone shopping for appropriate clothes. The five different outfits cost more than she usually spent on clothes for herself in a year.

She dressed carefully in a muted blue blazer and skirt and lighter blue blouse. Navy blue shoes with a medium heel and a matching purse completed the outfit. Her collar-length medium brown hair was turned under all around her head and face. It was a soft, neat, and flattering style without being fussy. A little lipstick, a light spray of cologne, and she was ready.

Steve was finishing a cup of coffee when she walked into the family room. He looked up and smiled. He got to his feet. "You look good, honey."

She took a deep breath and sighed. He knew she was nervous and there was nothing he could do about it. He took his cup to the kitchen, rinsed it, and put it in the dishwasher. Kathy was staring out the window when he returned.

"It's time to go, honey," he told her.

"Tell me it's gonna be all right," she asked.

He came up behind her and put his arms around her. "It's gonna be all right."

"I just wish it was over," she said.

"So do I," he agreed, holding her coat while she slipped her arms into it.

She turned and picked up her purse and they walked out the front door together.

* * * * *

Monday, January 3, 1977 - 8:55 a.m.

The gallery of the courtroom was empty except for Steve. John Everett and Kathy sat at the defendant's table. Lloyd Maddox sat at the prosecutor's table. A bailiff, a clerk, and the court reporter were present, all waiting for Judge Harrison to make his appearance. Suddenly, at nine-fifteen, the door behind the bench opened, the bailiff called for all to rise, and Judge Harrison stepped up to his bench.

"Be seated," he told them. "Is the state ready to proceed with the case of the State of Texas against Kathleen Mavis Cooper for the murder of Ray Jackson?"

"It is, Your Honor," Maddox declared.

"Is the defense ready?" he asked John Everett.

"Yes, Your Honor."

"First order of business, a jury panel. I've sent a bailiff down to the Jury Assembly Room for a panel of one hundred and twenty," the judge stated. "Are the questionnaires ready?" he asked the remaining bailiff.

"Yes, Your Honor."

"Have you gentlemen approved the questionnaires as printed?"

Both Mr. Maddox and John Everett stated that they had.

Kathy touched John's arm. He turned to her. "Why a panel of so many?" she asked, her voice almost a whisper.

"A hundred and twenty is usual in murder cases," he told her. "A lot of them will be eliminated during voir dire."

"To get twelve out of one hundred and twenty is only one in ten!" she said with surprise.

"We need fifteen. Twelve for the jury and three alternates," he informed her.

The doors at the back of the courtroom opened as a Deputy Sheriff, who was one of the bailiffs, brought the prospective jurors into the courtroom. He seated them in order in the pews behind the prosecution's table first, then on the defense side of the courtroom. He took the forms with the names to the judge, then stepped to one side of the courtroom.

"Good morning, ladies and gentlemen," Judge Harrison said to the prospective jurors. "Thank you for being here today. I know jury duty is an inconvenience. It is, however, a very important part of the justice system. A citizen's right to a jury trial is guaranteed by this country's constitution. Serving on a jury, when called on to do so, is a duty and a responsibility.

"I'm going to tell you a little about this case and the time I expect it will take. Then, if any of you have a problem with serving, I will consider those problems individually.

"This is a murder case," he stated.

Many heads in the jury pool glanced at Kathy. She didn't see them because she was concentrating on what Judge Harrison was saying.

"Jury selection and the trial will take six weeks, possibly eight. Therefore, we need to have you available for roughly the next two months. I ask you to make every possible effort to make yourselves available. This is an important case. A young woman's future depends on the outcome.

"Now then, if any of you have a problem with being available for the next two months, raise your hand and I will talk to each of you individually."

Kathy glanced around to see more than a few hands go up. The bailiff moved to the rail and had them line up in the aisle. One by one they approached the judge's bench and spoke to him. Kathy could not hear the reasons they gave the judge for being unavailable. He dismissed twelve of those who talked to him, which would shorten the voir dire by a day and a half, Kathy reasoned. Anything to get on with it.

"I thank the rest of you for making yourselves available," Judge Harrison told the remaining prospective jurors. "From this moment on it is important for each of you to avoid press, television, and radio coverage of this case. The reason is to find jurors who have no prior knowledge of this case. So, remember, no newspapers and no television or radio news until after the trial or after you are released from serving in this case. The defendant deserves an unbiased panel to decide her guilt or innocence. Is that clear?"

Heads nodded in the gallery. "Any violation of this could result in the jury being sequestered for the duration of the trial. None of us want that, least of all you and your families. However, I will order it if necessary. Is that clear?"

In the gallery, heads again nodded. "In addition, you are not to speak to the attorneys, the defendant, or any of the witnesses in this case, and they are not allowed to speak to any of you. Also, you are not to discuss this case among yourselves until you retire to the jury room to consider the verdict. You are not to discuss this case with anyone else, including your families, until the trial is concluded. Is that clear?"

Again the gallery nodded, and Judge Harrison continued. "The bailiff will give each of you a questionnaire. You will fill this out and return it to him before you leave here today. The questionnaire will give the attorneys in this case some background information on each of you. You are required to answer each question fully and honestly.

"The attorneys will have one week to review the questionnaires. Then, one week from today, voir dire will begin. Voir dire is from the French. It means, literally, speak true. The attorneys will question each of you to determine your acceptability to serve on this case.

"Voir dire may take up to fifteen working days. The attorneys can effectively question only eight to ten people a day. You will be told which day you are to report back here. A panel of fifteen jurors is required for a murder case. That includes three alternates. If fifteen people are chosen before all of you are questioned, the rest of you will be notified that you need not return.

"If fifteen jurors are not found among all of you, more prospective jurors will be brought in, and the process will continue until we do find fifteen suitable. Those of you who are selected will be notified when to report to this courtroom for the beginning of the trial.

"The bailiff will now give each of you the questionnaire you need to fill out and return to this courtroom. You may leave this courtroom to do that. The coffee shop downstairs is commonly used for that purpose. However, do *not* leave the building until you have completed it and returned it to one of the bailiffs in this courtroom. When you return the completed questionnaire, the bailiff will give you the date and time that you need to return for jury selection." He paused. "Does everyone understand?" He was answered with nods. "Does anyone have a question?" Heads shook. "This court's in recess," he concluded, with a bang of the gavel.

John and Steve stood up. Kathy remained seated. She looked up at John. "Now what?"

"The clerk will make copies of the completed questionnaires," he told her, "and call my office when they're ready. I'll send my clerk to pick them up. Then we've got a week to review them and prepare questions for voir dire."

"Will I get to see them?" she asked.

"No reason you need to."

"Just curious," she admitted, standing up. "And I thought maybe I could help."

"I have a paralegal in the office who is an expert at reviewing the questionnaires," John told her, "and finding areas I need to explore in the questioning."

"Isn't there something I can do? I'm tired of sitting home worrying," she stated.

He smiled and shook his head. "Things are starting to move, Kathy. Be patient a little longer," John said as he closed his briefcase and picked it up and left the courtroom.

Steve took Kathy's hand, hoping the physical contact would help her. It did, and it didn't.

Chapter 38

Monday, January 10, 1977 - Wednesday, January 19, 1977

Kathy was alone when she arrived at the courthouse a week later. Steve had decided to save his vacation days so he could attend the trial. Kathy had agreed, but now she missed his support. John showed concern for her, but it wasn't the same. So she just had to grit her teeth and bear up.

The first day of voir dire went slowly. The attorneys each had up to thirty minutes to question each prospective juror. The first was eliminated after only twenty minutes. In addition, three others were processed before noon. The other four were questioned that afternoon. At the end of the day, no juror was accepted by both the prosecution and the defense.

Kathy was disappointed. She hoped things would go faster. She understood the reasons that the jurors were eliminated. A few she didn't, and asked John about each. The next day she didn't ask anymore. She no longer cared. By the end of the third day, she was getting discouraged again.

Things went better the rest of the week, and by Wednesday of the following week they had a jury of twelve and three alternates. Judge Harrison informed everyone connected with the case to be ready to start at 9:00 a.m. on the coming Monday, January 24th.

Kathy thought things were looking up until the prosecutor approached her and John in the hall and asked for a meeting. They all entered a small conference room.

Lloyd Maddox, the prosecutor, spoke first. "We have a plea bargain offer for your client," he addressed John Everett, not Kathy. "For a guilty plea to manslaughter, we will agree to a probated sentence of five years. No jail time."

"Never!" Kathy exclaimed, jumping to her feet. "I'm not guilty of anything except…"

"Kathy!" John exclaimed as he grabbed her arm and squeezed. "You have your answer, Counselor." He stood up. "We'll see you in court on Monday." John picked up his briefcase and, still holding Kathy by the arm, guided her from the room.

"I know you were upset, Kathy," he told her. "But don't talk to him unless I say it's all right."

"Sorry, John." Kathy fought to control her indignation.

John smiled. "He made the offer because he has doubts that he can prove murder. The elements of murder just aren't there. We're going to beat this, Kathy."

"I may beat the rap, but I didn't beat the ride," she commented. "All right, John. See you Monday."

They shook hands and parted. He watched her walk away. John had heard that phrase, "he beat the rap, but he didn't beat the ride" many times from his father. It was a way of saying that the person was arrested more for his attitude than evidence, a practice still common in police work, particularly among the older officers. The suspect might walk away from the charge, but he would take that ride to jail first.

John's father, like most cops then, was a hard-nosed, old-school cop, and a strict disciplinarian. John talked back to his father only once. He thought his father was going to beat him to death. He didn't step out of line again until college.

He was studying criminal justice primarily because his father expected his four sons to follow him into law enforcement, as he had followed his father. One of John's friends was arrested for a misdemeanor offense he didn't commit. John attended the trial. The defense attorney representing his friend lost the case through incompetence, and his friend had to pay a fine and spend some time in jail. John rebelled. He went on to law school, determined to defend the unjustly accused. It was a choice his father never forgave him for making.

Most of John's clients were *justly* accused. Ethically, he was bound to give them the best defense possible, and he made a lot of money doing it. The wealth he earned defending the guilty allowed him to select deserving cases to defend. When opportunity occasionally presented a case like Kathy's, it was pure pleasure for him to act as defense attorney.

Chapter 39

Monday, January 24, 1977 - 8:50 a.m.

Kathy and Steve stepped out of the elevator in the County Courthouse. As they turned the corner of the hall leading to Judge Harrison's courtroom, Kathy came to a standstill. The area in front of the courtroom doors was full of people, including the media with microphones and cameras, many blacks, and police officers. She turned her back to the crowd, wanting to run away.

"Honey!" Steve said, grasping her arm.

"I can't do this," she said.

"Yes, you can. We can do it together," Steve told her.

She straightened up, knowing Steve was right. With Steve beside her, she could do anything. She nodded and turned back to face the crowd. As they approached the courtroom, the officers held everyone back, forming a corridor to the courtroom for Kathy and Steve. The press tried to stick microphones in her face. She ignored them. Others started chanting, "Murderer! Murderer!" She ignored them.

She looked from one familiar face to another among the blue uniforms. Some nodded, some smiled, some spoke, and Jesse Banks winked as he opened the door for Kathy and Steve and held it. After they entered, he let it close and stepped squarely in front of it. Nobody was getting inside unless they had business there.

The courtroom gallery was empty. Kathy and Steve walked to the front where John was waiting for them.

John greeted them both with a smile. "Are the officers outside friends of yours?" he asked Kathy.

She nodded, smiling at the thought.

"Some of them have been called as witnesses. It's important that you don't talk to them about the case," John informed her.

"All right," she stated. Kathy stepped inside the railing and sat at the defendant's table. Steve sat right behind her in the gallery. As the jurors arrived, they were sent to the jury room by a bailiff stationed just inside the door.

The last two jurors arrived. A few minutes later the bailiff announced, "All rise," as Judge Harrison entered and took the bench.

"I understand there is a crowd in the hall. Are there any objections to allowing them entry?" the judge asked. "At the first disruption, I'll have the court cleared and it will stay that way."

Neither the prosecutor nor John Everett had an objection.

"Bailiffs, you will frisk each person before they are allowed to enter, and search the women's purses. Get some of the HPD officers to help if you need them," the judge ordered.

The people were allowed to enter one by one. Four officers entered first and helped the bailiffs check a mixture of press, public, and officers. In the searches, they confiscated a couple of pocket knives. One black woman's purse yielded a pistol, a Saturday night special. The bailiff held it up to show Judge Harrison. Kathy was stunned. For the first time, she felt fear for herself.

John jumped to his feet. "Your Honor, the defense requests the gallery be kept empty. Obviously, my client's life is in danger."

"Request denied," Judge Harrison ruled. "Arrest that woman," he told the bailiff.

The woman was promptly handcuffed and removed from the courtroom. Another HPD officer stepped forward to assist. In fifteen minutes, both sides of the gallery were nearly full. The prosecution side filled mostly with blacks and press, and the defense side with officers. Two officers stood inside the courtroom doors.

Judge Harrison addressed the audience, "I will not stand for any demonstrations in my courtroom. Any disruption will result in immediate arrest for contempt of court. This is the only warning you will get!" He turned to the bailiff. "Bring in the jury."

The jury members filed in and took their assigned places in the jury box, which was on the prosecution side of the courtroom. After the bailiff read the indictment aloud, the judge turned to the jury.

"First order of business is opening statements," the judge stated. "The attorneys will outline the cases they will present. This is not testimony and should not be considered as such. The testimony given by witnesses under oath is all you will consider in reaching a verdict.

"Is the state ready, Mr. Maddox?"

"Yes, Your Honor."

"Please begin."

Maddox walked around the table and approached the jury box. "Ladies and gentlemen, you've been told this is a murder trial. Kathleen Mavis Cooper is accused of murder in the death of Ray Jackson. It is the State's responsibility to prove that.

"During the testimony, you will learn Ray Jackson was shot in the back. That shot was fatal. He had no weapon. We will prove," he turned to point at Kathy, "Kathleen Cooper fired that shot!"

A couple of soft amens were heard from the audience. The judge gave them a sharp look, but he said nothing.

"We will show that Kathleen Cooper was riding with an on-duty Houston Police Officer. She was an observer. A woman, unfamiliar with police procedure, she misinterpreted a situation and reacted in an irresponsible manner. You will learn that the officer's rifle was unsecured in the police vehicle, giving Kathleen Cooper access to it. She used the officer's rifle to shoot Ray Jackson.

"We have witnesses who will testify to her expertise with firearms. She could have wounded Ray Jackson. She chose not to. She chose to shoot to kill. And kill she did, leaving Ray Jackson's wife a widow and leaving his three children orphans."

Kathy sat with her hands in her lap, fingers interlaced, and tried not to get angry over the slanted presentation of the prosecutor. After all, that was his job. Still, it hurt to hear the facts told in such a brutal manner.

"Ray Jackson had no weapon. He was unarmed. There is no justification for shooting an unarmed man. None for shooting an unarmed man in the back. No justification for killing Ray Jackson at all.

"It might have been you, or one of your loved ones, that she killed. But it wasn't. It was Ray Jackson. A black man. An unarmed black man. Shot in the back. No attempt to wound. One... deadly...shot!" The prosecutor paused, then concluded with, "Thank you for your attention." He went to the State's table.

"Fifteen minute recess," the judge announced.

The jury filed out of the box and into the jury room. A few in the gallery left the courtroom. One of the bailiffs approached Kathy.

"Mrs. Cooper, if you are reluctant to go through that crowd to the ladies room, there is another you can use," he told her.

"Yes, please," she answered, getting to her feet. "May my husband come with me?"

"Of course."

Kathy and Steve followed him from the courtroom and through a door at the side near the defense's table. John remained at the table, going over notes he made during the Prosecutor's opening statement.

* * * * *

The recess ended and everyone returned to their places. Judge Harrison entered and called for the jury. When they were seated, the judge turned to John Everett.

"Is the defense ready, Mr. Everett?"

John rose from his chair. "Yes, Your Honor."

"You may begin."

John approached the jury box. "Ladies and gentlemen of the jury, yours is an awesome responsibility. You will be deciding the future life of this young woman," he turned to point at Kathy, "Kathleen Cooper."

"Much of what the prosecutor has told you is true. However, the truth can be distorted. The truth can be misinterpreted. It is true that Ray Jackson was a black man. It is true that he was shot in the back. It is true that Kathleen Cooper fired that shot. It is true that he died.

"It is the circumstances of the shooting that are important in this case." He paused to let them wonder about that for a moment.

"Kathleen Cooper was serving on one of the Harris County grand juries at that time. Riding along with on-duty police officers as an observer is a privilege offered to members of the grand juries. Kathleen Cooper accepted the offer to ride along to learn about the policing end of our justice system. Toward that end, she rode along on sixteen evening shifts. She also rode along on sixteen night shifts.

"Kathleen Cooper learned about police procedures, about the paperwork, about the frustrations, about the pressures, about the abuse the officers take from the public, about radio procedure, and about the dangers. And most important, she learned that when trouble starts, officers cover their partners' backs.

"During the night shift on that Sunday morning, she was riding with Officer Calvin Henson. At about five a.m., Officer Henson saw a man and a pickup truck on a construction site and stopped to investigate. After parking his police vehicle in the entrance to the site, Officer Henson walked over to talk to the man. Kathleen Cooper remained at the car, as she had on many occasions.

"Two more men appeared from the other side of the truck. Kathleen Cooper recognized the danger of the situation and took Officer Henson's rifle from the car. The three men jumped Officer Henson, knocked him to the ground, hit him, kicked him, and tried to get his pistol. A kick in the head rendered him unconscious. Ray Jackson picked up a piece of pipe. When he raised it over his head to hit Officer Henson, Kathleen Cooper shot him.

"You will hear Kathleen Cooper's story from her; hear what she was feeling and what she was thinking at the moment she fired. You will learn that the other two men surrendered.

"This shooting was not murder. Kathleen Cooper shot Ray Jackson in defense of another. In defense of Officer Calvin Henson. Killing in defense of another is justified under the laws of the State of Texas. This shooting was justified by the circumstances." John paused to look at each member of the jury. "Thank you." He turned and returned to the defense table.

"This court will recess for lunch. We will reconvene at one-thirty," Judge Harrison announced and brought his gavel down. Everyone stood while he left the courtroom.

John turned to Steve. "I think it would be best if you and Kathy come back to my office with me. I'll have lunch sent in. There's a room there where Kathy can lie down and rest until we have to be back here."

Steve and Kathy glanced at each other and both nodded.

"Chinese or Mexican?" John asked.

"We like both," Kathy said. "Chinese might be less likely to upset my stomach."

"Chinese it is," John agreed. "I'm going to phone my office and give this crowd a minute to disperse." He walked to the clerk's desk to use the phone.

Kathy turned and saw that the officers were guiding everyone out of the courtroom. When it was cleared, four of them remained. John returned.

Jesse Banks turned to her. "Where to, Kathy?"

"We're going to Mr. Everett's office," she answered. "Why?"

"Where is that, sir?" Jesse asked John.

"Two blocks west on Preston. It's in walking distance," John answered.

"Not today, sir. If you'll follow the officers, please," he requested.

"Jesse, what is going on?" Kathy asked.

He winked. "You'll see."

The four officers escorted Kathy, Steve, and John to the elevator and prevented anyone else from getting in with them. It went down to the basement level without stopping. The officers led them to the underground entrance where Sergeant Ralph Strong waited for them with his police vehicle.

He came around to greet her and introduced himself to Steve and John. He opened the door and held it for Kathy and Steve to get in the back. John sat in the front and gave Ralph the address of his office.

"Ralph,…who organized all of this?" Kathy asked.

"Who said it was organized?"

"You answered a question with a question!" she exclaimed.

"Did I?" he teased, as he drove up the ramp that led out from under the building and up to street level. "We take care of our own. You know that, Kathy."

"She isn't one of your own," Steve pointed out.

Kathy, surprised by the sharpness of Steve's tone, looked at him and wondered what he was thinking.

"Kathy saved the life of an officer when she shot Ray Jackson. We owe her," Ralph stated.

Steve looked at Kathy, stared at her in fact. He began to think he didn't know her at all. Was there more to it than just the shooting? What went on when she was riding along with the officers? He hadn't asked and she hadn't shared much with him, except for the details about the shooting. What kind of relationship did she have with the officers? Did he dare ask? He wanted to know, and asking was probably the only way he stood a chance of finding out.

Ralph stopped the car at the entrance to the building where John's office was located. The three of them got out. "What time are you leaving to go back to court?" Ralph asked.

"About one fifteen," John told him.

"I'll be here," Ralph stated. He drove off after watching them enter the building.

Chapter 40

Monday, January 24, 1977 - 1:45 p.m.

Court reconvened with the prosecutor calling his first witness, Calvin Henson. The prosecutor established that Calvin was a police officer and that he was working Radio Patrol out of the Northwest Station on the night of the shooting in a one-man criminal investigation unit.

"Was Kathleen Cooper riding with you that shift?"

"Yes."

"Had she ridden with you before?"

"Yes."

"How many times?"

"Twice."

"What happened at five o'clock on that Sunday morning?"

"I was taking Kath…Mrs. Cooper home. We spotted a pick-up truck and a man on the construction site at Mangum Road and Georgi Lane. We stopped to investigate."

"Why did you stop to investigate?"

"I knew there had been thefts of construction materials from that location."

"Continue."

"I parked the unit in the entrance…."

"Unit?"

"The police unit. The police car."

Mr. Maddox nodded and motioned for Calvin to continue.

"I approached the man at the pick-up truck."

"And where was Mrs. Cooper?"

"She was standing next to the passenger side of the unit, behind the open door."

"Did she have the rifle at that time?"
"No."
"Where was the rifle?"
"In the car."
"Where in the car?"
"Leaning against the front seat on the passenger side."
"Isn't that where Mrs. Cooper was sitting?"
"Yes, sir."
"Was the rifle secured in any way?"
"No."
"Was it locked in a holder?"
"No, sir. We don't have locking holders in the cars."
"Is this standard procedure?"
"Yes, sir. The guns need to be easily accessible," Calvin explained to the jury.

"Let me be sure I understand. You walked away from your police unit, leaving a civilian and an unsecured rifle behind. Is that correct?"

"Yes."

"What happened when you approached the man at the pick-up truck?"

"I asked him what he was doing there at that time of the morning."

"What was his answer?"

"That he was there to collect some trash."

"And then what happened?"

"Two more men came around from the other side of the truck. I stepped away and turned to keep all three men in view."

"Go on."

"That's when the three of them rushed me. They knocked me to the ground. I fought to keep them from getting my pistol. One of them kicked me in the ribs and in the head and I lost consciousness."

"Then you didn't see the shooting, Officer Henson?" Mr. Maddox asked.

"No, sir."

"No more questions," Mr. Maddox stated and returned to his chair at the State's table.

The judge looked toward the defense table as John stood up.

"I have no questions for this witness at this time," John stated. "The defense reserves the right to call Officer Henson as a defense witness."

Judge Harrison turned to Officer Calvin Henson. "You may step down, but keep yourself available."

"Yes, Your Honor," Calvin acknowledged as he stepped down.

Judge Harrison recessed the court for a mid-afternoon break. Kathy left the courtroom by the side door which led to the bathroom she'd used that morning.

Steve stood and stretched while he looked at the spectators. He noticed Sergeant Ralph Strong standing next to the doors at the back of the room.

He walked up to the sergeant. They greeted each other. Then Steve spoke, "You didn't answer my wife's question earlier."

"No, I didn't," Ralph admitted.

"I want an answer."

Ralph jerked his head in a motion indicating that Steve should follow him. He led Steve out of the courtroom and away from the people in the hall. When they were alone, he turned to Steve.

"We don't want Kathy to know what's going on."

"I'll decide what she should know!" Steve exclaimed.

"Officer Dean Driskell and Bob Richmond got a tip from their snitch that Kathy's life is in danger."

The shock was evident on Steve's face as the color left it.

"Evidently this snitch met Kathy one night when he told Driskell and Richmond about a dice game they later raided. He asked them if the white lady he met that night was the one charged with murder for shooting Ray Jackson. They told him she was. He told them that the word on the street was that she was a dead woman, and he wanted them to see that she was protected."

"The snitch wanted her protected?" Steve asked with disbelief.

"Yes, he did. Seems she made an impression on him when she asked why he was a snitch. Driskell and Richmond said he told her the truth. He talked to her like he had never done with them. The snitch has asked about her more than once since the night he met her.

"The snitch's tip went up the chain of command, and the approval to provide a police escort for Kathy came back down. Evening and night shift officers at Shepherd and Northwest Stations volunteered. Other officers also volunteered. We've had volunteers from all over the city."

"What about our sons? Do they need protection, too?"

"We've got 'em covered, Steve."

"They haven't said anything."

"I doubt if they know. Our undercover officers are good at their jobs," Ralph assured him.

"My God," Steve said. "I had no idea."

"We don't want Kathy and the boys to get any ideas, do we?"

"No! Definitely not!" Steve agreed.

"Good," Ralph said with a nod.

They returned to the courtroom as the judge reconvened the court. The prosecutor called Officer John Bailey to the stand. After he was sworn in and his status as a police officer was established, the questioning began.

"You were working night shift Radio Patrol out of the Northwest station on the Sunday morning in question?"

"Yes."

"Alone?"

"No. My partner was Officer Dennis Vaughn."

"What happened at about five o'clock that Sunday morning?"

"We heard Mrs. Cooper on the radio put out an *assist the officer* call. We were a couple miles away. We ran it with lights and siren. We were the first unit on the scene."

"What did you observe when you arrived?"

"A unit blocked the entrance to the construction site. Mrs. Cooper was standing at the passenger door with a rifle to her shoulder. Two men were facedown on the ground, about halfway between Mrs. Cooper and Officer Henson, who was lying on his back, and another man was facedown next to him."

"What did you do then?"

"I ran past Mrs. Cooper to check on Officer Henson. He was unconscious but breathing regularly, and didn't appear to be bleeding. His pulse was strong and regular. I knew that an ambulance had been dispatched."

"Continue."

"Another unit arrived while I was checking Officer Henson. Officer Oakes helped my partner handcuff and search the other two men. Officer Cannon went to the man lying facedown next to Officer Henson and handcuffed him. Additional units and the ambulance arrived. We put the two prisoners in separate cars."

"What happened next?"

"Officer Henson was loaded into the ambulance and taken away. Two detectives from Homicide arrived. They examined the scene, then instructed us to take the prisoners to Central and charge them with Aggravated Assault on a Peace Officer. We left the scene at that time."

"No more questions," the prosecutor stated.

The judge nodded to John, who seemed deep in thought as he approached the witness.

"Officer Bailey," he said. "I want to be sure I understand. You ran past Mrs. Cooper who had a rifle to her shoulder?"

"Yes."

"In a position to fire that rifle?"

"Yes."

"You turned your back on a civilian with a gun?"

"Yes."

"Do you often turn your back on a person with a gun?"

"No. Not ordinarily."

"But you did this time?" John asked.

"Yes."

"Explain."

"It was obvious Mrs. Cooper was holding the gun on the two suspects on the ground."

"You trusted that it was safe to leave the rifle in her hands?"

"Yes."

"Tell us why?"

"Mrs. Cooper had been riding along with officers every weekend for about two months. She had ridden along with me twice. I had observed her behavior at scenes. My fellow officers talked about the way she conducted herself at other scenes. I was confident that she presented no danger to me or to my partner."

"Thank you, Officer. That's all," John concluded.

"Redirect, Mr. Maddox?" the judge asked.

"No, Your Honor."

"Will you be recalling Officer Bailey for the defense?" the judge asked John.

"No, Your Honor."

"Officer Bailey, you are excused. This court will recess until nine tomorrow morning," Judge Harrison declared with a stroke of his gavel.

As people left the courtroom, four night shift officers from North Shepherd station approached Kathy and Steve. Kathy introduced Steve to them. Art Donahue asked for Steve's car keys and where the car was parked.

"I'll bring it to the basement entrance," he explained. "When the courtroom is clear, the others will escort you and Kathy down."

Steve handed over his keys, told Art where the car was located, described it, and pulled out his wallet for some money to pay the parking. Art refused the money and left.

"How you doing, Pretty Lady? How you holding up?" Donny Wells asked.

"Pretty Lady?" Steve questioned, sounding a little defensive of his territory.

"Donny calls all women, Pretty Lady. Don't you, Donny?" Kathy said.

"Yes, ma'am."

"I'm doing okay," she said with a smile, a genuine smile. The first Steve had seen in weeks.

Fred Oakes checked the hall, and the group left the courtroom.

"What have you guys been up to?" Kathy asked.

"You should have been with us last Saturday night," Donny stated. "We had a hijacker running. He was going westbound on…"

As he told of the chase and arrest, Kathy felt she had come home. Fred Oakes then told of another incident from a month back. They kept it up all the way to the basement and the arrival of Art with Steve's car. Donny opened the passenger door for Kathy. Steve walked around to the driver's door.

"In the morning," Art told Steve, "officers will meet you and Kathy here shortly before nine. One of them will park the car and the others will escort you and Kathy to the courtroom."

Steve nodded, but didn't know what to say. He was stunned at the caring and concern the officers showed for Kathy, and grateful for it. Still, he wondered if there was more to her relationship with the men than a desire to protect her and gratitude for saving an officer's life.

Chapter 41

Monday, January 24, 1977 - 6:45 p.m.

Kathy was rinsing the supper dishes and loading the dishwasher when Steve approached her. He stood and watched her for a moment, deciding how to start.

"Did you know all the officers in court today?" he asked.

"Most of them."

"How well do you know them?"

Kathy looked at him over her shoulder. "You sound…jealous," she said with surprise.

"I guess I am," he admitted. "You shared something with them you haven't shared with me."

"My experiences riding along."

"Yeah."

"I didn't know you were interested. You never asked," she pointed out.

"You know I don't pry. I'm just trying to understand your relationship with them," he stated.

Kathy turned off the water and turned to him, drying her hands. "Honey, I don't feel I can explain it to you so that you would understand."

Steve turned away from her. He was angry and hurt.

"Listen to me a minute, please," she begged.

He kept his back to her. "I'm listening."

"I took notes. I've typed them up. I'd like you to read 'em. Then we can talk about it." She waited for an answer.

"All right," he agreed.

"I'll get 'em," she said, stepping past him to go to the study. She returned with a three-ring binder that was over an inch thick. She handed it to Steve. "They're rough. Lots of typos, and not edited."

Steve opened it and flipped the pages with his thumb. They were typed, single-spaced, and numbered up to two hundred and forty-seven. He took the binder into the family room, sat in his recliner, and started reading at the beginning.

Kathy returned to the kitchen to finish the after supper cleanup. Steve was still reading her notes when she joined him in the family room. She picked up the murder mystery she was reading. Shortly before ten, she finished the book and decided to go to bed.

"I'm ready for bed, honey," she told Steve. "How about you?"

"In a little while. You go ahead."

She went to him, gave him a good-night kiss, and went down the hall.

Steve went back to reading her notes. He continued until he finished at a little after one. He closed the binder with a sigh and set it on the coffee table as he got to his feet. He turned off the lights as he headed toward their bedroom.

He stood in the doorway and watched Kathy sleeping in the soft light from the master bathroom. She had always been special to him. Now he knew that other people—other men—recognized it too. At first it worried him. He wasn't sure why. He trusted her. It was the men he didn't trust. He had known that she enjoyed being on the street with the officers. He learned that she had formed a comfortable relationship with them. When they gave her a bad time, she took it and turned it around on them. The result was a mutual respect. Yes, they teased her, some made passes, but she handled it all with humor. Her notes were surprisingly candid and honest. They showed her mistakes and vulnerabilities, her tough side, and her soft side. He never would understand her completely, but now he understood her more. As a result, he could accept the rapport she had with the officers and be thankful for it. It appeared that they were doing everything they could to protect her and the boys.

As he undressed, he thought of how lucky he was that she loved him. He sometimes wondered why. After eighteen years, he still didn't feel worthy of her. Few men would, he thought. He turned out the light in the bathroom and got into bed, being careful not to wake her because he knew how tired she was. She needed all the rest she could get to face another day in court in the morning.

Chapter 42

Tuesday, January 25, 1977 - 7:10 a.m.

The next morning, still in her pajamas and robe, Kathy was in the kitchen fixing breakfast when Steve walked in and put his arms around her from behind. He nuzzled her neck below her right ear, which always made her shiver.

"I love you," he said.

"I love you, too," Kathy answered, wondering where this was coming from. "What's gotten into you this morning? You haven't had your coffee yet."

"I don't need coffee to appreciate the woman I married."

Kathy stiffened. She turned within his arms to face him. "Is this about my notes?"

"Sort of."

"Do you want to talk about it?"

"I don't need to," he told her. "I found out what I wanted to know. I was worried about losing you."

"I told you I'd be careful," Kathy reminded him.

"Not that way. Well, yes, that way, but…men make passes," he added hesitantly.

Surprised to learn of his insecurity, Kathy stated. "I love *you*. They're no threat to you."

"Women seem to be attracted to men in uniform."

Kathy smiled. She had to admit that was true. "Yes, they are. I never saw you in your Navy uniform, except in pictures. I fell in love with you, not a uniform."

He pushed her hair back, held her face in both hands, and kissed her tenderly, but with passion.

"The sausage will burn," she informed him when he ended the kiss with a hug that pressed their bodies together. He let her go and she turned back to the stove.

"After the kids leave," he promised.

"After the kids leave, what?" Davy asked from the doorway.

"Never mind," Steve told him.

"Ooooh, that!" Davy said, rolling his eyes and going to the breakfast room table.

Kathy couldn't help smiling. Steve seemed uncomfortable, then he smiled and went to the table. It was a good start for the day.

* * * * *

Tuesday, January 25, 1977 - 8:55 a.m.

As promised, officers waited to escort Kathy and Steve from the basement entrance to the courtroom. Upstairs they found much the same crowd as the day before at the courtroom doors. The doors were opened for Kathy, Steve, and their escort. John Everett came in right behind them. Steve's keys were returned by the officer who took the car, who told Steve where he had parked it.

Judge Harrison entered the courtroom a little after nine. He ordered the spectators to be searched before they were allowed entry. No knives or guns were found this time, but one woman had brought her knitting. She protested when the bailiffs took it away. They explained that it would be returned to her when she left.

Judge Harrison brought the room to order, had the jury brought in, and told Mr. Maddox to call his next witness. He called Dan Cannon, who was sworn in, stated his name, and took his seat in the witness chair. He was in uniform, but Maddox still established that he was an officer with HPD.

"On the morning of September 26th, were you working night shift out of the Shepherd station?" Maddox asked.

"Yes, sir."

"Were you working alone that night?"

"No, sir. My partner was Officer Fred Oakes."

"What happened at about five in the morning?"

"We heard Mrs. Cooper put out an assist on the radio."

"What did you observe when you arrived on the scene?"

"One unit was parked in the entrance of the construction site with Mrs. Cooper standing beside it. A second unit beside the first was empty. One officer was handcuffing two men on the ground. Beyond them, Officer Henson and another man were on the ground. Officer Bailey was kneeling beside Officer Henson," Cannon answered.

"What did you do?"

"We bailed out. I ran to the man lying beside Officer Henson, handcuffed him, and felt for a pulse. There was none."

"You handcuffed a dead man!"

"I didn't know he was dead when I handcuffed him."

"What was the cause of his death?'

"Objection," John said, getting to his feet. "Calls for a conclusion Officer Cannon is not qualified to make."

"Sustained."

Maddox hesitated a moment before continuing. "Continue, Officer Cannon."

"Several other units arrived. Mrs. Cooper went to Officer Henson and knelt down beside him. When he started coming around, Kathy told him to lie still and that an ambulance was on the way. He wanted to know where he was and what had happened. Kathy said that the three men jumped him. He didn't seem to remember that. Kathy told him about stopping at the construction site and the three men that attacked him. He asked what happened. She didn't answer him. I asked her if she shot the man. She nodded. I told Officer Henson that she held the other two at gunpoint and called for assistance."

"And after that?" Maddox asked.

"The ambulance arrived and the paramedics came to Officer Henson. I helped Kathy to her feet and moved her out of the way so they could check Calvin. Officers Bailey and Vaughn put one of the prisoners in their unit. Officer Oakes put the other in our unit. The investigators from the Crime Lab arrived along with two detectives from Homicide. The detectives told us to take our prisoners to Homicide and to keep them separated. We left the scene at that time."

"What was Mrs. Cooper doing when you arrived at the scene?"

"She was standing next to Officer Henson's unit."

"Did she still have the rifle?"

"Yes, sir. She was holding it with the barrel pointed up in the air."

"A female civilian holding a rifle at the scene of a shooting? Did you ever consider that she might have shot the officer?"

"No, sir! I knew she had backed up the officer she was riding along with. She'd done it before."

"She'd shot someone before?" Maddox asked.

"No, sir. She got on the radio to get help for another officer."

"And this time she shot first and got on the radio after. Is that correct?"

"I don't know. I wasn't there," Dan stated.

"What did she say when she got on the radio?"

John stood up. "Objection, Your Honor. The defense will be submitting a copy of the tape of the radio calls relevant to this incident. The jury will hear exactly what Mrs. Cooper said at that time."

"Objection sustained."

"You stated that you ran out in front of Mrs. Cooper when you arrived, correct?" Maddox resumed.

"Yes."

"Weren't you concerned about leaving a gun in the hands of a civilian?"

"No, sir."

"Why not?"

"I knew that she knew how to handle it safely."

"How did you know that?"

"I taught her how to use it," Dan told him.

"When and where did you teach her this?"

"Four of us took her out to shoot."

Kathy's stomach knotted up. If they weren't in trouble about this before, they are now, she thought.

"Four officers?"

"Yes."

"To the department firing range?"

"No, sir. We took her out in the county, out West Montgomery Road, past all the houses, and shot at empty beer cans."

"When did this happen?"

"Early one Sunday morning."

"And Mrs. Cooper shot at the beer cans, too?"

"Yes, sir."

"What weapon did she use?"

"My thirty caliber carbine."

"Did she hit any?"

"Yes, sir. She hit two out of two."

"Is that all the shooting she did that night?"

"No, sir. One of the other officers let her try his twenty-five caliber semi-auto pistol."

"How did she do with that?"

"She hit six out of the first seven and seven out of the second seven."

"If I add that up right, she hit fifteen out of the sixteen beer cans. Is that correct?"

"Yes, sir! She surprised the hell out of us!" Dan said with a smile.

There were chuckles among the jurors and many of the officers. Steve looked proud and Kathy blushed.

"You did this while you were on duty?"

"Yes, sir."

"You left your patrol area to do this?"

"Yes, sir."

"Isn't this against department policy?"

"Yes, sir!"

"Does the department know about what you did?"

"Yes, sir."

"Were the four of you disciplined for it?"

Kathy sat up straighter, worry plainly evident on her face.

"Yes, sir. We each got a written reprimand and three days off without pay."

Kathy closed her eyes, hung her head and shook it. Three days off without pay meant just that. Three days they could not work or get paid. In addition, they could not work their extra jobs those days, so lost the pay for them also. Altogether that could amount to a several hundred dollar loss of wages for each of them.

"Kathy Cooper has some expertise at handling guns and shooting them. Is that correct, Officer Cannon?"

"Objection, Your Honor," John said as he stood. "Calls for an opinion."

"Sustained."

Maddox hesitated a moment. "You witnessed Mrs. Cooper hit fifteen out of the sixteen beer cans. Is that correct?"

"Yes."

"No more questions," Maddox told the judge as he returned to his chair.

"Mr. Everett," the judge said. "Will your cross-examination be lengthy?"

"No, Your Honor," John said as he stood up.

"Proceed."

"Officer Cannon, how did the department learn about the target practice?"

"Kathy called and told us that the homicide detectives wanted to know who taught her how to use a carbine. She said she would have to tell them. We went to Sergeant Strong and told him about the situation."

"The four of you admitted it?"

"Yes, sir."

"You admitted it, knowing you had violated department policy?"

"Yes, sir."

"You admitted it, knowing you would be disciplined?"

"Yes, sir."

"Do you resent being disciplined for this?"

"No, sir," he said with a smile. "It was worth it to see her shoot!"

More than a few chuckles were scattered around the courtroom.

"No more questions," John Everett stated to the judge.

"Redirect, Mr. Maddox?" the judge asked.

"No, Your Honor."

"You are excused, Officer Cannon," Judge Harrison stated. "We'll take a fifteen-minute recess." He stood and left the courtroom.

Chapter 43

After the recess, Maddox called Sergeant Watson to testify.

"Tell us what you observed when you arrived at the scene of the Ray Jackson shooting."

"Mine was the third unit to arrive on the scene," Sergeant Watson said, speaking not to Maddox, but to the jury. "Mrs. Cooper was standing next to Officer Henson's unit holding a rifle pointed up in the air. I walked up behind her and reached around to take the rifle. She resisted until she turned around and saw who I was. Then she released it and ran to where Officer Henson was lying on the ground. I secured the rifle in my unit and went to check on Officer Henson. He was conscious. One paramedic was checking him over. Mrs. Cooper was sitting on the ground near him crying. I went to look at the man the other paramedic was checking on. It was Ray Jackson. The paramedic said he was DOA. I got down next to Mrs. Cooper and asked what happened."

"What did she tell you?"

"Objection, Your Honor," John stated. "Mrs. Cooper will be testifying in this case."

"Approach, Your Honor?" Maddox requested.

Judge Harrison nodded. The court reporter picked up her machine and moved close to record the comments of Judge Harrison and the attorneys as part of the transcript of the proceedings.

"Your Honor," Maddox said. "Mr. Everett may decide later that Mrs. Cooper will not testify. Her statements to the officers should be heard by the jury."

"Mr. Everett," Judge Harrison asked, "did Mrs. Cooper give the police a sworn statement?"

"No, Your Honor."

Judge Harrison motioned them back to their places. "Objection overruled. You may answer the question, Sergeant," Judge Harrison stated.

"Yes, Your Honor," Sergeant Watson acknowledged. "She told me that they had stopped to investigate a man and a pick-up truck at that location. When two more men appeared, she got the rifle out of the unit. When she looked up, the three men jumped Officer Henson. She took the safety off the carbine and pulled the bolt back to put a cartridge in the firing chamber. When she looked up again, Ray Jackson was raising a piece of pipe over his head to hit Henson. She fired, got the other two men to move away from Henson, and got on the radio to get help."

"She said Ray Jackson had a piece of pipe in his hand?"

"That's correct."

"Was there a piece of pipe in Ray Jackson's hand when you saw his body?"

"No."

"Was it on the ground near his body?"

"No."

"Where was it?"

"We didn't find it."

"You did *not* find the piece of pipe?"

"That's correct."

"What happened after she told her story?" Maddox asked with skeptic emphasis on "her story."

"She asked if she had killed the man, if he was really dead. I told her, 'yes.' She wanted to see, and got up. I went with her. She looked at the body for a moment, then turned away. Officer Henson had been put on the stretcher to be moved to the ambulance. She took his hand and walked along with him. She watched while he was loaded and until the ambulance drove away. At that time, I suggested that she sit in my unit. She wanted to go home. I told that her she needed to remain at the scene, but that I would send an officer to tell her family what was going on. She then sat in my unit."

"You put her in your car where the rifle was?"

"No. The rifle was locked in the trunk of my unit."

"Then you did *not* trust her to be in the car with the rifle?"

"The rifle was in the trunk because it was evidence. When she sat in my car, my shotgun was in the unit where she had access to it."

"How long did she sit in your unit?"

"About thirty minutes, until the detectives took her to Homicide Division to make a statement."

"A sworn statement?"

"You'll have to ask them about that," the sergeant told him.

"No more questions," Maddox said as he stepped away from the witness box.

Judge Harrison turned to John. "Mr. Everett?"

John stood. "Sergeant Watson, you said that the man who the other paramedic was checking on was Ray Jackson. Did you recognize him at that time?"

"Yes."

"How did you recognize him?"

"HPD had handled him before."

"Objection, Your Honor!" the prosecutor exclaimed. "May we approach?" he asked.

The judge motioned him forward. The court reporter again joined the conference at the bench.

"The defense is attempting to put the victim on trial by bringing up his criminal record, Your Honor," Maddox stated.

"Your Honor, Ray Jackson's criminal record is a matter of public record," John Everett stated. "It proves that he had a propensity to commit violent crimes."

The judge shook his head. "Step back, gentlemen. Objection sustained." He turned to the jury. "The jury will disregard the witness's last statement. Proceed, Mr. Everett."

John considered a moment. "How long have you been with the Houston Police Department?"

"Twenty-five years," the sergeant answered.

"Mrs. Cooper told you that Ray Jackson had a piece of pipe."

"Yes."

"Did you see a piece of pipe?"

"No, I didn't."

"Did you doubt her story?"

"I thought she was mistaken about the pipe since it wasn't on the scene. However, I had no doubt that Officer Henson's life was in danger."

"Objection, Your Honor," Maddox said. "The witness is giving an opinion."

"Your Honor," John said, "Sergeant Watson's twenty-five years with HPD qualifies him as an expert on situations like this."

"I agree, Mr. Everett. Objection overruled."

John turned to the sergeant. "You stated that Officer Henson's life was in danger. Why do you say that?"

"He had been kicked unconscious. He could not defend himself or keep the three men from getting his pistol. It would have been easy for them to beat him to death or shoot him with his own weapon."

"Were the two men who Mrs. Cooper held at gunpoint arrested?"

"Yes."

"What were they charged with?"

"Aggravated assault of a peace officer, aggravated assault, and theft," Sergeant Watson answered.

"I understand the aggravated assault of a peace officer. What was the other aggravated assault charge for?"

"During the investigation we found that the security guard had been beaten and locked in the porta-can."

"And the theft charge?"

"Construction materials had been placed in the pick-up truck."

"Where are those other two men now?" John asked.

"Objection, Your Honor!" Maddox exclaimed as he rose to his feet. "This line of questioning has nothing to do with the circumstances of the shooting. I move it be stricken from the record."

The judge turned to Mr. Everett, who stated, "It establishes the motive for the three men to attack Officer Henson."

"I agree, Mr. Everett. However, their whereabouts at this time is not relevant. Objection to the last question is sustained. The prior testimony will not be stricken."

"Yes, Your Honor," John said, accepting the ruling. "No more questions."

"Redirect, Mr. Maddox?"

"No, Your Honor," Maddox answered.

The judge nodded. "You are excused, Sergeant."

"Yes, Your Honor."

"We will recess for lunch and reconvene at one-thirty."

As had happened the day before, officers waited for the courtroom to empty of spectators, then escorted Kathy and Steve from the courtroom and down to the basement entrance where Sergeant Ralph Strong waited in his unit. As he was driving up the exit ramp to the street, he asked where they would like to have lunch.

"Honey?" Steve asked.

"All I want is something light," Kathy stated. "Soup and a sandwich, maybe."

"That sounds good," Steve agreed.

"I know just the place," Ralph said. After a moment he chuckled and shook his head.

"What?" Kathy asked.

"You, hitting fifteen out of sixteen beer cans," he told her.

She moaned. "Three days off each, Ralph?"

"They admitted it. If the department had found out any other way, they could have been terminated," he informed her. "Besides, Kathy, I already suspected."

"How?"

"I smelled gun powder residue on them at end of shift one morning. And a couple nights later, I overheard Cannon compare you to Annie Oakley."

"It's my fault. If I hadn't shot Ray Jackson, it wouldn't have come up."

"If you hadn't shot Ray Jackson," Ralph stated emphatically, "Calvin Henson would be dead, and probably you, too!"

"What?"

"If you had seen them kill Calvin, what do you think they would have done to you?"

Kathy was suddenly chilled to the bone. She hadn't thought of that. She looked at Steve, who appeared equally stunned.

After a moment Ralph asked, "You enjoyed the target practice, didn't you?"

"Yes," she admitted.

"Well, in the future, if you want to do some shooting, let me know. I'll take you to the department range," Ralph advised.

"I will," she agreed.

Ralph joined them for lunch at a diner, entertaining them by telling of recent events at Station One. Kathy enjoyed catching up on what the officers had been up to. She had missed hearing the phrase, "You should have been with us…" that she had heard so many times while she was riding along. She also missed their teasing.

Their support of her now, during the trial, meant the world to her. They understood about the shooting on a level that Steve and her family never could, because they didn't have the street experience necessary. God, I miss it, she realized with surprise. She was trying to figure why, when Ralph announced it was time to leave.

Chapter 44

January 25, 1977 - 1:50 p.m.

When court reconvened, Maddox called Charlotte Saxon as his next witness, one of the homicide detectives. She and her partner had questioned Kathy on the morning of the shooting. Charlotte Saxon was sworn in, and her position with HPD was established.

"Tell us what you saw when you and your partner arrived at the scene of the shooting."

"Officer Henson was being loaded into the ambulance. Two suspects were in two separate police units. Sergeant Watson was with Mrs. Cooper. The victim was on his back, about eighty feet from Officer Henson's unit."

"What did you do?"

"First we asked about Officer Henson's condition. Then we looked at the scene. We asked Sergeant Watson what Mrs. Cooper had told him. He told us. We looked for a piece of pipe, but didn't find one. We did find an empty shell casing for a thirty-caliber rifle near Officer Henson's unit. We talked to the crime lab men and told them what we needed." She paused, then continued. "Sergeant Watson accompanied us to his car and introduced us to Mrs. Cooper. We informed her that we needed her to come downtown with us, and that we would see that she got home later."

"Did she go with you willingly?"

"Yes, sir."

"And when you got her downtown, what happened?"

"We took her to Homicide where we questioned her about what happened."

When she was asked what Kathy had told them, Detective Saxon related the same version that Sergeant Watson had told in court earlier.

"And did you find the pipe?"

"No, sir."
"She admitted shooting Ray Jackson. Is that correct?"
"Yes, sir."
"And you found no pipe or other weapon in the area. Is that correct?"
"Yes, sir."
"No further questions."
John rose from his chair but stayed by the defense table.
"Did you tell Mrs. Cooper that no pipe was found at the scene?"
"Yes, sir."
"How did she react to that?" Everett asked as he stepped to the witness box.
"She was shocked. She turned so pale, I thought she was going to faint."
"But she didn't faint?"
"No, sir. She was puzzled. She was certain she saw a pipe in Ray Jackson's hand when she shot him."
"Two suspects were arrested at the scene of the shooting. Correct?"
"That's correct."
"Did you question them?"
"We tried, but they both asked for attorneys and then refused to answer any questions."
"They never answered any questions?" John asked.
"No, sir. By the time we worked out a deal with their attorneys for them to get immunity, both of the men were unavailable."
"Unavailable? Explain please."
"Bucky Smith had been returned to prison in Huntsville for violating his parole. Two days later he was stabbed in a fight and died. Chico Costas' whereabouts are unknown at this time. He was released on bail and disappeared. We believe he fled to Mexico," Detective Saxon explained.
"Neither one of them said *anything* about the shooting?"
"That's correct."
"Bucky Smith had been on parole for what?"
"Objection, Your Honor," Maddox said as he stood up.
Judge Harrison motioned the attorneys forward and waited for Maddox to state his grounds for objecting.
"The defense is again trying to put the victim on trial. By bringing up Smith's prison record, Mr. Everett is casting guilt by association on the victim, Ray Jackson."
Judge Harrison turned to Mr. Everett.
"That was not my intention, Your Honor."
"Oh, I think it was, Mr. Everett. Objection sustained."
"No more questions, Your Honor," John stated and returned to the defense table.
"Redirect, Your Honor," Maddox announced.
The judge nodded.

"Detective Saxon, did you question people who lived near the scene of the shooting?"

"Yes, sir, but we didn't find anyone who had witnessed the shooting."

"No one saw anything?"

"One person said he saw the police unit at the scene with the emergency lights flashing. Another said he heard what he thought was a gunshot. However, neither of them *saw* what happened."

"So, as far as you know, there are *no* witnesses to the shooting."

"That is correct, sir."

"Thank you, Detective. No more questions."

"Mr. Everett."

"No questions, Your Honor."

"Will you be recalling Detective Saxon for the defense?"

"No, Your Honor," Everett stated.

"You're excused, Detective."

As she stepped down, the judge announced the mid-afternoon break. Thirty minutes later Maddox called Richard Wilson from the Crime Lab as a witness. He entered the courtroom with a good-sized piece of poster board in one hand. The bailiff brought out an easel, and the poster board was placed on it. It was covered with a piece of paper. Richard Wilson was quickly qualified as an expert and accepted as such by both the prosecution and the defense.

"Did you go to the scene of the shooting of Ray Jackson?"

"Yes, sir."

"What did you do there?"

"Took measurements, photos, and collected evidence."

"What can you tell the jury from the measurements, photos, and evidence you collected?"

"I've prepared a diagram of the scene and can explain best with that."

"Your Honor, I request that the diagram be entered as an exhibit in this case," Maddox asked.

"So ordered," Judge Harrison said.

Richard Wilson uncovered the diagram. Kathy couldn't see it clearly from where she was sitting because it was angled toward the jury, but she listened intently to his explanation.

"This rectangle," Richard Wilson explained, using a pen as a pointer, "marked eleven-fifty-seven, represents the police vehicle Officer Calvin Henson was driving that night. The KC next to the unit is where Kathleen Cooper was standing at the moment she fired. The small x to the right of her and the unit is where we recovered an empty shell casing. The outline marked CH is where Officer Calvin Henson laid on the ground unconscious. The outline marked RJ is the location of Ray Jackson's body. We recovered a thirty caliber carbine from Sergeant Watson. We also…"

Somewhere during Richard Wilson's testimony, Kathy tuned it all out. She knew what he was going to say. It all dealt with scientific tests and what the results proved. It was all unnecessary as far as she was concerned.

At about four-thirty that afternoon, Judge Harrison recessed the court. Kathy and Steve were escorted to the car. The drive home was silent for the most part. Kathy worried about the trial. Steve worried about her safety. They both worried about the boys.

Chapter 45

Wednesday, January 26, 1977

Testimony from the experts filled the third day of the trial. First, the Medical Examiner testified to all the gory details of the damage the bullet did to Ray Jackson's body, complete with color photos of the entrance and exit wounds. Kathy deliberately tuned out that information. It meant that the cause of death was a gunshot wound that entered his back, exited his front, and destroyed his heart on the way through.

Second, the ballistics expert from HPD testified that the shell casing found at the scene came from the thirty caliber rifle recovered from Sergeant Watson. He also stated that no bullet was recovered from the scene, in spite of a comprehensive search.

After the lunch recess, a fingerprint expert testified to finding Kathy's prints on the thirty caliber rifle that ballistics had proved the shell casing was fired from. Other prints on it were those of Officer Calvin Henson and Sergeant Watson.

Last was a sergeant from the Dispatch, who brought a copy of the tape of the radio calls starting with the *assist the officer* call Kathy broadcast, and continuing until the dispatcher announced that the situation at the location was under control. The jury listened to the tape several times. Kathy thought she sounded funny, not like herself at all. She could hear tension in her voice, perhaps even some fear. Well, that's what I felt at the time, she thought.

To everyone's surprise, after that witness left the stand, Maddox rested the case for the prosecution. Judge Harrison recessed the court for the day, instructing everyone concerned that court would resume at nine the next morning.

Kathy felt buried under the testimony given in the prosecution's case. She wondered if John could possibly dig her out of this hole. She wished she knew what happened to the pipe. How could it disappear? Could she have been mistaken? No, she told herself. I know what I saw!

Steve could tell that Kathy's spirits were really down. It didn't surprise him, but he didn't know what to do about it. They were escorted to their car and began the drive home. Kathy was unusually quiet. Concerned, Steve tried to think of some way to help her. The best he could do was to reach out and take her hand. She rewarded him with a little smile that quickly faded.

Chapter 46

Thursday, January 27, 1977 - 8:55 a.m.

When officers escorted Kathy and Steve to the courtroom, John Everett waited at the defense table. Kathy went inside the railing and sat next to him.

"Kathy, I'm going to put you on the stand this morning," John reminded her.

She tensed up. She was not looking forward to testifying.

"All you have to do is tell the truth. Don't leave anything out. Don't add anything. Take your time answering my questions. Carefully consider the prosecutor's questions before you answer. Do not let him make you angry."

Kathy nodded and promised to do her best.

The judge entered the courtroom a little after 9:00 a.m. The spectators were searched and the jury was brought into the courtroom.

"Mr. Everett, are you ready to proceed?" Judge Harrison asked.

"Yes, Your Honor," John answered, as he stood. "The defense calls Kathleen Cooper."

Kathy was sworn in and John began the questions.

"Mrs. Cooper, were you a member of one of the grand jury panels seated at the beginning of August of last year?"

"Yes."

"Which grand jury panel?"

"Judge Parker's."

"What are the duties of the grand jury?"

"To hear the facts in felony cases and determine if there is enough evidence to indict and try the person charged or not."

"You had additional duties, didn't you?"

"Yes. I was secretary of that grand jury."

"What were your duties as secretary?"

"To keep track of which cases were indicted, which were no billed, and to be sure that the foreman signed all the indictments."

"Grand jury members are also given privileges, aren't they?"

"Yes."

"Can you tell us what those consist of?"

"A tour of the county prison farm and of the state prison at Huntsville were organized for those members who were interested."

"Did you take those tours?" John asked her.

"No. They were scheduled for sometime in October. I resigned my position at the end of September."

"Were there other privileges offered?"

"Yes. Most of the police agencies in the county invited the jurors to ride with on-duty officers."

"You accepted that invitation, didn't you?"

"Yes!"

"Why?"

Kathy took a deep breath. "Because I wanted to see what police work is really like."

"Were you nervous?"

"A little, at first," she admitted.

"Were you ever scared out there?"

"Not for myself. A few times for the officers, but never for myself."

"How many times did you ride?"

"Sixteen times."

"When did you ride along?" John asked.

"Each time I rode along, the evening shift picked me up at home. I'd go to the substation at end of that shift and go out with the night shift officers. They would take me home near the end of their shift."

"You rode along with two shifts each time?"

"Yes."

"How many different officers did you ride along with?"

"Twenty-eight."

"How did the officers react to your presence?"

"Hesitant to begin with."

"Explain."

"The first officers I rode along with were Calvin Henson and John Bailey. I remember remarking that they didn't seem comfortable with me riding along. Officer Bailey told me, 'Partners take care of each other. Now we have to take care of you, too.' I tried to assure them that I would follow their orders. The last thing I wanted to do was distract them or get them hurt. After we handled a couple of calls, they relaxed some. By the end of shift, they seemed comfortable with me."

"How did the other officers react to you?"

"About the same at first. But after I'd ridden along a few times, they seemed to accept my presence."

"Now, I want you to think about the night in question when Calvin Henson was in a one-man unit and you were riding along with him. How did he treat you that night?"

"Almost like I was the man-on-the-ground."

"Will you explain that, please?" John asked.

Kathy turned to the jury. "In a two-man unit, the officer not driving is the man-on-the-ground. It is his responsibility to write down the radio calls as they get them and to do the paperwork. He is the one who writes the traffic tickets and any reports they need to file on incidents that occurred during the shift."

"And he treated you like the man-on-the-ground that night?"

"Yes."

"What exactly did you do?"

"I wrote down the locations of the calls as they came in. When we picked up a runaway juvenile, Calvin questioned him while we were on the way to Central. He asked his name, age, address, et cetera. I wrote it all down. When we arrested a drunk woman, he asked me to write down the information on her car: VIN number, license number, make, and model, so the car could be impounded. Things like that."

"You didn't write any traffic tickets, did you?"

"No. I just wrote down information he would use later."

"How did that make you feel?"

"Like I was part of it. It made me feel good."

"You enjoyed helping Officer Henson?"

Kathy smiled. "Yes, I did."

"Officer Henson testified that at about five o'clock that Sunday morning he was taking you home. Is that correct?"

Kathy's smile disappeared. "Yes, that's correct."

"Tell us what happened on the way to your house."

Kathy took a deep breath and braced herself. "As we passed the construction site, I noticed a pick-up truck and a man beside it. I mentioned it to Calvin, and the fact that it was about five on a Sunday morning. He went back, parked in the entrance, and walked over to talk to the man. I stayed at the unit."

"Why did you stay at the car?"

"Calvin told me to."

"Go ahead. What happened next?"

"Two more men suddenly appeared on the other side of the truck. I didn't like the odds of three men to one officer. So I reached in the car for the radio mike to call for a back-up unit. When I looked up again, the men rushed him and knocked him off his feet. I dropped the mike on the seat and took the rifle out, pulled the bolt back to put a shell in the chamber. I looked up. One of the men had a piece of pipe in his hand and he was raising it over his head. He was going to hit Calvin with the pipe."

Kathy paused, her mind focused on a memory, her eyes looking down toward the floor, but seeing nothing except the memory of what had happened next, as she had not previously perceived it. She remembered seeing the muzzle flash when she fired. She remembered seeing the bullet enter Ray Jackson's body. She shivered as she remembered seeing blood squirt from the wound.

"Kathy?"

She nodded jerkily as her attention came back to the present. Trembling all over from the shock of the vivid memory, she said, as though surprised, "I shot him."

John saw her physical reaction and turned to the judge. "Your Honor, request a brief recess."

"No!" Kathy stated.

"Are you able to continue?" the judge asked.

"Yes, sir."

"Continue, Mr. Everett," the judge urged.

"Yes, Your Honor." John turned to Kathy. He understood her need to get this over with. "What happened then?" he asked as gently as he could.

Kathy swallowed hard, trying to get control of her voice. "I ordered the other two men to get up and move away from Calvin and lie facedown on the ground. Then I got on the radio and called for assistance." She fought to maintain control, but couldn't stop shaking.

"You testified that the man, Ray Jackson, had a piece of pipe in his hand. Is that correct?"

"Yes."

"Which hand?"

"His right hand."

"Can you demonstrate how he raised it?"

"Yes." Kathy raised her right hand over her head.

"Thank you." When she had lowered her arm, John continued. "Will you describe the pipe, please?"

"It appeared to be about this long," she said, holding her hands about fourteen inches apart. "And about that big around," she added, making a circle of her thumb and middle finger. "It was dark."

"What was your intention when you got the rifle out of the car?"

"To stop them."

"How did you plan to do that?"

"I didn't have a plan. I just felt that if I didn't stop it, they'd kill him."

"At what moment did you decide to shoot?"

"When he raised the pipe over his head to strike Officer Henson with it."

"Who taught you how to shoot?"

"My father."

"How old were you?"

"About ten or twelve I think."

"Did he take you hunting?"

She shook her head vigorously. "No, no! Target shooting only, for marksmanship. I...I never shot at...at anything alive before."

"Would you do anything different if you had it to do over?"

"No!"

"Thank you, Kathy. No more questions," John concluded.

Judge Harrison turned to the jury. "Ladies and gentlemen, this court is recessed until two this afternoon," he announced with a stroke of the gavel.

The jury filed out. Kathy left the witness chair and was met halfway to the defense table by Steve, who hugged her tight.

"Are you okay, honey?"

She nodded.

They waited for the courtroom to clear, then the escort took them down to the basement where Sergeant Watson waited in his car. He introduced himself to Steve as they got in the car.

"Where to for lunch?" he asked.

Kathy just shook her head.

"Surprise us," Steve told him.

Before he drove away, he turned to speak to Kathy. "I want to thank you for what you did."

"For killing a man?" she asked him.

"Sometimes there isn't any other way. This was one of those times." He turned and put the car in gear and drove up the ramp to street level.

Sergeant Watson's approval, coming from a man she admired and respected, meant a lot to Kathy. She smiled, remembering the night he called her on the carpet for being *out of uniform*. It helped her calm down and begin to look forward to lunch.

They ate at a place just north of Central on Washington Avenue, in an old frame building that leaned to one side. The wood floors waved gently from uneven settling of the foundation piers. Few of the tables and chairs matched. The room was crowded with police officers, both in uniform and in plain clothes. Talk overheard by Kathy all had to do with police work. The selection of food from the steam table was varied and well prepared. The homemade rolls were hot, crisp on the outside, and melt-in-your-mouth soft on the inside. As a result, Steve and Kathy both overate.

Chapter 47

Thursday, January 27th, 1977 - 1:45 p.m.

The court settled down, the jury was brought in, and Kathy returned to the witness stand for the cross-examination by the prosecutor. She was nervous and kept thinking about John's instruction to "Think about the question before you answer."

"Mr. Maddox," Judge Harrison said. "You may begin."

"Yes, Your Honor," the prosecutor said as he stood. He approached the witness box slowly. "Mrs. Cooper, why did you resign from the grand jury?"

"I resigned because of the shooting."

"Did Judge Parker request your resignation."

"Yes, but I decided to resign before he asked me to."

"Why?"

"I felt I wouldn't be able to concentrate on the work."

"Was there any legal reason you were required to resign?"

"Not that I know of."

"Killing a person is a felony in this state. You were being investigated in connection with a killing, were you not?"

"Yes."

"So you were being investigated for a felony, weren't you?"

"Objection, Your Honor," John said. "The prosecutor is misrepresenting the law. A shooting is not a felony until it is ruled such by the investigating body."

"I withdraw the question, Your Honor." Maddox paused. "A few days later, you were indicted for murder, correct?"

"Yes."

"And arrested?"

She closed her eyes for a moment at the memory of that first night in jail. "Yes."

"Mr. Maddox," the judge said, "we all know she was indicted and arrested for murder. That's what we're all doing here. Move on, Mr. Maddox!"

"Yes, Your Honor. Mrs. Cooper, when were you married?"

"In May of nineteen-fifty-eight."

"When was your first child born?"

"Objection, Your Honor. Not relevant to this case," John stated.

"Approach," Judge Harrison said, motioning to the two attorneys. "Where are you going with this Mr. Maddox?"

"It brings her character into question, Your Honor. She had the baby seven months after the wedding," Mr. Maddox stated.

"So she was pregnant when she got married. That has nothing to do with this case," John argued.

"I agree. Step back. Objection sustained," Judge Harrison stated.

Mr. Maddox thought for a moment. "Mrs. Cooper, on the night of the shooting, what was the situation at the moment you decided to get Officer Henson's rifle out of the car?"

"Officer Henson was on the ground. The three men were hitting and kicking him."

"Tell us again, at what moment did you decide to shoot?"

"When Ray Jackson raised the piece of pipe over his head to hit Officer Henson with it."

"You could see that?"

"Yes."

"This happened before sunrise?"

"Yes."

"Was it still dark outside?"

"Yes."

"If it was dark, how could you see the pipe?"

"The headlights of the car were on high beam. They lit up the area really well."

"When you described the piece of pipe, you said, 'It *appeared* to be' so long and so big around. You also stated that it was dark. Which is true? Could you see it in the highlights, or was it dark?"

"I *could* see it in the headlights. The *pipe* was dark. Not white, like the plastic stuff they're using now," Kathy explained impatiently.

John Everett, who had been making notes, looked up with interest.

Maddox backed off. Her answer surprised him. He was looking for an inconsistency, to raise doubts about her testimony. He didn't find one.

"You stated you shot Ray Jackson to stop him. Is that correct?" he asked her.

"Yes."

"Were you aware that the shot would kill him?"

"No."

"Did you even stop to think that it might kill him?"

"No," she reluctantly admitted.

"You didn't care, did you?"

"I didn't think about it, one way or the other." Realizing how casually she had taken the most precious thing from the man—his life—brought tears to her eyes.

"Would you have shot him again if the first shot had not stopped him?"

"Yes."

"Then you admit you were willing to kill him?"

"If necessary to stop him, yes."

"What about the other two men? Were you willing to kill them, too?"

"If I had to."

"If you had to," Mr. Maddox repeated sarcastically. "But it wasn't necessary to kill them, was it?"

"No."

"They surrendered. Ray Jackson could have surrendered, too, if you had given him a chance, couldn't he?"

"I don't know."

"You didn't give him a chance to surrender, did you?"

"No. There wasn't time." Tears ran down her face and she sniffed noisily. "I'm sorry."

"Mrs. Cooper," the judge said.

She turned to face him as he handed her a box of tissues. "Thank you." After she wiped her eyes and blew her nose, she again apologized. "I'm sorry."

"You say there wasn't time. You say he had a piece of pipe. What you say, Mrs. Cooper, doesn't prove anything."

"Objection, Your Honor. The burden of proof is on the prosecution, not the defense!"

"Withdrawn," Mr. Maddox stated as he returned to the prosecutors table.

Judge Harrison turned to the defense. "Mr. Everett?"

John approached her.

"Kathy, tell the jury exactly what you were thinking at the moment you squeezed the trigger."

She took a deep breath and let it out with a sigh. "I thought that he was going to kill Calvin, and I was the only one that could stop him."

"Thank you," John said, turning to Judge Harrison. "No more questions."

"Fifteen minute recess," the judge announced.

Kathy stood and John took her arm as she walked back to the defense table. Steve waited with open arms to hug her.

"You did fine, Kathy," John told her.

Kathy had time to go to the ladies room during the recess. She washed her face, freshened her lipstick, and returned to the courtroom. The court was called to order, and things proceeded.

The judge asked, "Mr. Everett, are you ready to proceed?"

"Yes, Your Honor."

"Call your next witness."

"The defense calls Officer Calvin Henson."

The word was passed to the people in the hall, and Officer Henson promptly responded by coming through the doors. He approached and sat in the witness chair.

"Officer Henson, you are still under oath," the judge reminded him.

"Yes, Your Honor."

"Your witness, Mr. Everett."

John stepped forward. "Officer Henson, when Kathy Cooper rode along with you, what was your impression of her?"

"She was genuinely interested and extremely inquisitive about police work."

"How did you feel about having Mrs. Cooper ride along with you?"

"At first we were concerned about how she would act at scenes."

"You said 'we'?"

"Yes, sir. My partner, John Bailey and I."

"How did she act at scenes?"

"She showed good sense and always did what we told her to do."

"Can you give us an example?"

"Yes. We made a traffic stop. The driver had been drinking. We were talking to him, taking our time, trying to decide if we should take him to Central for a breath test. At one point, I thought that he was getting irritated with us, and I motioned for Mrs. Cooper to go back to the unit. She did, without any hesitation or question. She just did it."

"Why did you motion her back to the unit?" John asked.

"If he started swinging at us, I didn't want her close enough to get hurt."

John nodded and turned away, thinking a moment. When he turned back, he asked, "On the night of the shooting, you were in a one-man unit. Correct?"

"Yes, sir."

"Did you have any reluctance about her riding along that night?"

"No, sir. I was comfortable with it," Officer Henson replied.

"That was the third time she rode along with you, wasn't it?"

"Yes, sir."

"Except for being in a one-man unit that night, was there anything different about it?"

"She'd ridden a lot, and learned a lot. Her questions were more and more about the procedures and the details of our job. She was curious about every aspect of police work. Having her ride along was like having a rookie to train. She remembered what she was told."

"Can you give us an example?"

"Yes, sir. One of the calls we made that night…"

"Which night?" John asked, to clarify.

"The night of the shooting."

John nodded, "Go ahead."

"This call was a *burglary of a residence*. While I was checking for fingerprints and lifting a few, the woman told Mrs. Cooper about kids in the neighborhood putting firecrackers in their mailbox on their front porch in the middle of the night. Before I could speak up, Mrs. Cooper told them to call Station Five and file an *alert slip*. That would put the unit on that beat on notice to patrol that area more often about the time of those occurrences. She learned about alert slips from some of the other officers she rode along with, because it hadn't come up when she was riding along with me."

"Tell us about the incident that led to the shooting, in as much detail as you can."

"It was about five o'clock on that Sunday morning," Officer Henson began. "I was taking Mrs. Cooper home. A few blocks from her house there was a small construction site. There was a pick-up and a man on the site. She mentioned it, and I told her they were probably construction workers arriving early. She pointed out that it was five o'clock on a *Sunday* morning. I made a U-turn, went to the location, and parked in the entrance to the site. I put the headlights on high beam to light up the area. Mrs. Cooper got out. I motioned for her to stay at the car.

"I approached the man by the pick-up and was talking to him when two other men came around from the other side of the truck. I turned to keep all three of them in sight, and backed away a few steps. The two men came around the back of the truck and all three of them jumped me. I fought to keep them from getting my weapon. I knew that against three men it was just a matter of time and they'd kill me if they got it. One of them kicked me in the ribs. Another kicked me in the head. I lost consciousness."

A wave of nausea hit Kathy's stomach when she realized how frightened Calvin must have been.

"What was the situation when you regained consciousness?" John asked.

"Kathy was kneeling beside me. She told me an ambulance was on the way and to lie still. At first I didn't remember where I was or what had happened. She told me where we had stopped and why, and that the three men had jumped me. I asked what stopped them.

"An officer, Officer Cannon, I believe, asked her if she had shot the man. She nodded. He then explained that she had held the others at gunpoint and called for help." He looked toward Kathy. "She saved my life and probably her own."

"Objection!" Maddox said as he stood up. "Speculation, Your Honor!"

"Overruled!"

"What happened next?"

"The paramedics checked me, and the sergeant insisted that I go to the hospital. They loaded me on a stretcher."

"What injuries did you suffer from the attack by the three men?"

"Two broken ribs and a concussion."

"How long were you in the hospital?"

"Two days."

"And how long were you on sick leave?"

"Six and a half weeks."

John paused a moment to shift to another topic. "Were you carrying your flashlight when you approached the pick-up truck?"

"Yes."

"What happened to it?"

"I dropped it in the struggle."

"And after that?"

"One of the other officers put it on the gurney as it was moved to the ambulance."

"Describe your flashlight, please."

"It's a five D-cell flashlight in a metal housing."

Kathy gasped. Suddenly it was clear to her.

"How long is it?"

"I don't know exactly. About fifteen inches, I think."

"What color is it?" John asked Calvin.

"Black."

"Where is the flashlight now?"

"In my briefcase in the trunk of my car," Calvin told him.

"And where is your car?"

"In the parking garage behind the courthouse."

"Approach, Your Honor?" John asked.

The judge motioned for Mr. Maddox to join them. The court reporter also came forward.

"Your Honor, there is a possibility," John stated, "that Mrs. Cooper mistook Officer Henson's flashlight for a piece of pipe. I move that the flashlight be taken into evidence and checked for Ray Jackson's fingerprints."

"If this is a delaying tactic, Mr. Everett, I am going to be very unhappy," Judge Harrison told him.

"It is not, Your Honor. This is a possibility that the defense had not considered until this moment."

"Mr. Maddox, any objections?" the judge asked.

The prosecutor started to object, then thought better of it. The chances of finding any identifiable prints belonging to Ray Jackson were slim at best. It could work in the prosecution's favor. "No, Your Honor."

The judge motioned for them to step back. "Continue, Mr. Everett."

"Yes, Your Honor. I move that Officer Henson's flashlight be taken into evidence and checked for Ray Jackson's fingerprints."

"Granted," the judge declared. "When court is recessed, the bailiff will accompany Officer Henson to his vehicle, take custody of the flashlight, and deliver it to the fingerprint lab."

"Thank you, Your Honor." John turned to Calvin.

"Officer Henson, can you add anything else to your testimony?"

"Only that when Kathy Cooper saved my life," he told them, speaking directly to the jury, "I doubt she ever stopped to think about her own being in danger."

Mr. Maddox rose from his chair and started to speak, then shut his mouth and sat down.

"Thank you, Officer. No more questions," John concluded.

"Court will resume at nine a.m. tomorrow," Judge Harrison declared. "Court's recessed."

Calvin was more than happy to have the flashlight checked for Ray Jackson's fingerprints, but he had been using the flashlight for a couple months after returning to duty. He thought that the possibility of finding any useful prints was remote. But it was worth a try. He left the courtroom with the bailiff.

At the defense table, John, Kathy, and Steve had a quiet conversation about the long odds that anything probative would come from the fingerprint examination. It had been handled a lot since the shooting. If no usable prints were found, would the flashlight create enough reasonable doubt for acquittal? The possibility gave Kathy hope. She now knew that it was Calvin's flashlight she had seen in Ray Jackson's hand. She hadn't imagined it!

Her mood lightened by this development, as she listened to the escorting officers quietly discuss the slim to impossible chances of proving that Ray Jackson had held the flashlight. Still, they admitted, the fact that the flashlight was on the scene might help Kathy's case.

Chapter 48

Friday, January 29, 1977 - 9:20 a.m.

Court got underway with Calvin Henson taking the stand for Mr. Maddox's cross-examination.

"Mr. Maddox," the judge said, "proceed, please."

"Yes, Your Honor," Maddox said as he approached the witness chair. "Officer Henson, you testified that you approached the man at the pick-up without being aware that there were two other men present. Is that correct?"

"Yes, it is."

"Did you call out with the dispatcher?"

"No, I didn't."

"Then you didn't call for back-up either, did you?"

"No."

"Officer Henson, if Mrs. Cooper had not been with you that night, would you have handled that situation differently?"

"Possibly."

"Possibly? Explain, please," Maddox asked.

"I might have called for back-up before I approached the man. I might not have. So much depends on your feeling about a scene."

"A feeling?" Maddox questioned. "Something like ESP, perhaps?"

"A hunch. A feeling. Sometimes you sense that there is going to be trouble before anything happens."

"Did you get a sense of trouble that night?"

"No. I did not."

"Could that be because Mrs. Cooper's presence distracted you from your job?"

"No!" Calvin exclaimed emphatically.

"Why didn't you call for back-up that night?" Mr. Maddox asked.

"I've been a cop for over ten years. Some things you just do based on experience and instinct, without stopping to think about them consciously."

"And if you had stopped to think about it that night, what would you have done?"

"Probably the same thing I did."

"What did you think when the men jumped you?"

"That they would probably kill me unless Kathy put out an assist."

"You expected her to get on the radio?"

"Yes."

"Did you expect her to get the rifle out of the car and shoot them?"

"No, I didn't! But I wasn't surprised when I was told about it."

"You were told about it? That's right. You were unconscious when the shooting occurred, weren't you?"

"Yes."

"You do *not* know what the situation was at the moment she fired the rifle, do you?"

"No, sir."

"Then the only witnesses were the two other men who were arrested. Correct?"

"As far as I know."

"And they didn't say anything about it when questioned. We only have Mrs. Cooper's story. And no proof positive that it is the truth."

"Objection, Your Honor," John Everett said as he rose to his feet. "The prosecutor is testifying. Request the last statements be stricken from the record."

"Objection sustained." Judge Harrison turned to the prosecutor. "Mr. Maddox, I'll have no more of that in my court."

"Yes, Your Honor."

"The jury will disregard Mr. Maddox's last statements and they will be stricken from the record. Proceed, Mr. Maddox."

Maddox hesitated for a moment. "No more questions."

"Redirect, Your Honor?" John asked.

The judge nodded.

John approached the witness chair. "Officer Henson, if you had called for back-up before you approached the man by the pick-up, would the outcome have been any different?"

"Objection, Your Honor. He's asking for an opinion."

"Mr. Maddox, you raised the question of his options and opinions in your cross. Objection overruled. You may answer, Officer Henson."

"I doubt it would have changed anything, unless the back-up unit got there before the men jumped me, and that wasn't likely."

"Why not?"

"It happened so fast. There wasn't time. They probably wouldn't have gotten there soon enough to change anything."

"Thank you, Officer. No more questions."

"Mr. Maddox?"

"No questions, Your Honor."

"You're excused, Officer Henson," the judge told him. "Fifteen-minute recess." Judge Harrison left the bench, and the jury retired to the jury room.

Officer Henson stepped down from the witness chair. He walked directly over to Kathy and gave her a bear hug. She returned it. Steve watched, then offered his hand to Calvin. Nothing was said, but everything was understood.

The time for the recess was almost over when one of the bailiffs approached John Everett and whispered something in his ear. John glanced toward the courtroom doors, nodded, and thanked the man. He turned to Kathy and Steve.

"This may be the fingerprint report. I'll be right back."

John left the courtroom. Kathy and Steve looked at each other, both hoping for evidence that would help Kathy's case. John returned shortly after with papers in his hand, but before he could tell Kathy and Steve anything, the bailiff interrupted.

"All rise."

The judge sat at the bench, ordered the jury be brought in, and turned to John.

"Mr. Everett, you may call your next witness."

"The defense requests that James McCue be added to our witness list."

"Objection! The prosecution has received no notice of this addition."

The judge crooked fingers at both of them to bring them to the bench. "Explain, Mr. Everett."

"Mr. McCue is the fingerprint expert who examined Officer Henson's flashlight, Your Honor. His report was delivered to me just moments ago." John handed the report to Judge Harrison.

The judge read the report and handed it to the prosecutor. "Is Mr. McCue present at this time?"

"Yes, sir. He's standing by in the hall."

"Objection overruled. You may call Mr. McCue."

"Thank you, Your Honor."

The bailiff called the witness from the hall. Mr. McCue entered the courtroom carrying a clear plastic evidence bag containing a flashlight. The bailiff administered the oath, and John Everett quickly established McCue's experience and expertise.

"Mr. McCue, you examined Officer Henson's flashlight for fingerprint evidence?"

"Yes."

"Is that the flashlight in the bag you are holding?"

"Yes."

"Please tell the jury what you found," John requested.

"There were many prints on the flashlight. We lifted thirty-one. Most of those were grouped at the lens end of the light. Those we identified as Officer

Henson's. At the other end, we found three prints from Ray Jackson's left hand."

"Please show us where the prints from Ray Jackson were found."

McCue opened the bag, took the flashlight and held it in his left hand, about two inches from the end opposite the lens. "Ray Jackson held it in this manner," McCue stated. "We found his thumb print in this area, and his index and middle fingerprints here, all three from his left hand." He held the flashlight, turning it so the jurors could see how it was gripped.

"Is it possible that Ray Jackson picked up the flashlight with his left hand," John demonstrated as he spoke, "and transferred it to his right hand to strike with?"

"Objection, Your Honor," Mr. Maddox said, almost wearily.

"Sustained."

"Your Honor, permission to allow the jury to examine the flashlight?" John asked.

"Mr. Maddox?"

"No objection, Your Honor."

John took the flashlight to the jury foreman, who felt the weight and the balance when held the way the John had suggested Ray Jackson might have held it to strike a blow. A couple of the other men held it the same way and smacked it against their open palms. John waited for it to make a complete circuit of the jurors, then retrieved it. He turned to the witness chair.

"Mr. McCue, did you find any evidence that Ray Jackson did *not* grasp the flashlight in his right hand?"

"No."

"Then he could have?"

"Objection," Maddox stated.

"Withdrawn," John stated, then continued. "Were there any partial prints at the lens end that were not Officer Henson's?"

"All of the prints that were identifiable at the lens end were Officer Henson's."

"No more questions," John stated, then returned to the defense table.

Mr. Maddox stood and stepped to the witness box. He picked up the flashlight. "Mr. McCue, did you find any prints that conclusively proved that Ray Jackson held the light in his right hand at any time?"

"No, sir."

"That's all, thank you."

"Redirect, Mr. Everett?"

"No questions, Your Honor."

The judge excused Mr. McCue. "Call your next witness, Mr. Everett."

"The defense rests, Your Honor."

"Any rebuttal, Mr. Maddox?"

"No, Your Honor."

"All right, gentlemen. Closing arguments Monday. Court's recessed until nine a.m. Monday."

John turned to Kathy with a slight smile. Kathy returned it. For the first time since she had been arrested, she had hopes of being acquitted. Ray Jackson's fingerprints on the flashlight convinced her that she had seen the flashlight in his hand, not a piece of pipe. Intellectually she knew she had done the right thing. Emotionally, she still regretted taking Ray Jackson's life. Kathy's eyes met Steve's. They exchanged smiles and nods.

The atmosphere of the courtroom had changed. The blacks were quiet and thoughtful, where before they seemed angry and smug. The officers, who had been somber and quiet, nodded, smiled, or gave Kathy a thumbs-up sign. They were convinced. She just prayed that the jury was also convinced.

Greg Sampson left the courtroom with Steve's keys to retrieve the car. Kathy stood and, holding Steve's hand, they approached their escorting officers, Donny Wells, Art Donahue, and James Dickens. James checked the hall. As Kathy and Steve stepped out of the courtroom, the three officers formed a triangle around them.

When the elevator doors closed behind them, Donny Wells turned to her with a big grin.

"Pretty Lady, finding those fingerprints is…well, somebody up there is on your side."

"They'll have to acquit you now," Art stated.

"I hope you're right," Kathy admitted, still doubtful.

"The only reason for Ray Jackson to pick up the flashlight was to use it as a weapon," James said. "The jury will see that."

Donny and Art agreed.

Kathy shook her head. "You know the saying, 'a jury is twelve people too dumb to get out of jury duty.'"

"You'll be acquitted," Art insisted.

"And then, Pretty Lady, you apply to the Sheriff's Academy." It was more than a suggestion, but not quite an order.

Kathy shook her head. "I don't know, Donny."

"You'll make one damn good cop," Art stated.

"I'll partner with her right now," James declared.

Kathy turned to James, aghast and somewhat amused. "James, didn't you tell me women have no place in patrol?"

"Most don't, but you're a natural. You took care of business. You protected your partner and you did it without any training," James explained, his admiration for her obvious in his voice.

"You'll be as asset to any department," Art added.

The signal on the elevator sounded, indicating their arrival at the basement. The men turned quickly to face the opening door, stepped out, and checked the area. Kathy glanced at Steve. He was scowling. Without a word, they went to the car.

As Steve drove off, Greg Sampson joined the others. "What the hell happened? Kathy's husband looks ready to kill somebody."

"We were assuring her she would be acquitted, and Donny suggested that she apply to the Sheriff's Academy," James explained.

"So…?"

"I don't think she ever told her husband she wants to be a cop," Art offered.

"Oh, shit!" Greg exclaimed, looking toward the car as Steve drove up the ramp.

Chapter 49

Friday, January 29, 1977 - 11:45 a.m.

The drive home was a silent one. Steve wasn't much of a talker to begin with, and when it came to his feelings he didn't talk at all. He appreciated that the officers supported Kathy and protected her, but they had no right to suggest that she become a cop. When she objected weakly to the suggestion, they almost became insistent.

He admitted that the idea of her becoming a cop was contrary to his beliefs. Men protected women and children, not the other way around. She was small. In a fight, she would get hurt. He couldn't stand that. Worse than that, cops get killed. He could lose the most important person in his life. The thought frightened him.

Could he picture her in a uniform with a gun on her hip? No! That was too foreign an image. In spite of the fact that he knew that she shot and killed a man, he couldn't picture her doing it. She loved life so much, for her to take a life was unthinkable. And yet, she had. She had taken a life to save a life.

Steve worked so much overtime when the boys were younger that Kathy taught them to throw and catch a ball, to ride a bicycle, to dribble a basketball, to shoot baskets, and to roller-skate. Her tomboy side was evident in her notes, too. It showed in the persona she adopted to be accepted by the officers she rode with.

Her notes acknowledged the apprehension she felt for the officers before the raid on the dice game, the sadness of the tragic events, the frustration of the nonsense calls, the excitement of the hot calls, the boredom of the quiet hours, the satisfaction of witnessing a meaningful arrest, and the adrenalin rush of running with lights and siren.

She had surprised him one morning after she rode along with her need for sex. He learned from her notes that it had been a particularly hectic night, with tense situations and seeing death up close. In her notes, she referred to her need for sex that morning as an affirmation of life.

The question in his mind was, does she want to become a cop? Stupid question! All the signs were there. He had tried to ignore them. What he didn't understand was…why?

* * * * *

The silence in the car was stifling. Kathy sensed that Steve was upset. He had a right to be. Her actions had put him through hell the last six months. Riding along worried him. The events of the shooting and trial surpassed worry. She couldn't think of a word to adequately describe the emotional state they provoked. Donny's suggestion that she apply to the Sheriff's Academy, added to the other things, might be more than Steve could deal with.

The suggestion didn't surprise her, as it had Steve, because the possibility had been mentioned several times while she was riding along. It pleased her to know that they believed she could be an officer. She had doubts about her abilities, but none that lessened her desire to try to earn that uniform and badge.

Kathy never shared her dream of being a cop with Steve. It was a very personal and private dream. Before she could share it with him she became pregnant. Dismissing the dream as a childish desire, she became a full-time wife and mother.

Now she realized that the dream never died. It had manifested itself in the mysteries and true crime books she read, and in the television programs and movies she enjoyed most, while wondering if they were an accurate portrayal of police work. She learned, while riding along, that some were more realistic than others, but all contained some truths about police work.

How could she explain it to Steve? Was it possible for anyone with no exposure to law enforcement to understand? Her interest began with an act of kindness from an officer when she was a child. It grew into a desire that she put aside to fulfill family obligations. Because of her strong interest, she took advantage of the opportunity to ride along. It changed everything.

As the engine of the car died, Kathy looked up to discover that they were in their own driveway.

Silence continued as they entered the house. Kathy put her coat and purse in the entry hall closet. Steve hung his wind breaker in the closet and went to the kitchen. Kathy followed. Steve started a pot of coffee. Kathy put the tea kettle on the stove, then opened the refrigerator and started setting things out for lunch. Her stomach knotted at the thought of eating.

Steve set two places at the breakfast room table. He never looked at her. He didn't say a word as sandwich makings, chips, and cookies were arranged on the table. Except for the fact that he walked around her, she might not have been there at all. Steve poured a cup of coffee, took it to the table, and sat down. After making a cup of tea, Kathy joined him.

Steve built a sandwich by slamming everything onto the bread.

Kathy couldn't stand it any longer. "Honey, say something, please."

Without looking at her, he stated, "I have only one question. Do you want to be a cop?"

She took a deep breath and braced herself for his reaction. "Yes," she answered.

He looked up and met her eyes, completely mystified. "Why?"

"That's two questions," she said with a slight smile.

He was not amused.

"Sorry," she said.

"Just tell me why," he pleaded.

"I don't know if I can make you understand. I'm not sure I understand."

"Try," he asked.

She wondered where to begin, and decided the beginning was best. "When I was a little girl, about five, Mama took me shopping in a big store downtown. We got separated. I looked and looked for Mama, but I couldn't find her. I started crying. A big man in a blue uniform got down on one knee in front of me. 'Are you lost?' he asked. I said, 'No. Mama's lost.' He got out his handkerchief and dried my tears. 'I'll help you find her,' he said, and picked me up. He was so kind, so gentle; I knew everything would be all right. And it was. From that moment on, I wanted to be like him when I grew up. I wanted to help children when they were lost and afraid. And not just children, but anyone who needed help.

"Police work is not all car chases and shoot-outs. Every call is different. People expect the officers to solve their problems, because they don't know how. Some just need information about where to go for help. Others are lonely and just need someone to talk to."

Steve watched her face light up as she talked. She seemed to be more alive.

"Stopping a drunk and getting him off the street may not seem like much, but it may save somebody's life. Running with lights and siren to a shooting in progress may sound exciting, but it's scary, because you never have enough information about the situation until you get there. Whatever it is, you have to handle it. It's challenging, interesting, exciting, boring, and filled with paperwork. Yet, at the end of shift, you know you did some good out there."

Kathy suddenly realized that her phrasing didn't refer to the officers in the third person, but in the more personal second person, as though she were part of the "you." She lowered her head, the animation of a moment ago disappeared. She felt self-conscious.

"You really want to be a cop," Steve said, with wonder.

She nodded. "Yes," she said avoiding his eyes.

Stunned, Steve said nothing. He sat and stared at the woman who remained a mystery to him, even after eighteen years of marriage. So many things raced through his mind that he couldn't think. He couldn't speak, for fear of saying the wrong thing.

Ride Along

Kathy grew uncomfortable with the silence. "I'm not hungry," she told him, as she stood up. "I'm going to lie down." She stepped away from the table.

Steve reached out and took hold of her arm. "We need to talk about this, honey."

"There's nothing to talk about unless I'm acquitted," she stated flatly.

"You will be! We have to believe that!"

"I wish I could."

Steve released her arm and Kathy left the room. He turned and watched her leave with her head down, shoulders slumped, with sadness and the acceptance of loss on her face. He didn't understand her desire to be a cop, but he hadn't missed her passion for it.

He turned back to the table. The thought of finishing his sandwich revolted him. He discarded it and cleared the table. Quietly, he went to the bedroom to check on Kathy.

* * * * *

She lay on the bed, her back toward the door, sobbing like a child heartbroken over the loss of their favorite toy. It was not as simple as a lost toy. She had many reasons for the tears. Steve had told her that he would rather she didn't ride with the officers. To her that was the same as if he had said "no." For the first time in their marriage, she wanted something bad enough to do it spite of Steve's objection. Always before, she deferred to his wishes. After all, this was the man who married her when she got pregnant, the man who supported her and the children, the man she would have married pregnant or not, the man she loved, respected, and desired. In the past, when he said he would rather she did not do something, she deferred to his wishes.

She had gone against his wishes to ride along with the officers. Look what it had cost—nights when Steve didn't sleep for worrying about her on the streets, the death of a man who left a widow and three children, and her arrest and trial. Because she had selfishly done what she wanted to do, Steve, the boys, and her entire family had suffered.

If she was acquitted he would say "no" again. She would acquiesce, not for lack of desire, but from guilt for all the pain she had caused everyone involved. Events had awakened her dream, then cruelly snatched it away.

* * * * *

Steve approached the bed. He lay down beside her and rolled her toward him. He held her in his arms while she cried herself out and fell asleep. He blamed himself for her tears. If he had not gotten her pregnant, she would have followed her dream. But would she have married him? He never doubted her love; he doubted his being good enough for her. Thrilled when she became pregnant with his child, he had given no thought to what she might be giving up to become his wife.

He blamed himself for the pain she was experiencing. How could he make it up to her? He couldn't bring himself to encourage her to become a cop. Yet, he had no right to insist that she not become one. He had to let her know how he felt about it, then leave the decision to her.

* * * * *

It was a quiet weekend. Avoiding any mention of the trial or Kathy's desire to be a cop, she and Steve spoke to each other only when necessary. Davy and Jake knew there was a problem and wondered if their parents had argued, or if it was just tension over the trial. Sensing it was a private matter, they didn't ask.

The weekend passed slowly, but it did pass.

Chapter 50

Monday, January 31, 1977 - 8:45 a.m.

Kathy, Steve, their sons, Davy and Jake, and Kathy's parents and sisters arrived at the courthouse. They were met at the basement entrance. Three officers waited to park their cars. Upstairs, the corridor outside the courtroom was so crowded that the officers had trouble clearing a path for Kathy and her family. Except for obscenities and shouts of "murderer," there were no incidents.

Inside the courtroom, the gallery was already full to capacity, except the front row on the defense side which the officers had reserved for Kathy's family. Ray Jackson's wife and family sat in the front row on the prosecution side. Some of the public managed to get seats behind them, but most of the prosecution side was filled with press and television reporters. The defense side was full of officers in uniform. More people stood in the space behind the last row of seats.

John turned to her. "Morning, Kathy."

"Good morning, John."

"The case will go to the jury today," he told her.

Kathy nodded that she understood. John turned back to his outline for his closing statement. At nine sharp, the bailiff called for all to rise, and Judge Harrison came in and took the bench.

"Be seated," Judge Harrison said as he sat down. "Were all the spectators searched?"

"Yes, Your Honor," the bailiff answered.

"I want to remind all of you that I will not stand for any disruption of these proceedings. Any demonstration will result in the participants being arrested *and jailed* for contempt of court." He gave the audience a moment to think about that. "Counselors," he addressed the attorneys, "are you both ready to proceed with your summations?" They both said they were. "Bring in the jury," he instructed.

As soon as the jury was seated, Judge Harrison turned to the prosecutor. "You may begin, Mr. Maddox."

"Thank you, Your Honor," Maddox said as he stood up. He approached the jury box.

"Good morning, ladies and gentlemen. Thank you for the attention you have given to this case.

"Serving on a jury is a duty and a responsibility. An inconvenient duty, yet an important part of our criminal justice system. Without it, the guilty would go free to commit other crimes. It also protects the innocent from undeserved incarceration. *You* accepted this duty and responsibility when you made yourselves available to serve.

"YOU will consider the facts in this case and render a verdict. YOU will decide if Kathleen Cooper is guilty or not guilty of committing murder when she shot Ray Jackson. YOU, a jury of her peers, will make that determination.

"Ray Jackson did not have an opportunity to have his case heard by a jury. His right to an impartial trial was taken away from him when Kathy Cooper pulled the trigger of the carbine and shot him dead. No chance to defend himself. No way to appeal her judgment. She chose to be his judge, jury, and executioner.

"According to the Texas Penal Code, a person commits murder if he or she intends to cause serious bodily harm to another and commits an act clearly dangerous to human life that causes the death of the other person.

"Kathy Cooper intentionally shot Ray Jackson. Shooting a person clearly indicates an intent to cause serious bodily harm. In this case, it resulted in Ray Jackson's death. Her actions fit the definition of murder.

"The defense claims that the shooting was justified because Ray Jackson had a piece of pipe in his hand and threatened to hit Officer Henson with it. This is not supported by the physical evidence.

"The shooting occurred at a construction site. It was logical for Kathy Cooper to invent a piece of pipe to justify her actions. No piece of pipe was found at the scene.

"When Officer Henson testified that he lost his flashlight during the struggle, the defense changed their story. It wasn't a piece of pipe; it was Officer Henson's flashlight. It is true that Ray Jackson's fingerprints were found on the flashlight.

"Did he intend to use it as a weapon? Not necessarily. He might have had any number of reasons for picking up the flashlight. Perhaps he was going to steal it. We have no way of knowing why he picked up the flashlight.

"No witnesses to this incident have been found. All we have is the testimony of the woman who killed Ray Jackson. There is no physical evidence to prove that her version of the incident is the truth.

"Why was she there in the first place? The practice of allowing grand jurors to ride with on-duty officers is dangerous. Putting civilians in police cars with unsecured weapons is worse than dangerous; it is asking for someone to get killed. And someone did. Ray Jackson got killed.

"Shot in the back, by a woman who was curious about police work. Officer Henson stated that having her ride along was like having a rookie to train. She testified that he treated her like the man-on-the-ground that night. She took notes for Officer Henson. She gave advice to one couple about filing an alert slip.

"Perhaps that was the problem. Perhaps she was beginning to think that she was a police officer. She had NOT been trained as a police officer. She was NOT a police officer. Consequently, she misinterpreted the situation.

"Ray Jackson died because Kathy Cooper was there, and because a rifle was unsecured in the police vehicle when the officer left it unattended. She chose to take the rifle out of the car instead of getting on the police radio and calling for help. She chose to shoot Ray Jackson.

"Kathy Cooper was familiar with guns and how to use them. She had practiced shooting targets for marksmanship. Four of the officers took her out in the county to shoot at beer cans. One of the four taught her how to use a thirty caliber carbine. We heard how she hit fifteen out of the sixteen beer cans she shot at. She could have shot to wound Ray Jackson. She didn't.

"Kathy Cooper aimed for the center of Ray Jackson's body. Her aim was true. This was a killing shot. Ray Jackson was dead. She gave him no opportunity to surrender. She gave him no chance to survive. She shot him in the back with no warning.

"Kathy Cooper admitted on the stand that she was prepared to shoot again. She admitted that she was willing to shoot the other two men also. Fortunately for them, they had an opportunity to surrender. Ray Jackson was not given that opportunity. He was just suddenly dead.

"Kathy Cooper intentionally shot Ray Jackson with the intent to cause serious bodily harm, which resulted in Ray Jackson's death.

"Give Ray Jackson justice! Find Kathy Cooper...guilty...of murder." He looked at the jury members for a moment, then went to the prosecutor's table and sat down.

Ray Jackson's widow was crying quietly. Spectators began to talk to each other in soft tones. Judge Harrison picked up his gavel. "Fifteen minute recess."

The jury filed out but no spectators moved from their seats. They sat talking quietly. Some of the officers cursed softly. Some people speculated on what the defense would say in response to the prosecutor's statement. Some quoted odds on the outcome. No laughter was heard and no smiles were seen.

Kathy, shivering at Mr. Maddox's harangue, hugged herself in an effort to get warm. Her mother rose and took off her sweater, leaned over the railing, and placed it around Kathy's shoulders. Kathy looked around, nodded, and slipped her arms into the sleeves of the sweater.

The short recess ended with a hush falling over the room when Judge Harrison returned to the bench. After he called for order, the jury once more filled the jury box. At Judge Harrison's nod, John Everett stood and walked to the jury box.

"Good morning." A few of the jurors acknowledged his greeting by nodding their heads. "Justice, ladies and gentlemen. We're here to serve justice. The word justification is derived from the word justice. The circumstances and facts in this case provide justification for Kathleen Mavis Cooper's actions.

"Justification as a defense is defined in the Texas Penal Code as, 'It is a defense to prosecution that the conduct in question is justified under Chapter Nine, in using force or deadly force against another to protect a third person if the actor reasonably believes that his intervention is immediately necessary to protect the third person.'

"Consider the circumstances. Officer Henson was attacked by three men. Can one man win a fight against three? Only in the movies! This was not a movie! This was real. This was happening right in front of Kathy Cooper. It was happening quickly. How much time passed from the moment Kathy saw the other two men and the moment Ray Jackson raised something over his head to strike Officer Henson?

"Kathy saw the men appear. She didn't like the odds. She reached in the car, grabbed the radio microphone, straightened up, then saw the three men jump Officer Henson and take him to the ground. She dropped the mike, grabbed the rifle, took it from the car, and jacked a round into the chamber. She saw Ray Jackson raise something over his head to strike Officer Henson. She raised the rifle to her shoulder, took aim, and squeezed the trigger.

"How much time did it take for these events to occur? Think about it." He gave the jury a moment to consider. "Seconds, ladies and gentlemen. Seconds is all the time Kathy Cooper had to decide a course of action.

"In the heat of the moment, she thought the object in Ray Jackson's hand was a piece of pipe." Demonstrating with his hands, John repeated Kathy's description. "She testified that the object was about this long, this big around, and dark in color. Officer Henson's flashlight fits that description.

"We know Ray Jackson picked up the flashlight. His fingerprints were found on it. Why would a man pick up a flashlight in the middle of a fight? To use it as a weapon! All of you handled it. You felt the weight of it. Imagine what damage a forceful blow with that flashlight would have done to Officer Henson." Again John paused.

"Kathy Cooper believed that without immediate intervention, Officer Henson would suffer serious bodily injury, or even death. She was the only person who *could* intervene. She did the only thing she could do to stop the attack before serious bodily injury to Officer Henson occurred. She took aim and fired the rifle to keep Ray Jackson from striking with the flashlight.

"Kathy Cooper responded to the circumstances to protect a person who could not protect himself. She did *not* intend to kill Ray Jackson. She intended to *prevent* Ray Jackson from killing Officer Henson. Because Kathy Cooper chose to defend his life, Officer Henson is alive today.

"The circumstances justify this shooting. Kathleen Mavis Cooper is…not…guilty…of murder." John met the eyes of each and every juror individually. "Thank you for your attention." He turned, walked back to the defense table, and sat down.

The courtroom was totally silent. When Judge Harrison spoke, it seemed to break a spell.

"Mr. Maddox, your rebuttal."

"Yes, sir." Mr. Maddox rose and slowly went to the jury box. He was thinking hard.

"Undoubtedly the events of that Sunday morning unfolded in seconds. How many seconds does it take to shout, 'Stop, or I'll shoot?' With that warning Ray Jackson could have surrendered. He was given no warning. No opportunity to surrender.

"Kathy Cooper shot Ray Jackson without warning. She shot him in the back.

"Ladies and gentlemen, that's murder." He paused, then said, "Thank you." Mr. Maddox returned to his seat.

Judge Harrison looked around the courtroom. "Ladies and gentlemen of the jury, the next step in this case will be my instructions to you before you begin deliberating. Since it is nearing the noon hour, we will recess until two o'clock. Bailiffs will clear the courtroom during the recess."

Kathy and all her family waited for the courtroom to clear. Officers waited for escort duty. Not four as usual, but ten officers waited. They announced their intention to escort all of Kathy's family to the underground entrance where they would be taken to a place for lunch.

Downstairs, three cars were waiting for them. They left with two officers and three members of the family in each car. They were taken to the Spaghetti Warehouse, where the six officers stood guard on the private dining room occupied by Kathy and her extended family. It wasn't a party, but it had a hopeful feeling about it. They discussed the closing arguments. All agreed that John Everett's closing argument was powerful.

Kathy agreed. Still, she had doubts about the verdict, in spite of her family's efforts to assure her that she would be acquitted. She enjoyed having everyone together, in spite of being able to eat very little because of her state of mind.

Chapter 51

Monday, January 31, 1977 - 1:50 p.m.

The hall outside the courtroom was crowded when Kathy and her family returned from lunch, but the people parted and allowed her group to pass without comment or incident. Inside, the courtroom was again full. As she passed, several of the officers spoke words of encouragement. Their belief in her meant a lot to her, but it didn't relieve the knot in her stomach.

Judge Harrison didn't waste any time getting things started. As soon as the jury was seated, he began his instructions to them.

"Ladies and gentlemen, in a few minutes you will retire to the jury room to decide on a verdict in this case, to decide if Kathleen Mavis Cooper is guilty or not guilty of the murder of Ray Jackson. In order to make that decision, you must first understand the elements of the offense charged against the accused, and laws applicable to the case.

"The indictment states, 'In the name and by authority of The State of Texas, this indictment is presented to the One hundred and eighty-seventh District Court of Harris County by the Grand Jury, alleging that Kathleen Mavis Cooper committed murder on Sunday, September 26, 1976, at about 5:10 a.m., at Five Thousand Georgi Lane in Houston, Harris County, Texas, when the accused, with intent to cause serious bodily injury, shot the victim, Ray Jackson, with a thirty caliber carbine, causing his death, against the peace and dignity of the State.'

"The prosecution is required to prove each and every element of the offense charged, beyond a reasonable doubt. The Texas Penal Code defines Proof Beyond a Reasonable Doubt as, 'All persons are presumed to be innocent, and no person may be convicted of an offense unless each element of the offense is proved beyond a reasonable doubt. The fact that he or she has been arrested, confined or indicted for, or otherwise charged with the offense gives rise to no inference of guilt at his or her trial.'

"The defense is alleging justification as a defense to prosecution in this case. The Texas Penal Code on Justification as a Defense states, 'It is a defense to prosecution that the conduct in question is justified under this Chapter Nine.'

"The Texas Penal Code states 'A person is justified in using force or deadly force against another to protect a third person if, under the circumstances as the actor reasonably believes them to be, the actor would be justified under Section 9.31 in using force or deadly force to protect himself against the unlawful force or unlawful deadly force he reasonably believes to be threatening the third person he seeks to protect, and the actor reasonably believes that his intervention is immediately necessary to protect the third person.'

"The Texas Penal Code further defines Burden of Proof as, 'A defense to prosecution for an offense in this code is so labeled by the phrase {It is a defense to prosecution...}. The prosecuting attorney is not required to negate the existence of a defense in the accusation charging commission of the offense. The issue of the existence of a defense is not submitted to the jury unless evidence is admitted supporting the defense. If the issue of the existence of a defense is submitted to the jury, the court shall charge that a reasonable doubt on the issue requires that the defendant be acquitted.'

"To put it simply, ladies and gentlemen, to return a verdict of 'guilty,' the prosecution must have proved beyond a reasonable doubt each and every element of the charge of murder as stated in the indictment, and the defense must have failed to create a reasonable doubt with evidence presented for the defense to prosecution of justification.

"If any reasonable doubt as to the elements of the offense and/or the defense to prosecution exists, you must acquit the defendant by returning a verdict of 'not guilty.'

"The verdict must be unanimous. All twelve of you must agree.

"Are there any questions at this time?"

Many in the jury box shook their heads. No one raised a hand to ask a question.

"If you have any questions during your deliberations, you will put them in writing. The bailiff will bring them to me and return with my answer. Any questions?"

Again, no hand was raised.

"You may retire to the jury room to deliberate at this time."

Kathy was impressed with the way Judge Harrison explained things to the jury. She watched as the jury left the courtroom, trying to get a feel for what they were thinking. The jurors all looked solemn and serious, as though they understood the duty placed upon them, but showing no clue to their feelings or opinions.

Her future was in their hands. She tried to resign herself to the possibility that she would be convicted. At this point, she just wanted it over, an end to the uncertainty.

Judge Harrison remained on the bench. With the help of one of his clerks, he began to process some paperwork. The spectators started talking in muted voices. Occasionally one would leave the room and promptly be replaced by someone else.

Kathy tried talking quietly with her family, but she couldn't hold a thought long enough to carry on a conversation. She felt more in limbo than she had at any time since the shooting. Her emotional state was chaotic: worrying about the verdict, hoping it would be not guilty, and horrified at the thought of being found guilty and the family seeing her handcuffed and removed from the courtroom. The thought of returning to jail was sickening.

The scene of the shooting, the aftermath, her arrest, processing at the jail, and the trial played over and over in her head. She couldn't turn it off no matter how she tried to distract herself. The waiting for the trial to begin was nothing compared to the torture of this moment. She had chosen to be tried by twelve and now wondered if it was the correct choice.

John Everett had taken a book of New York Times crossword puzzles from his briefcase and was working one, in ink, seemingly unconcerned about the verdict.

Kathy wished she could be as unconcerned.

The atmosphere of the courtroom was something like a funeral. People talked in low voices. Her family exchanged comforting words. There was no comfort for Kathy. The hell of waiting continued. It felt like time had stopped. The hands on the clock appeared not to move. Kathy wondered if it was broken, but it wasn't. The adrenaline in her system had sped up her perceptions, making things only appear to slow down.

She thought she would scream if something didn't happen soon. One moment she wanted to cuss and throw things and the next she fought back tears. She regretted putting her family through this, but she knew she would have regretted the alternative more. She turned to look at the officers sitting behind her family and saw Calvin Henson smile and nod reassuringly.

Abruptly she turned away. The grip on her emotions was too fragile to risk looking at him again. She excused herself to go to the ladies room to wash her face and try to break the tension by doing something physical. She was drying her face when there was a knock on the door.

"Mrs. Cooper, you need to return to the courtroom. The jury has reached a verdict."

She opened the door. "Thank you." She walked past the bailiff and returned to her seat on legs that she had trouble making work properly. They felt all disconnected somehow. John held the chair for her as she sat down.

Judge Harrison called for order and the spectators settled down. "Ladies and gentlemen, the jury has informed me that they have reached a verdict. When the verdict is read I will tolerate no disturbance in this courtroom. If necessary, I request that the Houston officers present assist the bailiffs in maintaining order and in clearing the courtroom as quickly as possible."

Sergeants Watson and Strong both rose and consented to Judge Harrison's request.

Judge Harrison motioned for the jury to be brought in. When they were seated, he asked the foreman if they had reached a verdict. The foreman stated that they had. The form the jury was required to fill out was passed to Judge Harrison by the bailiff.

When Judge Harrison looked at it, his expression revealed nothing. He passed the form to the bailiff to be returned to the jury foreman. All the while, Kathy was afraid she would lose what little lunch she had managed to force down. She swallowed several times.

"The defendant will rise," Judge Harrison ordered.

Kathy struggled to her feet, unsure if her legs would hold her because they were shaking so badly. John stood beside her, took her hand, and held it. All the officers got to their feet, too, as though they were also on trial.

"Foreman of the jury, will you read the verdict, please."

"Yes, Your Honor. In the matter of the murder of Ray Jackson, this jury finds the defendant, Kathleen Mavis Cooper...NOT guilty."

Relief took all the strength from her legs. Steve vaulted the railing to catch her. Ray Jackson's widow wailed like a wounded cat. The press bolted for the courtroom doors leading to the phones in the hall. The officers broke into applause and cheers. Kathy's family hugged and cried and laughed. Judge Harrison smiled and indulged in the reaction for a moment before pounding his gavel and demanding order.

Steve held Kathy as she dissolved into tears of relief and joy. When she slowed down and began to smile, he took out his handkerchief and wiped her face tenderly. He raised her chin and kissed her, then turned to shake hands with John and say thank you.

Slowly order was restored.

"Mr. Everett," Judge Harrison said, "is there anything else?"

John turned to Judge Harrison. "Yes, Your Honor. I'd like to petition the court to expunge all records of this case."

"Granted, with pleasure," Judge Harrison proclaimed and then turned to the jury. "Ladies and gentlemen, thank you for your service in this matter. You are excused. Court's adjourned."

The officers formed a barrier around Kathy and her family to exclude the public and press. The jurors stepped from the jury box and several came over to shake Kathy's hand. She thanked each one.

Turning to John, Kathy hugged him. "I can't thank you enough," she said.

"You're welcome," he replied with a smile.

"Is the defense fund going to be enough to cover your fee?"

"There is no fee. This was a pro bono case."

Kathy was stunned. "That's not right!"

"Indicting you for murder wasn't right. I believe you did the right thing. My father was a cop. He was killed in a similar situation, while people who saw it did nothing."

Kathy gasped as she thought of how painful this case must have been for him. "Oh, John. I'm sorry. I didn't know."

John squeezed her hand. "It was a long time ago, Kathy. I've gotten over it."

When the crowd thinned out, many of the officers stepped forward to speak to Kathy. Three of them asked for the keys, locations, and descriptions of the family cars. Ten remained to escort Kathy and her family to their cars. They were Calvin Henson, Dean Driskell, Bob Richmond, Sergeants Watson and Strong, Art Donahue, Dan Cannon, Fred Oaks, Donald Wells, and John Bailey; officers who taught her the most during her riding along.

With hugs and smiles, Kathy and her family left the courtroom.

It was over, finally, to everyone's relief—except Steve's.

Chapter 52

Tuesday, February 1, 1977 - 6:30 a.m.

When the alarm went off, Kathy woke with a start, then sighed deeply. The trial was over. Her life could get back to normal. She headed for the kitchen to start coffee, breakfast, and lunches for Steve and the boys.

"Morning, honey," he said, as he entered the kitchen.

"Good morning."

Steve poured a cup of coffee, went to the table, and started reading the paper. Shortly after, the boys joined him at the table. Kathy put breakfast on the table. Steve opened the morning newspaper, took out the sports section, and passed the rest to the boys. Jake grabbed the section with the funnies. Davy checked out the city and state news section.

"Mom made the paper again!" Davy informed everyone. "Second section, page three," he added with disgust. "When you got indicted, it made the front page. Now that you've been acquitted, they bury the story!"

"That's not fair!" Jake exclaimed.

"You're not news anymore, honey," Steve said with a smile.

Kathy nodded. "Thank God."

After breakfast, Kathy cleaned up the kitchen while Steve and the boys got their things together for work and school.

"Take it easy today. Get some rest," Steve told her when he was ready to leave. With a hug and kiss, he left for work.

Shortly after Steve left, the boys left for school. Kathy made another cup of tea and sat down to read the paper. She read the brief article telling of her acquittal on the murder charge for the shooting death of Ray Jackson. This article did include information about his past criminal record and time served in prison. After dressing and getting the laundry started, she left for the supermarket.

After getting the groceries home and put away, she went to the study to check on the bills. They were up to date. The notebook containing her notes from riding along caught her eye. She still hadn't typed up her notes from the last two nights on the streets. She picked up her notepad and started reading the notes of those last two nights. They ended just before the shooting.

Again, events replayed in her mind—the shooting, her arrest, the trial, and the way the officers supported her during the trial. I must find a way to thank them, she thought. Homemade cookies? Not enough. Once they were eaten, they would be forgotten. Something lasting. She smiled. I know just the thing. She reached for her notebook.

Kathy spent the next couple hours going through the notes, making a list of all the officers she had ridden with, and their badge numbers. A letter of commendation naming all the officers would be lasting. It would go in their permanent personnel files. List complete, she started the letter and had a good rough draft by the time the boys got home from school. She finished it and called HPD to make an appointment to deliver it personally to Chief Ledford.

Chapter 53

Thursday, February 3, 1977 - 9:50 a.m.

When she arrived at Central just before ten, the front parking lot was nearly full, but she found a place next to a police unit. She entered the first floor lobby from the main entrance. The atmosphere was familiar and comfortable, but busier than she had seen it before. She looked, without success, for a familiar face among the many officers moving through the lobby.

Kathy pushed the button for the elevator and looked through the doors into Records while she waited. Unlike her visits on the evening and night shifts, every desk was occupied. She could hear telephones ringing and typewriters clattering as the clerks worked.

She rode the elevator to the third floor and walked down the left-hand hall to the chief's office. The receptionist told her that he would be with her shortly. Kathy took a seat. After only a few minutes the Chief's door opened. He escorted an officer out and approached her.

"Mrs. Cooper," he greeted her warmly. "Come in," he said as he motioned to his office. He shut the door behind them. "Mrs. Cooper, this department owes you a debt. What can I do for you?" he asked.

"Call me Kathy."

He nodded.

"I just wanted to deliver this in person," she said, holding out the envelope containing the letter, "and thank you for the opportunity to ride along."

"Sit down, Kathy. How are you doing?" he asked as he opened the envelope and withdrew the folded sheets of paper while meeting her eyes.

"Better, now that the trial is over."

Chief Ledford nodded, sat down, unfolded the letter, and began to read. At the bottom of the first page were two columns of officers' names and badge numbers. He nodded and turned to the next page where the columns continued. His mouth fell open and he looked up at her. "How many officers did you ride with?"

"Twenty-eight."

"That's remarkable," he told her. "Most women are scared to ride along."

"I was scared a couple of times."

"The shooting?"

Kathy nodded. "I was scared that I couldn't move fast enough to stop him."

"I know that feeling," he stated. "You said a couple times."

"The other time I was scared of you," she said with a mischievous smile.

"Me? Why?" he asked, mystified.

"I had to put out an *assist* one night. I was afraid that if you found out about it, you'd make me stop riding along."

He put the letter down. "What happened?"

"Sergeant Ralph Strong and I stopped to check a man in a car stopped at an intersection with the motor running. He was drunk and came out fighting...."

After Kathy completed her story, the chief told a story. Story followed story, as they slipped into the language that was so natural in telling about the streets. They talked, joked, and reminisced like old friends with a common history. Thirty minutes passed quickly, and Kathy realized she had taken more of the Chief's time than she should. She rose to leave.

"Have you ever thought about becoming an officer?" he asked as he got to his feet.

"Ever since I was six years old."

"We could use you."

"I'm past HPD's age limit," she said plaintively.

"You're kidding!"

"I'm thirty-six."

"There are other places. Have you considered the Sheriff's Department?"

"Not really. HPD would be my first choice."

"Then come in the back door."

"What back door?" she demanded.

"Two or three years with the Sheriff's Department with a good record and you can get in HPD as a Modified Entry Officer."

"Regardless of age?"

"Within reason. You'd still have to pass all the requirements—medical exam and drug testing, physical agility, polygraph, background check, psychological…Kathy, have you seen a counselor about the shooting?"

She nodded. "A woman. I wasn't comfortable talking to her about the streets. It wasn't helping, so I quit going."

"I'm going to have the department counselor call you," he informed her as he reached for a pen and a piece of paper. "What's your number?" She told him. "His name is Carter Walters. He can help. He used to be a street cop."

"I thought he only saw officers?"

"He'll see *you*."

"Thank you, sir," she said, deeply touched by his thoughtfulness.

He took her hand and held it. "You're welcome. Call me anytime, if I can help."

She nodded, turned, and walked to the door. He held it open for her as she left.

As she drove home, Kathy thought of the officers who told her she would make a good cop; officers she admired and respected. If she could get in with the Sheriff's Office and make it through their training, it would open that back door to HPD. I need to quit thinking in terms of "if I can," she thought. I need to decide to do it, and do it.

Still, she had to consider Steve's feelings about it, and she thought she knew what that would be. He would rather she didn't do it. Was she strong enough to go against his wishes and still keep their relationship from being affected adversely? She wanted to be a cop, but not at the expense of her marriage and family. What to do?

Shortly after she arrived home, Carter Walters called, and she made an appointment to see him the next morning. She hoped he could help stop the nightmares.

Chapter 54

Thursday, February 3, 1977 - 7:15 p.m.

Kathy approached Steve in the family room. "Can we talk?" she asked.

He had been expecting this since the trial ended. He knew what she wanted to talk about, and he knew it couldn't be avoided or ignored, as much as he wished it could be. He stood up and followed her to the study.

Davey and Jake exchanged glances, both wondering what was going on now.

In the study, a table and two chairs formed a sitting area in one corner. This was a favorite spot of Kathy's. She often sat and read in this corner. They each took a seat. Steve sat silently, waiting for Kathy to speak.

She spoke softly, hesitantly. "I…ah…saw…Police Chief Ledford this morning. I wrote a letter of commendation for the men I rode with and…wanted to deliver it personally. We talked. He is arranging for me to talk with a department counselor about the shooting."

"That's good," Steve offered.

"We also talked about…he suggested that…I found out there's a back door to HPD."

"Back door?"

"If I become a Deputy Sheriff with two or three years' experience and a good record, I can transfer to HPD."

"I don't understand. Why the Sheriff's Department?"

"Because I'm past HPD's age limit. The Sheriff's Department has no age limit." Kathy watched as a frown gathered between his eyebrows.

Steve looked away and leaned back in his chair. "There's no hurry then. You can wait until the boys are out of school."

"Jake will graduate in three years," Kathy said thoughtfully.

"I was thinking until they were out of college," Steve stated, looking at her.

"I'll be in my mid-forties!"

"So?"

Kathy looked away and sat back in her chair. I want it now, she told herself, not seven years from now. She shook her head. Three years, maybe, not seven.

Steve watched her consider. He could almost read her thoughts from the expression on her face. When she looked up he saw determination.

"In three years the boys will both be in college. They won't be home except on weekends and summers. Why should I be here at the house when I could be working, earning money to help with their college expenses?" she asked.

"We can afford to put the boys through college without you going to work."

"I know that. But it would make it easier. Or we could save more for our retirement." She could see that Steve wasn't buying it. "Why don't you just say you would rather I didn't become a cop!"

"You know that already."

"Yes, I do," she said, defeated, lowering her head to hide her disappointment.

Steve watched her slump in the chair. She wants it so bad. She's wanted it for a long time.

"Why?" she asked, looking up at him again.

Steve took a deep breath and sighed. "Isn't it obvious? I want you safe. The streets are dangerous."

"I wouldn't be on the streets. They're not assigning women to patrol!"

"Where are they assigned?"

"Juvenile, matrons in the jail, clerical positions in different divisions."

Steve was thoughtful for a moment. "I just want you to be safe."

"I know."

"I don't want you on the streets anymore."

"I understand," Kathy said.

"Can you wait until Jake graduates?"

"From high school?"

He nodded, reluctantly.

She sighed. Three years. I've waited this long. I can wait a little longer. She nodded. "Okay," she said. "I'll wait until Jake graduates from high school."

Their eyes met. They both nodded, got up from the chairs, and left the study, neither of them totally happy with the compromise. Steve hoped that in the next three years something would prevent her from becoming an officer. It made him feel like a cad. He wanted her to be happy, but he also wanted her safe.

Kathy was pleased they had reached an agreement without a heated argument. Not that she and Steve had ever had a heated argument. They had disagreed a few times, but she always deferred to him. She had done it again tonight, and wondered if she had the patience to wait.

Chapter 55

Friday, February 4, 1977 - 9:00 a.m.

Through the open doorway, Kathy entered the reception area outside Carter Walters' office. The small area was nearly filled by a desk and a couple of chairs. Nobody was at the desk. The inner door was closed. Should I knock on the door, or just take a seat, she wondered. The inner door opened before she decided.

"Mrs. Cooper?" a man in uniform inquired.

"Yes."

"I'm Lieutenant Walters," he said, extending his hand.

The lieutenant was in his mid-fifties and stood about six feet tall, with thinning salt-and-pepper hair and warm brown eyes in a fair-complected oval face. His well-shaped lips were partially hidden by a full brown mustache, carefully trimmed even with the corners of his mouth. He had kept in shape. The uniform fit him well.

"Come in, please," he requested. He stepped back and held the door open for her to enter, then closed it. "Have a seat," he said, motioning to a group of overstuffed easy chairs. "Would you like some coffee?" he asked in a pleasant baritone as he moved to a small kitchen area along the wall on the right.

"No, thanks. I don't drink coffee."

"A soft drink?"

"Yes, please."

Opening the fridge, he gave her a choice of three brands. As he filled a glass with ice cubes and opened the soda she chose, Kathy looked around the small room, which was softly lit from partially closed blinds on windows facing north. The colors in the room were restful, and the lamps, tables, and plants added a homey touch. It was a comfortable room. She looked at the framed certificates and diplomas on the walls.

"You're a psychologist, not a psychiatrist?"

"That's correct," he confirmed.

"Then you can't prescribe pills?"

"Do you want pills?"

"No, I don't."

"Good," he said, handing her the soda. "Go ahead and sit down." He returned to the kitchen area and poured a cup of coffee for himself.

Kathy looked at the chairs. "Which chair is yours?" she asked.

With cup in hand, he approached her. "Take your pick. They're all the same."

Kathy stepped to the one nearest the door, rather than one of the others which were located in corners, sat down, and sipped her soda.

He sat across from her and sampled his coffee. He waited for her to say something. When she didn't, he asked, "Mrs. Cooper…may I call you Kathy?"

"Yes, of course."

"How can I help you, Kathy?"

"I killed a man."

"You saved an officer's life."

"I was arrested and tried for murder."

"You were acquitted."

"Yeah. Well, you know what the public thinks."

"What do they think?"

"I got away with murder."

"Do you think you did?"

"I don't know. It's all mixed up," she said with a big shrug.

"We'll sort it out," he stated.

She sensed his sincere desire to help her. His gentle, friendly manner put her at ease. He had worked the streets as a cop. He would understand her feelings. She could talk to this man.

She nodded. "Where do we start?' she asked.

"With the shooting. Tell me about it."

Once more, Kathy told of that Sunday morning. She had been over it so many times that to her it sounded like a recitation. She stared at a point somewhere between herself and the windows behind the lieutenant. "I got on the radio and called for help. It seemed to take forever for them to get there," she concluded.

"How did you feel at that moment?"

"Relief. Concern for Calvin. How bad was he hurt? Then someone said he was dead. I thought they meant Calvin but they didn't. He was going to be all right. The man I shot was dead. I wanted to see for myself. He was lying on his back, his eyes and mouth wide open." Kathy closed her eyes at the memory.

"What did you feel at that moment?"

"I don't remember feeling anything. I was shaking and crying—and tired. I just wanted to go home and sleep." She paused. "I felt it was all my fault."

"Why?"

She sighed. "If I hadn't pointed out that it was five o'clock on a *Sunday* morning, Calvin would have dropped me off at home, patrolled a little longer, and OD-ed. It was my fault he went back to check. And it nearly got him killed.

"I've gone over it and over it and I keep wondering, did I miss something? Was there another way to stop it?" She looked up at him.

"Was there?"

She shook her head. "I don't think so. When the two other men appeared, if I had called for back-up it would have taken time that I needed to get the rifle, jack a round into the chamber, take aim, and fire. Too much time. He would have hit Calvin with the flashlight. And back-up wouldn't have gotten there in time to help.

"If I had tried to shoot the flashlight out of his hand or shoot him in the arm or leg, I might have missed him completely. I couldn't take that chance. With Calvin already unconscious, if I had hollered 'Stop or I'll shoot!' they might have rushed me. I doubt I would've been able to stop all three of 'em."

"Did you consider those options while it was happening?"

"Not consciously. I just reacted. I didn't have any choice. I didn't mean to kill him!"

He nodded in understanding. "Knowing you had no choice, how do you feel about Ray Jackson being dead?"

"I'm sorry he's dead, but…"

"But?"

"I'd never forgive myself if I'd let him kill Calvin."

"So you feel you did the right thing?"

"On a logical level, yes. Emotionally, I keep trying to second-guess myself; To find some way I could have avoided killing him—even though I know there wasn't any way and nothing is going to change the fact that he's dead. So if that's true, why am I having the nightmare?"

"*The* nightmare?"

"Yeah. The same one over and over."

"Tell me about it."

"It's a replay of the shooting, except when I shoot, I miss. He hits Calvin in the head with the flashlight and…" Kathy closed her eyes at the image in her mind, "and Calvin's head breaks open like a cantaloupe." She looked up at the Lieutenant. "I wake up screaming."

"Why do you think you're having the dream?"

"I don't know."

"Ask yourself, what does it mean?"

"It doesn't mean anything. It didn't happen that way."

"Is it trying to tell you something?"

"What?"

"Think about it. And think about what we've talked about today. Next week we'll talk about the dream."

Kathy looked at her watch. The time had gone so fast. She got to her feet as he also rose from his chair.

"Same time next Friday?"

She nodded. "Yes, thank you, Lieutenant."

"You're welcome, Kathy."

He opened the door for her and she walked away, her thoughts mixed but not as chaotic as in the past few months. He had said they would sort it out. Kathy began to believe they could.

*****

Friday, February 4, 1977 - 6:15 p.m.

At the supper table, Kathy told Steve of her session with Carter Walters. She explained that she was comfortable with him.

"He's easy to talk to," Kathy stated.

"I'm glad," Steve said, wishing she would talk to him. He stopped eating and stared at Kathy while he wondered what thoughts and feelings about the shooting she was holding back. Were they so horrific that she felt she couldn't share them with him? Was she afraid he wouldn't understand? That they would in some way cause him to stop loving her?

The boys were telling them about their day at school and their plans for the weekend. Kathy looked up at Steve suddenly.

Caught, Steve smiled guiltily, lowered his eyes to his plate, and began unnecessarily cutting up his pork chop into even smaller pieces.

There it is again, Kathy thought. That look, as if he wonders who I am. She had seen that same look on the faces of some friends and neighbors, some of whom had literally backed away from her. What is he thinking, she wondered. Are we ever going to get past this?

The atmosphere at the table had changed. The boys sensed it and exchanged looks of concern. They also knew that things had changed with the shooting. The tension of the past months had affected them all. Davey feared it was going to destroy his parents' marriage. Jake missed his parents' energetic, happy relationship of the past. Both boys wondered if things would ever return to normal.

Chapter 56

Monday, February 7, 1977 - 1:30 p.m.

Kathy had promised Steve she would wait until Jake graduated from high school before pursuing a law enforcement career. However, over the weekend she got to wondering about the Sheriff's Department. Were the requirements similar to HPD's? Was there a physical agility test she must pass? What about other tests? And documents? Height and weight? She wanted more information. When the time came to apply, she wanted to be ready with all the necessary paperwork, documents, and whatever else was required. That meant contacting the Sheriff's Department and finding someone willing to take the time to talk to her face-to-face and answer her questions.

With a couple of phones calls, Kathy found the right person. She met with Sarah Beaumont, a female deputy, at the county courthouse. Deputy Beaumont was near Kathy's age, about five feet eight inches tall, with brown hair worn in a short curly cut and expressive green eyes. She greeted Kathy warmly and led her to a small private office.

"So you're interested in becoming a deputy sheriff?" Sarah Beaumont asked.

"Yes, I am," Kathy confirmed. "I'd like to find out about the qualifications, application process, and anything else you can tell me."

"At the moment we aren't hiring. In fact, there are no plans for an academy class this year."

"I couldn't apply right now anyway."

"Oh?"

"I promised my husband that I wouldn't until the boys graduate from high school."

"When will that be?"

"Three years."

"I see." Deputy Beaumont opened a drawer in her desk and pulled out an information packet. "This will answer a lot of your questions," she told Kathy as she handed her the packet.

"Can you give me an idea of what the requirements are?"

"Sure. Applicants must be twenty-one years old, provide a statement from a doctor that they are in good health, have a psychological evaluation, be a citizen, have a valid Texas driver's license, a clean credit report, and a stable work history, and pass the agility and drug tests."

"A stable work history will be a problem. I haven't worked since I got married, nineteen years ago."

Deputy Beaumont considered for a moment. "If you got a job now and held it for a year or more, I think that we could make allowances for you."

"Make allowances?"

"Let's just say considering your history, you'll make a good Deputy."

Kathy nodded with understanding. It's the shooting. Would everyone she met from now on remember only that she killed a man?

"All the things that came out about you in the trial prove you'd make a good cop. Any police agency in the county would be honored to have you apply."

Then it hit Kathy. The deputy was looking at her as a heroine while she was still thinking of herself as a killer. That realization left her stunned and confused.

Kathy stood. "Thank you for this," she said, holding up the information packet. "I'll take a look at it." Kathy started to turn to walk away.

"Mrs. Cooper?" Deputy Beaumont realized she had made Kathy uncomfortable but she didn't know how.

"Yes."

"Call me anytime you have a question. If you'd like to tour some of our facilities, or ride along, let me know. I'd be glad to arrange it."

Kathy looked up sharply at the mention of riding along. Her heart skipped a beat or two. She held out her hand. "I will. Thank you."

"You're welcome, Mrs. Cooper." Deputy Beaumont shook Kathy's hand and wondered what she had said wrong.

Kathy left the Sheriff's Department Offices and the County Courthouse. When she reached her car in the parking garage, she sat for several minutes. Deputy Beaumont's words came back to her: "We could make allowances for you…considering your history, you'll make a good Deputy."

I'm not some kind of heroine, Kathy thought. The vivid memory of the bullet entering Ray Jackson's body and blood flying from the wound flashed through her mind. She closed her eyes not wanting to see, but it didn't help.

It was ugly! It was killing! How could anyone think that was heroic? The officers who came to court, is that why they came? Because they thought of her as a heroine? She had thought it was out of friendship, but was it? She did what she had to do. Still, she regretted that her shot had killed.

She forced herself to breathe slowly and deeply. It was several minutes before she started the car and drove home. The nightmare came again that night for the first time since she had seen Lieutenant Walters.

Chapter 57

Friday, February 11, 1977 - 8:55 a.m.

Kathy and Carter Walters settled down with coffee for him and a soda for Kathy. She took one of the corner chairs this time, feeling comfortable with him and the surroundings.

"Well, Kathy, how did your week go?"

"It was okay."

"But?"

Kathy sighed and thought a moment. "I talked to a deputy at the Sheriff's recruiting office. I've wanted to be a cop since I was a little girl."

"Why the Sheriff's Department? Why not here?"

"I'm past the age limit."

"Oh, I see."

"Steve wants me to wait until the boys are out of high school. I went to the Sheriff's Office to get some information about requirements and qualifications."

"Uh huh."

"One of the things I'll need is a stable work history. When I told the deputy I hadn't worked since I married, she said that if I got a job and held it for a year or more they could make allowances for me."

"So?"

"And she said some other stuff, too, about any agency being honored to have me apply." Kathy paused. "What about all the officers who came to court during the trial? Did you know they escorted Steve and me to and from the courtroom?"

"Yes, I did."

"And Chief Ledford arranging for me to see you. You're here for the officers. I'm a civilian. Am I getting special treatment because I…" Kathy stopped as memories of the shooting flashed through her mind.

"Because you what?"

"Killed Ray Jackson?"

"Do you think so?"

"They seem to be treating me like I'm some sort of a hero."

"What do you think you are?"

"Not a hero. A hero is someone who risks their life for something."

"Or someone who saves a life?"

Kathy shrugged. "I did what I had to do. That doesn't make me a hero. I'm uncomfortable with that."

"How often do you give yourself credit for what you do right?"

Kathy considered for a moment. "Is that what they're doing? Giving me credit for saving Calvin Henson's life?"

"Would you be more comfortable if they only looked at you as a killer?"

"No." She shook her head.

"That's what you've been doing, isn't it?"

She nodded. "I guess it is. I need to remember that Calvin's alive and stop thinking about the killing part."

He nodded.

"I'm just not used to being treated special."

"I know."

"I had the nightmare again that night."

"Which night?"

"After going to the Sheriff's Office."

"And?"

"I woke up. I wasn't screaming this time. I didn't even wake Steve. He slept right through it. You told me to think about the dream and try to figure out what it meant."

"Uh huh. Have you thought about it?"

"Yes, but I don't know if I've figured it out. When I woke up, I kept telling myself it didn't happen. Calvin's alive. It didn't happen. I stopped it. The good guy's alive. The bad guy's dead."

"Uh huh."

"It's the same thing isn't it? It's telling me I did the right thing."

He nodded.

"That makes sense," she said with a nod.

For the first time, he saw her smile, and he knew she had reached the point of understanding and acceptance. Still, it would take time for her to adjust.

Kathy folded her arms across her chest and got a thoughtful look on her face.

"What else is bothering you, Kathy?"

"What makes you think something else is bothering me?"

"Your body language."

"Oh." She unfolded her arms and frowned. "It's Steve. Every once in a while I catch him staring at me as though I'm a stranger."

"Why would he do that?"

"It was probably a shock for him to learn that his wife—the mother of his children—was capable of killing."

"And you think he's disturbed by this?"

"What man wouldn't be?"

"Why do you think it disturbs him?"

"It's a side of me he's never seen."

"Tell me about that side."

She hesitated a moment and sighed. "Looking back, I realize that when I left the house and got in the car to ride along, I took on a different personality. I don't know how to explain it."

He waited.

"After riding a couple of times, it was like I was one of the boys. I guess you'd call it my 'tomboy' side. The masculine side. For example, the men would bring pictures from accidents, murders, and suicides to roll call. Someone always said 'let Kathy see 'em.'

"One was a suicide by shotgun under the chin. It showed a man lying on the bed, with his lower legs hanging down from the end. The barrel of a gun pointed toward the ceiling between the man's knees. About two feet from the top of the man's head, a pink lump the size of a large grapefruit lay on the bedspread. It was his brain. From another angle, it showed that the inside of the man's head was empty.

"They kept testing me. I always looked at the pictures. They were waiting for me to barf or faint or something."

"And you didn't?"

"Hell, no! I found the pictures fascinating. How feminine is that?"

"Curiosity isn't limited to the male of the species," he stated with a smile.

"I guess not. But what would Steve think? What does he think? What should I do about him?"

"You know what to do, Kathy."

"We need to talk."

"Uh huh—and what else?"

Kathy shook her head.

"Communicating means more than just talking."

"Listening?"

"Yes, and?"

"Understanding?"

"Yes."

"I'll try tonight."

"Be honest with each other."

"Yes, sir."

The session ended with the understanding that Kathy would see him again the next week. Carter Walters entered his small private office through the door to the right of the kitchen area, picked up the phone, and called Chief Ledford's office. He was put through at once.

"Yes, Carter."

"Chief, I talked with Kathy Cooper this morning."

"How's she doing?"

"Better than I expected. Did you know she wants to be a cop?"

"Yes. She told me."

"She contacted the Sheriff's Department."

"What do you think?"

"About her becoming a cop?"

"Yes."

"She has some things to work through, but she's got her head on straight. She's intelligent and has good instincts. It's a shame she's past our age limit."

"Yeah. We could use her. Will you be seeing her again?"

"Yes, as long as she feels the need I'll be available to her."

"Thanks, Carter. Keep me posted."

"Yes, sir."

* * * * *

Friday, February 11, 1977 - 6:45 p.m.

As they finished dinner, Kathy told Steve she wanted to talk to him. He nodded. The boys exchanged a glance that asked, what now? They excused themselves and retired to their bedrooms to do their homework.

Steve and Kathy cleared the table. Kathy started rinsing the dishes and loading the dishwasher. Steve stood next to her, his back to the cabinet.

"What's on your mind?" he asked her.

"You are. Is something bothering you?"

"No," he answered with a frown. "Why do you ask?"

"Because every once in a while you look at me as thought you don't know who I am."

"Oh. No!" He hesitated. "No, honey. We've been married nineteen years. I think I know you pretty well."

"You didn't expect me to kill a man, did you?" she challenged.

"No, but it didn't surprise me."

"It didn't?" Astonished, Kathy turned to face him.

"No," he confirmed, shaking his head. "You're a woman."

"That doesn't make any sense."

"Sure it does. Maternal instinct. Females kill to protect their young. You killed to protect another person."

"Well...don't you think that's...macho? More something a man would do?"

"I think it makes you more of a woman."

Kathy stood looking at him with her mouth open, oblivious to everything except the look of pride on Steve's face.

"Look at it this way. A man thinks he can win a physical fight. That's macho. A woman knows she'll lose a physical fight with a man unless she's some kind of amazon."

"Oh," Kathy said, considering.

"Kathy, I love you. You did the right thing. I'm proud of you. It's the nightmare that concerns me. I want you to get over this and go on with your life. I don't want it to destroy you."

"Lieutenant Walters and I have talked about it. If Ray Jackson or Calvin was going to die that night, I'm glad it was Ray Jackson. I never would get over it if Calvin had been killed."

Steve smiled, took her in his arms, and kissed her soundly. Her hands made wet splotches on the back of his shirt and neither of them cared. They spent the evening talking about the past, the present, and their hopes for the future. In the end they understood each other's feelings, strengths, and weaknesses.

Kathy told him about visiting the Sheriff's Office to get some information about applying and her need for a stable work history. She was right. Steve did not like the idea of her getting a job.

"I'd rather you didn't get a job," he told her. "Mom worked the whole time I was growing up. Sis did as much or more than Mom did raising me. I don't want that for our kids."

"The boys aren't children anymore, honey."

"I know, and I know you need a work history. But I don't have to like it."

"No, you don't."

"What've you got in mind, job-wise?"

"A civilian position at HPD."

"I knew it," he said with a chuckle.

Steve offered no further resistance. He was beginning to understand the strength of her need to be a police officer. There was no denying that she seemed driven to do it or how animated she became when talking about it. In the end, he gave her his blessing. She should be safe working at Central, what with officers all over the place. The only danger there would be the men in uniform making passes at her.

They made love that night, with tenderness and passion. Both slept as untroubled as babies.

Chapter 58

Tuesday, February 15, 1977 - 9:45 a.m.

The day before, she had finally looked at the information packet from the Harris County Sheriff's Office. After her appointment with Carter Walters, she was beginning to understand her reaction to the deputy's comments at the Sheriff's Office. Kathy accepted the fact that she had taken a man's life. Still, it was going to take time to think of herself as other than a killer. But not as a hero. Never as a hero!

The packet detailed the qualifications and process for applying to become a deputy. She met most of the requirements, but she needed a work history and to get physically fit enough to pass the agility test. She had called Lieutenant Goodson in Public Relations, and through him made an appointment to talk to Sergeant Fleming about working as a clerk in Records Division.

When Kathy arrived at Central, she had to wait a few minutes for someone to vacate a parking place. The entrance to the building was busy with officers and civilians entering and leaving. Kathy walked up the steps, pushed through the double doors, crossed the lobby from front to back, entered Records Division, approached the counter, and asked for Sergeant Fleming.

Moments later an officer announced, "I'm Sergeant Fleming. Come in Mrs. Cooper."

He held the gate in the counter open for her. He was nearly six feet tall and about the same age as Kathy. Both his hair and his eyes were the same shade of brown. While his wavy hair seemed somewhat unruly, his eyes were disciplined and intelligent. They revealed nothing of what he was thinking. His "cop face," Kathy thought.

"Lieutenant Goodson tells me you're considering working for the department?"

"Yes. I'm just not sure where."

"Well, I'll do my best to convince you that Records is where you should be. Come on back to my desk." He walked beside her and past the five booths where the clerks usually sat taking reports. Only three of the booths were occupied. They also passed several desks where clerks were on the phones and others were typing index cards. He grabbed a chair and pulled it over to his desk, but made her sit in his padded chair. "Now tell me what you're thinking," he instructed.

"I want to be a cop with HPD but I'm past the age limit. I'm thinking about trying the Sheriff's Department, but I'm going to need a stable work history. I haven't worked since I got married nineteen years ago. I would like to stay involved with police work until the Sheriff's Office starts hiring again."

"And you want to have contact with the officers you rode along with, don't you?"

Kathy smiled and nodded. "Yes, I do," she admitted.

"Well," he said. "Records would be a good place for you. You've been here when the officers were dictating their reports, haven't you?"

"Yes. I even typed one for 'em one night. They had raided a dice game. Officers were waiting three deep when we came in. So the men got me a form and a typewriter."

"Then you already know what it's like to have officers come in, anxious to get the report done and get back on the street."

"Yes, I do."

He told her how Records is a service division and how much of the material within the department originates there. Accuracy is important because the reports are used in presenting cases to the grand jury and in court. He explained the shifts, the hours, and how much intelligent clerks were needed. Then he reminded her that she would be seeing officers and hearing what they did on the street.

As they talked, the sergeant's "cop face" became more animated and expressive. He asked questions about things Kathy had experienced while riding along, but he never referred to the shooting. He was as easy to talk to as any of the officers she had met. Just before noon, she realized she had taken up more of his time than she should have. She promised to think about working in Records and to call him if she had questions.

She didn't have to think about it for very long. By the time she got home, she knew she would apply for a job in Records Division of the Houston Police Department.

* * * * *

Tuesday, February 15, 1977 - 6:20 p.m.

During dinner Kathy told Steve and the boys that she was going to apply for a job as a clerk in Records at HPD. She wanted them to help her decide which shift would interfere with the family lifestyle the least.

"You're going to get a job?" Davy questioned.

"Yes. I need a stable work history to get into the Sheriff's Academy," Kathy started to explain.

"Sheriff's Academy!" Davy exclaimed.

"You wanna be a cop?" Jake exclaimed in amazement.

She nodded. "Yes."

"After what happened?" Jake demanded.

"Why, Mom?" Davy asked.

"It's complicated," she told him.

"I'd like to know why," Davy repeated.

"It's something I've wanted since I was a little girl." She hesitated. "This may sound idealistic, but it felt good serving on the grand jury. It's part of what makes our country work. I was proud to do it. Being a cop is another way to serve our country."

"You make it sound like you're going into the military," Davy said.

"In a way I am. Police departments are paramilitary organizations."

"What does that mean?" Jake asked.

"It's like the military with ranks and chain of command, but not as military."

She explained the hours of the shifts. Steve and the boys left it up to Kathy.

As she was loading the dishwasher her thoughts raced. Steve, the boys, the job, the future. Was she being selfish? She knew Steve's childhood had been difficult. His father had abandoned his wife and children when Steve was young, maybe five or six. Kathy didn't have any frame of reference for that. Her parents were still together after over forty years of marriage. She simply couldn't comprehend what Steve's childhood had been like.

On the other hand, she and Steve had provided a stable home for Davy and Jake. They both made good grades—not the best in their class, but good enough that getting into college wouldn't be a problem for them. Neither had ever been in any trouble at school or elsewhere. A much different childhood than Steve had experienced. She really felt that they would be fine with her working.

She wished she could talk to her mother or her sisters about this, but that wasn't possible. Her mother was old-school; the husband worked and the wife stayed home and raised the children. She wouldn't understand Kathy going to work when it wasn't necessary.

Her sisters both married the wrong men and both divorced after having a child. They both had to work, had to put the children in daycare. To them, Kathy was the lucky one, being able to stay home. They believed she had it easy. Why would she want to give that up to go to work when there was no financial need for it?

At least she and Steve were in agreement. More or less.

* * * * *

Ride Along

Tuesday, February 15, 1977 - 10:35 p.m.

Steve sat at the game table in the study. He had his favorite chess set arranged in a problem from a book of chess problems Kathy had given him for Christmas. He stared at the problem without seeing it, without attempting to solve it.

In the nineteen years he and Kathy had been married, she had never mentioned her childhood desire to be a police officer. If she hadn't ridden along, there wouldn't have been a trial and he might never have found out about it. Most women wouldn't have dared to ride along. But Kathy was not most women

She was a walking collection of contradictions. He saw her as artistic and athletic, a tomboy yet feminine, a good poker player who cheated at solitaire, comfortable in a fancy ball gown or under the hood of a car with a smear of grease on her face, having hands strong enough to give a relaxing rub down and dexterous enough to crochet a delicate lace doily.

Was she perfect? No. She had her faults. But she was perfect for him. When they first met he didn't think he stood a chance of dating her. But when he asked her out, she surprised him by saying yes. They went out to dinner and sat at the table talking for hours after they finished eating. The movie they had planned to see was totally forgotten. He fell in love with her that night.

He spent every moment he could with her after that first date. Every time they parted he wondered if he would see her again, or if she would realize he wasn't good enough for her and drop him. She liked to try new things, go new places. He liked a routine, settled life. She was an extrovert and he was an introvert. Nineteen years of marriage and he still wondered why it worked for them.

Now she wanted to get a job. The job would change their lives. Was their marriage strong enough to survive such a basic change? He didn't know. He knew she would take the job and he knew he had no right to try to stop her. She was his wife, not his property.

"Honey," Kathy said from the study doorway. "It's time for bed."

Steve nodded and stood up. He followed Kathy to the bedroom. As they undressed, they talked about the changes her working would require. They agreed to talk about it again, after Kathy worked for a month. They talked of their love for each other. When they retired for the night they expressed that love in the most intimate way.

Chapter 59

Thursday, February 17, 1977

Kathy drove Steve to the airport to catch a flight to Libya. He expected to be there on business for about three weeks. He always worried about Kathy and the boys while he was gone. Kathy worried about him, in the unstable Middle East. Still, they parted with hugs, kisses, and promises to each other to be careful. Kathy watched the planes until Steve's flight took off, then headed home.

Kathy hoped to start the job in Records and have the kids settled into a routine with any problems worked out before Steve returned. She called Sergeant Jack Fleming to tell him she had decided to apply for a job in Records. She asked how to go about it. He told her who to call.

"Looking forward to having you here," he told her.

She thanked him and called to make an appointment at the Civil Service office.

* * * * *

Friday, February 18, 1977 - 9:00 a.m.

Kathy was at Central again for her appointment with Carter Walters. She talked about the family's reaction to her decision to apply for a job in Records and her desire to do something to contribute to HPD. They touched on the shooting briefly. Three visits with Carter Walters and she was beginning to come to terms with the past. The memory would never set completely comfortably in her mind, but she would go on with her life and think of it less and less often.

Carter told her there was no need for him to see her any more, unless problems came up. Then she should call him. She promised she would.

When she finished her counseling session she drove to One Allen Center to apply for a job in Records Division at HPD.

On the 18th floor she filled out the application. Her typing and 10-key adding machine ability were tested. After passing both, she was interviewed by a Mrs. Miller, who sent her over to Central to see Sergeant Dunlap. He sent her to Records to see Sergeant Fleming. He took Kathy into the captain's office to interview her. After the time they had spent talking a few days earlier, it wasn't much of an interview.

"You're hired, Kathy. What shift do you want?"

"Days."

"What days off?"

"Monday and Tuesday."

"Done!" He told her how glad he was that she had decided on Records and assured her that she wouldn't be sorry.

"I'm looking forward to it. I feel so out of touch," she told him. "I don't know what's happening on the streets."

"Why don't you buy a scanner and listen to the radio calls?"

"Wouldn't I need some special authorization to do that?"

"Nope. You just need to know which crystal to buy to listen to the area you want." He told her where to buy a scanner and which crystal to purchase to listen to the units working out of the Shepherd and Northwest Substations.

She thanked him and returned to HPD Personnel. Sergeant Dunlap turned her over to Officer Byrd, who brought out a bunch of forms to be filled out. One asked for five references, which Kathy had no trouble providing. When Kathy finished, Officer Byrd went over the form, asked a few questions, and added things to what Kathy had put down.

"All the information you will be handling is confidential," Officer Byrd told her. "The Department has to ask some questions that might seem intimate or prying. We have to be sure there is nothing someone could use to blackmail you into revealing confidential information." He paused. "Is there anything in your background that could be used to blackmail you?"

Kathy blushed and reluctantly admitted that there was.

"Will you tell me what it is?"

"Do I have to?"

"If the department knows about it, then any attempt to blackmail you will fail."

"I had an affair once." Her blush deepened. Shame and guilt had nearly destroyed her at the time. Being reminded of it brought it all back and left her feeling completely unworthy. The department wouldn't hire me now, she thought.

"How long ago did this happen?"

"Eleven years ago."

"Are you still in contact with the man?"

"No. I don't even know where he is now."

"Okay," Officer Byrd said as he made a note.

"Are you writing that down?" she asked with distress.

"No, I'm not. I just noted that you were willing to tell us there was something in your past." He turned the form around so she could see. "Okay?"

Kathy nodded. So that was it. They wanted to know if she would admit it to the Department to keep someone from blackmailing her.

"I'll also be talking to your neighbors."

"A few of them I don't know," she told him. "They might not understand about the police cars at my house once in a while."

"Friends you made while riding along?"

"Yes."

"Are you seeing any of these officers?"

"Yes, I see them."

"Dating?"

"No!"

"Did you use any of them for references?"

"No."

"Why don't you give me their names?"

"I'll have to bring you a list. I can't remember all twenty-eight," Kathy told him.

"Twenty-eight! You rode along with twenty-eight different officers?"

"Yes, sir."

"Well just give me the names of two or three."

Kathy named Dean Driskell, Bob Richmond and Sergeant Ralph Strong because she had ridden along with them the most. She went to Identification Division to get pictures and fingerprints taken. She hand carried the pictures back to Officer Byrd, and he sent her with all the paperwork back to Mrs. Miller at the Civil Service Office. They were so busy that she was told to return on Tuesday, as the office would be closed Monday for President's Day.

She left One Allen Center and drove over to the Sheriff's Department. Might as well go all the way, she thought. From the lobby she called Sarah Beaumont and said she was ready to fill out an application. Who should she see? She was told to come on up, that Sarah would handle it.

Deputy Beaumont led Kathy to the small room where they had talked the first time. Kathy was given a five-page application for employment to fill out. The information required was general: name, address, phone number, Social Security Number, driver's license number, position wanted, education, time lived at present address, previous address and time lived there, and a detailed employment history. She completed everything except the employment history and took the form to Deputy Beaumont.

"I've applied for a job with HPD as a Records Clerk."

"Good. Working in records you will still be learning about police work. I'll just note that on here." Beaumont wrote a notation on the employment history page, looked over the form, and asked a couple questions to clarify things.

"That does it, Mrs. Cooper. When we start hiring again you will be contacted. Then the real paperwork will start."

On the way home Kathy stopped and bought a scanner and the crystal for the northwest area. That night she listened to the scanner while she crocheted, instead of watching television. At bedtime she took the scanner into the bedroom and turned it down low. As she was getting undressed, she heard unit eleven sixty-three checking wants and warrants on a traffic stop.

"Eleven sixty-three," the dispatcher called. "He's wanted twelve times."

"Eleven sixty-three," Officer Fred Oakes radioed back. "Please confirm DOB (date of birth). Man says he has a son with the same name."

It took a few more minutes to get the answer. "Eleven sixty-three, DOB is confirmed. He's wanted twelve times."

"Eleven sixty-three. Bless you! That's clear!"

The radio went crazy with other officers clicking their radio mikes. Kathy smiled, turned out the light, and drifted off while listening to the radio calls.

*****

Tuesday, February 22, 1977 - 9:00 a.m.

Kathy returned to One Allen Center to complete her processing. The physical exam was very brief. They took a blood sample and a urine specimen. The doctor asked her if she was healthy. Kathy told him yes. He passed her and that was that.

She took papers back to personnel at HPD where there were more forms to fill out—deductions, insurance, et cetera. When she finished the paperwork she was told that she was to report for work at seven the next morning.

Chapter 60

Wednesday, February 23, 1977 - Tuesday, March 7, 1977

Sergeant Fleming, the day shift supervisor, arrived in Records. He hung his jacket over the back of his desk chair and went to the break room to start some fresh coffee. This would be Kathy Cooper's first morning. He had some concerns about it. Ruth Bellows, the head-clerk, who would be in charge of training Kathy, reacted negatively when told Kathy had been hired.

"We need good clerks," she informed him, "not payback for some supposed heroine."

Like her, others would also think Kathy's job in Records was payback for saving Officer Henson's life. Few would understand her desire to contribute. He had talked to Kathy enough to know she was sincere. He also understood that she would be leaving in a couple of years to attend the Sheriff's Academy. In the meantime, Records would benefit from having her as a clerk.

As soon as Kathy and Ruth Bellows arrived, he introduced them. He kept an eye on things from his desk, wondering if Kathy would sense Ruth's hostility and how she would react.

At her desk, Mrs. Bellows handed Kathy three index cards.

"Type your name, address, phone number, and Social Security Number on each. I want two, letter perfect," she instructed Kathy.

It took only a few minutes for Kathy to complete the task, without needing the third card. Mrs. Bellows then instructed on how to type the index cards each report required. "If you have any questions, ask."

"Yes, ma'am."

Kathy took several reports and returned to her desk. She studied the page illustrating the way things were indexed and started typing them. At one point she ran across a Burglary of a Residence report filed by Jesse Banks. She took time to read it before indexing it. It wasn't anything special but still she found it interesting.

About ten percent of the cards she typed that day were returned by the checker for corrections or additions. By 3:00 p.m., the end of her shift, she was numb. She had not concentrated that hard or that long for years. She slept well that night with the scanner turned on for company.

The next day she began issuing case numbers when officers called on the phone, in addition to indexing reports. She learned to take notes on things that were new to her so she wouldn't have to ask the same question twice.

As she arrived at Central one morning she saw John Buford.

"Morning, John. Still working at the jail?" she asked.

"Yeah," he said with disgust. "Looks like it'll be a year before I can get back on the streets. After five years on patrol in Oklahoma City I don't need this. I miss the streets."

"So do I," she told him. "You know, there are usually several units parked out back. What do you say we hot-wire one and go to work?"

John laughed, "That's the best offer I've had lately. Love to have you as a partner."

They decided they had better not do it.

By the time she left work on Sunday afternoon, she was ready for a couple of days off. On Monday, she did the laundry, ran errands, paid the bills, planned the meals for the week, bought groceries, and cleaned half of the house. Tuesday she finished the house cleaning, baked a cake, talked to her mother and sisters, read part of a mystery novel, and prepared a nice dinner for herself and the boys. Wednesday morning she was ready, even eager, to go to work.

During the second week she began taking reports of stolen bicycles and car batteries over the phone. Dean Driskell was there one morning when she arrived. He was training a rookie and asked Kathy to take the report. She explained she wasn't doing reports from officers yet.

Another morning, Calvin Henson came into Records. He waved to Kathy, who set aside the report she was indexing and went to the counter to talk to him for a moment.

"So it's true!" he exclaimed. "I heard you went to work down here."

Kathy nodded.

"You're working the wrong shift. We need you on nights!"

"And the evening shift officers want me on evenings. I can't please all of you."

"You rode along both shifts. You can work both shifts," he teased, and they both laughed.

They visited for a few minutes. Kathy caught up on happenings at Station Five and learned that the department had started assigning women to accident and traffic units. Could patrol units be far behind, she wondered.

She was not as tired when her second week ended. In fact, she was pleased with herself. She had learned a lot in the past two weeks, but she knew she had a lot more to learn and looked forward to mastering it. She wanted to be the best clerk she could be.

Chapter 61

Wednesday, March 9, 1977 - 1:48 a.m.

Tuesday night, like every night since Steve left for Libya two weeks earlier, Kathy fell asleep with the scanner on low volume. It had awakened her several times when something happened on the street, so it was no surprise when she found herself suddenly awake. She turned up the volume thinking she had missed something, but the scanner was quiet for nearly a minute.

"Eleven sixty-one, my partner's been shot! Get an ambulance rolling!" an officer exclaimed and gave the location.

Oh my God! Her heart started pounding. Who's riding eleven sixty-one tonight? Art Donahue? Dan Cannon? Donny Wells? Fred Oakes? Units checked in, running it as an assist. The dispatcher did not acknowledge. The first unit on the scene was Art Donahue. Thank God he's okay!

The dispatcher advised that all traffic was being cleared all the way from the scene to Ben Taub Hospital. The ambulance arrived on the scene about three minutes after the call went out. Art disregarded Ben Taub. Paramedics were taking him to Parkway for stabilization. It was bad if the paramedics didn't think he would last code three (with red lights and siren) to Ben Taub.

Dispatch asked for the name. Barber, Art told him. It hit Kathy like a fist to the solar plexus. Jason Barber was in his mid-twenties. He had served in the military for four years, had come home, attended the police academy, and married his high school sweetheart about a year ago.

The ambulance left the scene. The dispatcher advised that the wounded officer's blood type was O positive. Several units with officers of that blood type checked in to say they were en route to Parkway.

Art put out a description of the car wanted in connection with the attempted murder of a peace officer. He also passed on to Donny Wells more information he had gotten from the wounded hijacker at the scene, then asked for an ambulance for the man.

Unit eleven sixty-six, Donny Wells and Fred Oakes, and others headed for Acres Homes to look for the car in which two hijackers got away. Unit eighty, Lieutenant Billings, called for all sixth district cars in service to meet him at North Shepherd and West Little York to set up the search for the car. District Three and Five cars were pulled into Sixth District to run the calls.

"Eleven sixty-four to unit 80." Kathy recognized Wade Ellis's voice.

"Unit 80."

"I have his wife. Where do you want her?"

"Take her to the front door. Deputy Chief McKnight will meet her there. Where was the officer hit?" the lieutenant asked.

"Lower left chest," Wade Evans told him.

All the officers' voices were tense. Units started checking in from Parkway and reporting to unit eighty, who was organizing the manhunt. Kathy had a bad feeling about this. It was too quick for them to have given blood and be ready to return to the streets.

She felt numb and pain at the same time, expecting the worst and praying for the best. Every muscle in her body felt tense, as though to protect herself from a blow. It must be worse for the officers, she thought. At least they were busy hunting for the shooter. There was nothing Kathy could do but wait and listen and worry about all of them.

At 2:35 a.m. Art called for at least two more rolls of film for the investigator and gave the type of camera. Eleven fifty-seven said he would pick up film at Station One and take it to the scene.

Unit eighty advised the dispatcher to notify the Sheriff's Department and Texas Department of Public Safety (State Troopers) and request all major highways out of town be covered by them. Several units informed the dispatcher they would be out on assignment as the lieutenant got the manhunt organized. He also called for a unit to talk to the wounded hijacker at Ben Taub to get a more complete description of the car and the other hijackers. Very few calls were going out on the radio. One unit called out to Homicide with witnesses from the scene.

At 2:50 a.m. an alarm dropped on a church near Kathy's home. One unit from Southwest Houston and two Vice units ran it. The Vice units advised the Southwest unit that they would be in plainclothes. Everyone will be a little trigger-happy tonight. Please God, don't let anyone else get hurt, Kathy prayed.

"Wanted for attempted murder of a peace officer," and the description of the wanted car was repeated every few minutes—the make, model, and the fact that it had Louisiana plates. That it was occupied by two black males was added to the information. Northeast units reported in service to run calls in the Northwest area. Unit eighty called out en route to Parkway. Unit nine twenty-two, Sergeant Ralph Strong, took charge at Shepherd and Little York. SWAT teams had been called in. Day shift SWAT teams were notified to report for work. Three Narcotics units called in, available for the hunt. The whole Northwest area was blanketed with units concentrating on the black neighborhoods, looking for the car. A description of another car the hijackers were known to have used went out on the radio.

Art's unit called out to homicide. Art and Donny kept getting on the radio, trying to remember every little bit of information they had collected on these hijackers who had been hitting area stores for several months. Kathy could hear the tension in their voices. Art sounded particularly bad.

At 3:45 a.m. one of the sergeants ordered the Station Five day shift officers to be called to report to work and to work their districts until further notice. All the Northwest night shift units were concentrating on finding the car the hijackers used. Units from Central, Northeast, Southwest, Vice, and Narcotics were running the few calls going out in the Northwest area.

Units were stopping every car that vaguely fit the description of the one wanted. Lots of wants and warrants were being checked. Lots of chatter between units, trying to get as clear a picture of the suspects as possible.

At 4:00 a.m. the dispatcher repeated the wanted order. "Wanted for attempted murder of a peace officer…stand by." There was silence for several moments. Then, "Wanted for Capital Murder of a peace officer." His voice broke before he could continue with the description of the car and the suspects. Kathy cried.

At four-thirty a.m. the units moved in on one location.

"We have Discharge of Firearms," came over the radio. "Get an ambulance rolling to stand by in case it's needed."

Minutes passed. Two long, long minutes.

"The suspects are in custody. Disregard the ambulance. No one is hurt."

Thank God, Kathy thought, crying with relief. It was too late to try to sleep, so she showered and dressed. She woke the boys, packed their lunches and hers, and started cooking breakfast.

When Davy came to the breakfast table he noticed there were only two places set at the table.

"Aren't you eating, Mom?"

"No."

He went to her and saw the tears running down her cheeks. "Mom, what's wrong?" he demanded, thinking something had happened to his dad.

Kathy fought unsuccessfully to stop the tears. "An officer got killed last night. I heard it all on the scanner."

Davy took the spatula from Kathy's hand. "I'll finish this, Mom."

Kathy nodded and fled to the bedroom. I've got to pull myself together, she thought. I've got to go to work. I need to stay busy. I wish Steve were here. No, I don't. It would just be one more reason for him to be against me becoming a cop. The tears stopped. She washed her face, repaired her makeup, and returned to the kitchen.

The boys were eating. From their looks of concern, she knew Davy had explained to Jake what had happened during the night. She got her coat from the closet and picked up her purse and lunch. She went to the table and gave each of the boys a kiss on the cheek and told them she would see them after work.

"Drive careful, Mom," Davy advised.

She nodded. "I will. Love you both. See you this afternoon."

"Mom..." Jake said. His concern showed in his face, but he didn't know what to say.

Kathy smiled, grateful for his concern. In spite of dealing with her own chaotic emotions, she reassured him. "I'll be all right." She headed for the front door.

Chapter 62

Wednesday, March 9, 1977 - 6:55 a.m.

Kathy arrived at Records and put her purse on the desk she would use that day and walked back to where Sergeant Fleming was sitting at his desk. When their eyes met, hers again filled with tears.

"You heard?" he asked.

She nodded. "I had my scanner turned on. I heard it all. Sergeant, can I get time off…."

"No, Kathy!" he interrupted. "You're not getting off today. This is something you need to deal with. You're going to stay and do your job like the rest of us."

Offended, she told him, "I'm here to work today. I'd like time off to go to the funeral."

"Sorry," he said chagrined, realizing he had misjudged her.

Kathy nodded. She knew that he and everyone else were in a highly emotional state.

"Of course you can go," he told her. "Had you ridden with Barber?"

"No. I'd met him. I didn't know him well. Still it hurts, thinking about his wife and parents, the other officers and what they're going through."

"You're learning, Kathy," he told her. "Probably no other civilian connected with this Department has been accepted as closely into the family as you've been. You know about the brotherhood of officers. You know the joy of being accepted as one of us. And now you're learning the price of belonging."

She nodded, tears again running down her face. The price is high, she thought, but worth it. I pray I never have to pay it again but I also know I will. And yet, I'll stay. I'll fight to remain a part of this family. She dried her eyes and went to her desk.

When her lunch break came she asked Sergeant Fleming to join her and talk while she ate. He agreed. Kathy asked what a policeman's funeral was like. She did not want any surprises.

He told her, "It's like any funeral but like none you've ever been to before. The officer was like a friend and neighbor, but the pain is for a brother. It's like burying a member of your own family. It's a moving experience. A painful experience. When an officer dies in the line of duty, it is almost always a young man taken much before his time, suddenly and violently. It's tragic, yet heroic. Painful, yet patriotic. He'll be in uniform. His badge will be removed before the coffin is closed, mounted on a plague, and later given to his wife.

"The honor guard is what gets you the most," the sergeant continued. "It will include officers from Departments all over the state. If there is beauty in a thing such as this, that is it. All the officers in uniform saluting as the coffin is taken from the church to the hearse. At the grave, there will be the folding of the flag and its presentation to his widow, the rifles firing the salute, and taps will be played."

Kathy thanked him for the information and they returned to work. The day passed fairly quickly, although there were moments when she found herself gazing into space, thinking about the officers she knew and how this must be affecting them. She thought the source of her greatest pain was knowing that it could have been any one of them.

That night Kathy tried to read a little but couldn't concentrate. She had trouble sleeping, in spite of sleeping very little the night before. Even the scanner turned low didn't help. It was after 3:00 a.m. when she finally drifted off for a couple hours of fitful rest.

Chapter 63

Friday, March 11, 1977 - 12:45 p.m.

Kathy wore one of her blue trial outfits to work. She left early to attend Officer Jason Barber's funeral. She found the church across the street from what had been a large discount store with a huge parking lot. The store stood empty. The lot quickly filled up with cars, many of them police units from police agencies in the Houston area. She also saw police cars from Dallas, Austin, San Antonio, Huntsville, State Trooper cars, and others from Oklahoma, Louisiana, Arkansas, and New Mexico. When the marked parking slots were all filled, the cars parked in double rows in the lanes between. Officers were arriving five and six to each police unit.

Kathy walked toward the church and saw funeral directors meeting the officers on the parking lot side of the street. Each had a roll of black tape. Each officer took a piece and covered his badge number. Like a mourning band worn on the arm, they put on mourning for their dead brother officer. Still, it was more than that. The badge number is their identity when they are in uniform. By covering the numbers on their badges they were all alike, all like the man in the coffin. The tape would remain on the badges until the officer was buried.

The officers gathered in small groups outside the church entrance. There was little talk, just sad faces. Kathy saw many of the officers she had ridden along with. They acknowledged each other with nods. No one wanted to talk. Not the officers and not Kathy. She reluctantly entered the church.

In the lobby there were two guest books, one for the civilians and one for the officers. After signing the book, civilians entered the sanctuary, walked straight down the center aisle to the coffin, then turned right to go up the right-hand aisle to sit in the pews on the right-hand side of the church. The family was already seated in the front pew. The pews on the left side of the center aisle were empty, reserved for the officers.

Kathy walked down the center aisle. At the coffin, she braced herself before she looked. Jason Barber was so young. Such a waste. She turned to the right, went up the right-hand side and found a seat on the aisle.

Soon the officers came in, pallbearers first, then the Mayor, Police Chief, the Sheriff, Deputy Chiefs, and other high-ranking police officers. Other officers followed down the center aisle, turned left, and filled the pews from front to back, then down the aisles on the left and right and across the back of the church.

At some signal Kathy didn't see, the officers all sat down. The noise of all the holsters and pistols hitting the wooden pews sounded as if a hundred gunfighters all dropped their guns on the saloon floor at the same time. It seemed oddly out of place in a church.

Several of the officers Kathy knew were standing in the aisle near her, Lt. Billings and Sergeant Schmidt among them. Art Donahue stood about six feet in front of Kathy and she couldn't help watching him during the service. Tears ran down his face much of the time, and Kathy's tears kept pace with his. His pain hurt her more than she thought possible.

When the service ended, the officers in the pews went first to the coffin, then across the front of the church and up the right-hand aisle. Many of them that Kathy knew nodded to her as they passed, including Chief Ledford. Some touched her shoulder in passing. This made her cry even more.

After the officers, the civilians left the church starting with the pews in the rear. When Kathy stepped outside she saw the honor guard standing in formation. Among them were officers in uniforms from other departments, just as Sergeant Fleming said there would be. The officers came to attention and saluted as the pallbearers and casket approached the doors, and remained that way until the doors of the hearse were closed. They were then dismissed and all went to their cars to form the procession to the cemetery.

The motorcycle escorts had diverted all traffic off the freeway in both directions all the way out to the cemetery. From the height at the top of the overpasses, Kathy could see neither the beginning nor the end of the procession. The flashing lights of the police units extended for miles in both directions.

At the cemetery the officers formed the honor guard again before the casket was brought to the grave site. The service was much shorter. The Department Chaplin offered a prayer and told the significance of each fold of the flag as it was folded for presentation to Jason's widow.

A light rain started, as though God joined their sorrow. Kathy flinched when the salute was fired, thinking gunshots were probably the last sound Jason heard. Taps was played. Jason's family returned to the limousine. Kathy went to her car and drove home.

Chapter 64

Friday, March 11, 1977 - 7:05 p.m.

Kathy and the boys finished supper and she cleaned up the kitchen. She was in a mood to watch some mindless television before bed. The phone rang. It was Steve calling from the airport. He was taking a taxi to the house.

An hour later, Steve arrived. The boys joined him and Kathy in the family room to catch up on things. He told about his trip and how different Libya was. The boys told him about their bowling scores in the school league and returned to their rooms to study, watch television, or read.

"Steve," she started hesitantly. "I took the job in Records."

He nodded, resigned to it. "I expected that. How is it?"

"I've got a lot to learn, but it's interesting."

"Which shift did you get?"

"Days, with Monday and Tuesday off. That way I don't have to do all my shopping and errands on Saturday, like everybody else who works."

"Days. That's seven to three?"

"Yes."

"Then you have to leave before the boys and get home after they do."

"A little bit. I fix their breakfast before I leave and pack their lunches. They get their own snacks after school."

He nodded. "Are they all right with it?"

"I think so. They got used to me being gone while I was on the grand jury. This isn't much different."

They were sitting next to each other on the couch. She snuggled down in his arms. "I missed you so much. I needed you today," she said, her tone so poignant that Steve pulled her close. "I went to the funeral of one of the officers I knew. He was killed in the line of duty on Wednesday morning."

"What happened?" he asked softly.

"He and his partner walked up on an armed robbery in progress."

"Have they caught the killer?"

"Yes."

"Was he one of the men you rode along with?" Steve asked.

"No." Before more tears started, she forced her mind back to Steve. "You must be tired. It took you a couple of days to recover from the jet lag last time."

"I could use some sleep," he admitted.

Kathy got up. "Come on," she said. "I'll put you to bed."

They rose. Steve went to check that the doors were locked and started turning off lights.

Kathy went to the boys' rooms. "Daddy and I are going to bed. You boys get to bed on time."

"There's no school tomorrow," Jake protested.

"Eleven o'clock, it's lights out."

"Yes, ma'am."

Steve came down the hall and told the boys goodnight. He and Kathy went into the master bedroom and Steve closed the door. As he undressed he watched her turn down the covers on the bed, set the alarm clock, and undress. She put on pajamas and went to brush her teeth.

She's trying so hard, he thought, to keep things as near normal as she can. He disliked having her working. Reluctantly, he accepted her need to do this, without understanding it. He wouldn't ask her to quit in spite of the officer's death, which renewed his fears for her safety if she became an officer. He would rather have her working at the Central Police Station. He hoped something would keep her from becoming an officer, because he didn't know if he could deal with that. They climbed into bed and snuggled lovingly, both too tired to make love.

Chapter 65

April, 1977

Kathy had settled in to the routine of working full time. She had progressed in her training to the point that she worked one of the booths most days. She saw officers she knew once in a while, giving her an opportunity to catch up on what the men were up to.

Steve and the boys seemed to have adjusted. They were spending more time on the weekends doing things together. She knew that Steve would still prefer she didn't work. She wished she could change that. Kathy loved him and was sorry for causing him distress, but she loved him all the more for allowing her to do what she felt compelled to do.

Kathy knew enough about the physical fitness requirements of the Sheriff's Academy to realize that she needed to do something about getting in better shape. She called the HPD Academy and asked for Lieutenant Carl Stewart and discovered he had been promoted to Captain. When he came on the line, she asked how best to prepare for the physical fitness requirements of the Sheriff's Department.

He gave her the name and phone number of an instructor who taught martial arts and also held special classes for officers on how to subdue and control suspects.

"That sounds perfect. But would he accept me as a student for that kind of training?" she inquired.

"With my recommendation. Have him call me," Captain Stewart told her.

She thanked him and made the call. The instructor, Mike Daniels, questioned her about what kind of training she was looking for, then said he would get back to her. When he called back he told her that Captain Stewart had said good things about her and yes, he would accept her as a student for the type of self-defense training she would need as a police officer. The price he quoted was within her budget. She started classes the following Monday morning and was surprised to learn that her lessons were private, just the instructor and her.

Mike Daniels was surprised with her natural athletic ability and how rapidly she progressed. She spent the first hour stretching and learning how to fall without hurting herself. She easily mastered falling backwards or to either side. Falling face forward was the most difficult because it went against all her instincts. She bumped her nose on the mat twice before she got the hang of it. After that she progressed quickly, in spite of the sore muscles and bruises.

* * * * *

July, 1977

Kathy had been working in Records for five months when Sergeant Fleming motioned for her to follow him to the captain's office one morning. She wondered if she had done something wrong. Sergeant Fleming sat at the captain's desk and waved her to a chair.

"The test for Clerk Two is coming up in a couple weeks," he informed her. "I think you should take it. It means more money and more responsibility."

"Sergeant, some of the other girls need the extra money. I don't."

"Cooper, didn't you tell me you wanted to contribute to this Department?"

"Yes, sir."

"You can contribute more as a Clerk Two."

"Yes, sir," Kathy said, thoroughly chastised. "If I take the test and pass, will I still be able to stay in Records and take reports?"

"Yes, of course, if that's what you prefer to do."

"In that case, I'll do my best."

"If you aren't in the top five, I'll take you and your family to dinner."

Two weeks later, on Wednesday morning, she reported to the convention center where the test was being given. She was surprised to find out that over two hundred people had signed up for this citywide competitive test for Clerk Two positions. Top five, she thought. This is going to cost the Sergeant a dinner.

The test questions were basic grammar, spelling, and math. She was concerned about one question. She thought that the phrasing was confusing and still wasn't sure of her answer when the time ran out. The proctors collected the tests and everyone was dismissed.

The next day after work, she called the Civil Service Office, as instructed. After identifying herself, she was given the results. Citywide, she had placed second with a score of ninety-eight out of one hundred possible points. She was stunned. Looks like I won't get that dinner from the sergeant after all, she thought.

The next day, Sergeant Fleming took her to the captain's office again. He congratulated her on the results of the test.

"I want to make it clear to you," Sergeant Fleming began, "if you wish to stay in Records on the day shift, you may. However, there are two other positions I want you to consider. "We need a Clerk Two on the Accident Desk. It is days, with weekends off. Also, the night shift needs a Clerk Two. In addition to the raise in pay as a Clerk Two, there's a shift deferential. You'd make more per hour than on day shift."

"I'm not interested in the Accident Desk. I want to continue taking reports."

"Would you be willing to consider changing to the night shift?"

The night shift, she thought. That's when the best reports are filed. Steve won't like it, she thought. The shift deferential and the pay raise as a Clerk Two would allow her to continue her private lessons and perhaps increase to two classes a week. It was perfect, if Steve would go for it.

"I'll have to talk to my husband. I'm interested, but he'll have to agree," she told him. "How soon do you need an answer?"

"Before your next days off," the Sergeant stated.

"Yes, sir."

He dismissed her and she went to work in one of the booths. By the time her shift was over, she realized how much she wanted the night shift position. Now she had to talk to Steve about it.

* * * * *

Kathy approached Steve after supper that evening.

"Honey, I told you I placed second on the Clerk Two test."

"Yes," he nodded.

"The sergeant pulled me aside today," she told him, "to talk about where they could best use a Clerk Two. They need one on the night shift and they offered it to me."

"In Records?"

"Yes."

"And you're interested," he stated.

"Only if it's all right with you."

Steve stared at her for a moment. The look on her face was like a little girl asking for something she wanted very much. "You don't need my permission. This is your job. You make the decision."

"We've always made decisions about your job together," Kathy reminded him.

"That's true." He thought a moment. "What are the hours for the night shift?"

"Eleven p.m. to seven a.m."

"And your nights off would be?"

"Probably the same, Monday and Tuesday. At least I'm going to ask for the same ones."

"It'll play hell with our sex life," he complained with a twinkle in his eye.

"We can make up for it on Mondays and Tuesdays," Kathy replied with a smile.

He nodded. "I like the idea of you being home during the day in case the boys need you."

"Then it's all right with you?"

"Yeah. But don't forget about Monday and Tuesday nights," he warned.

"I won't," she promised, as she kissed him. "Thank you."

He watched her take her favorite chair and pick up an afghan she was crocheting. Since she started working she seemed happier, things were more organized, the house kept better, and the meals more varied. It seemed to be good for her, and he and the boys were spending more time doing things together. He wasn't sure how having her on the night shift would work, but he couldn't turn her down. She would have been disappointed and the look on her face would have broken his heart. He loved her too much to do that to her.

* * * * *

August, 1977

The night shift, Kathy found, was different from the day shift in many ways. First, the parking lot which was so crowded during the day offered many places to park at ten-thirty at night. Most of the desks used during the day shift in Records were empty. There were three clerks manning the booths, three clerks on the phones, one clerk checking, two file clerks to file the index cards, and a sergeant and a lieutenant.

She started working in one of the booths her second week on nights. She saw a few evening shift officers and many from the night shift. They were surprised to see her working nights, and the evening shift still complained that she was working the wrong shift.

One night that week two officers came in who she didn't know. The two other booths were busy. The officer with the clipboard looked at Kathy and shook his head.

"Oh, damn! A new clerk!" he said with disgust. Then he leaned over the counter and in a condescending tone asked, "Can you type a report, honey?"

"Can you dictate one, darling?" Kathy answered in the same tone.

The officer jerked back as if she had slapped him, and he looked at her like something he had never seen before. Maybe he hadn't.

"Have you got a case number?" Kathy asked.

"Not yet," he answered.

She grabbed a notepad and asked for the offense, location, and the officers' names, and went to the Case Number form. She filled out the blanks, wrote the case number down, and returned to the booth. She inserted a form in the typewriter and started typing in the offense, location, and the officers' names.

The officer started dictating the report. Kathy had no trouble keeping up with him, and in fact, had to pause a few times for him to think about what to put next. When she finished the first page, he asked to see it. He read it over and handed it back to her.

"How long have you been in Records?" he asked.

"Six months," she told him, "on the day shift."

"Why didn't you tell me?"

"It was more fun this way."

He gave a dirty look to his partner who had started laughing, and handed the report back to Kathy. "You're doing a good job," he admitted.

"Thanks. You dictate all right, too."

"I guess I deserved that."

"You did," she said with a smile.

He held out his hand to her. "I'm Robert Baker."

Kathy nodded as she took his offered hand, "Kathy Cooper."

Still holding her hand, his smile faded. "Kathy Cooper! You killed that turd and saved Calvin Henson's life!"

Kathy nodded. Will we never get past that, she wondered. Is it always going to be the first thing people think when they meet me?

Baker took her hand in both of his. "Ma'am, I'm sorry I offended you."

Kathy smiled. "It's all right. It was mutual."

Baker released her hand, introduced his partner, and then he continued with the report. He apologized again before they left and thanked her for doing the report. Kathy told them anytime and laughed when they left, thankful for the nights she had spent riding along that gave her the ability to return his harassment.

* * * * *

October, 1977

Two officers, who had arrested a Harris County Deputy Sheriff for Driving While Intoxicated and Resisting Arrest, were dictating the report to Kathy when Sergeant Baxter interrupted and told her it was her break time. Another clerk would take over. Kathy looked at the clerk he had brought along to take her place and knew the girl would make a mess of it.

"Sir, this one is kind of important."

"All reports are important, Cooper!"

"Yes, sir," she said as she reluctantly stood up and left the booth.

The next night the sergeant called her back to his desk. He had a copy of the report he had taken her off of the night before.

"You were right, Cooper. This one was important," he admitted. "The sheriff complained to the deputy chief of Patrol. He passed it back to the captain, who gave it to the lieutenant, who kicked it back to me. I'm asking you to go to all the divisions involved, retrieve all the copies, and retype it."

She knew that was as close to an apology as she was going to get. "Yes, sir. I can do that."

With the botched report in her hand she started out at the top of the building and stopped at every division that had a copy of it. It took her nearly thirty minutes to get them all together. She then realized that for the last copy, she had to go to a different building. It meant walking a long city block, in the dark, which she was not comfortable doing. However, nothing happened and she was relieved to get back to Central. After that, she retyped the report and took it to Sergeant Baxter for his approval. She stood by while he quickly read it.

"Nice job. Thanks," he said when he finished.

"You're welcome," she said before getting back to work.

* * * * *

November, 1977

At 6:00 a.m. one Sunday, officers she knew from Station One came in. They told her they got in the mess involving three units, three locations, four offenses, two hit-and-run accidents, and three people arrested. The second unit was handling booking the perpetrators and the third was pulling wants and warrants. Those officers would be along shortly.

Kathy got a case number for them and they started the report. Soon the other officers arrived. She knew all but one of them, who turned out to be a rookie. When her shift ended at 7:00 a.m., the officers weren't anywhere near done with the report. Kathy excused herself and went to see Sergeant Baxter. She told him what the situation was and asked if she could stay and help the officers get the report finished.

He nodded. "Bring them inside and find a quiet corner. Let the day shift sergeant know when you leave, so we can put you in for overtime."

"Thank you, but I'm not asking for overtime, sir." She turned and went back to the booth. She and the officers moved to a desk on the far side of the room. Kathy called home to let Steve know she was working late. The officers took advantage of being able to sit down and even helped themselves to coffee from the break room. At 10:00 a.m. the report had been typed, read by the officers for accuracy, and approved. They thanked Kathy for staying and left Records.

Kathy turned in the report to the checker, gathered up her things, and went to tell the day shift sergeant she was leaving. Sergeant Baxter was still there. She thanked him for letting her complete the report and told him she was leaving.

After she left, he went to the checker and got the report she had stayed to finish. As he read it, he realized it was a good thing she had stayed, because it would have been difficult for another clerk to pick it up in the middle and make any sense of it.

A few nights later Sergeant Baxter called her back to his desk again and handed her a sheet of paper. "You are required to read this and sign it," he told her. "It will go in your permanent personnel file."

Puzzled, she began to read what turned out to be a letter of commendation for staying and completing the report from the six officers without asking for overtime. She was stunned and a little annoyed that the sergeant was making a big deal out of her doing her job.

"This isn't necessary."

"Yes it is. This is a service division. Your service to the officers is outstanding and deserves recognition. Afraid you're stuck with it. The lieutenant and the captain approved it," he told her with a smile.

"Yes, sir." She took the pen he offered and signed the letter. She returned his smile and went back to work.

* * * * *

1978 - 1979

So the months passed into years. About twice a year, Kathy would get a call from the Sheriff's Office asking if she was still interesting in becoming a deputy. The first few times she explained about having to wait until Jake graduated from high school. Later calls were to confirm her unavailability at that time. Each call reassured her that she had not been lost in the shuffle of paperwork. Each call also disappointed her because it meant another class was being started and she wasn't going to be part of it.

Jake graduated from high school in May of 1979. In June, Kathy called the Sheriff's Office to let them know that she was available and to ask when the next class would start, only to learn that a class started two weeks before and another wasn't scheduled for that year.

In August, both Davy and Jake left to attend Texas A & M. Kathy continued to work the night shift. She still enjoyed seeing her officer friends and hearing about what was happening on the streets. She just wished she was doing it, instead of just hearing about it. Maybe next year.

At home she and Steve settled into a routine that both were comfortable with. They made the most of the evening hours they had together and the nights she was off. Kathy continued to hope for a change and Steve continued to hope things would remain the same.

Chapter 66

Thursday, May 1, 1980 - 9:10 a.m.

Wednesday night had been brutal. The moon had been full. Two clerks were out sick. At times all the phone lines to Records were busy because officers were on hold waiting for a clerk. Three clerks were assigned to the booths but still officers were lined up waiting.

As checker that night, Kathy juggled taking reports and checking, but only managed to get further behind. At about five o'clock in the morning things began to thin out. However, Kathy didn't catch up completely by the end of shift. Driving home, she was too tired to enjoy the beautiful spring morning. She passed up eating and reading the paper to go straight to bed. When the phone rang it woke her from a sound sleep.

Struggling to croak out a sleepy "Hello," she wished she had unplugged the phone.

"Kathleen Mavis Cooper?" a strange male voice asked.

"Who's calling?" she asked, puzzled by the use of her full name.

"Deputy Barnes. Harris County Sheriff's Office."

"I'm Kathy Cooper."

"You filled out an application to become a Deputy Sheriff some time ago. Are you still interested?"

Suddenly, Kathy was completely awake. "Yes, sir."

"Report to the Academy on Rehab Road south of Atascasita at one o'clock for the reading comp and agility tests."

"Deputy Barnes, I worked the night shift last night. Can I schedule this for another time?"

"If you're interested, be there. Otherwise the spot will be filled by someone else."

"Where are Rehab Road and Atascasita, sir?"

"Do you have a Key Map, Cooper?" he asked curtly.

"Yes, sir."

"Learn how to use it," he ordered and hung up.

"Yes, sir," she answered to a dead phone.

One o'clock at the Academy, she told herself. She picked up the phone to call Steve. He did not want to hear this news. She put the phone down. Her thoughts were so mixed up; she had a difficult time sorting out how she felt. After years of waiting, the door was open. Could she pass it up? Not without being miserable. Not without regretting it the rest of her life. She had to do it now, if she was going to do it.

Steve would not try to stop her. He didn't have to. She knew how he felt. She also knew that he loved her enough to let her do what she wanted in spite of the worry it would cause him. She had to decide which was worse, her misery and regret if she gave it up, or his emotional distress if she didn't. It seemed selfish to choose her dream.

Would she be content to continue in Records? No! If she didn't try, she would have to quit working at HPD. It would be too painful to remain associated with the Department, to see officers every shift and know that she passed up a chance to become one of them. I've waited three years for this call. I have to try. I have to call Steve.

She picked up the phone and dialed his office number, only to find that he was in a meeting that would last all day. His secretary offered to take a message or have him call her when they broke for lunch. Kathy declined both and thanked her, knowing she would have to leave before Steve had an opportunity to return her call.

No longer tired from the night before, Kathy got out the Key Map to find out where the Academy was located. It was in northeast Harris County, east of Houston Intercontinental Airport. After studying the map and laying out the route she would take, she glanced at the clock and knew she had just enough time to eat a quick breakfast, shower, dress, and make the long drive from northwest Houston.

Chapter 67

Thursday, May 1, 1980 - 12:45 p.m.

The Rehab Center, someone's idea for a warm and fuzzy name, was still a jail. Kathy climbed the flight of steps to the entrance and walked into the lobby. At the rear of the lobby, a deputy sat at a desk in front of a door. Kathy approached the desk.

"I'm Kathy Cooper. I was told to come here for some tests."

"The Academy's upstairs."

She thanked him. The stairs started next to the entrance door, went along the front wall to a landing, then left up to the second floor balcony. A deputy with a clipboard stood at the top of the stairs.

"Name?" he demanded.

"Kathy Cooper," she answered.

"Cooper, Kathleen Mavis?"

"Yes."

"Yes, sir!" he barked.

"Yes, sir," she replied, with raised eyebrows.

"First row, fifth desk," he ordered as he motioned to the door across from the stairs.

"Yes, sir," she answered. I applied to a paramilitary organization, she reminded herself, which is going to require some adjustment in thinking and behavior.

Kathy entered what appeared to be a classroom. A few young men and one woman sat at the school desks. Kathy walked down the first row of desks and took her seat at the fifth one. When she observed one man chewing his lower lip and another drumming his fingers on the desk, she decided the others were as tense as she was.

As others arrived and took their seats, Kathy realized they were being seated in a checkerboard pattern, with an empty seat in front, behind and on each side of each applicant. There was no conversation, only an occasional nod of acknowledgment. At precisely one o'clock, according to the clock on the wall at the front of the classroom, the door deputy and a sergeant entered the room. They closed the door behind them.

The sergeant looked over the group. "Good afternoon," he said.

There was a scattering of responses.

"I can't hear you!"

"Good afternoon, sir," the group answered.

"I am Sergeant Rowe." He motioned to the other deputy. "This is Deputy Barnes. An academy class has been scheduled to start the first of October. The class will be limited to forty cadets. We have already qualified thirty-five. There are only five spots left to fill. Those of you who pass the reading comprehension test will take the agility test. Perhaps two or three of you will pass both.

"The tests will be passed out face down. Leave them that way until you are told to start."

He nodded to Deputy Barnes, who handed tests and pencils to the first person in each row. That person kept one of each and passed the others back to those behind him.

"On the first page fill in your full name, address, and phone number. You will have one hour to complete the test. When you finish, you will sit quietly until the time is up. Are there any questions?"

One young man raised his hand and the Sergeant Rowe motioned to recognize him.

"When will we know how we scored?"

"Stand up when called on!"

"Yes, sir," he said as he rose to his feet and repeated his question.

"You won't be informed of your score. This is a pass-fail test. If you pass, you will take the agility test. Also pass-fail. If you pass both you will receive a Pre-Employment Questionnaire and instructions for completing the process." He paused. "Any other questions?" There were none. "You may begin the test."

Kathy turned hers over, filled in the required information, and began answering the questions. The test emphasized reading comprehension, grammar, punctuation, and spelling. She thought of the five available spaces for the next class and remembered Sergeant Fleming predicting she would be in the top five on the first promotional test she took. He had been right that time. This time she *had* to score in the top five to be eligible.

Focusing on the test, she was still aware that the sergeant and deputy were proctoring the test by walking the room in a random pattern. When she finished, she reviewed her answers. Feeling she had done as well as she could, she turned the test face down and folded her hands in her lap.

She kept thinking about Steve and how he was going to react to this. It was distracting her. She shouldn't have anything on her mind right now except for the agility test. If I passed this test, she thought. Don't be stupid. You're a writer. Of course you will pass this one. She wondered what the agility test entailed. Kathy had talked to enough HPD officers to know the details of the HPD agility test. She didn't know any Sheriff's Deputies, so she had no idea what to expect. She hoped three years of martial arts training, exercising, and running had gotten her in shape to handle whatever was required.

"Time's up. Pass the tests to the front of each row," the sergeant announced.

Deputy Barnes gathered up the tests and pencils.

"Wait here," the sergeant told them as he and Deputy Barnes left the room.

They waited, fidgeting impatiently, talking little in near whispers, nearly thirty minutes before the sergeant returned.

"Leave the building if I call your name. Adams, Cooper, Edwards, …"

Kathy's stomach nearly rebelled. I didn't make it, she thought. I wonder if I can try again. And if so, how long will I have to wait? She descended the stairs to the lobby and pushed through the door to the outside. At the foot of the outside steps, Deputy Barnes motioned for Kathy to get in the van parked at the curb.

She got in. Others joined her. Altogether they were eight of the fifteen who took the reading comp test. Deputy Barnes got in the driver's seat. Sergeant Rowe got in the passenger seat. As the van started moving, Kathy noted that there were no windows except in the driver's compartment. She didn't have a good view of where they were going, but she was aware when the road surface changed from blacktop to gravel. Shortly the van stopped and they all got out into an open field in which an obstacle course was laid out. The applicants milled around trying to get a look at what they faced.

"Gather round," Deputy Barnes yelled and waited for them before continuing. "I'll walk you through the course. There are two parts to the test. Each is timed separately. The obstacle course is the first part. A quarter mile sprint is the second, which will immediately follow the first." He walked to the first obstacle.

"This is the low wall. Go over it. Next, the window. Go through it. The high wall. Get over it any way you can. The balance beam. If you fall off, go back and try again. The culvert; go through it. The monkey bars. Go up the ladder, across the bars hand over hand, using each bar, and down the ladder. The platform. This simulates the top of a box car. Go up the ladder, using every rung, cross the platform, and descend the ladder, again using every rung. The dummy; grab it and drag it across the finish line. Immediately sprint down the field to the marker and back.

"You will do this one at a time. Go back to the starting point and change into your gym clothes, if you have 'em. And get the lead out!"

Kathy looked up at the platform as she jogged past. From the ground it looked too narrow to walk across with any ease.

"Hi."

Kathy turned her head to the only other woman in the group. "Hi .What do you think of the course?"

"It should separate the men from the boys."

"I hope not the girls from the boys."

The woman smiled and held out her hand. "Ellen Swenson."

"Kathy Cooper."

At the van, they stepped to one side of the van. The men went to the other side. Kathy dropped her slacks and removed her blouse to reveal shorts and tank top underneath. Ellen Swenson also wore gym clothes under her street clothes. Both of them began stretching to loosen up and warm up for the test. The young men stood around talking. The men who Kathy judged to be ex-military were warming up in a variety of ways.

"Adams!" Deputy Barnes shouted. "Step to the starting line. Ready. Go!"

Adams, average build, height, and weight, was nondescript except for his red hair and freckles. Kathy and the others walked along beside the obstacle course as Adams scrambled through it like a kid on the playground. Sergeant Rowe and Deputy Barnes conferred, checking their stopwatches and making notes. They all started jogging back to the starting point.

I'm next, Kathy thought, breathing deeply and slowly in an attempt to control the rush the adrenalin gave her.

"Cooper, get ready, go!"

She heard the signal to go as if from a distance. She hurdled the low wall, pulled up on the window sill with her forearms and dived through the window. Next she faced the high wall, six feet of smooth wood siding. A rope hung down from the top. She took a couple running steps, vaulted up, grabbed the rope near the top, and walked up the wall and over. The balance beam, a six-by-six beam, sat about twelve inches off the ground. Kathy easily walked it. The culvert was too small to stand up in. The gravel and trash in the bottom of it discouraged crawling on hands and knees. Kathy duck-walked through it, wondering if she would be able to straighten up at the other end.

She paused at the monkey bars to wipe her hands on the seat of her shorts. Up the ladder she went, grabbed the first bar, swung out to reach for the second, and swung too far, grabbing the third. She dropped to the ground and began again. With very little swing, this time she was able to use every bar, as instructed.

She approached the platform. It must be thirty feet in the air, she thought as she climbed the ladder. The two-foot-wide platform provided adequate width to walk on, but the drop to the ground was unsettling. Kathy tried to focus on the far end, not the height, but she made the mistake of looking down at the ground. Her mouth went dry. Her heart pounded. She couldn't move. I have to do this, she thought. Look at the end of the platform, she told herself, but she couldn't drag her sight from the ground.

"Cooper!" a voice called to her. "Close your eyes. Raise your head. Look at me. I'm at the top of the down ladder."

Kathy looked up. Swenson stood head and shoulders above the end of the platform.

"Look right here," Swenson instructed, pointing her own nose. "Now, take a step. Good. Now take another. Keep walking. You're doing great. You're halfway. Keep come…"

Kathy swayed and fell on her hands and knees. From that angle, the platform filled most of her range of vision. She took a deep breath and started crawling. When she reached the ladder, Swenson moved to hang on the side of the ladder. Kathy descended slowly on shaky legs.

"Thanks," she told Swenson as she passed.

She approached the dummy, which lay on its back. Kathy pushed it to a sitting position, wrapped her arms under the dummy's arms and around its chest. She figured it weighed as much or more than she did. Using her legs she pushed backward, dragging the dummy with her. By the time she crossed the finish line her legs were trembling. She turned and starting jogging toward the marker. Gradually she increased her speed as her legs recovered, crossed the finish line, slowed to a stop, and stood gasping for breath.

"Cooper."

Kathy straightened up and turned to the sergeant. "Yes, sir." *This is where I get the bad news,* she thought.

"There's a first aid kit under the front passenger seat of the van. Go take care of your knees."

Kathy looked and discovered that her knees were scraped and bleeding slightly. "Yes, sir."

One by one they were called. Edwards was one of the men Kathy judged to be ex-military. Kelso was a dark-haired young man, and Lincoln was the only black in the group. All three of them had no trouble with the course. When they called for Phillips, he didn't step forward. Looking around for him, they saw him walking back toward the Rehab Center. The sergeant drew a line through Phillips' name and called for Swenson.

Kathy watched Swenson go through the course without hesitation, with smooth motions and surprising strength, practically jogging across the platform. In the sprint, Kathy thought she looked like a thoroughbred, running for the pure pleasure of running.

After Swenson, the last of the group took his turn with no problems. They returned to the van, were driven back to the Rehab Center, were and told to take a bathroom break and return to the classroom.

In the ladies room, Kathy again thanked Swenson. "I wouldn't have made it without you."

"Glad I could help."

"I doubt I made the time limit," Kathy said

"I guess we'll find out in the classroom," Swenson offered.

Chapter 68

Thursday, May 1, 1980 - 5:45 p.m.

Steve recognized the aroma of spaghetti sauce the moment he came in the front door when he got home from work. A spaghetti dinner was a just the right welcome home after an all-day meeting with a client who kept changing the specifications of the project.

He found Kathy in the kitchen spreading garlic butter on the French bread. He put down his briefcase, walked up behind her, wrapped his arms around her, and pulled her against him. As always she leaned into him, then turned around for a kiss.

"Hi, honey," she said.

"Hi, darling. Have I got time for a shower?" Steve asked.

"Sure. Go ahead."

Steve kissed her again and headed for the bedroom, stripping off his clothes as he went. He liked leisurely showers, but this time he showered quickly, looking forward to dinner. In clean casual slacks and T-shirt he returned to the kitchen, to find dinner ready to serve.

Steve talked about work and his frustrations from dealing with a difficult client. Kathy let him vent. That was what he needed. She only half listened. She had heard it all before over the past twenty-two years. By the time they finished dinner, Steve had wound down. He sat back to enjoy his iced tea.

Kathy got up and started clearing the table. Steve got up to help her. When Kathy closed and started the dishwasher, she turned to find Steve standing there watching her.

"What's going on, honey?" he asked with amused curiosity. When she looked puzzled, he continued. "My favorite dinner, listening to me complain about work without a word from you. What's going on?"

There was no way to soften the impact for Steve. "I got a call from the Sheriff's Office this morning," she stated. "They asked if I was still interested in becoming a deputy."

Steve's expression didn't change but he felt like she had punched him in the gut. The moment he had dreaded for three years had arrived. He had prayed this day would never come. He knew it would sooner or later, but it was too soon. He wasn't prepared for it. But then, he probably never would have been.

"What'd you tell 'em?" he asked.

"I said yes." She watched for a reaction from Steve. "They told me to report for the reading comprehension and agility tests this afternoon. I called to tell you before I left, but you were in a meeting."

"You took the tests?"

She nodded.

"How'd you do?"

"I passed both," she told him, thinking he looked like a deer caught in the headlights. "Honey? Say something."

"What's the...the next step?"

"They gave me a Pre-Employment Questionnaire to fill out, but I don't know if I should."

"What?"

She wouldn't meet his eyes. "If I become a cop you'll worry yourself sick. You nearly did when I was riding along."

He nodded. "Yes, I'll be concerned for your safety, just like everyone else who's married to a cop. That's normal. But you'll have the training." With a slight smile he continued, "I'll be proud, too."

Kathy looked up, studying the look on his face. All she saw was love. "You think I should go ahead?"

He nodded. "You've wanted this for a long time."

Kathy's eyes overflowed. Steve took her in his arms and held her. His heart nearly burst with love for this woman who loved him enough to consider sacrificing her desires for his comfort.

"I can't wait to see you in uniform," he teased, to cover up his anxiety.

"I thought men were turned off by women in uniform."

"Not true. There's something exciting and dangerous about a woman in uniform who carries a gun and handcuffs."

Kathy smiled. "They won't be fur-lined."

"Ooooh," he moaned, "too bad."

Chapter 69

Friday, May 23, 1980 - 9:50 A.M.

Kathy entered recruiting at the Sheriff's Office and was escorted to an interview room. It resembled the interrogation rooms at HPD, with a table and two chairs, one on each side of the table. She sat in the one on the far side and waited and waited. It had taken her three and a half weeks to get all the documents ready to submit. And she waited some more. She was ready to get on with the initial interview and wondered if they had forgotten her.

The door suddenly opened. Kathy rose to her feet. A stocky male deputy who looked about forty-five with salt-and-pepper hair entered. His expression said don't mess with me.

"Sit!" he ordered, in a surly manner.

"Yes, sir," she said as she sat back down.

"Kathleen Mavis Cooper?"

"Yes, sir."

"I'm going to go over your application line by line and I'll ask some questions that are not on it. Answer honestly and with complete information. Do not make me work for it!"

"No, sir."

He did as he said he would, questioning each line of information from her birth date to her current marital status and her reasons for leaving every job she ever held. The part-time jobs she had held during high school and college were varied and brief, but she never got fired, and that seemed to be what he was looking for.

The ages of the boys was questioned. Where were they were going to school? What were Davy and Jake majoring in at A&M? How were their grades? Had they ever been arrested? Every piece of information on the form Kathy had filled out was questioned for more information, even her work in

Records Division. All he had to do to get that information was pull her HPD personnel file. Kathy knew it would be reviewed before her application was approved.

Again, as when she interviewed for the job in Records, he asked about anything that could be used to blackmail her. She told him she'd had an affair. He wanted details: name of the man, frequency of their liaisons. There was only one. She ended it.

"What's the matter, wouldn't he go down on you?"

Kathy ignored the question. "The problem was my guilt."

"Then he did go down on you?"

"That is none of your business!" she exclaimed.

"Everything about your past life is our business! Everything!"

Kathy was embarrassed and angry at having this stranger pry into her sex life.

"No, he didn't go down on me. We did it in the missionary position," she told him defiantly. "It was about fifteen years ago. I felt so guilty that I threw up and prayed my husband would never find out."

"Have you had any contact with him since?"

"No!"

He went on to other things. The questions came and the answers went smoothly until he got to her criminal history.

"You were arrested, charged with murder and indicted, and you think you stand a chance of becoming a cop? We don't hire criminals!" he told her.

"No, sir."

"You killed someone," he stated.

"Yes, sir."

"And got off on a technicality."

"No, sir!" she objected.

"You're arguing with me?"

"No, sir. I'd like to explain."

He shook his head. "You can't explain away a murder charge."

"Will you let me try?"

"Why should I?"

"In the interest of being fair and getting the truth," Kathy suggested, angrily.

"Go ahead. Try!" he challenged, sat back, and folded his arms across his chest as though this was a waste of his time.

"I was acquitted because the evidence proved that the shooting was justified. I shot in defense of a police officer I thought was about to be killed. Sir!" she added forcefully.

"That doesn't earn you any special consideration here!"

"I don't expect any!"

He studied her for a moment. Her jaw was set. She was angry, but controlling it well.

"Do you think having killed someone is going to make you a good police officer?" he asked, then continued before she could answer. "We try to teach deputies to handle things without killing anybody."

"That's what I want to learn, sir."

"Why do you want to be a cop?"

"I was raised to believe in obeying the law, voting in elections, and serving on juries when called. Good citizenship was as important as church on Sunday. Serving on the grand jury allowed me to contribute something to the welfare of our society. And it gave me the opportunity to ride along with HPD officers and see what police work is really like.

"Being a police officer is another way to help people and contribute something to society," Kathy declared, daring him to try to keep her out.

"So, you rode with Patrol a few times and now you think you know all about police work," he commented sarcastically.

"No, sir, I don't, but I want to learn."

He glanced at the form in front of him. "You got out of the murder charge. What other felonies have you committed?"

"I carried a concealed weapon for protection," she admitted.

"Protection from what?"

"A man who made obscene phone calls and knew where I lived. I helped get him arrested, but they had to turn him loose. So I bought a pistol and carried it for a while."

"That's insulting. It implies the police were not capable of protecting you."

"I was concerned for the safety of my children. Under the circumstances, they issued a permit for me to buy the pistol and waived the three-day waiting period," she explained.

"There's no permit required and no waiting period," he said, puzzled.

"This happened in Oklahoma."

"They can't waive the waiting period."

"They predated the paperwork."

"You encouraged police officers to break the law? To give you special treatment?" he rose and shouted at her. "You're an adulteress, a felon, and a killer. You belong in prison, not in the Harris County Sheriff's Department!"

Kathy didn't say anything. She could feel her dream slipping away.

"Withdraw your application!" he told her.

"No, sir! I won't do that!"

"You might as well. You'll never make it!" He gathered up the papers, put them in a file folder, and walked out of the room, leaving the door open.

Kathy was shaking when she stood up. She wanted no special treatment, just the same opportunity to prove herself as anyone else. And it looked like she wasn't going to get it.

Chapter 70

Friday, May 23, 1980 - 7:10 p.m.

At supper, Steve could tell something was bothering Kathy. He waited until she was finishing the dishes to ask what she was upset about.

"I turned in my application this morning and had an interview. They don't want me," she told him.

"Honey," Steve took her hand. "Come sit down and tell me what happened."

They sat side by side on the couch in the family room.

"He called me a criminal," Kathy told Steve, "a felon, and a killer. He said it was an insult for me to apply and told me to withdraw my application."

Steve could see she was really down about this. "Did he say you were rejected?"

"No, but he might as well have."

"Are you going to withdraw?"

"No. I just..." She hesitated.

After a moment Steve asked, "You just what?"

"Just wish I understood his attitude," Kathy answered. "All I want is a fair chance, and this..." She could think of many things to call him, none of them nice. "This jerk acts like I'm public enemy number one."

"Honey, it's their game. You're going to have to play by their rules," Steve told her.

"Meaning?"

"It's like the Navy. You're going to have to put up with whatever they dish out if you want to be a cop."

"You know I do."

"Then don't let this discourage you. He's only one man. Shake it off," he advised her.

Kathy thought about it. She hadn't been rejected yet. Until that happened she had to keep trying her best.

"You're right, as usual."

"Have you taken your run today?"

"No, not yet."

He stood up and held out a hand to her. "Come on. A run will make you feel better. Let's change. I'll run with you."

Kathy smiled. "Think you can keep up with me?" she asked as she passed in front of him.

Steve smacked her playfully on the backside. "I'll be out front all the way!"

"You wish!"

The banter continued while they changed, both of them looking forward to some friendly competition.

Chapter 71

Wednesday, June 25, 1980 - 3:00 p.m.

A month passed and Kathy didn't hear any more about her application. She was beginning to wonder if they had rejected her and hadn't notified her, when she was contacted and informed of the time and place for her polygraph test. She didn't know what to expect on this one. Officers had told her only "tell the truth," which she planned to do. Still, what if she did and the machine said she lied? What then?

The examiner just talked to her for several minutes to help her relax. He also told her of what the test would consist. She verified that the information on her application was correct. When he hooked her up to the machine, her hands began to shake. She wondered if the machine would record how nervous she was. To record respiration rate, two bands were wrapped around her torso and abdomen. For sweat gland activity, metal contacts were attached to her ring and index fingers. The cuff on her upper arm would record blood pressure and pulse rate.

First the examiner asked control questions, instructing her to answer 'no' to all the questions, true or not. This would give him a baseline for comparison. He first asked if they were in Dallas. Then if they were in Houston. In addition, he asked similar questions about the month, the day of the week, and the time of day.

When he was satisfied that he had a good baseline reading, the relevant questions began. She was instructed to answer truthfully with 'yes' or 'no' answers. He started by asking questions to verify her name, address, marital status, education, and work history. She started to relax a little. Then the questions became more probing, asking about stealing, lying, alcohol and drug use, sexual practices, murder, and suicide.

After disconnecting the machine, the examiner told her, "There were a few questions that you reacted to that I need to clarify. First of all, is Kathleen Mavis Cooper your true name?"

"Yes," she told him.

"Have you ever used some other name?"

Kathy took a deep breath, "Yes, I have. I write under the name K. M. Beaumont."

"You're a writer?"

"I've written a few things."

"Have you published under the name K. M. Beaumont?"

"Yes."

"What types of things?"

"Articles, reviews of books and movies, interviews, and short stories," Kathy informed him.

He nodded. "You said you did not engage in or fantasize about bondage. Is that true?"

"Yes."

"The machine says that's a lie."

"What!" Kathy exclaimed, offended.

"You've never wondered what it would be like to be restrained? To be tied up or handcuffed?"

"I know what it's like to be handcuffed. I was arrested, remember."

"How did it make you feel?"

"Vulnerable," she admitted. "They tell you it's for your protection. I didn't feel protected! I felt vulnerable!"

"That probably explains your reaction," he acknowledged.

Kathy looked at him, wondering what he was thinking, but she saw no clue in his expression.

"We're finished," he told her.

Kathy got to her feet, walked to the door of the room, opened the door, then turned back to watch him for a moment. She was beginning to see a pattern in the testing and interviews, the pressure and stress. Keep the applicants off balance, she thought. See how they react.

He looked up. "That's all, Cooper."

"Yes, sir," she acknowledged with a smile, leaving him wondering what she was smiling about.

* * * * *

Thursday, July 10, 1980 - 9:00 a.m.

Kathy reported for the written psych test. The test itself made little sense to Kathy. The questions asked her preference between activities. Would she rather drive a truck or kiss a duck? Would she rather climb a tree or sew a

Ride Along

dress? They went on and on. In spite of trying, Kathy could discern no pattern or logic to them.

* * * * *

Tuesday, July 22, 1980 - 10:a.m.

    Kathy met with one of the department's psychologists for the psych evaluation. She talked with the psychologist for fifty minutes, mostly about her ride along experiences and the shooting, concentrating on her reactions and feeling. When the session ended, she stopped at the door and turned back to him.
    "You didn't ask me the one question I thought you would," she stated.
    "What was that?"
    "Why do I want be a cop?"
    "I didn't have to. You light up whenever you talk about it."
    "Oh," she said in surprise and smiled. "Thank you, doctor."
    "You're welcome. Good luck."

Chapter 72

Tuesday, August 12, 1980 - 9:15 a.m.

In the recruiting office of the Sheriff's Department, Captain Addison, Lieutenant Hoeffer, and Sergeant Rowe met in a conference room. The sergeant carried the files of five applicants. This meeting was to discuss acceptance or rejection for those five. If accepted, they would actually be hired by the Sheriff's Department and paid a salary while they attended the Academy.

The sergeant spoke briefly about each of the applicants he thought should be accepted. However, he had two he thought required in-depth discussions. The first was a man who had been involved in some domestic disturbances but was never charged.

"We know the police were called by the neighbors at least four times," the sergeant stated. "But the wife would never file charges against him. When I asked them separately about the incidents, I was told they had attended counseling and there has been no recurrence in the past five years. Evidently they had been going through some hard times financially. Also there was a lot of stress on them due to the illness of a family member."

"Sergeant," the captain interrupted. "You know how I feel about wife-beaters! There's no excuse for a man hitting a woman."

"Yes, sir. I know it would be taking a chance on him, but..."

"That's a chance I am not willing to take. He could make the whole department look bad. It's bad enough that some of these types get in the department in spite of all the checking we do, but when we know in advance, there is no way I'm going to approve hiring him." The captain paused. "Is that clear?"

"Yes, sir," the sergeant answered, closed the file, and set it aside.

"What else have you got?"

"Kathleen Mavis Cooper," the sergeant stated as he opened another file. "White woman, forty years old, sixty hours of college in liberal arts, has worked the past three-and-a-half years in Records Division of the Houston Police Department. Everything checks out with her—background, credit history, interviews, polygraph, everything, but...she was tried for murder."

"Murder?" the captain asked, not sure he heard correctly.

"Yes, sir. She was acquitted."

"Who did she kill?"

"One of three black men that attacked the officer she was riding along with."

"I remember the case," the lieutenant stated. "She was on the grand jury at the time, wasn't she?"

"Yes, sir."

The captain turned to the sergeant. "I vaguely remember. Do you have the details there?"

"Yes, sir." The sergeant proceeded to brief the captain and lieutenant on Kathy's shooting and murder trial. He concluded with, "The media crucified her. The Police Chief, the Mayor, and the District Attorney all felt the heat. It was an election year. In fact, the DA had to take it to a second grand jury to get an indictment after the first one no-billed her."

"The swine," the lieutenant muttered.

"John Everett was her defense attorney," the sergeant added.

"Well, that makes me wonder about her guilt," the captain stated.

"He did this one *pro bono*, sir," the sergeant said. "The HPD officers set up a defense fund for her. Everett wouldn't take it. He told them to donate it to the One Hundred Club."

"How much was in it?"

"Almost a hundred thousand dollars."

"Sounds like he believed in her innocence," the lieutenant put in.

"He used justification as her defense."

The captain nodded and sat back in his chair. He was thinking about the consequences of accepting Kathy to the Academy. Would it create another media storm? Would it bring criticism on the Department? If she made it through the Academy and as an officer had to shoot and kill someone else, what would the repercussions be? Not good! The Department's screening process and training would come under scrutiny. If any faults were found, or just implied, liability issues would surface, leading to possible lawsuits and costly settlements. It happened—not very often, but each time it damaged the credibility of officers on the street. It didn't seem to matter if it was a Sheriff's Deputy in the wrong or an officer from another department. It hurt the image of all officers.

She killed a man. How did it affect her emotionally, psychologically? There were many possible reactions to being involved in a violent incident: guilt, acceptance, paranoia, fear, depression, power, sadness, and others. He would have no control over her training but he would make sure the screening process on her application had no holes in it. Decision reached, he sat forward and spoke to the sergeant.

"Schedule another interview for Cooper with the three of us."

"The three of us?" the lieutenant questioned.

The captain nodded. "We're going to review her shooting as though she was one of our deputies when it happened."

"Is that fair?"

"It's necessary," the captain insisted. "Leave her file here. I want to look at it."

"Yes, sir," the sergeant answered, handing over the thickest applicant's file the captain had ever seen. "It includes a transcript of her trial" the sergeant explained.

The captain nodded and the meeting came to an end.

Chapter 73

Friday, August 15, 1980 - 9:55 a.m.

As ordered, Kathy reported to the recruiting office for her final interview. She knew what HPD's final interview was like. This one would probably be similar. As before, she wished it was not on a morning after she worked all night, but that seemed to be the pattern of all the tests so far. She wondered if it was deliberate. It probably was. It probably was another test of sorts.

She knew from experience that the shit usually hit the fan at the end of shift when officers were tired and ready to go home. Still, they were expected to deal with the situation no matter what. So I'll deal with this, she told herself as she entered the recruiting office.

The deputy at the desk told her to take a seat. She would be called shortly. Kathy knew what 'shortly' meant—anything from ten minutes to nearly an hour. Yes, there definitely was a pattern, she thought. She had suspected it. Now she was sure.

The wait was shorter than she expected, only fifteen minutes. She was escorted to an interview room. When she entered she was surprised to see three deputies waiting. They stood up when she entered.

"Good morning, Ms. Cooper," the man in the middle greeted her.

Kathy estimated he was in his late fifties. His full head of hair was completely gray over an intelligent, experienced face. His expression and brown eyes indicated that this was not a man to mess with.

"Good morning, sir."

"I'm Captain Addison." Motioning to his right he continued, "Lieutenant Hoeffer—"

"Lieutenant," Kathy acknowledged with a nod.

"—and Sergeant Rowe."

"Sergeant."

"Be seated, Ms. Cooper," he instructed, indicating the single armless chair positioned in front of the table at which the men proceeded to sit.

Kathy sat down, placed her purse on the floor next to the chair, crossed her ankles, tucked her feet under the chair, and folded her hands in her lap.

"Do you understand that your acceptance or rejection depends on this interview?" the captain asked in a warm, fatherly voice.

"Yes, I understand, sir."

"We have some questions about your background and past experiences."

"I'll do my best to answer them, sir."

"Good." He turned and nodded to Sergeant Rowe.

"You served on the Harris County Grand Jury in the fall of 1976. Is that correct?"

"Yes, it is."

"You rode along with HPD officers at that time?"

"Yes, I did."

"Was that what got you interested in police work?"

"No. I've wanted to be a police officer since I was a little girl."

"Why?"

"I got lost in a store downtown. I was about five, I think. A big man in a blue uniform dried my tears and helped me find Mama."

Lieutenant Hoeffer leaned forward. "You've been interested in police work ever since?"

"Yes, sir."

"Why did you choose to ride along with HPD?" the captain inquired.

"To find out what police work is really like."

"Was it what you expected?" the lieutenant asked.

Kathy smiled and shook her head. "No. It was better."

Captain Addison smiled and the lieutenant chuckled.

"You rode a lot." Sergeant Rowe stated.

"As much as I could."

"How many times did you ride along?" Lieutenant Hoeffer inquired.

"I rode evening and night shifts every Friday and Saturday for two months."

"Why?"

"Because the more I learned, the more I wanted to learn."

"If my calculations are correct, you rode along on thirty-two shifts."

"I believe that's correct, sir."

"How did you get along with the men?" the captain asked.

"We got along well, I think. They seemed to enjoy talking about their job, what they did, and how they did it to maintain officer safety."

"What area of Houston were you riding in?" Lieutenant Hoeffer asked.

"I rode out of Northwest and Shepherd stations."

"What kinds of calls did you answer?

"All kinds. Alarm calls, burglaries, both in progress and for reports, a couple of shootings, stabbings, domestic disturbances, fights, traffic stops, criminal mischief, and public intoxication calls."

"They taught you about officer safety," the sergeant stated. "Did they also teach you to aim at center body mass?"

Here they come, Kathy thought. Questions about the shooting. "They explained quite a bit about firearms training, and yes, they mentioned that they were trained to aim at center body mass."

"Did they tell you this is often a killing shot?"

"No, sir. They said aiming at the largest target increased chances of hitting and stopping the suspect."

"Stopping the suspect, not killing him?"

"No, sir."

"Did they ever draw their weapons while you were with them?" the captain asked.

"Yes, sir, a few times."

"Under what circumstances?"

"A kidnapping-hostage situation, a couple of burglaries in progress, and twice when they attempted a traffic stop and the suspect didn't stop right away."

"Did they fire their weapons in your presence?"

"No, sir."

"That's a lie!" the sergeant challenged angrily. "They took you out for target practice!"

"I thought the captain was referring to..."

"Did they," he interrupted, "or did they not fire their weapons in your presence?"

"They did."

As the pace of the questions increased and became more demanding, Kathy sat up straighter and became completely focused on the questions. She tried unsuccessfully to take her time, to think about the question before answering, but the pace became unrelenting.

"Is that when you learned how to use the carbine?"

"Yes, sir."

"According to the transcript of your murder trial, you shot at sixteen beer cans and hit fifteen. Is that correct?"

"Yes, sir."

"That makes you an expert shot! Why didn't you shoot to wound Ray Jackson?"

"Because I didn't want to take a chance on missing."

"You didn't miss. You killed him. How did you feel about that?"

Kathy hesitated, trying to sort out the feelings she remembered at the moment she learned Ray Jackson was dead.

"Answer the question!"

"At first I thought I'd missed him. Then he fell and I felt relief."

"Be honest. You got a rush out of it, didn't you?"

"No, sir!" Kathy exclaimed forcefully, appalled at the suggestion.

"Admit it. It gave you a thrill."

"It did not! It made me sick."

"You were glad he was dead!"

"Yes!" she admitted. "Better him than Officer Henson!"

The captain had watched Kathy's posture change from relaxed and open to a position on the edge of the chair, poised for flight or fight.

"Had the men taught you how to use the radio?" the lieutenant inquired mildly.

"Yes, sir."

"When you saw there were three men, why didn't you call for backup?"

"By the time I got the mike and looked up they had jumped Officer Henson and taken him to the ground."

"Did you put out an assist at that time?"

"No, sir. There wasn't time. Everything was happening so fast."

"And you were moving so slow."

"Yes, sir," she agreed, grateful for his understanding. Then it hit her. They were using the good cop, bad cop technique.

"You didn't even shout a warning! The sergeant accused. "You just shot him. In the back!"

"His back was toward me."

"He didn't know you were there."

"No, sir."

"And you killed him without warning."

It was a statement Kathy refused to acknowledge.

"Do you enjoy shooting?" the sergeant continued.

"Yes, sir."

"Hunting?"

"No, sir. Target shooting for marksmanship."

"Did you see a counselor after the shooting?" the lieutenant asked.

"Yes, sir."

"Who did you see?"

"Carter Walters over at HPD."

"He's a department counselor. How did you manage that?"

"Chief Ledford arranged it."

"Special treatment for a hero?" Disgust and sarcasm dripped from the sergeant's question.

Kathy did not lower herself to answer that.

"Are you a hero?"

"Heroes don't get as scared as I was."

"What were you scared of? You had the carbine."

"That Officer Henson would be killed if I didn't stop it."

"You did stop it. But you killed a man to do it. We train officers to handle things without killing."

Kathy clenched her teeth and her fists. Her lips were a thin line. She fought to control her temper.

"You made mistakes, Ms. Cooper," the captain stated. "When you saw there were three men you should have called for backup. When they jumped Henson you should have put out an assist. Before you shot you should have given Ray Jackson a chance to surrender. When you shot, you should have shot to wound him."

Kathy had heard all this before and hearing it again, knowing she did the only thing she could do, made her angry. Never breaking eye contact with the captain, she took a deep breath. In a very controlled tone, she stated, "With all due respect, sir, you were not there. I was! I did what I had to do!"

The captain and Kathy stared at each other, each trying to outlast the other. Kathy was not going to give in. Seconds passed. The room was dead quiet. More seconds passed. The lieutenant and the sergeant moved only their eyes back and forth from Kathy to the captain. Still more seconds passed.

"That will be all!" the captain suddenly exclaimed.

"Yes, sir!" Maintaining eye contact with the captain Kathy reached down for her purse and rose from the chair. She turned and left the room, wishing she could slam the door behind her. Unfortunately, it had one of those door closing gadgets on it to prevent it from slamming. She wanted to cuss or cry and fought to not do either anywhere in hearing or sight of the Sheriff's Office.

Kathy was frustrated, angry, and hurt. *I did the right thing. I didn't have any choice. It was Ray Jackson's life or Calvin's. I was cleared of the murder charge. The shooting was justified. How could they question it?*

By the time she reached the street, she decided that if they didn't accept her, she would find another police agency that would. Some police agency out there would hire her. She had to believe that. Surely the shooting wouldn't make her unacceptable to all of them.

Fatigue and disappointment left her shaking by the time she got to her car. *I blew it,* she thought. *I got angry. I shouldn't have.* But she had never been good at that when someone was attacking her. It did feel like an attack.

She took several deep breaths and rolled her head around to relieve some of the tension. *So I'll start over.* She started the car and drove out of the parking garage, thinking only of getting home and climbing into bed.

Chapter 74

Saturday, August 30, 1980 - 4:10 p.m.

Kathy woke slowly. Today was one of the best day's sleep she had gotten all week. She stretched and turned over onto her back, wondering what Steve and the boys had been up to all day. Yawning and stretching some more, she got to her feet and stumbled to the bathroom. Letting the water in the shower run, she brushed her teeth while she waited for the water to get warm. In the shower she quickly became fully awake.

When she returned to the bedroom Steve was waiting. He looked at the towel she had wrapped around her body and shook his head. "I heard the shower. Thought I might catch you naked," he teased, "but I can fix that," he said, making a wild grab for the towel.

Kathy sidestepped and found herself in a corner. Steve blocked her way out and slowly pulled the towel away. She let him. He took her in his arms and kissed her thoroughly.

"You taste of toothpaste."

"You taste of coffee," Kathy countered.

"You're no fun when you first get up," he complained.

"Neither are you!"

Steve let her out of the corner. "We're going to the Steak House for dinner tonight," he told her.

"What's the occasion?" she asked as she began dressing.

Steve watched, appreciating her fluid movements and trim figure. "We haven't been there in a while and I'm hungry for steak."

"Sounds good," she stated.

At 6:30 p.m. Kathy, Steve, and their boys walked into their favorite place for a steak dinner. Steve gave his name and they were taken immediately to a small private dining room. Kathy's whole family was there: her parents, her sisters, her niece, and her nephew.

"What is going on?" she demanded.

"Well," Steve hesitated. "We're not sure. This could be a celebration. If not, you'll have the family around you to sympathize."

He handed her an unopened envelope with the Harris County Sheriff's Office as the return address. Kathy took it as though it might bite her. Steve pulled out a chair for her and held it for her as she sat down. She looked around the table at her family members. They looked as apprehensive as she felt. At the same time, they all encouraged her to open the letter.

Finally, with a deep breath she picked up the steak knife and used it as a letter opener. In near slow motion she took the letter out and unfolded it. With a swallow she began to read it and suddenly burst into a brilliant smile.

"I've been accepted!" she exclaimed unnecessarily.

There were applause and cheers from the family and a hug and a kiss from Steve.

"I'm proud of you, honey," he told her.

"Mom's going to be a cop!" Jake exclaimed.

"That's cool!" her nephew put in.

Her sisters were smiling, as was her father. But her mother was crying. Kathy got up and went around the table to her.

"Mama, please don't cry," Kathy begged.

Her mother shook her head. "These aren't sad tears. I'm happy for you, Kathy. I know how much you wanted this and how long you've waited."

Kathy hugged her mother and kissed her cheek. Her father wrapped Kathy up in a bear hug and made her promise to be careful. Then her two sisters ganged up on her with hugs and laughter. Gradually the celebration calmed down and they ordered dinner. They joked and laughed and told stories while they ate. In spite of wanting to keep her weight down, Kathy and her two sisters shared a frightfully decadent dessert.

The party broke up at about eight-thirty. Kathy had plenty of time to get ready for work. She read the letter again and got more details out of it this time. Her Academy class would start October first. In the meantime, she had to turn in her resignation to Sergeant Baxter in Records. If she gave the two weeks notice that was typical, she would have two weeks before the Academy started. She could use it. Maybe she and Steve could take a short trip, spend some time together. There would be darn little opportunity after the Academy started.

She would also have to give some thought to how attending classes during the day would change the schedule at home. After working the night shift for over three years, adjustments were going to be necessary. But she would work things out. She sighed. It's true, she thought.

In one month I'll begin training.

The End